FIRE IN THE CANYON

Over the pounding of hooves, Armbruster heard a rifle shot, and then another. He looked up, eyes frantically searching the canyon walls for the source of the gunfire. He saw a Navajo and he jerked with all his strength on the reins. The horse nearly tumbled over backward in trying to stop, but Armbruster was paying the animal no mind. He had slid off the horse, rifle in hand.

Armbruster dropped down to one knee and brought the rifle up. He ignored the sweat rolling down his face as he aimed, waiting for the Navajo to show himself again. When the warrior did, ready to shoot at the soldiers once more, Armbruster fired. The warrior fell, bouncing down the rock-studded slope of the canyon wall.

Armbruster swung about, dropping his rifle and reaching for a pistol at the sound of someone approaching . . .

SIEGE AT FORT DEFIANCE

JOHN LEGG

ST. MARTIN'S PAPERBACKS

SIEGE AT FORT DEFIANCE

Copyright © 1994 by Siegel and Siegel Ltd.

The Forts of Freedom series is a creation of Siegel and Siegel Ltd.

ISBN: 0-312-95307-0

Printed in the United States of America

St. Martin's Paperbacks edition/November 1994

10 9 8 7 6 5 4 3 2 1

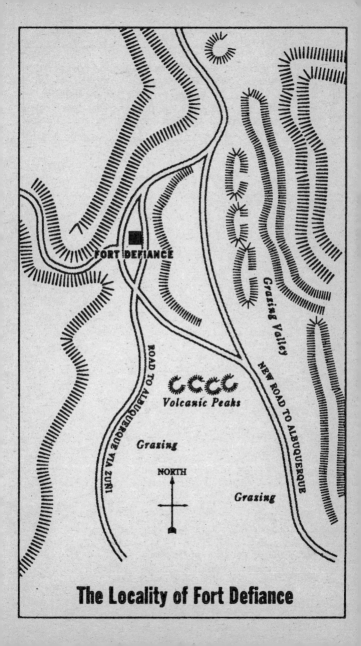

The Locality of Fort Defiance

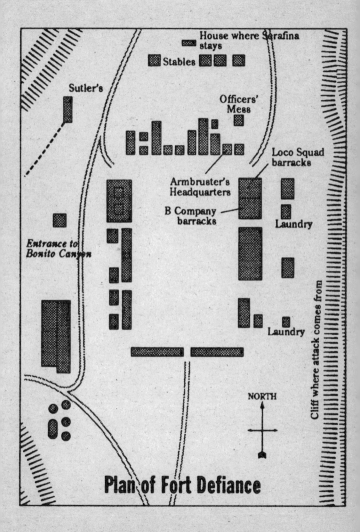

Plan of Fort Defiance

House where Serafina stays

Stables

Sutler's

Officers' Mess

Loco Squad barracks

Armbruster's Headquarters

B Company barracks

Laundry

Entrance to Bonito Canyon

Laundry

NORTH

Cliff where attack comes from

The persistent rumble of the drums calling the Long Roll woke First Lieutenant Edward Armbruster from a deep sleep. By the time his socks hit the floor, he was reaching for his pants. He had just gotten them buttoned and sat to tug on his boots when Sergeant Clancy Cavannaugh burst into his quarters.

"It's the goddamn Navajos again, isn't it?" Armbruster asked, looking up while jerking on one boot.

"Yessir. And I reckon we're in for one hell of a mornin'."

Armbruster tugged on his other boot and stood, reaching for his pistol belt with the two .44-caliber Colt Dragoons in flap holsters and the pouch of paper cartridges. The sound of shots filtered into Armbruster's adobe quarters.

"We'd best hurry, sir," Cavannaugh said almost eagerly. The sergeant enjoyed a good fight.

"Right, Sergeant. Go and form up the men. I'll be there directly."

"Yessir." Cavannaugh spun on his heel and tromped out.

Armbruster swiftly checked his pistols and then dropped them back into the flap holsters and closed them. He buckled on his sword, then reached for his shirt. He shrugged, deciding he didn't need it, and grabbed his rifle instead. In his long-underwear shirt and striped blue pants, suspenders hanging limply down, Armbruster headed outside.

Armbruster was surprised that the camp was rather calm. He had expected chaos. His men were waiting, formed in solid ranks. As always, they looked confident and prepared.

Private Sean O'Leary trotted up, puffing a little. "Beggin' your leave, sir," he said in a thick Irish brogue, "but Major Brooks wants you and Loco Squad to defend the east flank. He says to make sure you don't let the savages make it down that cliff."

Armbruster nodded. He was not happy with it. The cliffs, only yards from the eastern edge of the fort, rose up a hundred feet. With the advantage of the height, the Navajos had no real reason to come down off the cliff. That meant he and his men would have to go up and get them, but that would keep him out of the fight down here in the fort where the action was. He sighed. "Anything else, Private?" he asked.

"Yessir. The major estimates that we're facin' maybe two thousand of those savages," O'Leary said flatly.

"The Navajos'd be hard-pressed to field half that many warriors," Armbruster muttered under his breath.

"Beggin' your pardon, sir?" O'Leary questioned.

"Nothing, Private. Go on back to Major Brooks and tell him we'll defend our side to the last man." He wasn't being too sarcastic.

When O'Leary left, Armbruster turned to face his men. "Any of you like to sit here while those Navajos chuck rocks and shit down on us from the goddamn cliff?"

As he had figured, he got no affirmatives. He nodded in pride. "Sergeant Cavannaugh, take a third of the men from First Unit, and go up the south side of that cliff. Knock the Navajos off it any damn way you can. Shoot them if you want; push them if you have to."

"You sure about that, Lieutenant?" Cavannaugh asked with a grin.

"I'm sure, Sergeant," Armbruster said, returning the grin.

Cavannaugh nodded and began calling out names.

"Sergeant Goettle," Armbruster said, "you keep a third of Second Unit here. You'll be reinforcements for Sergeant Cavannaugh or me, if needed, and a last line of defense if the Navajos come roaring down off the cliff."

"Where're you going to be, sir?" Cavannaugh asked. He was ready to move out with his men, and wanted to be sure he knew whatever plan the lieutenant had come up with.

"I'll take the rest of the men and head toward Webber's. If the Navajos have any kind of plan, it probably includes seeing what they can grab there before taking on our storehouses."

"You watch your ass, Lieutenant," Cavannaugh said. One of the many things he liked about serving under First Lieutenant Edward Armbruster was that Armbruster didn't treat his men like dirt. He allowed a certain freedom of camaraderie. Sometimes enough to bring the post commander down on his own head, but always enough to let his men know he cared about them.

"The same, Sergeant," Armbruster said. He liked Sergeant Major Clancy Cavannaugh considerably; considered him an excellent top sergeant and relied on him. He had never been disappointed. "All right, men," he said, "let's move out. Keep low and move quickly." He turned and started north at a trot, his men doing the same behind him.

He headed for the stables sitting well back from officers' row. There were four stables, three of them bunched up, with the fourth some yards west of them. A little behind the stables sat a house all by itself. The ramshackle adobe was where Cruz Martinez, an itinerant trader, stayed when he was at Fort Defiance.

Armbruster knew the inside of that little house quite well, as he did Martinez's daughter, Serafina. The lithe, dark-eyed beauty traveled with her father on his trading runs to the Navajos and would stay at the fort when he did. Armbruster had thought her crazy when he first heard about it, until he learned that Serafina's mother was one of the Diné, as the Navajos called themselves.

Armbruster was somewhat glad that Serafina was not there; that Martinez had not listened to him and left his daughter there when he had gone. He also was worried, though, since Martinez and Serafina had been gone only two days. They could very well be dead if the Navajos had found them. There was no real reason to think that, but on the other hand, there was no real reason for the Navajos to attack the fort.

He found the stables guarded by a few nervous soldiers, who had seen no Indians but were sure they were going to die any minute anyway. Armbruster turned and led his men toward the west. The sound of more gunfire was ringing out steadily.

In minutes Armbruster and his men were standing at the door to the fort's sutler. Armbruster pounded on the wood door. "John!" he bellowed. "Open up, John! It's Ed Armbruster."

There were clunks and clacks and then the door swung open. "You got any of those goddamn savages after your tails?" he inquired.

"Yes," Armbruster snapped. "There's a thousand of them right there behind us. They're so damn close they're about to bugger us all."

"Well, hell, you'd probably marry the first one got to

you," Webber said roughly. Then he laughed, the sound a wheezing, snarling cacophony. John Webber was a big, gruff man with a wild beard and hair to match. But he was an honest and generally peaceful man.

"You had any trouble, John?" Armbruster asked when the sutler had calmed down.

"Not much. A few of them dusky bastards tried breakin' in the back door a little while back. There's at least a couple Diné ain't gonna do no more goddamn raidin':"

"Christ, John, don't sound so joyous about it," Armbruster said, a little annoyed.

"Hell, Lieutenant, you know I don't mean nothin' against the Diné. But I ain't gonna let no one—red nor white—try'n kill me without I don't extract a full measure of payment from 'em." He ran a gnarled hand through his hair. "So, what brings you to these parts, Lieutenant?"

Armbruster wasn't sure but he thought Webber was being sarcastic. Then he decided it didn't matter. "We come to make sure you weren't entertaining some of those Navajos. Maybe supplying them with guns and powder and such."

Webber laughed again, boldly and raucously. "Hell, Lieutenant, have you ever known me to *give* anything to anybody?"

Armbruster grinned a little. "Can't say I have," he agreed. He sighed and looked around. Gunfire was still popping regularly from all over the fort—except where he was standing. It was almost as if he and his men were in a world completely removed from the one the rest of the world inhabited. It created an odd and unpleasant feeling in him.

Webber broke his concentration. "Well, you boys best come in—or take off. I ain't gonna stand here with my dick flappin' in the open, so to speak, with every goddamn Navajo in the territory runnin' amok out there. No, sir. So it's either all in, or all out.''

Armbruster pondered that for a moment. Then a bullet plowing into the wood frame of the doorway made up his mind for him. "We're in," he said forcefully. He didn't know where the bullet had come from nor who had fired it, and he was not about to stand there and get killed trying to find out.

He waited aside, however, as his men filed quietly, though swiftly, into the sutler's, Armbruster being the last. Webber slammed the door and slid the thick piece of wood into the iron hooks to make sure it stayed closed.

Webber's wife, one of the few white women in the territory, passed around coffee as the men found spots to wait. Armbruster took a position at a shuttered window that gave him at least some view toward the parade ground. Dawn was edging into the sky opposite him, and he could begin to see figures up on the tall, rocky cliff. They were backlighted by the sun's effort to rise. The fort was still in darkness.

"Jesus," Sergeant Rick Bauer breathed. He had moved up next to Armbruster and peered through cracks in the wood shutter. "There's a hell of a lot of them, ain't there?"

"The thought had occurred to me," Armbruster said dryly. "Someone said there was a couple thousand, and I didn't believe him. I'm thinking I might could change my mind about that, though, once the sun comes full up."

"I think we are in some deep shit here, Lieutenant," Bauer said in a voice that was, for him, hushed and awed.

"It certainly would seem that way, Sergeant."

Webber strolled up behind Armbruster. "Who would've thought we'd end up dying at the hands of the Diné?"

"Well," Armbruster said with a quiet smile, "I did—when I first got here. I thought I'd been sent to the ends of the earth." Armbruster's speech was soft and far away, almost as if he were talking to himself.

When Armbruster had arrived at Fort Defiance a little more than three years ago, he was a second lieutenant and fresh out of West Point. He had visions of fighting dashing Indian warriors, and of winning swift promotions for himself. That seemed so long ago now.

December 24, 1856
Fort Defiance, New Mexico Territory

Lieutenant Edward Armbruster dismounted and tried to stomp some feeling back into his legs. After six weeks or so of almost constant riding, he wasn't sure he could walk yet. Most of the other men he had ridden into Fort Defiance with were not in much better shape, which made Armbruster feel a little better. These men were used to working as couriers, spending days on end in the saddle. More importantly, though, he would hate to have himself be seen as weak as his first impression on the men of the fort.

Armbruster was a tall, gawky young man of twenty-one. His face was red from the cold and contrasted with the mussed, medium-length straw-colored hair and the bright hazel eyes. His nose and Adam's apple were prominent, in stark relief to his gaunt face and thin neck. His fingers under the thick, warm gloves were long and slender, almost delicate. His face and eyes were expressive, and now were bright with interest in Armbruster's new surroundings.

The fort did not impress Armbruster in the least. All he saw was a miserable collection of squat mud or log buildings clustered around a bleak parade ground.

"These buildings are of adobe, like those I saw in

Santa Fe, aren't they, Sergeant?" Armbruster asked of First Sergeant Carl Burghalter.

"Yessir. It's the most common buildin' material in these parts."

"You ever been posted here, Sergeant?" Armbruster asked, looking at Burghalter.

Armbruster had been surprised when he had first met Burghalter, since the sergeant looked so Germanic. Yet he had no German accent at all. It had perplexed Armbruster for a day or two, before he got used to it. Burghalter was a tall man of about thirty with blue eyes and wheat-colored hair. He had broad shoulders and an expansive midsection. His wide, weathered face showed some signs of dissipation, but he still seemed in complete control of himself. Armbruster had heard some stories back at Fort Marcy about Burghalter, but he discounted at least half of them as merely the talk of gossips and jealous men.

"No, sir. I've been at Fort Marcy for better'n five years now. But I make the ride with the courier fairly often, so I'm pretty familiar with Fort Defiance and hereabout."

A light snow began falling as Armbruster asked, "The Indians around here cause much trouble, Sergeant?" He sounded as if he wished they did.

"The Navajos? Enough, I suppose. They raid a lot and stir things up some. Most of their raids're for stealin' horses and cattle and whatever else. Generally they stick to themselves, tendin' their gardens and watchin' over their sheep. They're not born killers like some others. The ones you got to watch out for in that are the Apaches. There's several large bands of 'em, most of 'em well south of here. The nearest ones are the Jicarillas, though they're a far piece northeast. They don't come ridin' over this way too much since the Navajos can kick their asses."

"What're the . . . Navajos, did you call them? . . . like?"

"Like any other goddamn redskins." Burghalter spit out a long, thick stream of tobacco juice. "They're goddamn thieves, each and every one of 'em. Christ, they'll steal your teeth you smile too wide." He spit again. "They're not as fractious as the Apaches—like I said, they mainly stick to their gardens and sheep—but even if they generally are more peaceable than other Indians, they're redskinned savages all the same."

Armbruster nodded. He was not happy with the report. He wanted to fight Indians, but certainly not tame ones like these Navajos sounded to be. No, he wanted to face the fierce Apaches—he had heard of them even way back east. Comanches, too, and Utes and Cheyennes and Sioux and Blackfoot. He could see no glory in making war on farming Indians.

The chill began seeping under Armbruster's coat, and he rubbed his hands together to try to get the circulation going again. As he did, he looked across the parade ground. The east side of the fort was dominated by a rocky cliff that rose to perhaps a hundred feet in height. The buildings—Armbruster took them for barracks—on the east side were set close to the cliff, a big disadvantage for defense, he thought, if he remembered some of his classes from West Point well.

Remembering such things shouldn't be all that difficult for Armbruster. After all, he had just graduated from the Point this past summer. He had spent a month afterward at home, showing off his fancy blue uniform with the second lieutenant's insignia on the shoulders to the young women. Then he had reported to Fort Leavenworth in the Kansas Territory, before finally receiving orders to report to the Third Infantry at Fort Defiance, New Mexico Territory.

The journey in and of itself had been a whole new experience for Armbruster. First there had been an interminable ride across the endless wastes of the prairie until reaching the mountains and Fort Marcy near the old Spanish town of Santa Fe. The fort was nothing special, but Santa Fe, well, that was another matter. He was surprised to find it a drab, brown little town, not the glittering cosmopolitan city he had expected. Once he got over that surprise, though, he was somewhat awed by the city—or, actually, by the residents of the city. Particularly the women.

After only three days at Fort Marcy, Armbruster had been sent on the last leg of his journey, nominally in charge of the detail escorting the mail-carrying courier to Fort Defiance. Armbruster might be fresh from the Point, but he knew that Sergeant Burghalter was in charge of the small group.

"It doesn't look like much, does it, Sergeant?" Armbruster asked.

"It ain't my place to comment on the design or construction of the fort," Burghalter said flatly. "Sir," he added after a moment's pause, not wanting to insult the lieutenant. On the ride from Fort Marcy, Burghalter had come to find that Lieutenant Armbruster was a decent man. True, Armbruster was still wet behind the ears—but he knew it. Armbruster was friendly, interesting and fairly lenient. Still, Burghalter wasn't sure how far he could trust Armbruster, even with a seemingly innocuous question such as the one Armbruster had just asked.

"I understand, Sergeant," Armbruster said. He knew he had put Burghalter on the spot and he regretted it, since that had not been his intention.

"However," Burghalter said with a sudden conspiratorial grin, "was I to make a comment about such a thing—which I'm not doin', mind you—I'd have to say that building the fort like this was pure, simple, outright, goddamn foolishness." Again he tacked on a "Sir" after several moments. "And it looks like shit."

Armbruster laughed. "I'll forget you said that, Sergeant," he noted.

"You'd best report in, Lieutenant," Burghalter said. "Major Brooks doesn't like dawdlers, and he'll be expectin' us."

"I think you're right, Sergeant," Armbruster said with a sigh. He had another look around, taking in the windswept cliff and the snow-covered buildings and parade ground. "You know, Sergeant," he said quietly, "being posted here's going to be a godawful thing to bear."

Burghalter grinned slyly. "That's why the men in this godforsaken hole call it Hell's Hollow."

Armbruster chuckled despite his growing annoyance at being stuck in such a place. "I wish you'd told me that earlier, Sergeant."

"Beggin' your pardon, Lieutenant, but if I'd've done that, you'd've skedaddled. Then I'd've had a devil of a time explainin' it to Major Brooks. Unless," he added with another grin, "I'd've gone with you."

"A tempting thought, Sergeant. I wonder how we would've fared." Armbruster sighed again. "Well, Sergeant, the major awaits our pleasure."

Moments later, Armbruster and Burghalter entered the office of Major William Thomas Brooks. Both snapped to attention in front of the spacious wood desk and brought up crisp salutes. Brooks returned the salute with a vague wave of the hand.

Brooks didn't appear to be too tall, but he had a certain strong bulk about him. His hair was sparse at top, but what was left was wild, curly and snow-white. His face was ruddy and creased from a life outdoors. It was marked by a flattened nose and a thin slit of a mouth. His entire being exuded command and authority, though a certain warmth lurked beneath the surface.

Before Armbruster could say or do anything,

Burghalter moved forward and placed a leather pouch on Brooks's desk. "Dispatches and mail for the men, sir," Burghalter said, stepping back.

"Thank you, Sergeant." Brooks left the pouch where it was. Then he looked at Armbruster, a question in his eyes.

"Lieutenant Edward Armbruster reporting for duty, sir," Armbruster said in militarily clipped words. He reached into a pocket, retrieved a piece of paper, stepped forward and handed it to Brooks. "My orders, sir." Then he stepped back and into attention again.

"Fresh from West Point, are you, Lieutenant?" Brooks asked without looking at the paper.

"Yessir." Armbruster was a little perplexed. "If you don't mind my asking, sir," he ventured, "how did you know that?"

"There's a certain look we have when we're just out of the Point, Lieutenant," Brooks said with a shadow of a smile. "West Point, 'forty-four."

"Yessir," Armbruster said, not knowing how else to respond.

"At ease, you two." Brooks picked up a pair of spectacles and eased them on. Then he leaned back in his chair to read over the papers. When he was done, he flicked them on the desk and then leaned forward so his elbows were on the marred wood surface of the desk.

"Lest there be any confusion, Lieutenant," Brooks said gruffly, "you've been posted to a shit hole of a place. There is little here to relieve the boredom. There is no town nearby where one might blow off some steam with a few snorts of whiskey and a roll in the hay with some money-grabbing trollop. Winters're often colder than a witch's left tit, and summers hot enough to fry a man's brains right inside his head."

Brooks pulled off his glasses. After dropping them

gently on the desk, he picked up a cigar and lit it from the lantern. He leaned back once more.

"We are plagued," he continued, "by exasperating Indians in the form of goddamn Navajos. They're not mean enough to bring us to war, but they're not peaceable enough to leave completely alone. If you're looking for glory fighting Indians, Lieutenant, you've been posted to the wrong place. About the only real Indian fighting we do here is when we make an expedition, and that's damn infrequent.

"I do not like fighting among my men, and I expect reasonably strict discipline to be administered whenever and wherever needed. Any questions, Lieutenant?"

"No, sir," Armbruster said flatly. He did have a couple: wanting to know how he could get out of here and how soon he could do so. But he knew that even hinting at such a thing would not be good for his career.

"Good. Welcome to Fort Defiance, Lieutenant." Brooks glanced over at Burghalter. "You have a good trip, Sergeant?"

"About usual, sir. A little more snow than the last, but no trouble."

"Good, good. Well, Sergeant, please take Lieutenant"—Brooks looked at the paper—"Armbruster and introduce him to B Company. You can leave him in First Sergeant Cavannaugh's care. And, considering the date, you and your men can stay over a day or two. You can bunk with B Company. I think there's enough room, though some of you might have to double up."

"Yessir. Are any special 'services' planned to mark the occasion?"

"I believe the men have something planned," Brooks said lightly.

"Special services?" Armbruster asked dumbly.

"I'll explain later," Burghalter interjected hastily.

"Indeed," Brooks commented. "On a more serious

note, Captain Goodwin will hold services tomorrow morning in the hospital."

"I didn't know Captain Goodwin was a preacher," Burghalter offered.

"He's not. But he's the closest thing this post has to one, and a number of the men requested the service."

"It mandatory?" Burghalter asked.

"Hell, no," Brooks growled.

"Then with your permission, sir," Burghalter said, snapping to attention once again, "we'll take our leave."

Armbruster was a moment slower in coming to attention, but his salute was smarter than Burghalter's.

Brooks returned the salutes, but then said, "One more thing, Sergeant. Show Lieutenant Armbruster to his quarters first. He's been assigned to the second one in from the east. The one between Captain Gilmore and Lieutenant Knudson."

Outside, Burghalter said, "Please wait here, Lieutenant. I'll only be a moment." He stepped down off the porch and issued orders to his men. He pulled his saddlebags and Armbruster's off their horses, and then the other soldiers led the horses toward the stables.

"This way, Lieutenant," Burghalter said. When Armbruster joined him in the still-falling snow, Burghalter turned and headed to a small line of buildings forming the northern perimeter of the fort. There were no stockade walls here; no battlements or bastions, just the buildings in a rude rectangle around the flat, desolate parade ground.

For some reason, Armbruster felt as if he were going to his doom.

{3}

First Sergeant Clancy Cavannaugh was a burly, hard-muscled man, but a friendly smile under a wild reddish brown mustache kept him from looking too mean. Still, Armbruster figured he would not want to mess with this particular sergeant.

Cavannaugh jumped up and shouted, "Attention!" when Armbruster followed Burghalter into the room.

Forty-three men—virtually all out of uniform—jumped up and stood at attention next to their double bunks.

"Sergeant Cavannaugh," Burghalter said, "your new company commander, Lieutenant Edward Armbruster."

Cavannaugh made a smart salute. "B Company mostly present and accounted for, sir!"

"Mostly?" Armbruster asked, eyebrows raised. He made a swift count, finding that the company was at least seven men short.

"Yessir. We've been shy three men from our regular compliment for some months. Plus, Corporal Bauer and Privates Finney, Olson and Vickers are all over in the hospital. Dysentery."

"Is that common, Sergeant?"

"Yessir. Out here anyway."

Armbruster nodded. Then he pointed. "Is that whiskey I see there, Sergeant?" he asked without inflection.

"Yessir," Cavannaugh answered tentatively.

Armbruster smiled. "That's right, I've interrupted your Christmas celebrations, haven't I?" he asked rhetorically. "Well, I'll leave you to your festivities, men. Sergeant Cavannaugh, please report to me tomorrow —at whatever hour you deem reasonable. Good night, gentlemen." He turned and walked out. He stopped just outside.

The late afternoon was gray and cold. Snow still fell, and it seemed to have increased some. Its shining whiteness did nothing to make the dismal fort any more cheerful.

A moment later, Burghalter came outside. "Sorry, Lieutenant," he said.

"No need to apologize, Sergeant." Armbruster grinned a little. "You had to have a few moments to tell them you and your men'd be back in there as soon as you got rid of me."

Burghalter smiled back. "Something like that, sir. Come on, I'll show you to your quarters." As they walked the short way, Burghalter said, "You can join us in the celebratin', if you're of a mind."

"That'd really liven things up, wouldn't it," Armbruster responded with a laugh. "It'd be the damned dullest Christmas celebrating anyone's ever done."

"If you say so, Lieutenant," Burghalter said quietly.

"I do."

Burghalter smiled into the snow. His already high impression of Armbruster rose even more. He stopped at a small adobe house and opened the door. He went in first, and groped around a little, until he found a lantern and got it lit. "Come in, sir," he announced.

With a little trepidation, Armbruster did. As he had feared, the single room was as dreary on the inside as it was outside. It had a table with two plain, solid-looking chairs. A pitcher, basin, cake of soap and small towel were on the table. As was the flickering lantern, which sent a sickly pale yellow light around the room. The bed in one corner was of wood with a rope "spring" and hay filled mattress. Two thin Army blankets were spread over the mattress. A tall chest of drawers was in another corner, and there was a small desk next to it. A small stove was centered on the wall between the table and desk.

Armbruster walked into the room, stopping at the bed to drop his saddlebags on it and to test the ticking's freshness. Then he wandered to the desk. On it sat a small, full inkwell, some blank sheets of paper, two pens and a blotter. The drawers of the chest were empty. All in all, the room resembled a hermit's cave. He glanced at Burghalter, who seemed antsy to get back to the barracks. "Are the officers celebrating, too?"

"I expect so, sir. But I don't know for sure, or where they might be gathered. I can find out for you."

"I'd appreciate that, Sergeant, if you'd let me impose on your kindness just this once more."

Burghalter had not wanted to do it; he had wanted to get his hands wrapped around a bottle of whiskey and get some good, hot food in his belly. But with Armbruster being so polite and self-effacing, he could not refuse. "I'll be back in a minute, Lieutenant," he said.

He was true to his word, but he did not come alone. Sergeant Cavannaugh was with him. "Sorry, sir," Cavannaugh said. "I wasn't thinking before. Since you've just come on the post, you couldn't know where things were. The officers are to meet in Captain Gilmore's quarters, next door on your right when you step outside. Beggin' your pardon, sir, but officers don't confide in sergeants, so I'm not sure what time the festivities begin."

"But . . . ?"

"But I've heard it's seven o'clock."

"Thank you, Sergeant. Both of you."

"Anything else you need, Lieutenant?"

"There somewhere I can eat?"

"Kitchen and officers' mess is out back, almost directly behind your quarters, sir," Cavannaugh said. "Supper's about six o'clock, which won't be long in comin', sir."

"Thank you again, Sergeant." Armbruster sighed. He was tired and felt beaten down. "Go on with your festivities."

"I'll send one of the men over to get your fire going, sir," Cavannaugh said. "It won't take long."

"That won't be necessary, Sergeant," Armbruster said. "Let the men enjoy themselves."

"You certain, sir?"

"Yes."

"Wood's out back."

"Thank you, Sergeant."

The two sergeants left. Armbruster stood there for a few moments, rubbing his face. He was having serious doubts all of a sudden about his choice of career. The thought of spending the rest of his career in bleak posts like Fort Defiance was enough to make him want to give up his commission. Then he scowled at himself. "Jesus, Lieutenant," he muttered sarcastically, "you've been on the post all of a half an hour and you're already ready to quit. Christ, give it a couple of days."

Having chastised himself, he went outside and around back, where he found a neat stack of split firewood. He was relieved to see that there was a supply of tinder, too. He had never been the best at starting fires. Gathering up an armful of wood and some tinder, he went back inside. It took him ten minutes, but he finally had a decent fire going.

Armbruster pulled a chair close to the stove, sat and

pulled off his boots. With a sigh of relief, he leaned back, stretching out his legs. He was nodding off when a knock on the door startled him. With a grimace, he pushed himself up and opened the door.

"Lieutenant Armbruster?" the officer standing there asked. He was as tall as Armbruster, but even thinner. His hair was almost as white as Major Brooks's. His mustache was the same color, making it difficult to see even though it was lush and thick. He wore only his regular army blouse, though it was cold out. He seemed none the worse for it.

"Yes."

The man stuck out his hand. "Lieutenant Hans Knudson. I'm B Company's other junior officer. Welcome to Fort Defiance."

Armbruster nodded and shook the man's hand.

"I'd like to invite you to a small gathering of the officers tonight to celebrate the Christmas."

"I'd be honored to attend," Armbruster said sincerely. Not only would it allow him to meet all the other officers, it would also show him to be a man who knew how to get along with others.

"Good. Seven o'clock. Next door." Knudson pointed.

"I'll be there, Lieutenant. Thank you."

"One more thing, Lieutenant." Knudson grinned. "You must be hungry."

"I am, considerably."

"I thought so. The officers' mess is serving now."

"Come in, Lieutenant," Armbruster said, stepping back out of the way. "I must've left my manners back on the trail somewhere. I need to tidy up a bit."

Knudson nodded and entered. "Cheery little place, isn't it?" he asked facetiously.

"Quite nice," Armbruster said flatly. He poured some water into the basin and washed his hands and face. As he toweled himself off, he asked, "Is yours as well appointed?"

"Every bit as luxurious." Knudson took the other chair and sat. "I guess we shouldn't complain too much, though. After all, we could be in the barracks with the enlisted men."

"A thought I'd not like to dwell on," Armbruster said with a laugh. He sat and pulled on his boots. Then he stood. "Well, sir, I believe I'm about ready as I'm going to get."

They left, Armbruster not bothering to put on his heavy coat. They were not going far. There were only two other officers in the mess hall when Armbruster and Knudson entered. Knudson introduced them to Armbruster as Captain Josiah Goodwin—the highest ranking officer of B Company—and Lieutenant Hugh Mosely.

"Will you be attending services tomorrow, Lieutenant?" Goodwin asked.

"If I can wake early enough, Captain," Armbruster said evenly. "It was a long arduous trip, and Major Brooks said it'd be all right if I skipped reveille in the morning," he added, lying about the last.

"Oh? Where did you come from?" Goodwin looked displeased.

"Fort Leavenworth."

"A fair piece, Lieutenant. Well, I still hope to see you at services."

Armbruster nodded, and then was taken to meet Mosely. He was a small, thin man with very large ears and a devil-may-care look in his eyes. His slim little mustache wriggled when he talked.

"So, are you plannin' to be at the festivities tonight, Lieutenant?" he asked.

"I do so, yes."

"Good. We can chat then. Right now I'm more interested in eating," Mosely said bluntly.

"Me, too," Armbruster agreed.

He and Knudson took another small table and ate what was put in front of them. Armbruster didn't much care what it was; he was that hungry. He was pleased, though, to see nicely seasoned mutton, from the Navajo herds, he assumed. There were also potatoes, corn, beans and corn bread. Armbruster stuffed himself.

"A cigar, Lieutenant?" Knudson asked. "Or may I call you Edward?"

"Ed'll do. And, yes, a cigar'd be nice about now."

Knudson nodded and handed Armbruster a cigar. "Good. Call me Hans."

Armbruster leaned back in his chair once his cigar was going, and he alternately puffed the cigar and sipped coffee.

Finally Knudson pushed himself lazily up. "It's almost time for celebrating," he said with a grin. "I want to clean myself up a little before I go."

Armbruster nodded and also stood. "Is special attire required for this thing?"

"No. It's rather informal. Or at least as informal as things ever get around here. A word of advice, though," Knudson continued as the two wandered outside. "I'd advise you to be on your best behavior tonight. You might feel the urge to hit the whiskey a good deal, but you'd make a hell of an impression on Major Brooks and the others if you were to get yourself three sheets to the wind, to use a term from our naval brothers."

"No, I expect that wouldn't be wise," Armbruster said dryly.

Knudson nodded. "I didn't mean to insult you, Ed," he said evenly. "It's just that newcomers sometimes forget themselves, especially after such a long trip. And some seem to think that because we're having a party that it's an excuse for them to get a little wild. I just wanted to make sure you knew that Major Brooks frowns on such behavior at the best of times.''

"I'm obliged, Hans," Armbruster said truthfully.

"I'll knock on your door when I'm ready," Knudson said as he stopped at his own small house. It was next to Armbruster's and looked to be about the same size and configuration.

Armbruster met all the officers—except one—at the gathering that night. The only one he didn't meet was one he had met already: Captain Josiah Goodwin. The pious officer wanted no part of such sinful activities as drinking in celebration of the Lord's birth. Major Brooks stayed only a short time, as did Lieutenants Frank Saxbury and Andy Emerson. The three were the only married officers on the post, and wanted to spend the evening with their families.

Armbruster paid attention to how much he drank, knowing how easy it was to get carried away with such things. He almost lost his resolve when he got cornered by Lieutenant Hugh Mosely, who proceeded to tell Armbruster everything he could possibly want to know about Fort Defiance, and then some. He knew—or thought he knew—everything that went on and how everything on the post operated. Even worse, he was distressingly cheerful throughout it all.

Knudson finally rescued Armbruster, who sighed with relief. "He always like that, Hans?" Armbruster asked.

"Yeah. He loves to see new officers come to the fort so he can do what he just did. Everyone who's been here more than a couple days knows what an insufferable idiot he is and avoids him when possible."

"Too bad, I guess. He seems like a decent enough fellow all in all."

"Yeah. But he can't control his urge to annoy folks

with his chatter.'' Knudson yawned. ''Well, it's about time I was in bed.''

''Getting some sleep sounds like a hell of a good idea. What time's reveille around here?''

''Daylight. Usually between five and six this time of the year. I think it'll be a little later tomorrow. Major Brooks might be a hard ass, but he's not unreasonable. He knows most of the men are celebrating tonight, and that many of the enlisted men will be rather under the weather. So he'll be a little more lenient. Unless, of course, they cause trouble. Then they'll feel the lash like as not.''

''Well, I hope that if the men get drunk and want to blow off steam that they'll do it quietly.''

{ 4 }

Armbruster opened the door to his house about six the next morning and gazed upon the bleary, sickly countenance of Sergeant Clancy Cavannaugh. The sergeant was weaving a little as he tried to stand at attention, and his salute was limp.

"You look like shit, Sergeant," Armbruster said brightly, returning Cavannaugh's salute. "Feel like it, too, I suppose?"

"Yessir." Cavannaugh belched and then grimaced, as if the burp had been painful.

"There much on the duty roster for today?" Armbruster felt only a little sorry for Cavannaugh. After all, the sergeant was old enough and experienced enough to know better than to get drunk. On the other hand, he had been in the same spot a few times and knew just how poorly Cavannaugh was feeling.

"Not much, sir. Five men're assigned to guard duty, and five to stable duty."

"You able to find ten men not hungover enough to be able to perform those duties?"

"Probably not." Cavannaugh wanted to vomit but wouldn't allow himself to in front of his new immediate commander. He held it back by sheer strength of will. "There's maybe six or seven who are. I'll put five of them on guard duty. With your permission, of course, sir."

"That'd be wise," Armbruster said dryly. "The others'll be sober enough to handle stable duty?"

"Yessir," Cavannaugh said. He nodded, too, and it started a heaving revolt in his head and stomach. He sucked wind in through his teeth trying to settle the rampaging sickness. "The rest of the men are at your command, Lieutenant." The thought of doing anything but sleeping off his hangover made Cavannaugh's agony that much worse.

"Well, Sergeant, I suppose I should get acquainted with the fort. And I think I can probably do that on my own. You and the men rest up and enjoy your Christmas day as best you can."

"Yessir!" Cavannaugh said with a wealth of enthusiasm. He couldn't believe his good fortune. He began to think that having Armbruster as one of his company commanders might work out well. If Armbruster was this pliant, Cavannaugh figured he should be able to control things—including Armbruster himself. "Anything else, sir?" he asked.

"Yes. Don't think that I'm a pushover because I am being a little lenient here, Sergeant. I won't be played for a fool. I'm young, it's true, and have little real experience in command. But I see myself as a commander, and a damn good one. I believe grown men should be treated as such. However, I won't be taken advantage of. If you and the men of B company want to be treated like men, you and they will have to show me the respect I deserve simply because of my rank. I hope to earn more respect by my behavior."

Cavannaugh was a little stunned, but once he could think about it—which was difficult considering how hungover he was—his respect for this new leader edged up. He even managed a small smile. "I'll have the men toe the line, sir. But . . ." He stopped, cursing inwardly that he had added the last word. He knew he should not continue.

"But what, Sergeant?"

"Nothing, Lieutenant."

"Bullshit," Armbruster snapped, eyes narrowing a little in anger. He figured it was time to show a little strength and leadership. "You appear to be a big, strong man. Have the courage of your convictions. You have something to say to me, come out with it. Don't back out once you've started."

"I'm not certain I should speak any further, sir. It might play hard on me."

"How many times've you lost rank, Sergeant?" Armbruster asked.

Cavannaugh offered a weak smile. "More'n once," he allowed.

"So if I were to bust you down a grade or two, it wouldn't be anything new, would it?"

"No, sir."

"You've known me but a short time, Sergeant, so you can't know this: I want a top sergeant who's not afraid of me because of my rank. I don't want one who tries to run roughshod over me, of course, but I do want one who's not afraid to tell me what he thinks, especially when he thinks I'm wrong. I had thought you to be such a man, Sergeant. Perhaps I was wrong."

"No, sir, you weren't," Cavannaugh growled. He straightened a little, trying to ignore the hangover. "What I was about to say, sir, was that I'll get the men to toe the line for a while, but you're going to have to prove yourself to them. You'll need to show 'em you can lead men—in battle. Then you might gain their respect."

"I'm aware of that, Sergeant. And I plan to do just that." He wasn't as sure as he sounded, but he would not permit any weakness to show.

"Yessir."

Armbruster nodded. "Go on and sleep it off, Sergeant. And have the men do the same. If anyone is in your condition tomorrow, he'll do thirty days on bread and water. Any above the rank of private who are in such condition will also be broken in rank."

Cavannaugh managed another weak grin. "Rightly so, sir. And I assure you, sir, that I won't be one of them."

"I didn't think you would be, Sergeant. Dismissed."

It did not take long for Armbruster to get acquainted with the fort, and then he spent the last few days of 1856 getting to know the men of B Company some.

What he had was forty-plus men of all shapes, sizes, intelligence, nationalities and disposition. At least half spoke and understood only a few words of English. Fortunately, Armbruster thought, many of the other men spoke two languages, and could translate for their comrades.

As with any group of men, there was a fair share of shirkers and complainers, as well as bullies, braggarts, drunks, timid souls, hard workers, spit-and-polish men and fools.

Despite their overall motley and inept appearance, they proved to be halfway decent soldiers, at least marching around on the parade ground. Armbruster was eager to see how his men performed in battle. He was also eager to see how he did under tense situations. He was not a vain man, but he held a certain confidence in himself. It galled him that he had no war experience. The latest war had ended eight years ago or so. At the time, he was still a boy, just hitting his teenage years. While he did not expect to be able to hide the fact that he had no battle experience, he had hoped that no one would make an issue of it. That had fallen by the wayside on his third night at the fort.

As usual, Lieutenant Hugh Mosely was expounding

on whatever flittered into his head in the officers' mess. Armbruster and Knudson were at another table, but it was hard to avoid what Mosely was saying. Armbruster cast a disparaging look at Mosely when Mosely said something about how he had been so heroic in the war with Mexico.

Mosely spotted Armbruster glaring at him and smiled cruelly. "I expect you wouldn't know about such things, would you, boy?" he said with a smirk. "Seein's how you've never faced an enemy."

Armbruster's look was venomous, but he could not say anything, considering that Mosely was telling the truth.

"Jesus, Hugh," Knudson snapped, "you ain't the only one fought in that war."

"That's a fact. But he's the only damn one here didn't fight then."

"So? None of us fought in the war with the British back in 'twelve."

"Hell, none of us was born then, except Major Brooks."

"Exactly," Knudson said with a nod, waggling his fork in Mosely's direction. "It's only a matter of the timing of his birth that kept Lieutenant Armbruster out of the Mexican War. It has nothing to do with bravery or anything else."

"Shit," Mosely said with a sneer. "Little baby-face there ought to be wearin' dresses."

Armbruster was shocked. Mosely had always been personable, if not exactly likable. He could not understand why Mosely had seemingly turned completely against him.

"That's about enough from you, Mosely," Knudson said angrily, starting to rise from his table.

Armbruster grabbed his arm and pulled him back down. "I'm obliged for the help you've given me, Hans," Armbruster said harshly. "But I can stand up for myself.'' He gazed across the room, eyes fiery with anger. "I'd be obliged if you were to answer one thing for me, Lieutenant,'' Armbruster said stiffly.

"And just what's that?'' The smirk seemed a permanent fixture on Mosely's face now.

"If you were so all-fired heroic in the war, how come you're still a lieutenant? I mean, jeez, loads of heroism, and eight years removed from the end of the war, one'd think you could've made captain, at least.'' He returned Mosely's sneer, though he was worried about offending Knudson, who was in the same position as Mosely.

Knudson did not seem to mind, but Mosely's eyes widened as his faced colored in rage. He suddenly slapped his hands on the table and shoved himself violently up, his chair crashing to the floor. He stood for some moments, too angry to speak. Finally he said icily, "You're lucky, boy, that I'm a kindhearted man, else I'd whip your ass up and down the compound.''

"Oh, I don't think it's because you're kindhearted,'' Armbruster said with a sneer. "It's just that you're a chickenshit. And if you didn't outrank me, I'd take you outside and kick the tar out of you.''

Mosely half climbed over his table, heading for Armbruster, before two other officers grabbed him and slammed him back into his chair. He sat there stewing for some moments, trying to get a handle on his rage. Gradually he was able to, and he stood slowly, face frozen in icy calm. He pulled off his uniform blouse and dropped it on the table. "No more lieutenant,'' Mosely said. "You got the nerve to take me on now, boy?''

"You promise you won't pull rank on me?'' Armbruster countered.

Mosely looked around at the others. He had planned to file charges with Brooks as soon as he beat the hell out of Armbruster—charges of striking a superior officer. But Armbruster had called him on that.

That increased his ire even more, as did knowing that he had no choice but to answer, "I promise."

Armbruster nodded. He wondered what had come over Mosely. He was not fond of the officer, not since Mosely had bent his ear the first night he had been at the fort. But he didn't hate Mosely, and he could not figure out why Mosely seemed to hate him now. He stood, pulling off his own uniform blouse. "Out back," he stated, and he headed for the only door, in the front. He still wondered what was wrong with Mosely, but he knew puzzling over it would not answer it.

With Knudson at his side, Armbruster stepped outside into the crisp cold afternoon, turned left and then left again to walk alongside the east wall of the kitchen. Close behind were all the other officers who had been in the kitchen.

Just as he got around to the back of the building, Armbruster fell on his face, a maniacal Mosely on his back, pounding the back of his head with insane fury.

Knudson and Captain Gilmore dragged Mosely off of Armbruster, and Mosely stood there roaring and snapping.

Armbruster rose slowly, brushing snow off his front with one hand and gingerly feeling the back of his head with the other. He glared angrily at Mosely. This suddenly was more than a challenge; it had become an insult to Armbruster.

"Let me go!" Mosely bellowed. "You two sons of bitches, let me go!"

"Not till Ed's ready," Knudson said calmly, though he, too, was getting rather heated. Like everyone else, he was bewildered at Mosely's behavior. "You aren't about to go jumping him from behind again."

"Let the dumb bastard go," Armbruster said evenly.

Knudson and Gilmore did, and Mosely charged forward as if he were berserk. And ran right into Armbruster's hard right forearm. Mosely's feet, on the slick snow, skidded out from under him, and he went down like a broken sack of horse grain.

Armbruster considered letting Mosely get up again, but then he decided that as crazy as Mosely was being today, there was no reason to do so. Instead, he stomped on Mosely's chest, twice. It wasn't as hard as he could have made it, but he figured he had done some damage.

Armbruster stepped back. "You want some more, I'm waiting," he said quietly.

Mosely only groaned.

"I think he's had enough, Ed," Knudson said dryly. "We best get him inside before he freezes to death. Give me a hand with him."

"No, sir," Armbruster said flatly.

Knudson glared at him for a moment, then grinned. "Hell, son, you knocked him down, you might's well help him back up."

Armbruster thought of refusing again, but knew he would be in trouble if he did. He nodded and helped Knudson lift Mosely. Holding him under the arms, the two carried Mosely toward the kitchen, his feet dragging in the snow. They plopped him unceremoniously in his chair and left him.

Armbruster picked up his uniform blouse and pulled it on. "I think I'll go back to my quarters," he said.

Knudson nodded. The enjoyment had gone out of lingering around the table with coffee and cigars.

Back in his small house, he lay on his bed, fingers laced behind his head. Mosely's behavior still baffled him. The more he thought of it, the more aggravated he got, until he had to get up and pace. Finally he lay down again and at last drifted off to sleep.

Knudson's pounding on his door the next morning woke Armbruster. He stumbled groggily to the door and opened it.

"Major Brooks wants to see you, Lieutenant," Knudson said flatly. "As soon as you can make yourself ready."

"It won't be but a moment," Armbruster said, growing more awake with each moment. He waved Knudson in and then turned. Quickly he splashed some water on his face and hair, ran a brush over his wet hair, tried to bat some of the wrinkles out of his pants, and finally put on his uniform blouse. "I take it this is about last night's ruckus?" he asked as he and Knudson went outside.

"What else."

They marched quietly across the parade ground to Brooks's office. Brooks was pacing slowly behind his desk. He turned when they came into the room. Mosely sat in a chair facing Brooks's desk.

Brooks returned the salutes given by Armbruster and Knudson, but the two stayed at attention. "Did you attack Lieutenant Mosely last night, Lieutenant?" Brooks asked.

"No, sir," Armbruster said honestly.

"You lying son of a bitch," Mosely snarled. He half swung in his chair, then groaned as his injured insides shifted and ground together.

"Lieutenant Mosely says differently," Brooks said.

"I told the truth, sir."

"Do you deny you gave Lieutenant Mosely his injuries?" Brooks demanded.

"No, sir."

"If you gave him the injuries, how can you say you didn't attack him?" Brooks was more than a little mystified.

"He attacked me, sir," Armbruster said simply.

"Goddammit, you lyin' bastard!" Mosely bellowed.

"Play another tune, Mosely," Armbruster said flatly, harshly. He was still at attention, and had not even looked at Mosely.

"That's enough, both of you," Brooks snapped angrily.

"Lieutenant Armbruster's telling the truth, sir," Knudson offered.

"Explain it," Brooks ordered.

"Lieutenant Armbruster and I were eating in the single officers' mess when Lieutenant Mosely began running down Lieutenant Armbruster, who took exception to it, and rightly so. Lieutenant Armbruster said he'd kick the shit out of Lieutenant Mosely if Lieutenant Mosely didn't outrank him. Lieutenant Mosely removed his blouse and said he was no longer a first lieutenant for the time being. On the walk outside to settle matters Lieutenant Mosely jumped on Lieutenant Armbruster from behind. Captain Gilmore and I pulled him off. When we let him go, Lieutenant Mosely charged Lieutenant Armbruster, who flattened him and then stomped on him a couple of times. Lieutenant Armbruster could've done Lieutenant Mosely a lot more damage if he wanted, but he backed away once Lieutenant Mosely was down."

"It's all lies," Mosely bellowed.

Brooks looked from Mosely to Armbruster to Knudson, wondering. Then he looked back at Mosely. "I don't know what's come over you, Lieutenant, but you'll be held in the guardhouse until a court-martial can be convened." Then he bellowed, "Orderly!" When Private Vickers entered, Brooks said, "Get a detail to escort Lieutenant Mosely to the guardhouse."

When Mosely had been taken away—mouthing curses and imprecations—Brooks said, "Such a strange thing. Very strange."

"Yessir," Armbruster and Knudson said in unison.

"At ease, men," Brooks said. He went to sit behind his desk. "Do either of you have any idea of what's brought on Lieutenant Mosely's peculiar behavior?"

"No, sir," Armbruster said. "It struck me as very

odd, though. It's not like Lieutenant Mosely at all. Or, rather, nothing like I've seen from him in the short time I've been at Fort Defiance."

"I think he's completely lost his reason, sir," Knudson volunteered.

"I'm afraid you might be right, Lieutenant. We should know by the time we convene the court-martial." He leaned back in his chair, senses a little dulled by aggravation. Finally he looked up. "Dismissed."

5

Armbruster was watching Company B drill on the parade grounds when the gunfire erupted. There was one shot, then another, a brief pause, and then a small fusillade. He whirled toward the cliff, expecting an attack by Indians. A slug tore through his coat, between his side and arm. A moment later, one of his men fell.

He whirled again, as more gunfire cracked out. He saw a soldier go down face first, shot by two others who had stormed out of the guardhouse. It took Armbruster a moment to realize that the fallen soldier must be Lieutenant Hugh Mosely. He ran toward him, noting that soldiers were pouring out of most of the buildings.

Armbruster was the first to reach the body—after the two soldiers who had shot him. Armbruster knelt and gently eased the body over onto its back. It was Mosely, and he was not quite dead yet.

Mosely tried to say something, but no words came. Then the light in his eyes faded. He sighed once, and then was gone, wide eyes not seeing the bright expanse of blue sky. Armbruster gently swept his hand over Mosely's eyes, moving the lids down to cover them. Then he rose.

"What the hell happened here?" Brooks growled as

he puffed to a halt near the body. "Lieutenant?" he asked, looking at Armbruster.

"Lieutenant Mosely's dead, sir. He was shot by those two," Armbruster said, pointing to the two guards.

"Why?" Brooks asked, mystified.

"I have no idea, sir."

"Well?" Brooks asked, turning his fierce gaze on the two men—Corporal Rick Bauer and Private Don Vickers.

"He . . ." Bauer started, then hesitated.

"Out with it, man," Brooks growled.

"The lieutenant was trying to escape, sir," Bauer said firmly.

"But how . . . ?"

"Somehow someone got him a pistol, sir," Bauer continued. "He's still got it in his hand. He . . . Well, dammit . . . pardon me, sir . . . he killed Private Endicott and started to run. That's when we—"

"You better explain it more fully than that, Corporal," Brooks interjected.

"Yessir." Bauer paused a moment. He was a little shaken by what had happened. He seemed a little steadier than Vickers, but not much.

"You ever killed a man before, son?" Brooks asked.

"No, sir."

"It's not pleasant, is it?"

"No, sir. Not one goddamn bit, beggin' your pardon, sir."

Brooks nodded, then gently urged, "Continue, Corporal."

"Private Endicott was bringing the lieutenant his noon meal. I don't know where he got the pistol, but we figure that as soon as Chuck—Private Endicott—opened the cell door, the lieutenant blasted him. We went runnin' back there to see what the gunshot was all about. Lieutenant Mosely charged out, firing a couple times and burstin' through us as he ran for the door. It's a wonder he didn't hit me or Private Vickers with any bullets. As it was he knocked Don on his ass.''

He paused a moment, trying to bat down his nervousness. "Then he was outside and runnin'. Me and Don come out, yelled at him once to halt, and then fired at him when we saw he wasn't about to stop.''

"And almost killed me in the doing," Armbruster said, sticking a finger through the bullet hole in his coat. He was shaking a little, now that things had calmed down. He hadn't had time before to be scared.

"And, even worse, sir," Sergeant Cavannaugh said gruffly. When all turned to look at him, he said sadly, "A stray bullet took the life of Private Yankelovich."

Bauer began to cry. He was quiet about it, not blubbering and sniffling, just releasing a steady flow of tears and an occasional sob.

Vickers stood with a blank look in his eyes, as if he had just been hit in the forehead. He was too dazed to say or do anything.

Brooks looked from one to the other, trying to fathom how badly the two men must feel after all this. He was sympathetic, but he could not be overly solicitous; they were soldiers and would have to act like it. "Lieutenant Armbruster," he said. "Have someone escort Corporal Bauer and Private Vickers to the post surgeon's. Maybe Doctor Fournier can help them be at ease soon and return to duty."

"Yessir."

"Then have some of the men take Lieutenant Mosely, as well as Privates Endicott and Yankelovich to be prepared for burial," Brooks continued. "Once that's in progress, I want you and Lieutenant Knudson to go through Mosely's quarters—with a fine-tooth comb if need be—to see if you can find anything there that might give us a clue to his strange behavior of late. Oh," Brooks tacked on, "and while you're in there, pack his personal effects for shipment back to his family.''

''Yessir.'' Armbruster issued orders as Brooks and the other officers left. Then he and Knudson headed for Mosely's quarters.

''This ought to be fun,'' Knudson said glumly while they walked.

''Indeed.'' Armbruster was distracted, trying to sort out things. He had never come so close to death before. He was surprised now that when that bullet ripped through his coat he was as calm as could be. He thought that was good, but he wasn't quite sure.

At the same time, he had never seen a man killed right before his eyes either. He had seen the dead of course—all embalmed and peaceful looking. Not one that had just had two large-caliber rifle balls enter the back and blow out two large, gushing holes in the front. It certainly wasn't as glamorous as he would have liked to believe.

All in all he was glad, though, that someone else had done the killing. He might've learned today that he was cool under fire—or, he thought ruefully, that he had been so scared as to only think he was cool—but that didn't mean he wanted to actually try killing another human being. Not even an Indian. And that, he knew, could put one hell of a crimp in his military career.

He tried to shove the gloomy thoughts out of his mind when he and Knudson entered Mosely's quarters. It was a duplicate of each of theirs, except in the sparse personal possessions scattered around.

Armbruster felt like a ghoul as he began going through Mosely's personal effects, starting with the obvious—the razor and mug of shaving soap by the basin and pitcher, the toothbrush and cleaning powder. He tossed the items in a wood box he found in a corner.

He noticed that Knudson had started with the chest of drawers.

With a sigh of fatalism and dislike, Armbruster headed for the small desk. The surface was a mess. The top of the inkwell was off, and one of the pens was in the bottle. The other pen, nib thick with dried ink, lay on the desk. Some ink was spilled on the blotter, and papers were scattered around.

Armbruster sat in the chair and picked up the papers, tapping them edgewise on the desk to neaten the pile. There were a few words written on several pieces of the paper, but nothing distinguishable. The rest of the papers were blank. Armbruster threw the marred ones into the stove, and the good ones into the box.

He placed the other loose items from the top of the desk into the box. There was little of interest—a pocket watch, a pipe, tobacco and tamper, a small magnifying glass, a few lead balls, a needle to which was attached a small streamer of thread, and two buttons. Then he reached for the stack of letters sitting on a corner of the writing desk.

The letters were loose, so Armbruster leaned back, not comfortable but knowing he had to do this. He pulled the top letter out of the envelope, opened it and began to read. It contained nothing more than a mother's letter to a favored son. The second was the same, the third a similar one from a brother.

Armbruster worked his way through the small stack of mail, learning nothing, and almost falling asleep in the process. He still felt uncomfortable with going through someone else's personal mail. He would not like it if anyone were to read his.

Next he picked up one by one the four books on the desk and ruffled through the pages. There was a Bible, an army manual, and one of Armbruster's favorites—*Moby Dick*. Being from Connecticut, Armbruster had been fond of whaling stories, and considered *Moby Dick* the best of them. The fourth was something titled *Uncle Tom's Cabin*. He put the first three in the box, but a letter was stuffed into the latter book. He pulled it out and dropped the book into the box. He opened the letter and began reading. The first few paragraphs were the usual pleasantries exchanged in letters by family members to one another. But then he found:

As we told you some time back, son, we moved into the Kansas Territory to keep all those nigger-lovers from taking over any more territory. But the fight's going to be harder than we had expected.

It's become bad of late with all those miserable, low-down free staters causing ruckuses all over the territory, shooting at peaceable folk for no good reason other'n to spread their vile ideas. They've caused so much trouble for us decent folk that we've had to form a militia. For a while there, the governor was one of us, and he was all for the idea. We figured that while we had us a man of reason and sense, we were in a position to boot the free state scum out of the territory once and for all. But not long ago, we got us a free stater for territorial governor. And he's caused us no end of hard times. I can only pray that Mr. James Buchanan wins the election in a few days from that insufferable Frémont feller. That happens, we'll have our way in the territory, as is right and proper.

To show you what we're facing out here, I've sent along a book—a sure sample of the trash that's being written and spoken here. Once you've seen what we're up against, you'll find us completely justified in what we've done.

There is good news, though. Your brother Cecil joined the militia straight off, and was made a corporal. But soon after—late in August—he and the other men fought valiantly at Osawatomie, which had been overrun by those suck-eggs free staters. Drove that scum clean out. Colonel Maggard of the militia was so plumb pleased with Cecil that he promoted him right there on the spot! Made him a major! He was . . .

Armbruster sat there stunned, holding the thin, crinkly paper, no longer really seeing it.

"Ed? Ed?" Knudson called. "You all right?"

Armbruster came out of his fog. "Yeah," he said. "But I think I've found out why Hugh went crazy."

"Let me see." Knudson strode across the small room and took the paper out of Armbruster's hands. He stood there for some seconds, reading. Then he stopped, eyes wide. "Jumping Jesus!" he exclaimed. "One damn battle and this damn fool of a colonel promotes him from corporal to major? That must've eaten at Hugh something awful."

"I expect it did. And then when he started riding me about not having fought against Mexico, and I rode him back about how he'd been a lieutenant since then without a promotion . . ."

"Jesus, no wonder he set on you like that. Who could've known?"

"Maybe nobody," Armbruster said quietly. "But I was the one drove him to all this."

"Like hell you did," Knudson snapped, tossing the letter on the desk. "He was half-crazy all along. Hell, I'm no lover of darkies, but that letter there is downright odious."

"I find it repellent. Utterly repulsive."

"You one of those folks they call abolitionists?" Knudson asked.

Armbruster looked up and half smiled. "I don't

know as if I could be called that, no. But I don't understand how people can think they can own people."

"I'm not sure darkies're people."

"Well, I expect they're close enough to make me mighty uncomfortable in thinking of owning some." He smiled wanly. "I never meant to say anything to you or anyone else about this. It's a sure way to cause trouble."

"It is that," Knudson said thoughtfully. "On the other hand, I've never looked at it in that light." He shrugged, knowing he was not explaining very well. "I just looked on nig— on black-skins as . . . hell, I don't know . . . slaves I guess. There weren't many of them in Minnesota, where I come from." He tapped the letter that was lying on the desk. "But if this is to be believed, everyone's going to have to start thinking about it." He grinned a little. "I might as well start now as later."

Armbruster nodded, and then sighed. "Let's get the rest of this stuff packed up. I suddenly feel a need for some fresh air."

Half an hour later, the two officers walked into Brooks's office. "Everything of his is packed and sitting in Hugh's quarters, sir," Knudson said. "I'll assign a detail to prepare it for shipping, if you want, sir."

"Please." Brooks paused and ran a hand through his silver-gray hair. "Did you two learn anything?"

"Yes, sir," Armbruster said. He stepped forward and placed the letter on Brooks's desk.

Brooks glanced up at Armbruster, a little surprised, then turned his attention to the letter. It took him only moments to read it, shaking his head most of the while. Finally he was finished. "Discounting his family's views on free state versus slave state," Brooks said quietly, "since that doesn't really matter, any man who aims to commit suicide because his brother outranks him in a

6

Armbruster put Mosely out of his mind as best he could and turned his thoughts to spring. He was eager for the change of season for several reasons, not the least of which was that he was plumb sick of winter. He would find out soon enough that spring was not the kind season he was used to; rather it was a stormy, often cloudy, and thoroughly muddy time. There was no getting away from the mud—deep, thick, goopy, rich red mud that clung to the boots and tried not to release the unfortunate victim. It splattered on everyone and everything, dried and then fell off in clotty chunks.

Armbruster had other reasons for wanting spring to arrive. It would mean the beginning of patrols. He looked forward to them—and hoped he might encounter some hostile Indians. It wasn't that he was bloodthirsty, or an Indian hater; it was what he was trained for, and he thought he was long overdue in getting on with that work. He did retain a sense of fear about it all, not knowing how he would react when really under fire. It was a test he looked forward to and dreaded.

With him so aware of each passing day, though, the time seemed to drag on and on. Two warm days in late

March had him convinced that spring had at last arrived, but the temperature the next day was down below freezing, dashing his hopes.

Still, spring had to arrive some time, and it finally eased its way into the high country, and Brooks passed around word that the men should begin preparing for patrols.

It had taken Armbruster some little time to get used to the fact that while he and his men were in the infantry, they would travel by horse. Distances were so vast out here that a true infantry was impossible. Here at Fort Defiance—and he suspected in many other western forts—the infantryman had really evolved into more of a dragoon, where they would ride until they found the enemy, then dismount and fight on foot. Armbruster found it disconcerting at first, but soon began to get used to the idea.

Armbruster never knew why Brooks picked him to lead the first patrol out after word had come that Navajos had raided a few farms. Hoping his worry did not show, he mounted up with Cavannaugh, Corporal Bauer and a dozen men. They had enough provisions for a week. After that they would have to fend for themselves.

"Sergeant Cavannaugh, lead the way," Armbruster said officiously. In a few moments, he was out of the fort.

Most of the men with him had been posted to Fort Defiance for a year or more, and so they knew the territory and the routine far better than Armbruster did. Unlike many men in his position, Armbruster was willing to admit he had much to learn.

Soon after leaving the fort behind, Cavannaugh dropped back until he was riding next to Armbruster. "Beggin' your leave, Lieutenant, but I don't usually ride out on the point."

"I didn't think so, Sergeant. What's the usual procedure?"

"You—or I—assign one or two men to ride out front, sir. Maybe two more behind them. Then us. The rest of the boys follow." He grinned a little. "That way the important folks like you are as protected as much as possible, sir."

"Not to say anything about my intrepid sergeant, eh?" Armbruster said with a small laugh. The release of some tension with the laugh helped him settle down a little.

"Well, sir," Cavannaugh said with a straight face, "I've got to stick close to you in case you need to issue orders."

"Indeed." Armbruster paused, uncertain, then shrugged. "Who usually chooses the point men, Sergeant?" he asked.

"You do, sir," Cavannaugh said flatly. He was still feeling out the lieutenant, even as he knew Armbruster was testing him.

"I'm not so sure you're being truthful, Sergeant," Armbruster responded in kind.

Cavannaugh glanced at Armbruster. In the few months he had been under Armbruster's command, Cavannaugh had become fairly sure he could trust Armbruster to say what he meant and mean what he said. He thought that was the case now. "I usually do, sir. At least with a man of your . . . limited experience." He figured that if he was going to get reamed out, now would be the time.

But Armbruster just nodded. "That makes sense, Sergeant," Armbruster said seriously. "Do it, then."

"Yessir." Cavannaugh wheeled away and trotted up to one soldier. He spoke briefly, and then repeated it with three others. Moments later those four men had ridden out in front of the column, spaced as Cavannaugh had said they would be. Cavannaugh came back to ride alongside Armbruster.

After riding a little distance in quiet, Armbruster asked, "What can we—I—expect on this patrol, Sergeant?"

"The truth again, sir?" Cavannaugh asked boldly.

Armbruster nodded.

"More than likely not a goddamn thing but a sore ass and a pocketful of boredom, sir."

"That's usual?" Armbruster tried not to sound too disappointed.

"Yessir. The Navajos're a little more settled than the Apaches or the Utes, but they can still cover ground with the best of 'em. It figures like this—by the time we get word some places've been raided and get a patrol up, those red bastards're long gone. We can track 'em, but if they put their minds to it, they can about disappear. Most times like this, we go out, follow the trail a couple days or so, and then ride back to Fort Defiance."

"Sounds pretty dull all right."

"Yessir. But keep to mind that it's a heap better this way. There's many a man—officer and enlisted man alike—that thinks he's going to be covered with glory by ridin' out and killin' some red devils."

Armbruster nodded. "You don't like Indians much, do you, Sergeant?" he asked.

Cavannaugh shrugged. "I don't dislike 'em just 'cause they're Indians. I just don't take kindly to anyone tryin' to kill me, and that's just what the Navajos or any other red bastards'll do if we catch 'em." He paused, gnawing on the ends of his red mustache. "I once thought I'd come out here, kill me some Indians and go home a hero. But in the couple years I've been posted out here, I've altered my thinkin' on that."

"How so?"

"There ain't a hell of a lot of glory in gettin' killed

by redskins, or by anyone else for that matter, sir. Not that I'm a coward, or that I'm tryin' to shirk my duty. No, sir. I just decided a while back that I'd much rather die of old age next to a toothless old wife than dyin' young from a Navajo arrow." He glanced over at Armbruster.

"Not a foolish idea, Sergeant."

"Thank you, sir." He paused. "Remember this, though, sir," he added. "I'll fight like a son of a bitch if we do catch these Navajos, or any others that've been causin' a ruckus. And if I'm sent across the divide in the doin', well, then so be it, and I'll leave my fate to the Almighty. But I ain't about to start trouble with no Indians that don't start something first."

"Nor is that foolish thinking, Sergeant," Armbruster said quietly.

"Another reason I like to be the one pickin' the men, both for patrol and to ride point, is that I know the men pretty well. I know the ones that hate Indians, the ones who think it's glorious to kill Indian women and kids, ones filled with an unhealthy malevolence."

"I don't know about the other officers at Fort Defiance, Sergeant, and I don't have a whole hell of a lot of experience, as you full well know, but I've never subscribed to the idea of running roughshod over my sergeant. I'm obliged for the help you've given me so far, and I'll continue to look to you for guidance. Not decisions, mind you. That's what they pay me for. But guidance I'll take all I can get of. It ever gets to the point where I think you're taking advantage or something, you'll be the first one to learn about my displeasure."

Cavannaugh didn't think that would be so bad. Armbruster had already shown himself to be a man of sense and vision. "That's as it should be, sir," Cavannaugh said diplomatically.

* * *

Four days out, Armbruster was certain they would never find any hostile Navajos. They had found two small enclaves of Navajos, but all the Indians in them seemed to be concerned about nothing more than their sheep, their horses and their fields.

Armbruster was fascinated, though, at seeing Navajos close up for the first time. They were taller and thinner than he had expected. Their eyes were expressive and alive, unlike those of the Osage and Kickapoos he had seen back in Kansas Territory. They had looked dissipated, beaten down by life's cruelties. The Navajos, though, appeared healthy and attractive. The women had small, delicate hands and feet, and their faces were long and thin, with full lips, dark eyes and prominent noses.

Also of interest were the homes the Navajos lived in. He had seen the buffalo-skin lodges of the Plains Indians; and he had encountered the pueblos, those adobe multistoried apartment buildings. But he had never encountered a hogan. They were odd-shaped abodes of logs and dirt, the doorway always facing the east to greet the day's rising sun. There were almost a dozen hogans in the first place Armbruster and his men stopped, not quite a village, but it was fairly close.

They rode out of the first one and by midmorning the next day they had found the second gathering of Navajos. They learned nothing there about the raiders either, and left straight off. A storm boiled up in the west that afternoon, and by the time they had made their camp, a steady, chill rain was falling. Lightning the likes of which Armbruster had never seen in frequency, severity and display flashed and flickered across the rocky, barren countryside. Thunder growled at them, until Armbruster suspected that the Navajo gods were angry at them.

He found it hard to lose the feeling even the next

morning. The rain had stopped, but the skies were still sullen and swollen. Armbruster huddled, feeling miserable, in his coat. This was not what he had expected it to be like out here. He expected grandeur and wonder. He had found those things, but he had also smacked face first into the reality of life in this harsh corner of the West.

Still, there was nothing grand or heroic about miles of mud. Or poor food cooked on furtive flames. Or thousands of sheep tended by diffident Indians. Or trying to sleep in the open when worrying about rattlesnakes, lizards and lord knew what else. Or having a sore rump all the time. Or of being cold one minute and sweltering the next. Only the land had any grandeur. That and the spreading immensity of the sky.

Sergeant Cavannaugh's arrival snapped him out of his gloomy thoughts. "May I speak, sir?" Cavannaugh asked.

"Of course, Sergeant," Armbruster said. "Sit. Have some coffee."

"Don't mind if I do, sir," Cavannaugh said. He sat and poured coffee, tasted it, then said, "I think we should head back to the fort, sir."

"Why's that?"

"To be blunt, sir, we don't have a pig's chance of findin' any hostile Navajos now."

"So we should just pack up and run?" Armbruster asked heatedly.

"We've been out here four days, sir, and haven't even cut sign of the hostiles. And as sure as my aunt Maggie's got corns on her feet, the hostiles aren't going to come out and announce their surrender."

Armbruster sat, anger growing. He knew what Cavannaugh had said was true, but he didn't like it one iota. He was certain that if he rode back into Fort Defiance empty-handed, as it were, that he would be the laughingstock of the post. That ate at his insides.

Cavannaugh knew what Armbruster was thinking. He had felt much the same himself when he had first arrived at the post. "There ain't a man in Fort Defiance who hasn't been in this situation, sir," he said softly. "Believe me, sir, this isn't new. It's one of the many frustrations of being posted out here."

"I wish I could believe that, Sergeant. I . . . I . . ." He paused, then snapped, "Dammit all."

"There'll be other times for fightin' Indians, sir," Cavannaugh said. He stared down into his coffee cup. He knew what Armbruster was going through, but he could not force the officer to believe him, or to feel better. Armbruster would have to do that himself.

"Yes, I know," Armbruster said, his irritation not lessening.

Cavannaugh looked at his commanding officer. He also smiled. "Besides, sir, we're getting low on rations. And it appears Private Davidson's come down with the ague or something, and Private Killian's showin' signs of it, too."

"You don't have to give me false reasons for going back, Sergeant," Armbruster said irritably.

"If I might be blunt one more time, Lieutenant," Cavannaugh said, figuring the risk was worth it.

"Speak your mind, Sergeant."

"Neither I nor you need any fuckin' excuses for doin' what makes sense. Sir." He chewed on his mustache some more. "I'm tellin' you, sir, that there's no one in the fort going to think bad of you for turnin' back now. You'll get your chance to play Indian fighter."

Armbruster battled down the sudden burst of fury. When he managed to control it, he realized that Cavannaugh was probably right. "Get the men moving," he said evenly. "And, Sergeant," he added as

Cavannaugh rose, "if you're lying about this, you'll re-gret it."

Cavannaugh grinned. "I'll take the chance, sir."

Armbruster felt a little better.

{ 7 }

With every yard closer he got to Fort Defiance, Armbruster grew more worried. Despite Cavannaugh's insistence that all the officers of the fort had led useless patrols, Armbruster was not convinced. He thought he did a pretty good job at concealing his concern, and since Cavannaugh didn't mention it, he figured he had succeeded.

Steeling himself, Armbruster finally led the way into the unenclosed fort, braced for jeers and taunts. He was mildly—though pleasantly—surprised when none were offered. The troops drilling on the parade ground ignored the new arrivals, while several officers and other enlisted men stopped and watched with only mild interest.

Armbruster and his men went straight to the large stable at the southwest edge of the post and dismounted in the corral. Armbruster walked slowly toward Major Brooks's office to report, while the men began tending to the horses. Armbruster tensed again as he neared headquarters. Surely Brooks would have something derogatory to say to him, he figured. He reported in, snapping up a crisp salute.

"At ease, Lieutenant," Brooks said. "Take a seat."

When Armbruster had, Brooks asked, "Well, how'd things go?"

"Not very well, sir. We didn't see hide nor hair of any hostiles. We came on two . . . villages, I guess you could call them . . . but they were friendly. The only rounds we fired were hunting twice."

Brooks nodded, nonplused. "That's about the usual," he said. "But never fear, Lieutenant, you'll get your chance to fight Indians sooner or later. You can be sure of that."

"Yessir." Armbruster suddenly felt much lighter of heart.

"Anything out of the ordinary to report?"

"No, sir."

"No discipline problems or anything."

"No, sir. Sergeant Cavannaugh keeps a firm hand on the men."

"He's one of the best," Brooks acknowledged. "Well, if there's nothing else, you're dismissed, Lieutenant." He paused. "But I wouldn't get too comfortable if I were you. Now that good weather's here, Indians—both Navajos and Apaches—will be raiding regularly. We often have several patrols in the field at any one time. Indeed, Lieutenants Emerson and Saxbury have E and G Companies out now. I expect we'll send another one, maybe even two, by week's end."

"Yessir," Armbruster said. He rose, saluted and then left. He headed straight for his quarters, where he took off his uniform and stuffed it into a canvas bag. In nothing but his long underwear, he washed some of the reddish dust off himself and began to shave. He was about halfway through that when someone knocked on the door.

"Who is it?" he shouted.

"Hans."

"Come on in."

Knudson entered and shut the door behind him. "Welcome back. You have yourself a grand adventure?" Knudson asked with a grin as he sat in a chair. He pulled out a pipe and began filling the bowl.

Armbruster squinted at Knudson to see if his friend was chiding him or just joking. He decided Knudson was teasing. "Heap big adventure," he grunted.

"Didn't see shit, did you?" Knudson asked, laughing. He lit his pipe.

Armbruster wiped his razor off on a towel, and then looked at Knudson. "Saw a couple of groups of Navajos tending their sheep and their gardens. That was about the extent of my excitement." He began scraping the soapy whiskers off his face again.

"Get used to it," Knudson said, blowing out some smoke.

"I suppose I'll have to if what I've heard is true." He finished shaving and wiped his face and then the razor off one last time. He stuck the towel into the bag with his dirty uniform. Then he pulled on another uniform.

"Hungry?" Knudson asked.

Armbruster nodded. "I haven't had a decent meal since I left here."

Knudson laughed. "Trail cooking does leave something to be desired, doesn't it?"

"Indeed." Armbruster sat on the bed to pull on clean socks and then his boots.

"Well, the mess is pretty much open all the time. Old Bessie's there from before dawn till after dusk."

"Good." Armbruster rose. "I just want to drop my things with one of the laundresses."

"Have one of your men do it."

"Nah. They're all still tending to the horses, and I'd just as soon get it done with."

Knudson shrugged. He stood and the two men left. Knudson waited outside the small laundress building—three sparse rooms, one for the washing, one for the drying, and the one in which Alma Vickers, the wife of Private Don Vickers, made her home.

"Well, how-do, Lieutenant," Alma drawled, baring her grayish teeth, a few of which were missing.

"Alma," Armbruster said noncommittally. He was uncomfortable around Alma Vickers. He was not sure why, but because of it, he would have preferred using the other laundress, Enid Coffey. But Enid was the wife of one of the men in Company G, and Armbruster thought it only right that he should support the wife of one of his own men.

"Well, ain't you glad to see me, Lieutenant?" Alma asked, feigning that she was hurt.

"Sure, Alma," Armbruster said flatly.

"Well, you sure as hell don't seem like it," Alma said with a hoarse laugh. Alma Vickers was a medium tall, heavily built women with almost no shape to her. Her features were coarse, as were her voice, language and manners. Stringy, mouse-colored hair poked out from under a too-small bonnet. Her breath and body odor were offensive.

"Just tired from the patrol is all," Armbruster said lamely. He held out his bag, wanting Alma to take it so he could get out of there as quickly as possible. "Can you have these done in a couple days?" he asked, trying to dredge up some civility.

"I can have 'em for y'all by late this afternoon, Lieutenant," Alma said boldly, "if I was to be given some little encouragement." She stared brazenly at him.

It was all Armbruster could do to suppress his shudder of disgust. Just the very thought of lying in a bed—or anywhere else, for that matter—with this grotesque creature repulsed him. "That wouldn't be nice to Private Vickers," he managed to say in fairly flat tones.

"He ain't gonna hear about it from me, that's for goddamn sure, lieutenant pretty face."

Armbruster wanted to run, but he stood his ground.

He had tried refusal and failed, so he figured he'd try another tack and pray that it worked better. "Truth to tell, Mrs. Vickers," he said evenly, "you're too much of a woman for me. You sure are." He wasn't sure, but he thought she blushed. The sight was repellent.

"Ah, well, Lieutenant," Alma said, taking his bag, "one of these days I'll latch onto you."

Armbruster nodded, not trusting himself to say anything, and then left.

"Jesus, Ed," Knudson said as the two moved off. "You look like you've seen a ghost or something."

"More like I met the devil in person," Armbruster said, his relief at having gotten out of there almost palpable.

"Alma?" Knudson asked, eyes wide.

Armbruster nodded.

"What the hell'd she do?"

"Nothing. It was what she said."

"Just what did she say?" Knudson asked, interested.

"She invited me to . . . well, hell, you know . . ."

"You're lying, aren't you?" Knudson asked, worried that Armbruster wasn't.

Armbruster shook his head. "It was as plain as day."

"Jesus," Knudson breathed, stunned. Then a clearer picture of what Alma Vickers looked like leaped into his mind. "That's enough to make a man sick."

"My thoughts, too," Armbruster said dryly.

"Well, well, well," Knudson said in mock sarcasm, "you must be the fort's new stud bull." He tried to sound awe-inspired, but the laughter that began ended that prospect.

"I can't help it if the ladies like me," Armbruster said, shuddering a little, but smiling, too.

"Ladies?" Knudson sputtered in laughter. "Ladies? You call that . . . that . . . thing in there a lady?"

Armbruster's face flamed red, and he said nothing. He did get a little angry, though, as Knudson's laughter continued for a while. His anger dropped as Knudson's humor with the situation dwindled. Both men had calmed down by the time they entered the officers' mess. They were the only ones there, since this was midafternoon.

"What can I do fo' you officers?" Old Bessie asked. She was a tall, slim, rather regal-looking woman somewhere in her forties. She had dark chocolate skin and thick lips. The skin of her face and hands was wrinkled some. Soft, almost brooding eyes stared out over a lightly splayed nose. Her head was capped by a crown of short, graying, tightly kinked hair. Armbruster thought she would have been a beautiful looking woman when she was young. The thought surprised him.

Armbruster remembered when he first heard about her, when Knudson had mentioned the name.

"Who's Old Bessie?" Armbruster had asked.

"One of Major Brooks's darkies. He brought several slaves with him, so we hired Bessie from the major for our mess. He didn't mind too much, since he kept the better of the two cooks he had."

"Hired?" Armbruster had asked, surprised. "You pay her?"

"Of course not. We pay Major Brooks. We do pay for two Tewa Indians from one of the pueblos to help out. They do the serving and cutting firewood and anything else Bessie wants them to do." He had chuckled. "I can tell you one thing, Bessie might be a darkie, but there's no doubt who's in charge of that small kitchen."

"Lieutenant Armbruster's the hungry one, Bessie," Knudson now said. "He's the one been out on patrol nearly a week."

"I'se got some fresh po'k from a hawg we kilt day befo' yestidday, Lieutenant."

"You have any chops left?"

"Sho' do."

"I'll take a couple of those, with whatever else you got to hand on the side. Except okra and broccoli. I can't stand those two things."

"Yassuh. You want coffee?"

Armbruster nodded. "Bring that straight off."

"Yassuh." Bessie turned to Knudson. "You want anythin', Lieutenant?" she asked.

"Just coffee for now. I might have some cobbler or something later, if Lieutenant Armbruster has some."

"Yassuh." She shuffled off.

"So, what'd you think of your first patrol, Ed?"

"Wasn't much different than the journey out here. The only excitement we got—or at least I got—was seeing a few Navajos up close. That and the night a panther run through the camp and scared the bejesus out of everybody." He paused, thinking back on the journey, then added, "This is some countryside around here, though. I've never seen anything even close to it. The red dirt, the odd rock formations, the canyons, everything was new and strange. But strangely beautiful."

Knudson grinned. "See, I told you this was a pretty place when you first got here. Now maybe you'll believe me when I tell you something."

"Bull," Armbruster said with a laugh. "I'm not going to trust a one of you boys. Soon's I did that, you and some of the others'd play some nasty prank on me or something, sure as hell."

"Been found out already, have I?"

"Yessirree."

"Damn." Knudson laughed some more.

Armbruster's meal came and he paid attention to that. Knudson prattled on just to keep himself occupied. Armbruster found the pork to be fresh and succulent. He wondered if perhaps his judgment wasn't clouded a little by a week of eating trail food, and several months of eating whatever Bessie could come by in purchasing from Indians or by the men hunting. Then he decided it didn't really matter. The meal was excellent, and he enjoyed it.

"You got room in yo' belly for some of my cobbler, Lieutenant?" Bessie asked as she cleared away Armbruster's plates.

"I believe I do, Bessie. And more coffee, if you don't mind."

"I don't mind, suh. And how about you, Lieutenant?" she asked, facing Knudson.

"Only if you give me a heaping helping, Bessie," Knudson said with a twinkle in his eye.

"Yassuh. You want mo' coffee, too?"

Knudson nodded.

Minutes later, Armbruster and Knudson were digging into heaping bowls of thick, sugary peach cobbler, washing it down with harsh, hot coffee. Finally both sat back. Armbruster felt bloated.

Knudson reached into an inner pocket and produced two cigars. "A meal like that one deserves to be topped off with a fine cigar, don't you think, Ed?"

"Indeed. Too bad we don't have any brandy, though."

"Ah, yes." He handed Armbruster one of the cigars. "Last two I have," he said sadly. "Won't be any more till the supply train gets here."

"When's that going to be?"

Knudson shrugged as he bit off the tip of the cigar. "Should be here almost any time. Those wagons have a hell of a time getting through the mud."

The next few days were filled with routine, but then a shout went up. Armbruster, who was inspecting Company B's barracks, strolled outside. Spotting Knudson, he called, "What's up, Hans?"

"Supply train's coming in."

Armbruster dismissed his men and headed out. The men poured out of the barracks behind him, as did the men of most of the other barracks. The first of the mule-drawn wagons rolled into the post between the two long buildings that served as storerooms, guard-house and headquarters. It cut hard right and stopped near the end of the building. Others came in, some going left, some going right, until all but one were parked there. The other one moved up past the corral toward the sutler's.

Armbruster joined the other officers in directing some of his men to begin unloading the wagons. The soldiers who had driven the wagons, as well as the ones who escorted them, all headed toward one of the enlisted men's mess rooms.

Since the dust took a while to settle, it was only after moving out across the parade ground that Armbruster saw the pack train of laden mules. Two people were driving the mules slowly across the camp. Suddenly Armbruster started. ''Who the hell is that, Hans?'' he asked with something like wonder in his voice.

Knudson looked at where Armbruster was pointing. Then he shrugged. "That's just old Cruz Martinez."

"Who's the woman?" Armbruster asked, mouth dry.

"Cruz's daughter, Serafina."

"What're they doing here with all those mules?"

"He's a trader. He comes up this way every year with the supply train. He brings goods for John Webber, and a bunch for himself. He'll spend a few days here letting his animals rest up a bit, then he heads out. He spends the summer trading with the Navajos and whatever other Indians he can find."

"What's she doing here?"

"You aren't interested in her, are you?" Knudson asked, disapproval in his voice.

Armbruster shrugged. "I've never seen anyone like her."

"Most likely you haven't." Knudson paused, watching the small pack train. "She's a half-breed. Her mother was a Navajo. From what I've heard, she had been captured by some Mexicans and taken down to Santa Fe. Cruz met her there and eloped with her, going to Albuquerque. She died sometime later, but not before she was able to teach Serafina some of the Navajo ways. Cruz was trading with the Pueblos down around Albuquerque and Santa Fe at the time, and he decided he'd try trading with the Navajos, too.''

"Why? That must've been dangerous.''

"Yeah, it could be dangerous. But there's a heap of Navajos out there, making it a big market.''

"Makes sense, but still . . .''

"Well, he figured to use his daughter to get an introduction to the Navajos. He met some Navajos who had gone down to Albuquerque to trade. He explained about Serafina and her mother, and asked them to take word back to their people. The next year when they came to trade there, they told Cruz to come ahead for trade, but he had to bring Serafina. He's been coming all these years now, and bringing Serafina with him every time.''

"How do you know all this?'' Armbruster asked, surprised.

Knudson shrugged. "It's sort of common knowledge, I guess. I can't swear that all of it's true, but it certainly seems like it.''

"Where're they going?''

"The Indian house at the far end of the post. He'll stay there a few days and then move on. Sometime in late summer, maybe early fall, he'll be back and stay there again before heading to Albuquerque for the winter.'' Knudson paused, staring at Armbruster. "I'm asking you again, Ed, are you interested in her?''

"Might be,'' Armbruster said with a shrug.

"Such things aren't done, my friend,'' Knudson cautioned.

Armbruster looked sharply at Knudson. "Well, if I am interested in her, which I'm not saying just yet, it's just for something exotic. It's not like I was planning to marry her or something.''

Knudson grinned. "Well, now, that's all right then.''

Armbruster smiled, but there was no feeling in it. He could understand why Knudson was so dead set against a marriage with the woman. He even sort of felt the same himself. After all, it wasn't natural for a white man to want to marry an Indian or a Mexican. The combination of those two was the absolute worst. But it didn't please him that Knudson had been ready to condemn him right off.

He turned to watch the work going on, but within moments he was looking back at Cruz Martinez and his daughter again. They were most of the way across the parade ground and he could barely see her. But the few seconds that he had seen her earlier attracted him with a power he had never felt before. He vowed then and there to get to meet her somehow. Then he would consider what to do beyond that.

He turned his attention back to the unloading, hoping that he had received some mail from his family in Connecticut. Mail delivery by courier was a chancy proposition during the winter, and there had been no delivery for the better part of two months.

The entire fort took on something of a festive air that evening. There were fresh foods, ones not had in some months, to be eaten in both the enlisted men's and officers' mess areas. A new shipment of whiskey had come with the supplies, too, and small measures were passed around to each man. There were renewed supplies of cigars as well as pipe and chewing tobacco.

Mail was delivered to the men—and Armbruster was pleased to see that he had gotten four letters, three from his parents, the fourth from his sister, Adeline. He put them in his pocket where they would be safe for the time being. He would open them when he was alone so that they could be savored.

The officers' mess was crowded that afternoon, and Armbruster had to wait until space came open, which took more than two hours. He spent the time in his room, reading through his mail. There was little of interest, or rather news, but he enjoyed them all the same, reading each three or four times. Afterward, he placed them neatly on his desk, to be read again later.

There was finally room in the small mess hall. So much room that he, Knudson and Captain Ambrose Gilmore were the only ones in there. Bessie looked frazzled when she came to the table to see what they wanted. Her son, Isaac, looked about as tired as his mother as he cleaned up the flotsam of earlier meals.

The three men ate a leisurely supper and then leaned back in their chairs with cigars and a cup of whiskey each. It was almost dark when Armbruster wandered back to his quarters. He pulled off his boots and his blouse and sat at his desk. He read his letters one more time before taking pen in hand to respond.

He had trouble writing, though, since he kept seeing in his mind a tall, slender young woman, wrapped in a blanket and riding a mule across the Fort Defiance parade ground. Finally, aggravated at himself, he dropped the pen and sat back, thinking.

He wanted to meet Serafina Martinez, but the problem was how he should go about it. He didn't think it was proper to just march up there, knock on the door and ask Cruz Martinez to let him see his daughter. And he didn't expect Serafina to just wander around the fort. With a couple of hundred crude soldiers who considered Indians, Mexicans and half-breeds as inferior, she would be an easy target of some unscrupulous thug as soon as she was out of her father's sight.

Still bothered by it all, he drank the last of his small allotment of whiskey and went to bed. The whiskey helped him sleep but he still felt lousy when he got up. He went through his ablutions absentmindedly and then headed for the officers' mess, hoping it was empty. It was, surprising him. He wondered whether he was the only slugabed of an officer who had slept late, or if he perhaps wasn't ahead of them all.

"What you want, Lieutenant Armbruster?" Bessie asked. She looked a little refreshed.

"Some bacon, if you have it. Might be nice to taste a couple of eggs, too." He looked up at her hopefully.

Bessie grinned. "I'se got some I'll whip up fo' you."

"Obliged, Bessie. Some biscuits'd be good, too. But first, coffee."

"Yassuh." Bessie hurried away but was back minutes later with a mug of steaming hot coffee.

Armbruster took the cup and eased some of the liquid down his throat. The hot splash in his stomach felt good. Before long he was done eating and felt better. He lingered over a last cup of coffee—his fourth—before strolling out. The day was ablaze with blue, and a soft, warm wind carried the scents of cedar and pine, manure and hay, smoke and spring.

He was surprised when he saw some Navajos riding into the post. He had never seen it before, mainly, he figured, because he had arrived here in the heart of winter. He had heard the men talk of it, of course, but until actually seeing it he had not been sure whether to believe it. He stopped and leaned against the corner of Knudson's quarters, watching.

The dozen Indians rode in from the southeast. Half cut off and went toward headquarters. The other six moved toward Armbruster, and then passed within a few yards of him. He turned to follow them with his eyes when they had gone by. The Navajos rode straight to the Indian house, where Martinez was staying. None dismounted, but moments later Martinez came out of the house and talked with the Indians.

The Navajos turned and rode back down toward the post, moving close by Armbruster again. They went to headquarters and stopped where five of their friends waited. The last of the Navajos was inside headquarters. That one came out before long and then the Navajos rode away again, heading the way they had come. They moved slowly and appeared unafraid to be amid so many white men.

Armbruster walked to the B Company barracks. His men were trying to recover from the previous day's high living. None was hungover, but most were lazy, feeling bloated and cantankerous.

Armbruster was feeling odd himself, mostly from a restless night wondering about Serafina Martinez. So it was with a small dash of cruelty that he rousted the men out of the barracks and put them through a grueling several hours of drilling, horse tending and marksmanship training. Even Sergeant Cavannaugh was shooting daggers at Armbruster from his eyes by the time Armbruster dismissed the men and let them drag themselves back to the barracks.

It helped him keep Serafina out of his mind somewhat. And doing so became easier over the next couple of days because he didn't see her again. He began to think that he had conjured her up out of loneliness.

He did see her again, though. Four days after the supply train had arrived, Armbruster stepped out of his quarters to head for his morning meal. As he turned the corner to head behind officers' row, he stopped, seeing Martinez riding toward him. The trader had a fairly long string of mules behind him. And bringing up the rear of the little column was Serafina Martinez.

Armbruster stood stock-still, heart pounding. He wasn't sure whether that was because he was about to see Serafina again, or because he was afraid she might not be anything close to what he had imagined.

Serafina barely glanced at Armbruster as she rode slowly by, but it was enough for him. He knew he had not made her more beautiful in his mind than she really was. She was fairly tall, slender though shapely and had a long, thin face dominated by a nose of the same proportions and a thick-lipped mouth. Her hair was long and of a sleek raven hue. Her hands, one loosely holding the reins; both resting lightly on the saddlehorn, were work hardened and delicate at the same time.

Armbruster stood there for some minutes after she had ridden away, watching the thin trail of dust the pack train kicked up. But in his mind he still saw Serafina riding a few feet away. Finally, though, he turned for the mess hall, but he was dazed and ate without really tasting any of the food.

It took him another day and a half to get over seeing Serafina. In a way, it was easier this time, since she was not at the fort any longer. Time also helped—the longer she was away from the fort, the less real she became.

Even still, he wondered about her now and again. Mostly he wondered why he had been so struck by her. He had never been affected by a woman like that before. He finally put it down to his being lonely, and Serafina having such an exotic—to him—look about her.

The day after the Martinezes left the fort, Captain Gilmore and his patrol returned. The following morning, Major Brooks called Armbruster into his office.

"Time for you to hit the trail again, Lieutenant," Brooks said.

"Yessir. Where and when?"

"First thing tomorrow. Take a dozen men plus a corporal or a sergeant. Go northwest and west. About as far as the Kinlichii area."

"Where?" Armbruster asked, then remembered to add, "Sir?"

"Kinlichii. Here." Brooks pointed it out on a map. "It's the best we can do with the Navajo word for the place. I hear it has something to do with a red house or a red spot. Don't ask me what it all means, though."

"Yessir."

"We have a Tiwa scout to go along this time. Nobody

knows what his real name is, so we all just call him 'Chief.' He speaks barely passable English—enough to understand him. He's generally useful.''

"Yessir." Armbruster left and hunted up Cavannaugh. "We're heading on another patrol tomorrow, Sergeant," he said. "I'd like you to come along again. Pick a dozen men and fall in at the quartermaster's an hour before dawn to draw supplies. Have another dozen or so saddle our horses and have pack mules ready at the quartermaster's at the same time. There's no reason men going on patrol should have to saddle their horses or load supplies. And leave Corporal Bauer behind in charge of the men here. He'll report to Lieutenant Knudson while we're gone."

"Yessir. Anything else?"

"We have a Tiwa scout. Somebody named 'Chief.' "

"As much as I dislike having scouts along, Chief's a pretty good man, sir. He don't cause any trouble, and he knows his place. He's also a pretty good tracker—for a Tiwa."

"You have something against Tiwas, Sergeant?"

"Not particularly, sir. It's just that the Tiwas are Pueblo Indians, and they're mostly sedentary. They don't do a lot of hunting or go to war much, so they don't have much in the way of tracking skills and other such skills that go along with warfare."

Armbruster nodded. It was another piece of information learned. One never knew when such knowledge might come in handy.

"I'll hunt up Chief and let him know our plans, sir."

"Thank you, Sergeant."

{ 9 }

Armbruster didn't get much of a look at Chief before that evening. Since it was still dark when they rode out, Armbruster had not really seen the scout. Shortly after leaving the post, the Tiwa headed out ahead of everyone, doing his job.

They rode much like they had on the last patrol, though with only two soldiers out at point since Chief was far ahead of them.

"What do the men do about women, Sergeant?" Armbruster suddenly asked sometime during the morning.

Cavannaugh looked at Armbruster, his eyes raised in question.

"Surely the army doesn't expect the men to live without some fraternizing with the fair sex."

"Well, no, not exactly, sir," Cavannaugh said with a chuckle. "You really want to know, sir?"

"Yes, Sergeant."

"The previous commander started sendin' ten or twenty men with the couriers every couple of weeks. They'd ride to Albuquerque, deliver dispatches and such, then have two days or so to . . . ah, sample the delights of Albuquerque before comin' back here. The next time we send a courier, another group of men'd go. That way everyone on the post got there maybe twice a year. It wasn't great, sir, but it was better than nothin'. Major Brooks has had the foresight to continue that policy."

"How long's it been since you've taken such an excursion?"

"Too damn long." He glanced at Armbruster and grinned. "Sir."

Armbruster smiled. "We might have to do something about that, Sergeant. As soon as we get back to the fort."

"Yessir," Cavannaugh said with some enthusiasm.

"What about the laundresses?" Armbruster asked.

"What about 'em, sir?"

"They ever . . . well, you know . . . offer themselves?" His face was pink with embarrassment.

Cavannaugh laughed. "It's been known to happen, sir. Still, most of 'em're married. Not that that'd stop some of the men, but regulations frown on such activities. That's a sure as hell way to cause trouble. But the ones that haven't married or have been widowed're free to seek men as they desire, as long as it's done discreetly. We've only seen one laundress at the post who hasn't been married and she wasn't single long. Same with widows. They're usually married up again within six months or so. It don't set well with some to have unmarried women romping around an army post."

"I suppose it wouldn't."

"You fixin' to get down to Albuquerque sometime soon, Lieutenant?" Cavannaugh asked, glancing askance at Armbruster.

Armbruster felt a blast of anger, but he quickly stifled it. Cavannaugh had asked a reasonable question, after all. "Well, Sergeant," he finally said, "let me put it this way. I sure as hell wouldn't object to it if Major

Brooks was to request me to escort a courier down that way."

He and Cavannaugh laughed.

Finally a halt was called for the day. Chief had picked out a spot and left some sort of sign for Cavannaugh to find. Camp went up smoothly, and before dark they were supping. It was then that Chief rode back into camp. He unsaddled his horse and took care of it, and then squatted at Armbruster's fire.

Armbruster took the opportunity to study his scout. Chief was short, bandy-legged and runty looking. He was scarecrowlike in his thinness, and his skin was extremely dark. His eyes under a prominent brow were hooded, his nose narrow and straight except for a bump in the middle of the top, and his lips were thin. His hair was shoulder length, matted and dirty. He wore greasy, highly stained buckskin pants, shirt and moccasins, all pocked with holes. Whatever of his flesh protruded was filthy.

All in all, Armbruster concluded, Chief was an ugly human being and a poor excuse for a man. Still, Brooks and Cavannaugh seemed to think he was capable. Armbruster still found it hard to think this man could be competent at all.

"What village—or, rather, pueblo—do you come from, Chief?" Armbruster asked.

"Sandia."

"Where is that?"

"Near town you say Albuquerque. North of there."

"Why are you scouting against the Navajo?"

"Hate Navajo. Kill family. Hate Jicarillas. Kill friends."

Armbruster nodded and quit asking questions. He suspected that Chief was trying to be polite but really didn't care to be questioned much. At least not about his personal life.

Chief was gone by the time Armbruster woke the

next morning. "He's out ahead, scouting again, Lieutenant," Cavannaugh said when he spotted Armbruster looking around in surprise.

The next three days were more of the same—riding through lands of odd rock formations, under clear blue skies, amid constantly rising temperatures, following an almost invisible trail left by Chief. They would make camp an hour or so before dark and be on the trail again shortly after dawn.

After supper on the fourth night out, Armbruster said to Cavannaugh, "I'm thinking of turning back tomorrow, Sergeant. What do you think?"

Cavannaugh was about to answer when Chief began jabbering excitedly.

"You understand anything of what he's spouting, Sergeant?" Armbruster asked, looking at the Tiwa in surprise.

"Not a goddamn word, sir. But I'll try'n get him to speak what English he can. Maybe we can figure something out." He grabbed the Indian by the shoulders. "Stop, Chief!" he roared. "Stop."

Chief stumbled to a halt and looked dazedly from Cavannaugh to Armbruster and back again.

"Speak English, Chief," Cavannaugh said. "Talk slow."

"Jicarillas," the Tiwa said, jabbing a finger in half a dozen directions. "We find. Tomorrow."

Cavannaugh looked at Armbruster. "He might be full of shit, Lieutenant," Cavannaugh said. "But he's usually right about such things."

Armbruster thought it over for a few moments, then nodded. "We stay on the trail tomorrow. But, if we've not found anything by sunset, the next morning we turn back for the fort."

"That all right, Chief?" Cavannaugh asked, looking at the Indian.

Chief nodded once, curtly and firmly.

About midmorning, Armbruster was beginning to doubt Chief's abilities. Then the Indian came riding swiftly back to the army column.

"You seen something . . ." Armbruster began to ask. Then he heard a few gunshots, which made that question moot. So he asked, "What is it, Chief?"

"Jicarillas. Five. They attack two traders."

"How far?"

"Half-mile."

Armbruster nodded. "Sergeant," he said with a touch of nervous excitement, "let's get there. But I want the men to stay quiet. I'd rather not scare those hostiles off with a lot of noise."

"Yessir." He quickly spoke to the men, and then he and Chief led the group off up a faint track they had been following.

The gunfire had stopped, and Armbruster hoped he and his men would get there in time to save the traders. He was almost relieved when he heard two more gunshots.

Suddenly Chief stopped and flapped an arm, telling everyone to slow down. Armbruster and Cavannaugh walked their horses up to him. "We close. Go on foot now."

Cavannaugh nodded and made some hand signals to his men, who dismounted. Three of the men pulled the horses off behind a pile of reddish rocks. The rest moved forward, until they were bunched up behind Chief, Armbruster and Cavannaugh.

Chief motioned to the men to get down. They all slithered forward until they were on the lip of a high, rounded hill. Chief pointed. Less than a quarter of a mile away, five Jicarillas lay on a slightly lower, red-soil, grass-stubbled hill, looking down into a depression, out of which rose a tall sandstone spire. Chief said, "Traders stay in rocks. No other cover." He waved his hand along the horizon.

"Soon's night comes, those Jicarillas'll be on those two poor traders," Cavannaugh said.

"Then we've got to stop them before night," Armbruster said simply.

"Hell of a lot easier said than done," Cavannaugh said. "Sir."

"I didn't say it was going to be easy. Any ideas, Sergeant?"

"Not much creative, sir. Only thing I can think of to do is just shoot those sons a bitches from here."

"At least two of them're almost out of view. And the other three don't make such good targets either."

Cavannaugh shrugged. "Only other choice I can see is tryin' to creep up on 'em."

"Think we can do that?"

Cavannaugh shrugged again. He looked out across the quarter-mile of nothingness. "I'm game if you are, Lieutenant," he finally said. "They see us comin', maybe they'll stand up or something and we can get a clear shot at 'em."

"Might work. You lead that assault, as it were, Sergeant."

"You going to stay back here with the others, Lieutenant?" Cavannaugh asked, turning his head to stare at Armbruster in surprise.

"No, Sergeant," Armbruster said solemnly. "I aim to take a few men around that way"—he pointed northeast—"and get around the other side of the hill and hopefully get down in those rocks with the traders. Offer them some protection in case any of those Jicarillas get away."

"We'll leave at your command, Lieutenant," Cavannaugh said.

Armbruster drew in a deep breath and let it out slowly. His heart was thumping. *The time's finally come,* he thought. *Now I'll find out what kind of man—and officer—I really am.* "Privates Vickers, Finney and Olson, you'll come with me. You other six men go with Sergeant Cavannaugh. Chief, you can go with either of us. Or you can wait here.''

"I watch. Make sure no Jicarillas leave."

Armbruster fought down a shudder. "Let's go, men," he said, hoping it sounded forceful.

They moved back down the hill and then hurried east. Armbruster felt an exhilaration he had never experienced before, and he liked the feeling, which worried him a little. When he thought he and his men had gone far enough, they walked up the hill again, flattening onto their stomachs just before they reached the top.

Armbruster peered over and nodded with relief. He could see most of the base of the rock spire, where piles of boulders presented a natural fortification. They would have to go down the hill and across a wide flat to get to that haven. About three-quarters of the way around the spire was the hill on which the Jicarillas lay. This was the only side where there was no second hill.

A pop of gunfire and an accompanying cloud of smoke came every now and again from the boulders, so Armbruster knew the two traders were alive, even if he couldn't see them.

Armbruster waited a few minutes, wanting to give Cavannaugh and the others time to at least get partway up the hill toward the Jicarillas. There would be a few dozen yards or so where Armbruster and his small group would be within rifle—or arrow—range of the Apaches.

But his adrenaline was pumping, and he found he could not stay there any longer. "Rifles ready, men?" When he got three softly grunted affirmatives, he asked, "Pistols ready?" Again he got a chorus of affirmation. With a deep sigh, Armbruster said, "Let's go."

Armbruster popped up and ran, bent over. He

hoped his men were following him, but he was not about to look back to see.

Suddenly gunfire broke out from up on the hill. Then there were shouts. Armbruster glanced up and saw a Jicarilla charge down the hill.

Armbruster slammed to a stop and dropped to one knee. Feeling his blood racing through him, he raised his rifle and fired. He felt a new burst of exhilaration when he saw the Apache tumble down the hill. The excitement fled a moment later when he realized that he had just killed a man, even if he was an Indian.

He forced those thoughts out of his mind and got up and ran again. His three men had passed him by while he stopped for the shot at the Apache, but he quickly caught up with them.

The haven seemed miles away, but the distance shrank quickly. Then Armbruster and his three men were in amongst the rocks. Armbruster shifted a little, heading toward the sound of skittish mules. He tripped over a small rock and went down hard.

"Shit," he muttered, bothered more that he had fallen like a clumsy oaf than by actually being hurt. He jumped up and began running again.

He only had time to note that the traders were Cruz Martinez and his daughter, Serafina, before he plowed into a Jicarilla who had suddenly appeared on a large boulder behind Martinez and jumped at the trader.

⊸❴ 10 ❵⊷

Armbruster hit the Apache in midleap, his head landing in the Indian's stomach. Both men tumbled to the ground and rolled. Armbruster lost his rifle in the collision, as he bounced on stones and rocks, grunting the whole while.

The Apache made no sound after the initial contact, which had knocked some of his wind out. He was up in an instant, face contorted with anger; a large, wood-handled knife in hand. He charged at Armbruster, knife raised.

Armbruster got an arm up and stopped the swiftly descending blade. He got a foot up and into the Ji-carilla's stomach and shoved the Indian away. The Apache's foot hit a stone and he fell, dropping his knife.

Armbruster got up, but he could not take advantage of the Indian's fall. He was more prepared this time, though, when the warrior charged. It didn't help much, since the Apache drove him backward until his back slammed up against the side of a mule's rump.

The Apache head-butted Armbruster, who sagged a little. The already nervous mule bucked, throwing Armbruster forward into the warrior. The Apache, who had been trying to knee Armbruster, was off balance. When the mule-propelled Armbruster crashed into him, the Apache staggered back a few steps.

Though he was still a bit dazed, Armbruster jumped forward and hammered the Indian's face with a fist. The warrior fell back a few more steps, and Armbruster pounded him again and again. The Jicarilla still managed to kick Armbruster in the stomach. Armbruster sank to his knees. He saw the Apache wobble toward him, and Armbruster scrabbled for the pistol in his flap holster.

Armbruster got the pistol out, but the Apache was almost on him. He fell to the side as the warrior tried to kick him in the face. He hit and rolled. When he stopped, he nervously shoved up to one knee and swung around, wincing as a stone ground into his kneecap. He got the cap-and-ball Colt cocked and fired when the Indian was only two feet away. The .44-caliber lead ball punched the warrior in the stomach, knocking him down.

Armbruster stood shakily. The Jicarilla was trying to get up again. Trembling, Armbruster stepped forward and shot the warrior in the forehead. Then he sank to his knees and vomited.

When his stomach was empty, he stood again. His hands were still shaking and he looked around as if he did not know where he was. Through dazed eyes, he saw Private Vickers grappling with another Apache. He had no idea of where Privates Olson and Finney were. But he could see that if Vickers lost his battle with the Apache—which seemed quite possible—Serafina Martinez would be in danger. He tottered forward, wondering where these warriors had come from.

Before Armbruster could quite get there, the Apache had flung Vickers to the ground. Then the warrior spun and grabbed Serafina's arm. The woman fought, kicking and hitting, until the Apache clouted her hard on the side of the head. As Serafina sagged, the Jicarilla ducked and scooped Serafina up and over his shoulder. He took a step forward and kicked Vickers in the face.

Armbruster was regaining some of his faculties and increased his speed a bit. The Apache had still not seen him, since the warrior's back was toward him. As the Jicarilla hopped over the prostrate Vickers, Armbruster picked up his pace even more.

A groggy Serafina half looked up and saw Armbruster. She seemed about ready to scream, or say something, but Armbruster put a finger to his lips. A moment later he was right behind the Apache, who had stopped for a moment to look around. Armbruster creased his head a good shot with his pistol.

The Indian grunted and sagged. It was enough to allow Serafina to squiggle out of the warrior's grip. As she stepped away from the Apache, Armbruster moved up, placed the muzzle of his pistol lightly against the back of the Indian's head and fired.

Armbruster fought to keep from getting sick again. Not that there was anything left in his stomach to come out, but he would feel like an utter fool to be suffering a case of dry heaves in front of Serafina.

"*Gracias,* Teniente," Martinez himself said, his voice harsh and flat, as he walked up. He always sounded as if he were about to rip someone's head off. He could be a wildcat when he was drunk or if he or his daughter were in trouble, but he was a generally peaceful man, something many people had trouble believing once they heard that rasping, gravelly voice.

Armbruster shook himself to break out of the sickness swamping him and put his pistol back into the holster.

As soon as he did, Martinez grabbed his hand and pumped it vigorously while thanking the officer profusely.

Cruz Martinez was short and thin, but he looked

hard as a rifle barrel. His long, greasy black hair was splattered with gray, as was his short, skinny mustache. Dark, devilish eyes almost overwhelmed the cheery, crooked smile he could conjure up at will.

"You're quite welcome, Mister Martinez," Armbruster said shakily. "I was just doing what needed doing is all."

"Like hell, Teniente," Martinez said with a wide grin. "If you hadn't come along, my Serafina would be in the clutches of that son of a bitch." He pointed to the bloody remains of the Apache.

Armbruster managed to avoid looking at the body. He had never realized what damage a .44-caliber pistol could do to a man when fired from less than an inch away. It was not a pretty sight at all.

Serafina Martinez looked at the tall, still gangly soldier with interest. She had seen him at the fort watching her while pretending not to. He did nothing for her then. She was not attracted to Anglos who towered over her and had too little meat on their bones. Besides, she had figured him for one of the usual American soldiers—arrogant, full of himself and thinking that all Mexican or Navajo women were there solely for them.

Now, though, she saw him in a slightly different light. Not only had he saved her life, he had been sick when he killed that first Apache. She realized that this young officer was no violence-hardened man. He had feelings for others. She had at times thought such a thing impossible for an American soldier.

Serafina smiled sweetly and said in a soft, melodious voice, "And I add my thanks to you, Señor. Without you, I . . . Well, I . . ."

"No need to say more, ma'am," Armbruster managed to squawk. His voice was not working properly. Not in such close proximity to this woman.

Serafina Martinez was maybe five-feet-two and

couldn't weigh much more than ninety pounds, Armbruster figured. He almost blushed when he thought that those ninety or so pounds were well distributed on Serafina's frame. She was not overendowed either at bosom or derriere, but Armbruster didn't mind. She was built perfectly as far as he was concerned. Almost-black, secretive eyes stared boldly out beneath thick, dark eyebrows. She wore a buckskin dress and leggings. Armbruster thought she looked just fine in them, but he had the fleeting thought that he would like to see her in something like the women in Santa Fe wore.

"But there is," Serafina protested. She had little accent, and what was there was unlike anything Armbruster had ever heard. "You saved my life and"—she lowered her eyes—"my virtue."

"It was a pleasure, Miss . . . ?" He did not want to let on that he already knew her name.

"I am Serafina Martinez," she said, eyes locking again on his.

Armbruster could feel his heart pounding again, and he all but forgot about the battle and the bloodshed around him. "Lieutenant Ed Armbruster," he said in a slightly strangled voice. He didn't know what came over him, but he reached out, took one of her tiny hands in one of his large ones. Then he bent and lightly brushed the excitingly dark skin of the back of her hand with his lips.

Serafina was very surprised. As a half-breed Mexican-Navajo, she was not used to such treatment, though some of the young *caballeros* in Albuquerque exhibited considerable charm at times. Nor did she expect such a gesture from an American military officer. She had never once seen something like that from the Americans.

Her bright smile beamed forth again. "I'm very pleased to meet you, Lieutenant Armbruster."

"Please, call me Ed." Once again he stunned himself by managing to turn away from that delightful face and disarming smile. Privates Finney and Olson had walked up while Armbruster was talking with Serafina, and they stood there waiting patiently. It was something they were used to. "You men all right?" he asked.

"Yes, sir," Olson answered for them both.

Armbruster nodded and walked to where Vickers was sitting holding his head in his hands. Kneeling next to Vickers, he asked, "How're you doing, Private?"

"I've been better," Vickers complained, then remembered to add, "sir."

"I suppose you have." Armbruster rose. "Stay there, Private," he commanded, as he turned to greet the small group of men led by Sergeant Cavannaugh.

"All present and accounted for, sir," Cavannaugh said. "Except Chief, of course. He's still back on the ridge. Maybe he's takin' scalps."

Armbruster suppressed a shudder. "You get all the Apaches up there?"

"Yessir." Cavannaugh pointed. "I see they weren't the only ones."

"They sure as hell weren't," Armbruster said strongly. "And it leads me to distrust Chief's abilities."

"Don't go doubtin' him too much just yet, sir," Cavannaugh said. "Chief's a good man. These Jicarillas here could've been a completely different bunch, sir, or maybe they waited near here for the others to finish up a raid or something. It's hard to tell with Indians, Lieutenant."

Armbruster nodded. "Yes, you're probably right."

"You're lookin' a little sickly, Lieutenant. You all right?" Cavannaugh asked. "You're not hit or hurt or anything, are you, sir?"

Armbruster grinned weakly. "I had a little bout of sickness a while ago, Sergeant."

"One of the Apaches hit you a good one, sir?"

Armbruster could hear the implied derision in Cavannaugh's words and see it on the sergeant's face. Still, he thought Cavannaugh was not so much making fun of him as he was sort of inviting him to join a special club. At least that's what Armbruster hoped Cavannaugh was doing. He smiled weakly once more. "No, Sergeant," he said in a level voice, "I was puking my guts out a little while ago. I . . . Well, dammit, there's no hiding it—I never killed anyone before."

"Not a real good feeling, is it, Lieutenant?" Cavannaugh asked quietly, though some of the men were snickering.

"No, Sergeant. No, it was not."

"Well, sir," Cavannaugh asked, still with a straight face, "what next?"

Armbruster thought it over for a few minutes, then said, "We'll stay here tonight. Mister Martinez, can one of my men use one of your mules to get our companions?"

"Sí." Martinez walked off to get a mule.

"Sergeant, have a detail get rid of these bodies here. We don't need scavengers disturbing our slumber."

"Yessir. Anything else?"

"Pick a man to ride out and retrieve our horses and the men holding them. Also have a small detail try to find some fuel for a fire and begin preparing a meal." The thought sent a queasy feeling through his stomach.

Martinez came back leading a mule—his own. Private Olson climbed onto the animal. "This is a good mule, Señor," Martinez said. "You be good to him."

Olson nodded and trotted off.

Armbruster walked off and sat on a rock. He was still shaky and needed to sit for a while. Martinez and Serafina wandered over and sat nearby. "You don't mind that we stay here tonight, do you, Mister Martinez?"

Armbruster asked. It was the first time he had thought that Martinez might object.

"No, no, no," Martinez said vigorously.

Serafina smiled, and Armbruster felt a certain stiffening of his backbone and squaring of his shoulders. "We'd be upset if you were to take your soldiers away, Lieutenant," Serafina said.

Armbruster nodded. "I'd be obliged, though, if you two were to make your own accommodations a little away from ours, Mister Martinez. I'd not want to tempt the men too much." Armbruster wasn't sure he could trust himself around the desirable Serafina, let alone the men.

"Sí," Martinez said, understanding.

"However, I'd be pleased to have you both as my supper guests."

Armbruster finally leaned back to allow the day's worries to drift away from him. It was the first time since early afternoon that he had been able to relax even a little.

Three fires had been made, and food was cooked. Armbruster, Martinez and Serafina ate at one fire. Cavannaugh and the men split into two groups, each sharing one fire. After eating, Martinez broke out enough cigars for everyone and brought out a small bottle of whiskey—just about enough for the men to have two fair sips each.

When the cigars were smoked down, night had fallen. Martinez and Serafina rose. "We have a long day tomorrow, Lieutenant," Martinez said. "So, *buenas noches,* Teniente."

"Good night, Mister Martinez, Miss Serafina." Armbruster stood and once more gallantly, gently kissed the back of Serafina's hand. Then he finally sat back to relax.

Soon after, Sergeant Cavannaugh came by. "A word with you, Lieutenant?" he asked.

"Of course, Sergeant," Armbruster said wearily. "Sit."

Cavannaugh did. He worried his lip a little before starting. "I think you noticed before, Lieutenant, that some of the men were having a little amusement at your . . . discomfort?"

"I did, Sergeant." The words were flat and ugly. Armbruster didn't like admitting it, or even thinking it, but there was no choice.

"Well, sir, I wanted you to know that it was not meant with any disrespect." Cavannaugh smiled a little. "Every man comes out here has to go through what you did today sooner or later. It's kind of an initiation, and the men were welcoming you." He looked embarrassed.

Armbruster nodded. "I was hoping as much, Sergeant," he said quietly. "I'm afraid I didn't acquit myself very well."

"You did just fine, sir—if you don't mind my sayin' so."

"I don't mind, Sergeant," Armbruster said with a smile. "Now you better get your rest." He chuckled. "Actually, I think I should get some rest. But in either case, we have a long day tomorrow."

{11}

Chief, the Tiwa scout, had come into the camp sometime during the night, Armbruster found out when he woke in the morning. The Indian was sleeping, curled up with his back against a rock. But as soon as he heard people awakening, Chief rose. Without waiting for an invitation, he went to one of the soldiers' fires and squatted. He rubbed his hands before the flames a few times and then poured himself some coffee.

"You think old Chief there can find us any more Indians, Sergeant?" Armbruster asked Cavannaugh after breakfast.

"I don't know, sir, though I suppose so. Why? If you don't mind my askin', Lieutenant."

"I don't mind." Armbruster sighed. "We've been out here a week or so. I figure it's about time we headed back to the fort. But if these Jicarillas were running around, there might be others. I'd sure hate to go back with some of the 'red devils' still chasing across the countryside."

"I'll go talk to Chief, sir," Cavannaugh said, pushing himself up. He wanted nothing more than to just sit around doing nothing except perhaps taking regular pulls from a whiskey bottle.

"Thank you, Sergeant."

"You know, sir," Cavannaugh said after a moment's hesitation, "if you want to head straight back, no one's going to hold it against you."

Armbruster glared for a moment. Then he relaxed and nodded. "Thanks, Sergeant. But I—we—have to do the job right."

"Yessir." Cavannaugh moved off. He returned a few minutes later. "Chief says he can hunt us up some more Jicarillas—if the soldier chief wants that."

"Soldier chief?"

"That's you, sir," Cavannaugh said with a grin.

Armbruster grunted, not sure he liked being called soldier chief, and not sure about why. Then he shrugged. "What do you think of what Chief had to say, Sergeant?"

"I think he's full of shit, sir, and he just wants to prolong things a bit to get a few days' extra pay."

"Can't blame him for that, Sergeant."

"No, sir. And I'm not doing so."

"Well, then, Sergeant, I expect we all can bear up under a few more days' worth of bad food."

"Yessir."

"The men all right? Ready to move?"

"Yessir. The only one injured in that melee yesterday was Private Vickers, as you know, sir. He's painin' some, but he can travel."

"Thank you, Sergeant."

As Cavannaugh headed back to the men, Cruz Martinez strolled up and squatted at the fire near Armbruster. "Me and Serafina will be pulling out now, Lieutenant," he said quietly around the *cigarillo* stuck between his lips.

Armbruster looked at the small, wiry Mexican, and thought Martinez seemed nervous. He decided after a few moment's thought that Martinez was perhaps a little afraid that other Jicarillas were in the area, and that he and his daughter would be in danger traveling alone as they were.

"Would you like an escort to the next Navajo village, Mister Martinez?" Armbruster asked.

Martinez's relief was visible, but he said, "I don't want you to go out of your way, Lieutenant."

"My job is to patrol the area, Mister Martinez. Accompanying you could be considered part of a patrol."

"Well, Señor Teniente, if that's the way you feel, how can I refuse such an offer?" He shrugged and grinned.

Armbruster smiled. He decided he liked Martinez, and not only because of the Mexican trader's daughter. "Which way is the next village? And how far?"

"A day and a half ride northwest. But . . ." He stuttered to a stop.

"Go on, Mister Martinez," Armbruster urged softly.

Martinez hesitated only an instant. "I must ask that you and your men stop and turn back before we reach the village."

"Why?"

"The Navajos are a suspicious people around outsiders. They wouldn't like me to come riding into the village escorted by American soldiers."

"I can see how that'd bother them." He nodded. "Well, you just tell us when you want us to stop and that'll be the end of it."

"*Gracias,* Señor Teniente. *Muchos gracias.*"

"It's nothing," Armbruster responded offhandedly. "*De nada.*"

"What's that?"

"*De nada.* It means 'thank you'—or 'it's nothing'—in my language."

Armbruster nodded. "I'll remember that."

"I thought you would." Martinez rose, once again looking edgy.

"You have something else to say, Mister Martinez?" Armbruster asked.

"I'd like to know when . . ."

"When we're going to leave?"

"*Sí.*"

"I'd say half an hour or less, Mister Martinez. As soon as the men get ready." He watched as Martinez walked back to his daughter and their supply mules. Armbruster had never heard much of Mexican people back in the east, and the little he had heard was not good. Mexicans were a lazy lot, the men mostly ne'er-do-wells or illiterate peons; the women given to loose morals. At least that's what he had heard. A little of that had been borne out in Santa Fe, but Armbruster had put much of that down to the Mexican people not liking American rule, even though the Americans had been there a decade already. But Martinez was not like that. He was independent, hardworking, and pretty fierce when pushed to it, if his activity in yesterday's fracas was any indication.

Armbruster rose, reluctantly, and moved about the camp, not really having much else to do. Cavannaugh saw him and came over. "Somethin' I can do for you, Lieutenant?" the sergeant asked.

"Not really, though there has been a slight change in plans."

"Oh?" Cavannaugh suddenly was a little wary.

"We're going to escort Mister Martinez and his daughter to the next Navajo village. Mister Martinez says it's about a day and a half ride northwest. If Chief's ready to ride out, you'd better have him go scout out that way."

"Yessir."

"How long before the men are ready to leave, Sergeant?"

"Shouldn't be no more than fifteen, twenty minutes, Lieutenant. I can push the men if you're in a hurry, though, sir."

"No, Sergeant. That'll be good enough. Carry on."

Armbruster walked off. He tried to keep out of the men's way, and so wandered out to the edge of the rock wonderland and stood there looking at the landscape. It was still a strange place to him, with the barren hills and the towering, odd rock formations, despite his having just come down one of those rocky ridges yesterday. But it was like he was seeing it for the first time. A few minutes later he turned at the sound of a horse and saw Chief riding out of the camp.

Bored, Armbruster went back into the camp and began saddling his own horse. It kept him occupied, which is what he wanted right now. He did not need to be thinking too closely about the past twenty-four hours. He still felt somewhat queasy at the remembrance of the damage he had done to the two Apaches with his pistol.

Finally, the column moved out. Two privates rode first, followed by Armbruster and Sergeant Cavannaugh, then came Martinez and Serafina, trailing their mules, and then the rest of the soldiers.

The landscape lost its interest for Armbruster in the long, dull ride. Despite the different rock formations, everything looked the same: flat, barren, dry land broken by the rock spires and by the heat waves shimmering in the distance; a never-ending expanse of blue sky above. Dust rose from under the hooves of the horses and mules, hanging in the still air until it coated the lungs or clothes of the riders.

Armbruster still did not want to think about the results of his battle, so he gladly shifted his thoughts to Serafina Martinez. He wished she were riding ahead of him instead of behind. That would allow him to watch her as well as keep at least some of the other men from watching her. He decided somewhere during the morning, though, that with all the dust kicked up by Martinez's dozen mules, the men back there couldn't see much of anything anyway.

They stopped for a midday meal of jerky, hard biscuits and canteen water. Chief rode in and reported to Cavannaugh that he had seen nothing out of the ordinary. Cavannaugh relayed the message to Armbruster.

"Chief know of a place we can bed down for the night, Sergeant?" Armbruster asked.

"I can check with him, sir. But to tell you the truth, I think Martinez'd probably be the better one to ask."

Armbruster nodded. He walked to where Martinez and Serafina were sitting on rocks and asked his question.

"*Sí,*" Martinez said with a nod. "There's a spring at the south end of Salahkai Mesa."

Armbruster nodded and, through Cavannaugh, passed the information to Chief. The Indian nodded, grabbed some food and left.

Not long afterward, the men—and woman—pulled themselves wearily into their saddles. Armbruster thought the day would never end. He was tired of the heat, tired of riding, tired of the endless countryside, and the malevolent, clotted ball of a sun. Finally, though, the mesa came into view off in the distance, restoring Armbruster's hope a little.

The campsite, when they got there, turned out to be a pleasant little oasis in the midst of all the heat and emptiness. The spring itself was a refreshing spot of cool, clean water. Reeds grew in profusion around the spring, and there were some small narrowleaf cottonwoods near the water. A few stunted junipers cast meager shadows.

The procession pulled to a stop and let the dust settle for a moment. Then everyone dismounted and began sluggishly going through the motions of setting up camp.

Tired and somewhat irritable, Armbruster began unsaddling his horse. Cavannaugh hustled over to him. "No need for you to do that, Lieutenant," he said a little nervously. "I'll have one of the men do it straight off, sir."

"I'd as soon do it myself, Sergeant." He looked at Cavannaugh and smiled weakly. "I sometimes feel rather useless, Sergeant," he said almost apologetically. "This'll keep me busy for at least a couple of minutes."

"You certain, sir?" Cavannaugh asked skeptically.

"Yes, Sergeant. I'll be fine. See that the rest of the work is done soon. The men're tired and hungry. Oh, and detail two men to help Mister Martinez unload his mules."

"Yessir." Cavannaugh wandered away, looking back once in worry. Armbruster seemed mighty subdued, and it was not normal. Then Cavannaugh sighed. Armbruster was a grown man, an officer, and he would have to handle things in his own way.

Armbruster took his time tending his horse, not being in any real hurry to just sit around doing nothing. Still, he could not take all night at it, so he finally tied the horse to a picket rope and placed a feed bag over his head. Then he strolled over to see how Martinez was doing. Or that's what he silently told himself, not being willing to let on even to himself that he really just wanted to see Serafina.

They were almost done, having been helped by Privates Finney and Heywood. Both were big men, with bull necks and broad shoulders. But where the former was a genial giant, the latter was a nasty-tempered misfit. Heywood had been brought along mainly because he was a hell of a man to have on one's side in any kind of fight.

Armbruster sent Heywood and Finney back to the other soldiers and then sat on a rock near Martinez and his daughter. "You two are more than welcome for supper at my fire tonight," Armbruster said softly. He could not understand why he was so skittish. He real-

ized that some of it was due to being so close to Serafina, and that some was the result of the battle—was it
only yesterday?—but that could not be all. He wished
he could figure it out and so deal with it.

"Muchos gracias, Teniente," Martinez said with a
grin.

Supper, when it was made, was a quiet affair. Almost
everyone seemed a little beaten down after the battle
and a long day of travel through the heat. Just after the
meal was over, Cavannaugh came to Armbruster's fire
and saluted smartly.

"What is it, Sergeant?" Armbruster asked, a little
surprised. In the months Armbruster had been commanding Company B, he and Cavannaugh had
reached something of an understanding, where their
formality was somewhat less than might normally be
had between a company commander and his top sergeant.

"The men'd like to have a little music, Lieutenant."

"They have their instruments?" Armbruster asked
with a smile.

"Yessir."

"Do you think it's safe?"

"I expect so, sir. If there were hostiles about, Chief'd
most likely have brought us news of it. Unless they got
him first. But I've not seen any sign."

"Then, by all means have at it, Sergeant."

"Would you mind my sitting in, Sargento?" Martinez
asked.

Cavannaugh shrugged. "I wouldn't expect so. You
play something?"

"Guitar."

"Well, come along then."

Cavannaugh left, heading back to his men, while
Martinez went off to get his guitar. It left Armbruster
alone with Serafina. His heart pounded with excite-

ment, but he had no idea of what to say to her. And it was she who spoke first.

"I never did get a chance to thank you for real, Lieutenant," she said, her voice soft and smooth as a baby's breath.

"For what?" Armbruster asked in strangulated tones.

"For saving my life."

"But you already—"

Serafina pressed a slim, warm finger against his lips. "Never really. But maybe some day I will." Her smile sent sparks of excitement crashing through Armbruster's body.

Armbruster was quiet, uncertain of his voice if he tried to speak. He was also trying to decide if he should say what he wanted to. Finally he cleared his throat and tried: "I might be out of line, Miss Serafina, and if so, you just tell me, and I'll back off . . ."

"You'll have to tell me—or ask me—whatever it is you want to before I can decide that," Serafina said with a small laugh.

"I'd like to court you, Miss Serafina," Armbruster said, his voice sounding to him like someone else's. "Or as much as possible when you come back to the fort."

"We usually stay only a few days, Lieutenant," she said.

"I know." Armbruster hoped he had heard a note of regret in Serafina's words.

"Well, we'll see when I return there." She smiled brightly. "But I would think the answer will be yes. At least from me. My father, he might have other ideas."

"Then we'll leave it at that," Armbruster said, both crushed and elated.

The two quieted, listening to the sounds of Martinez's guitar, Finney's harmonica and Vickers's concertina.

{ 12 }

Armbruster woke, unsure of why. He had had trouble getting to sleep anyway, what with thoughts of Serafina Martinez pounding in his heart and blood and brain. Still, he had finally drifted off, and now here he was awake again, eyes gritty with tiredness and dust.

He heard something and nodded, figuring that Chief had just come into camp. As he closed his eyes and settled himself in his thin blanket again, another sound startled him. He thought it had sounded like a muffled scream, quickly and surely squelched.

Armbruster flipped off the blanket, rolled and gently pushed up to one knee. His eyes scanned the dark camp. Most of the men were snoring softly, but all he could see were huddled shapes. Then one of the shapes moved. It appeared to be a gigantic shadow against the darker shadows. Then it shifted once more and Armbruster again heard a sound. He was sure now that it was a muffled scream, and a rather high-pitched one, which meant that it could only have come from Serafina.

He sat and swiftly pulled on his boots and then rose to his feet. As he moved off toward where Martinez and his daughter were sleeping, he undid the flap of his holster. He saw more activity and he went that way, moving quietly despite having increased his speed some.

The dark shapes quickly turned into a struggling Serafina Martinez over whom hulked Private Fenton Heywood. The giant soldier had a ham-sized hand over Serafina's mouth. His other hand was invisible, heading up into the darkness of her dress.

Armbruster's eyes grew wide with hate and anger. He jerked his pistol out and stepped up behind Heywood. "You son of a bitch," he muttered harshly just before slapping Heywood along the left temple with his pistol barrel.

Heywood grunted and fell a little to the side. He caught himself before he went down. Then he snapped his left elbow back, catching Armbruster in the ribs.

With the hard, callused hand gone from her mouth, Serafina screamed, which roused the entire camp.

Armbruster had his hands full. After the initial blow Heywood had dished out, Heywood shoved his bulky body up and backward, slamming into Armbruster. The lieutenant staggered away.

Heywood took a step toward Armbruster, but a flying Cruz Martinez suddenly slammed into the private. The small Mexican managed to knock Heywood down. Heywood angrily threw Martinez off him and started to rise.

By then, though, Sergeant Cavannaugh and the other men were there. Cavannaugh had his pistol out and cocked. Heywood knew damn well that Cavannaugh would not hesitate an instant to kill him. Still, he was not happy with it. "Chickenshit son of a bitch," Heywood snarled. "Protectin' that scrawny little bastard." He pointed to Armbruster.

"Back off, Sergeant," Armbruster commanded harshly before Cavannaugh could respond to Heywood.

"You sure, sir?" Cavannaugh asked, startled. He did not take his eyes of Heywood, nor did his pistol waver.

"Yes. Just relieve him of his revolver."

"Gonna shoot me down when I'm unarmed?" Heywood sneered.

"I don't need a pistol to take the likes of you, Heywood," Armbruster said calmly.

Heywood snorted in derision. He eased his pistol out and tossed it into the darkness.

"Private Finney," Armbruster said, holding out his Colt, "take my weapon."

When Finney had done so and moved out of the way, Cavannaugh eased down the hammer of his Colt and slid it away. Then he stepped back.

"Well, well, well," Heywood sneered, "the little lieutenant's got some sand in him after all."

"Before we begin this little fracas," Armbruster said sarcastically, "you might want to shove your limp pecker away."

"Afraid of it?" Heywood boasted, thrusting his pelvis out a little.

Armbruster laughed harshly. "No, not at all. It's just that when I knock the piss out of you, I'd rather it went in your pants instead of on mine."

Several of the soldiers snickered. Heywood's back stiffened, and then he self-consciously put himself away.

Armbruster moved up a few steps while Heywood was fixing himself. There was a decent-sized moon and plenty of stars. Now that his eyes had adjusted, he could see well enough. He felt strangely calm, almost at ease despite facing a foe who was as tall as he and outweighed him by forty pounds or so.

"You done playing with yourself now, Private?" Armbruster asked, a smirking tone in his voice.

Heywood grinned and then spit, "Have at me, you puny little shit."

Armbruster moved cautiously forward, hands held loosely in front of his middle. He jiggled his hands, trying to loosen his wrists and arms.

Heywood stood there with his hands on his hips, waiting arrogantly for Armbruster to do something. The pistol blow on the head had hurt but hadn't quite stunned him, and he figured that was in the back of Armbruster's mind.

It was, but Armbruster also had sense enough to know that he had not swung the pistol all that hard, and that Heywood's thick hair had blunted the blow even more. Still, he was wary. Heywood was a large—and extremely tough—man. Armbruster's ribs also hurt from where Heywood had elbowed him. He tried to keep his mind off the pain and concentrate on Heywood.

Armbruster's left hand flicked out, snapping on Heywood's nose. The jab had no effect on Heywood, other than to make him sneer a little more. Twice more the hand snapped out, popping on Heywood's face. Then, suddenly, Armbruster kicked Heywood in the knee.

Heywood yowled and instinctively bent. As he did, Armbruster jerked his own knee up. He smiled when it connected with Heywood's nose, breaking it and producing a quick rush of bloody snot.

Armbruster swiftly swung the pinkie side of his right fist at the sore spot on Heywood's temple. It connected, and Heywood grunted.

But Heywood was neither down nor out. He suddenly jerked his torso upward and backhanded Armbruster hard across the face. Armbruster staggered backward and almost fell. Serafina screamed.

Heywood barreled toward Armbruster and swept him up into his bearlike grasp. He lifted Armbruster off his feet and squeezed.

Armbruster could feel his innards being squashed,

but he kept his head. With his right fist he flailed at Heywood's temple. With the other fist, he pounded on Heywood's already broken nose. Neither worked to free him from Heywood's death grip, so he changed tack, pounding both fists repeatedly into Heywood's ears as hard as he could manage.

Armbruster could hardly breathe and the exertion was taxing his system further. Still, there seemed nothing he could do. Once more he changed his attack, reluctantly jammed his thumbs into Heywood's eyes. Then he pushed hard and rotated the thumbs, grinding them into Heywood's eyes as hard as he could.

Heywood took it for a few moments, but then he roared, and threw Armbruster down. He staggered back a few steps, his own hands rubbing at his eyes.

Armbruster landed hard. Seeing Heywood out of the fight mostly, he took his time getting up, trying to suck in deep draughts of air to make up for what he had missed. His ribs hurt like hellfire and he was a little worried that his jawbone might be cracked. His hands ached and they felt as if they were already swelling.

"Best finish him off, Lieutenant," Cavannaugh said quietly as he helped Armbruster up. Cavannaugh's respect and admiration for Armbruster had increased considerably in the past few minutes. Few men, let alone officers, would dare to go toe-to-toe with the hulking Fenton Heywood. It showed Cavannaugh just what kind of man Armbruster was.

"I'm not planning to kill him, Sergeant," Armbruster said flatly. He was standing with hands on knees, hoping he didn't fall on his face.

"You don't have to kill him, sir. Just put him out. And soon. He gets his eyes back, and you're gonna be in deep trouble. Sir."

Armbruster glanced sharply up at Cavannaugh, then nodded. He straightened and marched toward Heywood, stopping a foot away. "You ready to submit, Private?" he asked levelly.

"Fuck you." Heywood snapped. Suddenly he lashed out and a meaty fist caught Armbruster in the left eye. Armbruster fell on his rump, and then on his back.

Heywood leaped for him, but Armbruster managed to roll out of the way. Heywood landed on his stomach in the dirt. Armbruster swiftly rolled back to Heywood, grabbed Heywood's left arm and twisted it as he stood, slapping a foot down on the back of Heywood's neck.

Breathing heavily, Armbruster said, "You have one more chance, Private. Submit now and you'll face a fair court-martial."

"And if I don't?" Heywood wheezed.

"I'll break your goddamn arm for starters. After that, who knows? Perhaps I'll allow Mister Martinez to work on you for a while. That'd be interesting."

Heywood suddenly roared and surged up with all the power in his stocky legs. Armbruster was startled, but managed to keep his balance, as well as his grip on Heywood's arm, at least for a time.

Heywood felt his arm break, but then he was up on his feet. Armbruster had to release the arm and he wobbled backward, fighting to keep on his feet. Heywood slammed into him, and the two crashed to the ground.

Armbruster scrambled free as Heywood bellowed in pain when his broken arm hit the ground. Armbruster hopped up, a little unsteady, and stomped on Heywood's broken arm. Then he kicked Heywood in the face. Then again. He was about to do so again when Cavannaugh stepped partly in front of him.

"He's had enough, Lieutenant," Cavannaugh said quietly. "Unless you changed your mind and kill him." The latter was a question.

Armbruster drew in a ragged breath, then shook his head. "No, Sergeant, I'm not planning to kill him. I just wanted to make sure he wasn't going to get up anymore. Jesus, he's got more lives than a cat."

"He's a tough one, all right. And a nasty bastard."

Armbruster nodded. "I want him tied up tight and under guard until we get back to Fort Defiance."

"Yessir. Should we fix his arm?"

"If you can."

"You going to be all right, sir?" Cavannaugh asked, worried. Armbruster looked about done in.

"I think so." He paused. "Or maybe I just hope so."

"I'll help him, Sergeant," Serafina said quietly. She and her father stopped on each side of Armbruster.

"That be all right, sir?" Cavannaugh asked almost possessively.

"Yes, Sergeant. Take care of Heywood and detail a couple men to guard him. Let the others get back to sleep as soon as you can."

"Yessir." Cavannaugh stepped out of the way.

Serafina and Martinez gently took Armbruster under the arms and the lieutenant allowed the two to help him toward their small camp area. After setting him down with his back against a rock, Serafina retrieved her small medical kit. Martinez got more fuel and built the fire up so his daughter could see better.

"Some water, Papa," Serafina said as her father returned to her side. When Martinez had left, Serafina gazed into Armbruster's eyes. "What you asked me last evening, Lieutenant?"

"Yes?"

"I will talk to my papa. I think he will allow it." She smiled.

Armbruster returned the smile, then asked, "So, all I had to do to get you was beat the snot out of someone?" He laughed a little. "If I'd known that, I would've picked on someone a lot smaller than Heywood."

Serafina giggled, then turned serious. "It wasn't so

much that you fought a man," she said. "It was more the fact that you fought one of your own men to save a half-Mexican, half-Navajo. Not too many Anglo men'd do that."

"I'm not most Anglo men," Armbruster said with a touch of pride.

"I've noticed."

Martinez returned with some water. Serafina cut a small piece off an old blanket, dipped a corner in the water and then dabbed at the cut on Armbruster's face. Then she gently prodded his jawline and the socket around the eye where he had been punched.

"I don't think anything's broken there," she said.

"Sure feels like it."

"I bet it does. You want me to check your ribs?"

"If that wouldn't be improper."

"It will be all right, Señor," Martinez said.

Armbruster relaxed as Serafina opened his shirt. He found it hard to stay calm as her gentle fingers touched his skin. He leaned back, closing his eyes, trying not to let the excitement get the better of him.

"Nothing broken there either," Serafina finally announced.

Armbruster opened his eyes and looked straight into her wide, dark eyes, and almost got lost in them.

"Let me see your hands," Serafina ordered.

Armbruster lifted his right hand. The knuckles were cut and bleeding some. Serafina washed them, as gently as she could, but Armbruster still sucked in a sharp breath once. Serafina stopped immediately and carefully poked around. When she got another hiss, she nodded. She looked at Armbruster and grinned. "Well, we've finally found a broken bone." She pointed to Armbruster's right pinkie.

"Gee, how wonderful," Armbruster said dryly.

Serafina giggled again. "Let me check the other hand, then I'll fix the break for you."

It was not long before Armbruster had a crude splint on his pinkie and Serafina had cleaned up her materials.

It took Armbruster even longer this time to get to sleep.

❧{ 13 }❧

Armbruster was considerably relieved to get back to Fort Defiance. Though bound on his horse, the hulking Private Fenton Heywood had tried to cause whatever trouble he could on the journey back. He got so bad that Armbruster twice ordered the private gagged.

Armbruster ordered Heywood taken to the guardhouse, and then he rode to the stable. He was still sore, as well as being hot, tired and dusty. And, despite his relief, he felt a little sadness, too, at being back at the fort. It meant he was no longer with Serafina Martinez, and he would not see her again until late summer or early fall. On top of that, he was worried about her. If one group of Apaches had found the woman and her trader father, another one could. They were in that vast wilderness alone.

Armbruster turned his horse over to one of the men on stable duty, and trudged to Major Brooks's office and reported in.

"I hear—or maybe see—that you had some trouble on this patrol, Lieutenant," Brooks said. "That right?"

"Yessir. We ran into a band of Apaches attacking Mister Martinez and his daughter."

"Since you're standing here, I assume you were victorious against the Apaches?"

"Yessir. We—"

"Sit, Lieutenant. You've had a tough patrol."

"Yessir. Thank you." He sat. "We killed seven, or maybe it was eight, Jicarillas, without any loss to ourselves or Mister Martinez."

"Looks like you took a good thumping in the victory."

"No, sir. I'll explain my battered appearance later. The only casualty—if that's what you want to call it—of the Apache fight was a slight concussion suffered by Private Vickers."

"He's recovered?"

"He seems to be, sir. But I've ordered him to report to Doctor Fournier directly."

"Good." Brooks paused, then asked, "You kill any of the Apaches?"

"Yessir," Armbruster said quietly. He shuddered involuntarily at the remembrance.

"Are you square with that, Lieutenant?"

"Yessir."

"You certain?"

"Yessir. I . . . I got sick just after I did it, but I'm over it. I still don't like having done it, and I certainly got no pleasure out of it, but—"

"Just as long as you can do it again when it's called for," Brooks said harshly, making the statement something of a question.

"I can, sir."

"Good. Now, what about your injuries?" Brooks pointed. "You're a rather colorful specimen. How'd that occur?"

"In a tussle with Private Heywood. . . ."

"That large, overstuffed son of a bitch?" Brooks asked in a rush of words. He was surprised.

"Yessir, that's the one." Armbruster grinned a little, which it still hurt to do. "He tried forcing his way on

Miss Martinez. I caught him at his filthy deed and objected to it. He—"

"She's a half-breed Mex-Navajo," Brooks said flatly.

"She's a woman, sir," Armbruster responded defensively.

"And a mighty damned attractive one, too," Brooks conceded. "But she . . . her people aren't like us. The Indians and Mexicans both are a lot more . . . shall I say free? . . . with such things. They're of loose morals. Adulterous and immoral."

"Be that as it may," Armbruster said stiffly, "she's still a woman, and at the time she—as well as her father —was under my protection, as it were."

"That's a telling point."

Armbruster nodded. "Anyway, Heywood attacked me, and I was forced to defend myself against him."

"You went toe-to-toe with that hulk?" Brooks asked, surprised again.

"Yessir. He thumped me pretty good, but he looks as bad as I do."

"I'll have to go see that for myself. Where is he?"

"The guardhouse. I intend to file formal charges against him and see that he faces a court-martial."

"For trying to hump a half-breed Mex-Navajo?"

Armbruster was taken aback at Brooks's attitude, but, since he could not change it, he tried to ignore it. "If you have some objection to that, sir," Armbruster said flatly, "I'll not press the point. He still needs to account for attacking me."

"Well, yes, that certainly would be right." Brooks rested his elbows on the desk and laced his fingers. "We can't have such hooligans attacking officers. But I would be . . . grateful . . . if you were to avoid mention of the . . . incident . . . as much as possible."

"Yessir." Armbruster felt the tiredness and the pain of his wounds creeping up on him. He just wanted to get out of there, go clean up and then rest for a week or so. "Is there anything else, sir?"

"No, Lieutenant. You look tired. Go get some rest."

Armbruster stood. "Thank you, sir." He saluted, and clumped wearily across the compound to his small quarters. It took a few moments for his eyes to adjust to the dimness enough to allow him to light a lantern. Then he stood there, smoking match in hand, wondering just what had gone on.

The only furniture left in his simple one-room quarters was the stove. The bed, desk, chest of drawers, coat rack, all were gone. So were his clothes, including the ones he had had on a pole stretched catty-corner from front wall to side wall.

Armbruster turned slowly, eyes searching the walls, floor, everything. Then he spotted a piece of paper pinned to the back of the door. He pulled it free and went back to the lantern to read it. It left him even more puzzled.

> Lieutenant Armbruster:
> Due to a shortage of officers' quarters on the post, your quarters have been reassigned so a higher-ranking officer may move into your former quarters, small and stark as they are.
> Your new quarters are in Building Four some yards directly to the north from your old quarters. I hope you find them satisfactory, since they're all you're going to get.
> Respectfully yours,
> Capt. Lansford Hastings
> Housing Officer
> Fort Defiance, New Mexico Territory

Armbruster stood there a bit, tapping the note on a thumbnail while trying to sort things out. There was a puzzle here, and not everything was as it should be. He knew the note contained clues, but his tired, shocked brain made figuring them out difficult.

He looked through the note again. "Building Four," he murmured. "There's no such thing. Except . . ." His eyes widened when he realized that building 4 could only be one of the smaller stables north of officers' row. There was no way he would've been assigned to live in a stable. Not unless they converted one of the stables while he was gone. He did not figure that likely, but he had to keep open to the possibility of it.

Something else about the note—the name signed at the bottom—also bothered him. There was no officer by that name at Fort Defiance. Or at least there hadn't been when he had left. Still, the name seemed somehow familiar to him. He began pacing the room, brow knitted in concentration.

Suddenly he stopped. "Son of a bitch!" he mumbled, as things clicked into place, at least somewhat. He remembered now that Lansford Hastings had written a monograph titled *Emigrants' Guide*, perhaps a dozen or so years ago. He had studied it a little at the Academy. For several years travelers west had used it to lead them. Until word had gotten out about one party who had tried to follow it. The party ended up snowed in somewhere in the High Sierra, and were forced to dine on each other to survive. Once that became public knowledge, Hastings's small opus fell into some disrepute.

What all that had to do with Armbruster's predicament, he was not sure. But he began to suspect that the name was used to let him know—if he was able to figure it out—that this was all a hoax.

Half-angry, half-happy, he went outside and turned north, heading for the stables. Entering the fourth one, he found his possessions, set up almost exactly as they had been in his quarters, although in here it was among the horse manure and stench of the stable.

Hans Knudson stepped out of a horse stall near the back. His face was split by a wide grin. "Welcome home, Lieutenant," he said. "How do you like your new quarters?"

"I'm unimpressed with them," Armbruster said, smiling weakly. "Cute trick, Hans, but I'm not really in the mood for it. I'm tired and hungry and thirsty, sore and fed up. I want to get some grub, have a quick wash-off and then catch up on some sleep."

"Everything's ready and waiting," Knudson said, still grinning.

"Hans, listen," Armbruster said slowly, "I'm going to get myself some food. If all my things aren't back in my quarters, where they belong, I'm going to kick the shit out of you."

The smile froze on Knudson's face. He took a few steps forward and caught a good look at Armbruster's face. That told him two things: one, that Armbruster was not joking; and two, that Armbruster had good reason to be annoyed. "What the hell happened to you?" he asked.

"I was forced to teach Private Heywood some manners."

"Jesus," Knudson breathed. He shook his head. "I was just pulling a prank on you, Ed. I didn't mean—"

"I know all that. But I had a rough time of it out there this time." He looked a little embarrassed. "I killed my first man—men, actually. Two Apaches. Then I had the run-in with Heywood."

"Say no more." Knudson smiled crookedly. "Hell, what a waste of a good prank, though."

Armbruster managed to work up a small smile. "Sorry."

"Don't worry about it. I'll get you better next time." He sighed at all the work done for nothing. "Go on over to the mess. By the time you get back to your quarters, your shit'll be back in place—or there'll be a few men from Company B living in the guardhouse.''

"Thanks, Hans.'' Armbruster turned and started to head out. Then he stopped and looked back. "I really am sorry I spoiled your joke.''

"There'll be more, don't you worry.''

Armbruster nodded and left. He suffered Bessie's almost effusive welcome, and then ate a leisurely meal of roasted pork, potatoes, and biscuits, followed by apple cobbler, all of it accompanied by hot, black coffee. He seemed not to be able to get enough of the latter. It was as if he had not had any coffee in weeks. Considering how poor the trail coffee was, that wasn't too far from the truth, he decided after a while.

Finally he rose and walked outside. It was still a little hard for him to believe it was only early afternoon. He strolled to his quarters. Three enlisted men were just hustling out, leaving Knudson standing in the doorway.

"Well, it was close, but we made it,'' Knudson said with a grin. Then he held out a small, unopened bottle of fine Scotch whiskey. "My way of apologizing, Ed,'' Knudson said.

"That's not necessary, Hans,'' Armbruster responded.

"I didn't say it was. But if I'd had any brains at all, I would've waited to see what frame of mind you were in. Hell, often enough we all come back from those damned patrols hurt or angry, worried or scared to death. It's not the best time to pull a prank on someone.'' He shrugged. "Since I can't take back what's done, I thought maybe I could make up for it in a small way.'' He thrust the small bottle toward Armbruster again.

Armbruster took it, nodding. "Well, I'm grateful. I don't really figure I'll need help getting to sleep, but this'll still go down smooth and welcome.'' He grinned. "I don't suppose you'd want a sip or two of this before I hit the hay."

"No, of course not," Knudson said with exaggerated gestures of protest.

"Didn't think so. See you tomorrow." Armbruster laughed at the shock on Knudson's face. "You aren't the only one who can play pranks on folks, Hans," he said gleefully. "Come on, let's open this thing up."

"Why, you son of a gun . . ." Knudson said, then grinned.

Armbruster went inside and stopped, surveying the room. As far as he could tell, everything was back in its old position. His spare clothing hung on the rod, his few books were lined up properly on his desk. The bed was neatly made, and his firebox was full. He nodded and tossed the bottle on the bed. After he pulled off his uniform blouse and threw it aside, he sat on the bed, picked up the bottle, opened it and took a healthy swallow. "Not bad," he said as he handed the bottle to Knudson.

"Not bad, my ass," Knudson said before swallowing some. "It ought to be great considering how much I paid for it." He took another swallow and then passed it back. "Was it really that bad out there this time?" he asked.

"Bad enough." As he and Knudson passed the bottle back and forth, Armbruster told of the trip, all of it except his feelings for Serafina Martinez. After Brooks's reaction when Serafina was mentioned, Armbruster had decided to be as wary as he reasonably could where she was concerned.

The bottle and the story ended at roughly the same time. Knudson nodded. "All of us've been on as bad, or worse, but no one's going to make light of this one against you, Ed. We all remember the first time we had to kill someone. It's something that doesn't ever leave a man. You'll get used to it, but you'll never forget the first." Knudson pushed himself up. "Well, friend, it's about time you got yourself some shut-eye."

Armbruster nodded. He dropped the bottle on the floor and stretched out on the bed.

{ 14 }

One of the storerooms next to the guardhouse had been converted to a courtroom for Private Fenton Heywood's court-martial. Major Brooks was presiding. The rest of the panel was made up of Captains Josiah Goodwin and Ambrose Gilmore. Armbruster was to present his own case. First Lieutenant Frank Saxbury was to represent Heywood, who was in the "courtroom." The rest of the room was packed by whoever could cram himself inside.

Armbruster stood when Brooks called the court-martial into session. His face was still rather colorful and his pinkie bandaged and splinted. He was nervous, knowing that everyone in the room was looking at him with interest. He figured the audience was about equally divided between those who wanted to see him do well and those who wanted him to fall on his face.

"Sirs," he said slowly, "I have accused Private Fenton Heywood with attacking an officer of the United States Army—said officer being myself, Lieutenant Edward Armbruster."

"Take a seat in the witness chair, Lieutenant," Brooks said evenly. When Armbruster did, Brooks said, "Lieutenant Saxbury, you may question the witness."

Saxbury nodded and walked toward Armbruster,

stopping a few feet away. "Tell me, Lieutenant," Saxbury said with a tinge of dislike in his voice, "just what precipitated Private Heywood's attack on you."

"Private Heywood was in a place he shouldn't have been, doing something he shouldn't have," Armbruster said flatly. He wanted to try to avoid as much as possible bringing Serafina's name into this. There were many men here—apparently including Brooks—who would think that what Heywood had been trying to do was nothing to be concerned about.

"And just where was he that he wasn't supposed to be?"

"In a section of camp reserved for traders."

"Traders? Plural? Not just *a* trader?"

"No, sir. Two traders."

"Who were they? What were their names?"

"That doesn't matter," Armbruster said, tension increasing.

"Let the court-martial decide that, Lieutenant," Saxbury snapped.

"Answer the question, Lieutenant," Brooks said.

Armbruster glared at the commanding officer a moment, then turned his gaze back to Saxbury. In calm, measured tones, he said, "Mister Cruz Martinez and his daughter, Serafina."

"Then there was only one trader?" Saxbury pressed.

"I believe Mister Martinez considers his daughter a trader."

"Surely you jest, Lieutenant," Saxbury said with scorn. "A half–Mexican–half–Navajo trollop a trader?" He looked smug.

Armbruster's knuckles on the arm of the chair were white as he fought to control the sudden burst of rage that flashed through him. He finally succeeded. "We're all aware of her parentage. We also know that without her, Mister Martinez would have little chance of trading with a good many of the Navajos." Armbruster surprised himself with the evenness of his voice.

"That's all well and good, Lieutenant. I—"

"I'm not finished yet," Armbruster snapped. He knew he was making an enemy of Frank Saxbury, but right now he did not care.

"Oh?" Saxbury asked, surprise stamped on his face.

"There are two points here that need to be considered, Lieutenant," Armbruster went on, voice just a tad harsher. "One is the fact that I'm not the one being court-martialed here. Private Heywood is. The second is that this line of questioning has little to do with the matter at hand."

"Is that so?" Saxbury sneered. He was sure he had regained the upper hand.

"Yes, that's so."

"But," Saxbury added smugly, "didn't your altercation with Private Heywood begin because of the whore?"

"What whore?" Armbruster countered. His innocent look belied the anger still raging in his chest.

"That half-breed mongrel trollop who—" Saxbury slammed to a stop. He suddenly realized that he was letting himself get carried away, goaded on by his desire to destroy Armbruster.

"Yes?" Armbruster asked, still looking like a wide-eyed innocent.

Saxbury paced a bit, allowing himself to cool down so he could think more clearly. Finally he turned back to look at Armbruster from across the room. "Answer me this, Lieutenant," he said calmly. "How did the altercation begin."

"I already answered that. Private Heywood was doing something he wasn't supposed to in an area he wasn't supposed to be in." Armbruster's voice was every bit as calm as Saxbury's.

"Could you please be more specific, Lieutenant? Exactly where was Private Heywood? And exactly what was he doing?''

"He was in Mister Martinez's section of the camp, which I had placed off-limits to the men.''

"Why was it off-limits?'' Saxbury was beginning to gloat again, thinking he had Armbruster on the run.

"Mister Martinez has just started his trading for the year, so he still had several thousand dollars worth of supplies.'' Armbruster favored Saxbury with an insulting little smile.

"No other reason?''

"No, sir.''

"Not even because of the bi—'' Saxbury turned away, cursing silently at himself for having allowed Armbruster to drag him down again. He turned. "What exactly did Private Heywood do to precipitate the alleged attack on you, Lieutenant?''

"The what?'' Armbruster responded blandly.

"The alleged a—'' Saxbury blew out a long breath. "The attack on you.''

Armbruster knew this was the crux of the matter. There was no way he could gloss over it, but at the same time, telling it would give Saxbury an opening to exploit. He sighed. There was no getting away from it. "The private was in the midst of trying to rape Miss Serafina.''

"Oh, come now, Lieutenant,'' Saxbury snorted. "Rape? Surely you must be mistaken.''

"I am not, sir.'' Armbruster felt his face flame hotly.

"How do you know she just did not make an 'arrangement' with Private Heywood? An arrangement in which for certain remuneration, she would bestow her illicit favors on him?''

"I don't believe,'' Armbruster said dryly, "that she would've been trying to claw Heywood's eyes out if she had arranged to copulate willingly with him.''

Saxbury flushed angrily as laughter flittered around

the room. "Goddammit, Armbruster," Saxbury snapped, "I'll not be spoken to in such a manner by the likes of you." He advanced threateningly.

Armbruster rose, fists balled. "I kicked the shit out of Heywood," he snapped. "I sure as hell won't have any trouble doing the same to you."

"Lieutenants!" Brooks bellowed. "Enough of this." He waited a moment, then continued. "Lieutenant Saxbury, as much as I might hate to admit it, Lieutenant Armbruster is right in many things. It doesn't matter that this . . . woman . . . might have encouraged Private Heywood's advances. If she did, he should have refused, knowing that Lieutenant Armbruster placed the area off-limits to all the troops, for whatever reason he had. Nor does it matter, really, why Heywood attacked Lieutenant Armbruster. Unless Lieutenant Armbruster did something so heinous to Heywood to turn the private against him, Heywood had—has—no reason to have attacked the lieutenant. Perhaps you should turn your questions in another direction."

"Yessir," Saxbury said flatly. He was humiliated. "What happened then, Lieutenant?" he asked dully.

"I found him causing trouble for Miss Martinez and I stopped him," Armbruster said, thinking that he managed to keep the crowing of victory—as well as the surprise at Brooks's change of heart, if that's what it really was—out of his voice. "When I did that, he objected with an elbow to the ribs. Things kind of picked up from there."

"Did you encourage him any in his attack?" Saxbury was grasping at straws now.

"Well, sir, I was not going to stand there and let a man the size of Private Heywood stomp me into the dirt."

"Of course not. But I have heard that you actually challenged Private Heywood. Is that true?"

"We sort of challenged each other," Armbruster admitted.

"Oh? Would you care to explain that?"

Armbruster shrugged. "Sergeant Cavannaugh and the other men were about to grab Heywood and confine him. I offered Heywood the chance to not have that done."

"So," Saxbury said, feeling a little better, "what you're saying is that you invited Heywood to attack you. Is that it?"

"Not exactly."

"Let me get this straight. You challenged Heywood; practically told him to come and kick your ass, but you didn't encourage him to attack you?"

"I'll say it slow this time, Lieutenant, so even you can understand it," Armbruster said. He waited for the chuckles to subside, enjoying the choler on Saxbury's face. "When I stopped Heywood from attacking Miss Martinez, he attacked me so strongly that I thought several ribs were broken. He also hit me several other times. At that point, Sergeant Cavannaugh and some of the other men intervened. They were about to arrest Heywood when I offered him a chance . . . to redeem himself somewhat, I guess you might say."

"And then you attacked him, and he had to defend himself?"

"Not quite. He attacked me. After a fight of some minutes, I came out victorious."

"You expect this court-martial to believe that a man of your slimness and inexperience beat a man like Heywood, a man known for his prowess in brawling, a man much larger than you?"

"Yes," Armbruster said simply. "But if you have doubts, I'd be glad to give you a personal demonstration of my prowess, Lieutenant."

More chuckles floated across the room, and even Brooks and the pious Captain Gilmore smiled.

"Besides, Lieutenant," Armbruster went on, "my charges against Heywood stem from his initial attack on me, not the latter attack."

Saxbury felt a flush of excitement. He saw another small opening, and he went for it. "So, Lieutenant, what we have is your word that Private Heywood was trying to accost that . . . woman . . . and that you interfered and Heywood attacked you."

"That's right."

"But how are we to know you didn't initiate the attack? Answer that, Lieutenant. How are we to know that perhaps it wasn't you trying to rape that wh— woman and that Private Heywood tried to stop you?"

Armbruster shrugged. "I am an officer and a gentleman, sir," he said proudly. "And I would think that my word would count for a little more than the word of a thug."

Many of the officers in the room nodded. It made sense to them. To attack Armbruster's credibility that way was to attack the credibility of all of them.

Cavannaugh stood from his seat in the audience and saluted smartly. "Major, sir," he said in a strong voice, though he was nervous, "if I might speak, sir."

"You'll be able to spread some light on this matter, Sergeant?" Brooks asked.

"Yessir."

"Then proceed."

"Yessir. I heard something that night, sir. It woke me. I came out of my blankets and saw Private Heywood in the firelight. He was trying to rape that unfortunate girl," he lied smoothly.

Armbruster quickly covered up his astonishment.

Cavannaugh paused. "She might be a damned half-Mexican, half-Navajo, but she's still only just a girl, sir. Anyway, I was about to stop him when I saw Lieutenant Armbruster heading there. I stopped to wake some other men. When I next turned back, Heywood was clobbering the lieutenant. That's when me and the other men intervened.''

"That all, Sergeant?''

"I believe so, sir, yes.'' He shrugged. "I was going to arrest Heywood, like Lieutenant Armbruster said. But then the lieutenant made us back off, saying he could handle it.''

"Thank you, Sergeant,'' Brooks said. "You may take your seat.'' Brooks glanced from Gilmore on his one side to Goodwin on the other. Then he looked at Saxbury. "Anything further, Lieutenant?'' he asked.

"No, sir,'' Saxbury answered sourly.

"Captain Gilmore?''

"I think it's all been explained,'' Gilmore answered. "A most unfortunate thing when men cannot control their immodest urges.''

"Indeed,'' Brooks said dryly. "Captain Goodwin?''

"I think Private Heywood should have a chance to speak his piece.''

"Right you are, Captain.'' Brooks glared balefully out at Heywood. "You have anything to say for yourself, Private?''

"No, sir,'' Heywood grumbled. He was still angry at Armbruster, but he was more angry at himself. He should have been able to squash Armbruster with ease. Yet the tall, thin lieutenant had bested him, in a fair fight! That galled him no end. And, even if he had something to say to defend himself, he knew he wouldn't. Anything he said now would make him even less of a man than he was by having lost to Armbruster. Now he began to worry about what his punishment would be.

"Well, then,'' Brooks said, "the panel will convene outside to determine Private Heywood's guilt, and to determine what—if any—punishment is warranted.''

"Ah, Jesus, Ed," Knudson almost whined. "Use your head."

"I am," Armbruster snapped. "Like I said, you don't want anything to do with her—or me because I like her —fine. Just don't get in my way. And keep your opinions to yourself." Armbruster sighed. "I value your friendship, Hans, but not at the risk of going against my deepest feelings."

"Your what?"

"Maybe I should've said my deepest beliefs." He smiled ruefully. "Even though I'm not really sure what all those are. Just like my being out here, I'm feeling my way along, trying to find what I believe in, and what I don't. I've found I don't mind Mexicans and Navajos —or at least some of them anyway—all that much. I've also found that I don't much like sanctimonious folks who think they're better than everyone else."

Armbruster had surprised himself with the little speech. He had been pondering such things since beginning the trip back to the fort after his fight with Heywood. But he hadn't thought himself capable of giving voice to any of them, at least not for a while yet.

Knudson looked angry and perplexed. He wasn't quite so dead set against Indians or Mexicans or anyone else as much as many of the other officers were. But he was the kind of man who tried to make as little trouble as possible for himself—except when it came to pulling practical jokes. He went through life bending with whatever wind was blowing at the moment. With Indian haters, he could give as good as anyone. When he was with Mexican haters, he could spout all the slurs known to mankind about those people. Now, though, Armbruster was trying to force him to make a decision about such matters, and he did not like that thought. If he sided with Armbruster, he would lose some other friends on the post. If he did not side with Armbruster, he would lose the closest thing to a real friend he had

had in years. Besides, he didn't know himself how he really felt about such matters. He had spent so long not making decisions in those areas that he was no longer sure he could have an original thought about them. He sighed.

"I don't really know what to say, Ed," Knudson offered lamely. "I've never given much thought to—" He stopped as Brooks, Gilmore and Goodwin entered the room again.

The three officers sat and waited until there was silence.

"There's no doubt whatsoever," Brooks began, "that Private Fenton Heywood attacked Lieutenant Edward Armbruster. Even if Lieutenant Armbruster had challenged Private Heywood right from the beginning, Private Heywood should have backed down. He knows —or he damn well should know—that attacking an officer is wrong. And stupid."

Brooks paused, looking around the room. "With that as a given, it falls to Captains Goodwin, Gilmore and I to find a suitable punishment. Had Private Heywood had no record of infractions, he might've been gotten off with a small sentence. However, the private has something of a reputation as a bully and a troublemaker. He has been in the guardhouse countless times and has suffered other punishments. None of those has increased his wisdom or common sense, nor have they brought any beneficial changes to his behavior."

Brooks paused again. The silence was complete in the room, and one could feel the expectancy.

"Therefore, it is the order of this court-martial that Private Fenton Heywood should suffer fifty strokes of the lash, forfeit pay for two months and spend one month in the guardhouse on bread and water. The lashes will be administered three days hence." Brooks rapped the table with the butt of his Colt pistol.

Everyone in the room sat in stunned silence for

some minutes, then began filing out. Even Armbruster was shocked at the stiff sentence. If he had realized that such would be the result, he might've never made the complaint, or at least toned his complaint down some.

Armbruster stopped and realized he was alone. Knudson was walking away, head down, either in thought or disturbed. Armbruster shook his head sadly. "Damn, you really made a mess of things in a hurry, didn't you, son," he muttered to himself.

"What's that, sir?" Cavannaugh asked.

Armbruster turned and smiled weakly at the sergeant. "Just remonstrating myself, Sergeant." He pulled out a cigar and held it out. "Care for one, Sergeant?" he asked.

Cavannaugh rarely got to smoke a good cigar. All he could afford on his pay were foul-smelling stogies. Still, he was not about to take his commanding officer's last cigar. "Well, sir . . ." he said, eyes focused hungrily on the cigar.

"Hell, take it, Sergeant. I have more," Armbruster said with another weak smile.

"Thank you, sir," Cavannaugh said. He took the cigar and sniffed at it for some moments. He lit it, and then held the match out so Armbruster could light his cigar.

Armbruster nodded thanks. After puffing a moment, he looked squarely at Cavannaugh. "Just what the hell possessed you to lie your ass off in there, Sergeant?" he asked. He grinned a little, letting Cavannaugh know he wasn't angry about it; just curious.

Cavannaugh shrugged. "Don't know if I can explain it, sir. I can't stand Heywood. Never could. He's a cowardly pissant peckerwood, sir."

Armbruster looked around. He and Cavannaugh were alone. "You can cut the 'sir' crap every two seconds, Sergeant. At least for now."

"Yessir." He grinned. "Besides, Lieutenant, I knew you weren't lyin'. Heywood's the kind of egg-suckin' son of a bitch'd try to force himself on a woman. That's enough right there to raise my dander, dammit."

Armbruster's eyebrows raised. "You don't believe the way the rest of these men seem to—that because Serafina's a Mexican-Indian that she's no good and only got what she deserved?"

"Hell if I know what I feel, Lieutenant," Cavannaugh said flatly. "All I know is no real man's gonna go rape a girl." He shrugged again. "I reckon I might think a little different if you was to suddenly up and decide you wanted to marry her. But, then again, maybe not."

"You have a daughter about that age, don't you, Sergeant?" Armbruster asked suddenly, on a hunch.

Cavannaugh smiled sadly. "Yessir. Molly. She'd be about seventeen, maybe eighteen now."

"And?"

"And what, sir?"

"And you're not going to let me stand here and wonder about her, are you?"

Cavannaugh smiled. "Reckon not, sir." He paused, puffing his cigar a little. "Molly was almost eight years old when we went to war with the Mexicans. I up and joined a militia unit back in Tennessee. Wound up fightin' all the way to Buena Vista with General Taylor."

"The late president?"

"Yessir. Anyway, after the war, I mustered out and went back home. We had us a hardscrabble farm, and I worked it as best I could, but it never brought us much. I worked whatever extra jobs I could find, but times was hard." He stopped, staring off into the vast blueness of the sky. "Maggie—that was my wife—she died of the cholera in 'forty-nine, leavin' me and Molly. I knew I couldn't raise Molly by myself. Not and do right by her, so I turned her over to Maggie's sister, Mary.

"I went back to that hole of a farm, but I couldn't stand it. There wasn't much work around, and about the only thing I knew besides farming was soldiering, so I signed up again. I'd been a top sergeant in the war, and it didn't take me too long to reach that rank again." He smiled wanly. "And now here I am."

"I suppose you haven't seen Molly since you signed up again?" Armbruster asked.

"Once. I was being posted to Fort Marcy, and on the way out, I stopped by Mary's place. It was only a year after I'd left Mary there, but she seemed so different."

"You've had a hard life, Sergeant," Armbruster said sincerely.

"No worse'n a lot of other folks, Lieutenant," Cavannaugh said with a shrug. "I've got my health. I've got a calling I'm good at. I've seen a fair piece of country, and I've served under some of the best men to ever wear a uniform. That's a hell of a lot more than many a man's got, sir."

"Yes, Sergeant, yes it is. But at what cost? You've lost a wife and a daughter. You have little chance of finding another of either."

"I reckon that's so, sir. But . . . well, I sort of look at the men as my family."

"It's not quite the same."

"That's a fact." Cavannaugh smiled again. "Still, it ain't so bad."

"Well, Sergeant, I do appreciate what you did for me in there." Armbruster pointed his cigar at where the court-martial had been held. "I suppose I would've won out eventually, but I can't be certain of that. And you made things go a lot more smoothly. I'm in your debt."

"I ain't worried about it, Lieutenant," Cavannaugh said bluntly. "You don't *owe* me nothin'." He paused.

"Maybe I'm speakin' out of turn here, Lieutenant, but you showed me somethin' when you took on Heywood. I've seen my share of new lieutenants come and go. Most of 'em're assholes, begging your pardon. They're either all fired up for killin' Indians, or they think they're gonna change the goddamn army all by themselves. They generally treat their top sergeants like shit, and the other enlisted men worse. But you ain't ever done any of those things. You ain't chummy with the men, but you're not supposed to be. Still, you give me respect, and you give the other men respect—if they deserve it." Cavannaugh shrugged. "Maybe I ain't explainin' things too well, Lieutenant, but I think you get the drift."

"I do indeed. And I tell you frankly, that I'm honored to serve alongside a man like Sergeant Clancy Cavannaugh."

"You're gonna make me blush, sir," Cavannaugh said with a grin.

"Sure. When hell freezes over." He sighed. "Well, Sergeant, I expect we'd better get back to playing soldier."

Three days later, the entire fort—those men who were not out on patrol—fell out onto the parade ground. Lined up in ranks, they waited almost patiently as Private Fenton Heywood was escorted from the guardhouse.

A pole had been set into the ground in the center of the parade ground. From near the top hung a pair of shackles. They replaced the shackles Heywood had worn from the guardhouse. Because of the splint on his broken arm, Heywood was shackled around the biceps.

One of the guards pulled a large pocketknife and cut through the back of Heywood's shirt, exposing his entire back. The guard put his knife away, got the nasty-looking cat-o'-nine-tails and presented it to Brooks.

"Lieutenant Armbruster," Brooks said. "You were the one he attacked. To you falls the privilege of wielding the lash." He held the whip out. "If you want it."

"I'd rather pass it along to someone else, sir," Armbruster said bluntly.

Brooks shrugged. "As you wish, Lieutenant."

Armbruster took the lash, and walked slowly along the ranks of the men of Company B. He stopped in front of Cavannaugh and held the whip out. "I'd be obliged if you'd do the honors, Sergeant," he said.

Cavannaugh's eyes widened in surprise. Then he grinned and removed his coat. He took the lash and walked toward Heywood, flexing his shoulder and back muscles. He stopped a couple of feet behind Heywood.

"Who's that?" Heywood asked. "Who's got that goddamn whip?"

Cavannaugh grabbed Heywood's hair and pulled his head back some. "It's your old friend, Sergeant Cavannaugh."

Heywood tried to spit at Cavannaugh, but only managed to get the spittle on his own chin and arm.

"There's a passel of the boys here gonna get a heap of pleasure watchin' you get your ass whipped."

"Fuck you, you fuckin' worm."

"Ah, such talk," Cavannaugh said almost pleasantly. "Just remember, son, that long after the welts've healed—if they ever do—you're gonna have to live with the knowledge that some scrawny-ass lieutenant"—he winked at Armbruster, who was standing not far away—"fresh out of the Point stomped your ass into the ground and then got you court-martialed."

"I'm gonna kill you the first fuckin' chance I get," Heywood growled. "Then I'm gonna kill that shit-ball lieutenant." He paused a beat. "And then I'm gonna go finish the job I started on that half-breed bitch."

Cavannaugh shoved Heywood's head forward hard enough that the private's nose bounced off the post. He stepped back a pace, raised the lash, and then whipped it forward.

Heywood grunted a little, determined not to show any signs of weakness. By the eighth lash, he was screaming. By the twenty-seventh, he was back to groaning—small, mewling, weak little moans. By the fortieth, he was barely conscious, but still the whip kept coming.

{ 16 }

Armbruster felt more isolated as the days passed. Knudson avoided him as much as possible, and then took out a patrol. Even his company commander wanted little to do with him. He expected that of the men of his company, and so was not surprised when he found it to be so. However, the snubbing by the officers struck him as odd, until he concluded that they were angrier at him for having protected Serafina Martinez than they were about his bringing charges against an enlisted man. Armbruster figured that would blow over, but he did not want to be at the fort while the other officers were shunning him.

So, a week after the court-martial, Armbruster went to Brooks. "I'd like to take another patrol out, Major," he said firmly.

"You're not fully recovered, Lieutenant," Brooks said diffidently.

"The only thing that's not healed is my finger, and that won't interfere with my duty."

"Why do you want to go back out already, Lieutenant?" Brooks seemed bored and irritated.

"I think you know the answer, Major," Armbruster said flatly.

"Indeed," Brooks responded dryly. "You do know,

though, don't you, Lieutenant, that you brought all this on yourself?"

"I suppose I did, sir." Armbruster wanted to add— but did not—"And I expect it'll get worse before it gets better. If it ever gets better." What he did add was, "But I still think I did the right thing. Others don't, well, I can't do anything about that, sir."

Brooks was quiet for almost a full minute, then he nodded once. "I suppose it won't do any harm to let you head out again. In fact, it'll probably go a long way to easing some of the tensions around the fort." He sighed. "All right, Lieutenant. Take ten men. I suppose you'll want Sergeant Cavannaugh to go along?" he asked, not happy about the thought. He felt that the sergeant was getting entirely too close to the lieutenant. He frowned upon such fraternization.

"Yessir. He's a good man."

"Yes, he is. Well, so be it. Dismissed."

"Thank you, sir." Armbruster went straight from Brooks's office to the barracks, where he found Cavannaugh. "We're pulling out at dawn tomorrow, Sergeant," he said. "On a new patrol. Pick ten men. Have them draws rations and supplies for three weeks."

"Plannin' to stay out a while this time, Lieutenant?"

"Yes, Sergeant. The longer I'm away from the post, the better off it'll be for everyone concerned."

Cavannaugh nodded, understanding, and not needing to comment on it. "Anyone you don't want along?"

"Private Vickers," Armbruster said after a moment's thought. "I'm not sure he's fully recovered. And I don't think we need to pull him away from his wife any more than necessary. That's about all, though, unless you know of any men who're pals of Private Heywood."

"Believe it or not, sir, there are a few of 'em. Damn fools. I'll make sure they don't come along, even if they volunteer."

"Particularly if they volunteer," Armbruster said sourly.

"Why's that, sir?" Cavannaugh asked, puzzled.

"If they're friends of Heywood's, they just might get it into their minds to put a bullet in the back of my head while we're out among the hostiles."

"That they would," Cavannaugh said with a nod, understanding immediately. "I'll make doubly certain that even anyone who's ever had a kind word for Heywood doesn't come along." He paused. "You want Chief to scout for us again, Lieutenant?"

"If you trust him, and if he's available, I have no quibble with that."

"I trust him about as much as a white man can trust any goddamn Indian." He paused again, not sure he should speak, then deciding Armbruster would not mind. "Chief's asked to come along any time you lead a patrol, Lieutenant," he said softly. "Says he won't go out with no one else."

Armbruster's eyes widened. "Has word of that gotten around the post?" he asked.

"I expect it has, sir, since several of the officers have left out and he hasn't gone with any."

"No wonder the officers are shunning me. First I protect an Indian—rather a half-Indian—then for some unknown reason this scout won't go out with anyone but me." He shook his head in annoyance.

"If I may speak freely, sir?"

"You have all along, Sergeant. No reason to change now."

"His reasons are known. Or at least he's told me his reasons. I don't expect he's lyin'."

"And what are these reasons?" Armbruster was not really sure he wanted to hear them.

"One of 'em's got to do with you savin' Miss Martinez. Chief told me that's the first time he's ever known of a white man—an army man—to help an Indian,

even one who's not a full-blood. You also gained a-
heap of respect from him by knockin' the shit out of
Heywood. And you gained more when you took out
two Apaches all by your lonesome, sir."

"Great," Armbruster snapped. "Just goddamn
great. Every officer at Fort Defiance is snubbing me,
and yet I've won the undying gratitude of an Indian
scout."

Cavannaugh allowed himself to smile just a little.
"Chief isn't the only person's undyin' gratitude you've
gained, sir."

"What's that supposed to mean, Sergeant?" Armbruster was irritable, and growing more so at every
minute.

"It means, sir," Cavannaugh said with smiling caution, "that I believe you've also won the undyin' gratitude of Miss Martinez."

"I suppose you think that's humorous, Sergeant,"
Armbruster rasped.

Cavannaugh's eyes narrowed, and the smile fell from
his face. "On the contrary, sir," he said in his most
military voice. "I had thought you would like that. I
don't know if you're sweet on her, Lieutenant, but I
know you like her more than a little."

"And just how do you know that, Sergeant?"

Cavannaugh snapped to attention, clapping his lips
tight at the same time.

"Oh, for Christ's sakes, Sergeant," Armbruster
snapped. "You've been open with me all along. Now's
not the time to shut up."

Cavannaugh believed his commanding officer. "I
can see it in your face, sir," he said quietly.

"Shit and roses!" Armbruster spouted. He turned
and paced a little.

"Beggin' your pardon, sir, but what's the problem
with that?"

Armbruster stopped pacing and looked at Cavannaugh. "Because," he said tightly, "if you can see it, so can every goddamn one else. Christ, another reason for the other officers to give me the cold shoulder." He sighed. "You know, Sergeant, I'm beginning to think I ought to just leave the post on patrol and stay out there until I retire."

"You'd be mighty lonely, sir."

"Yes, Sergeant, I suppose I would." He sighed again. "I've really dug myself a hole, haven't I?"

"Depends on how you look at it, sir. Would you rather have the officers' company? Or Miss Martinez's?"

"Looked at that way, Sergeant," Armbruster said with a small smile, "it's an easy question to answer. However, in the cold light of reality, it's not that easy."

"You're gonna have to make that choice sooner or later, Lieutenant."

"I know. Well, nothing can be done about it now. Get the men ready, Sergeant. I'll meet you and the patrol at the stable before first light."

"Which way you want to go, Lieutenant?" Cavannaugh said as the men formed up on horseback just outside the stables.

The question took Armbruster by surprise a little. He hadn't really thought of that before, but he would have to make a decision. And soon. "Let's ride south, Sergeant. We'll check on those folks who're trying to settle in that place Sieneguilla de Maria."

Cavannaugh nodded. It didn't matter to him which way they went.

The men were quiet—as quiet as they could be with the creak of saddles, the clink of bridles and bits, the clank of equipment, and more—as they rode out of Fort Defiance. The only ones awake besides them were the few men posted as guards.

They moved slowly, since it was still dark. The first

specks of the new day soon began spreading, casting elongated, wavering shadows. And with them came the heat. Armbruster had already come to hate the heat, and that malignant blot of sun from which there was no escape. He had thought more than once since being at the fort that he was glad that he wasn't farther south. The men had talked of the desert down there, a place where a man's brain could fry right inside his head, where his eyes would dry up, giving up their precious moisture to the suffocating, arid heat.

By midday, they had come to the few scattered adobe shacks that some Mexicans were trying to make into a settlement. An adobe church was being built, its wood skeleton stark against the horizon and sky.

Raul Sanchez was the burgeoning settlement's nominal leader, and he was in a highly agitated state when the army patrol rode in. He sat with Armbruster under a canvas ramada and tried to control his agitation enough so that his English was understandable.

"Navajos. They steal three sheep, all our horses," Sanchez said.

"When was this, Raul?" Armbruster asked.

"Two days ago. I wanted to go after them, but we got no horses now. Those sons of bitches took all of them."

Armbruster nodded. He looked up as Cavannaugh stepped under the canvas roof. "The men have water, Sergeant?" he asked.

"Yessir."

"The horses been seen to?"

"Yessir. The men'd best have some food, though, since it looks like we're gonna be on the trail of some goddamn horse thieves soon."

"Good idea, Sergeant. Have—"

"We will feed your men, Teniente," Sanchez interjected. "We've got fresh mutton and plenty of beans."

"I'd not want to put you out any, Raul."

"You won't. If your men can get our horses back, that'll be payment for us. If not . . ." He shrugged fatalistically.

Armbruster nodded.

Sanchez rose and walked away. He stopped to talk with three women, pointing and gesticulating. The women nodded and hurried off. Then Sanchez spoke with Cavannaugh, who directed the men where to sit after loosening the saddles of their horses. Finally Sanchez returned to the battered wood table at which Armbruster was sitting.

Before long, the women were serving up bowls of rich mutton stew and side bowls of hot beans and chunks of Indian fry bread with which to sop up the rich juices. With Armbruster's approval, wine was passed around to the men, but only one cup each.

After the meal, Armbruster leaned back, not wanting to move. He could tell that the men felt the same way. Still, he knew he had to get on the trail of the raiding Navajos. They had had two days' start, and could be almost anywhere by now.

"You know who was leading the Navajos, Raul?" Armbruster asked. He figured asking a few more questions would give them all just a little more time for their food to settle.

"Gordo Nalgas," Sanchez said with a straight face.

When Cavannaugh laughed a little, Armbruster glanced at him. "Why's that so humorous, Sergeant?" he asked.

"You don't know what that means, Lieutenant?"

"No," Armbruster snapped.

"Sorry, sir. I forgot you don't speak any Spanish— yet. The translation of Gordo Nalgas is Fat Ass."

Armbruster laughed. "Now I understand. Is he a funny fellow, then?"

"No, sir. You see, the Navajos ain't as warlike as many other tribes. Not to say that they're as peaceable as the pueblo dwellers, but they don't make a religion out of war like some others. Still, they're some mean bastards when they need to be. You ever get the chance, ask some Apaches about how tough the Navajos can be. Unlike the Apaches, they generally don't kill for the hell of it. There are exceptions at times, though."

"Like Fat Ass?" Armbruster asked.

"Yessir. To tell you the truth, Lieutenant, I'm surprised he didn't kill anybody when him and his men raided here."

Sanchez grimaced. "We had a little warning," he said flatly. "We hide."

Armbruster nodded. "How many men did he have with him?" he asked.

"Six, I saw. He might've left others behind somewhere, though."

"Which way'd he go when he rode out?"

"West. But I don't think he'll keep going that way."

"Why not?"

"Not much out there. I think he'll turn north, back toward where most of his people live."

Armbruster nodded and rose. "Thank you for the food, Raul," he said. "I hope we can get your horses back." He turned. "Sergeant, get the men moving."

⊰⟨ 17 ⟩⊱

Chief picked up the Navajos' trail just outside the forlorn attempt at a settlement. As Sanchez had said, it went west. They followed for five miles. Then, as Sanchez had forecast, the tracks turned north, heading slightly upward, as if on an incline. The land here was vast and open, stretching off endlessly into nowhere, unless interrupted by some volcanic upheaval or sandstone monolith.

Armbruster decided he did not like it out here. The land was too big, too grandiose, too frightening. He preferred the close confines of Connecticut and New York State, where rolling hills were framed by thick forests. There was water back there—big, wide, powerful rivers; roiling, monstrous waterfalls; the ocean, with its waves and its temperamental nature; small, bubbling brooks; and rushing, fractious streams.

Out here there was nothing like that. It hardly ever rained, and when it did, it was usually a hellacious storm that came, pounded the earth and its inhabitants into submission, and then fled, leaving behind a new expanse of perfect blue. Out here there were few real watercourses. There were plenty of washes, but they were dry ninety-five percent of the time.

Even more troublesome, at least to Armbruster, was

the starkness of this hellish land. There were few trees —in many places almost no vegetation at all. There was nothing to stop, or even slow, the interminable wind, which swept the harsh dust ahead of it as if it were God's broom. The sand cut and bit at a man, and the wind was enough to drive a body mad. And while the odd rock formations were interesting to look at, they provided no comfort to the eye whatsoever. Not the way the forests and tidy settlements back east did.

Armbruster wondered how any man could find a home here. There were no people, no towns, nothing but desert, sand, wind and emptiness. He shuddered involuntarily at the thought of perhaps being sentenced to spending the rest of his life out here.

Cavannaugh saw it and asked, "You all right, Lieutenant?"

Armbruster shook himself out of the trancelike state in which he had found himself. "Yes, Sergeant," he said quietly.

"You certain, sir?"

Armbruster grinned weakly. "Yes, Sergeant." He sighed. "I was just thinking what a harsh, desolate land this is. And I must admit, I'm not at all comfortable with it."

Cavannaugh nodded. "I know what you mean, sir. I prefer the creeks and hollers back in Tennessee. But this land"—he swept his hand across the vista—"grows on a man after a while. Not to say that I'd not rather got back to Tennessee, but I could make my life out here now if it was asked of me."

"It has been asked of you, Sergeant," Armbruster said with a laugh. "That's why we're on this miserable mission."

"Yessir."

They rode on in silence for a little, before Armbruster said quietly, "There's something I've been meaning to say to you for several days, Sergeant, and I've not had the opportunity.''

''What's that, sir?'' Cavannaugh asked, wondering.

''First, let me say that I don't want you to take this the wrong way, and that I want you to hear me out.''

''Yessir.'' A little worry mingled with the curiosity.

''I appreciate your loyalty to me, Sergeant, but I wonder if it might bring a bad end.''

''You don't want my loyalty, or my service, sir,'' Cavannaugh said with an unusual stiffness. ''I'll see to it you're not bothered again.''

''I told you to hear me out.'' Armbruster sighed and scanned the countryside. ''It's not me I'm concerned about, Sergeant. It's you. You throw in with me, the way those folks back at Fort Defiance feel about me these days, and you're likely to hurt your career considerably.''

Cavannaugh threw his head back and laughed, loud and hard. The sound, so strange in this odd land, spooked a few horses, and the men had to fight a little to regain control over them.

''I say something humorous, Sergeant?'' Armbruster asked, startled and confused.

''You know what I got to say to that, Lieutenant?'' he demanded, still smiling. ''Fuck all them sots. That's what I got to say.''

''But the army's been your life for a long time now, Sergeant.''

''That's true enough. But what's that gonna get me, sir? Hell, if I make it long enough to retire, I'll get a pension so goddamn small I won't be able to feed a cat on it. No, sir, all the army's gonna do for me is to bend me over, ram me hard up the ass a few times and then send me on my merry way without so much as a thank you kiss.''

Armbruster laughed at the imagery. ''I'm sure the

army holds the same favorable opinion about you as you do of it, Sergeant,'' he said, still chuckling. Armbruster realized it felt good to laugh again. He had done precious little of it since the court-martial.

"The army don't give a donkey's dick for me, you or anyone else. Sir."

"Funny," Armbruster said with a sly smile, "I don't remember them teaching us that back at the Point."

"I wouldn't know about such things, sir."

Armbruster wasn't quite sure whether Cavannaugh was teasing him or was serious. He decided it didn't matter. "I just wanted to warn you, Sergeant, in case you hadn't thought of it. Stick with me and you'll get splattered with shit when all hell breaks loose.''

"You know, sir," Cavannaugh said solemnly, "a man like me doesn't have much in life. I ain't gonna get rich, and ain't no one gonna make me president. So all I got, really, is my pride, and the respect of people I have to deal with. And all I got to give is my loyalty and my respect. There might be many a man who gives those things freely, but I ain't one of 'em, sir. I'm real penurious when it comes to such things. I've judged you to be a man of honor; a man worthy of my respect and loyalty. The rest can kiss my ass at church on Sunday mornin'.''

Cavannaugh looked straight into Armbruster's eyes. "If that makes you uncomfortable, sir, or if you're not desirous of havin' my loyalty, you let me know."

Armbruster was a little self-conscious about all this, but he kept his eyes on Cavannaugh's. "I'm always uncomfortable when people try to make me out a better man than I am. And I'm ill at ease accepting something given so somberly. At the same time I'm honored, but I'm not quite sure how to thank you.''

"You can thank me by shutting up about all this crap," Cavannaugh said bluntly. "Sir."

Armbruster smiled. "Jesus," he said quietly, "now he's giving me orders."

"Only when needed, Lieutenant," Cavannaugh said so softly that Armbruster wasn't sure he had really heard it or had only thought it.

That night Chief found a campsite the raiding Navajos had used. "Two nights ago," Chief said.

"They don't seem to be in any hurry, then, do they?" Armbruster said more than asked.

"No," Chief responded. "They think they safe."

Armbruster nodded. "Sergeant, reveille will be an hour earlier than usual tomorrow. And maybe the next several mornings. I want us out on the trail as soon as it's light enough for Chief to see the tracks. We're also going to push as hard as reasonably possible. We do that, we might catch them in a couple more days."

"Yessir."

But Chief lost the trail the next afternoon. The soldiers stopped and waited while the Tiwa scoured the ground, practically crawling to spot some sign.

"What the hell happened, Sergeant?" Armbruster asked after sending Cavannaugh out to talk to Chief. "I thought he was a good tracker."

"He is a good tracker, sir," Cavannaugh said in a little irritation. "Several things've combined to throw him off. The ground around here is hard rock. Usually there's sand over it that'll give you some idea. But that godawful wind we had all day's blown the dust to hell and back. There ain't shit Chief can do about it except hope that something'll allow him to pick up the trail again."

Armbruster nodded. He was irritated at it all, but he knew Chief was not at fault. He also knew that his own anger and irritability would not change the situation, so he concentrated on trying to calm himself.

The column edged forward throughout the day.

Chief would finish checking out one spot and then move on maybe a quarter of a mile and begin the laborious process all over again. By nightfall, though, he had still not picked up the trail. So Armbruster called a halt.

After supper, Armbruster leaned back with his pipe and watched as Cavannaugh and Chief held an animated discussion off in the shadows. Cavannaugh then came over to Armbruster's fire.

"Sit, Sergeant," Armbruster said.

"Thank you, sir." When Cavannaugh was comfortable, he said, "Me and Chief've decided that we think we know where those Navajos're goin', Lieutenant."

"Where's that?"

"Place called Canyon de Chelly. It's something of a Navajo stronghold. Has been for all time, I suppose."

"There're likely to be many Navajos there?" Armbruster asked.

"Hard to tell, Lieutenant. I don't think so. They go through there all the time, from the way I've heard it. But if they fear widespread attack, they'll go there and hole up. It's got wood, water, good grass. It's got steep cliffs and many caves, plus a bunch of ruins. All that makes for a good defensive position."

Armbruster nodded. "How far is this . . . what did you call it?"

"Canyon de Chelly. It's a day's ride, maybe more, depending on where we want to enter it."

"It'll be a day's ride, Sergeant."

"Yessir." Cavannaugh pushed himself up. "You sure you don't want your tent set up, Lieutenant?" he asked. "It's gonna be a windy night, and cool, I figure."

"If you and the men can sleep in the open, so can I, Sergeant." Armbruster was a little pricklish about it. Suddenly he grinned. "Unless there's rain expected."

"No rain, sir," Cavannaugh said with a little laugh. "Well, good night, Lieutenant."

They stopped just before nightfall the next day near the entrance to the canyon. Since dark was almost on them, Armbruster wisely decided that trying to get into the canyon now would be foolish, if not disastrous. Camp was quickly made, and the men were in their bedrolls early.

During the ride down into the depths of the massive, sprawling canyon, Armbruster began to revise his thoughts about this hard land somewhat. Though most of the ground was sandy, a shallow, wide stream coursed through the canyon, giving life to cottonwoods and willows, as well as thickets of brush. Peach-colored walls, some of them sheer, rose a thousand feet up. In places the stone of the walls was darkly stained.

Cavannaugh pointed to a tall rock spire standing off to itself. "It's called Spider Rock, Lieutenant," he said. "From the tales we've heard, the Navajos think Spider Woman lives there. They say she takes bad children up there and eats them. If you look real close, you can see their bones way up atop there."

"Gruesome," Armbruster said flatly.

"No worse than some of our own tales, Lieutenant."

Well into the canyon they came to a small village of Navajos. The hogans were nestled in amongst the trees, in the shadow of the high cliffs, beneath an ancient Indian ruin that looked as if it had been there since time began.

The headman of the village greeted the soldiers, though he was less than pleased at this invasion of his home. Armbruster directed the men off to the side, a little outside the village. They stopped near the water and loosened their saddles. Then they sat around, nervous to be among the Navajos like this, and ate jerky.

Armbruster, Cavannaugh and Chief sat down with

the headman—Anciano, Old Man. Chief was to do the interpreting both ways.

"We're looking for some of your people who have been raiding," Armbruster said, while Chief translated it. "They stole horses from the people near Sieneguilla de Maria."

"These men are not here," Anciano said.

"Have they been here and left?"

For a few minutes, Anciano debated whether he should answer truthfully, then decided there was no reason not to. These foolish white men would never be able to catch up to Gordo Nalgas. And even if they did, by happenstance, come upon Gordo Nalgas, they would be defeated easily. "They were here," he said. "But they're not here now."

"Where'd they go?"

Anciano shrugged. "I don't know. I'm not the keeper of those men."

"You know which way they went?"

"North and east. I think they're headed for the Chuska Mountains." Anciano smiled inwardly. Gordo Nalgas was indeed headed for the Chuska Mountains and the old man thought it would be humorous to send the soldiers after the Diné raiders. Gordo Nalgas would run the white soldiers ragged in the mountains and then kill them.

"You know where that is, Chief?" Armbruster asked.

The Tiwa nodded, though he was staring at Anciano.

Armbruster nodded. "Thank you, Anciano," he said as he rose. He reached into a pocket and pulled out a small cloth pouch of tobacco and handed it to the old man. "A small sign of my thanks," Armbruster said almost lamely.

Anciano picked up the pouch and tossed it in the air a couple of times, nodding.

"Let's get the hell out of here," Cavannaugh said. "Sir."

{ 18 }

The men of the column rode just far enough to figure they were unlikely to be attacked by Anciano's men, and then they pulled into a camp. As was somewhat usual, Cavannaugh came to Armbruster's fire just after eating. He had gotten in the habit of doing so to see what Armbruster's plans were for the next day and such.

"You look troubled, Sergeant," Armbruster said.

"Chief thinks Anciano was givin' us a line of shit back there, Lieutenant," Cavannaugh said perfunctorily.

"How so?"

"Chief ain't sure, but the impression I got from him is that Old Man had a shit-eatin' grin on his face when he told us Fat Ass was headin' for the Chuska Mountains."

"You think Old Man was lying?"

"I don't know what I think. I know the Navajos go into the Chuskas quite often. I've heard it's a right pretty place up there."

"You must have some thoughts about it all, Sergeant," Armbruster prodded.

"Reckon I do, sir. You mind if I smoke, Lieutenant?"

"Of course not, Sergeant."

Cavannaugh quickly rolled a cigarette and lit it from the fire. After blowing out a column of smoke, he said, "I figure it's one of two things, sir. Either Old Man's lyin' and Fat Ass and his boys were sittin' over in that village. Or else Old Man *wants* us to find Fat Ass."

"Why the hell would he want us to do that?"

Cavannaugh shrugged. "Don't know, sir. I might hazard a guess and say that Old Man figures Fat Ass and his boys'll kick our asses."

"Well," Armbruster said dryly, "that could happen at any time."

"Yessir. But I'll say this. If that's what Old Man's doin', and we do get our asses kicked, I'm gonna be some aggravated at Old Man."

"Yes, something like that would require we repay him a visit." He thought for a little. "Well, Sergeant, what's your recommendation?"

"Go back there and slap Old Man around until we get the truth out of him." Cavannaugh was highly irritated by the thought that Anciano might be playing him and all the others for fools.

Armbruster looked at his sergeant in surprise.

"Ah, hell, sir, I don't really mean that. Chief thinks —and I agree—that we ought to head for the Chuskas and look for Fat Ass."

"I also agree."

The next morning, Chief led the way up the meandering canyon floor, heading roughly northeast. The canyon was a beautiful place, Armbruster thought, though many of its features were odd.

By the late afternoon of the following day, they were making their way into the Chuska Mountains. Armbruster was rather surprised. From the barren, desolate flats they had entered a wonderland of tall, sturdy pines. And the change had come about in a relatively short time.

They spent a few more days prowling through the

mountains, looking for the Navajo raiders. Chief picked up their trail the second day in, but lost it again a day and a half later. The Tiwa growled around camp that night, muttering dark-sounding phrases in his own language.

Finally, Armbruster said, "Sergeant Cavannaugh, see just what's got Chief's dander up."

"Hell, sir, he's just angry at himself for losing the trail—again."

"I said go see what's wrong with him, Sergeant," Armbruster snapped.

"Yessir," Cavannaugh responded, a little surprised. He spoke with varying degrees of heat with Chief for some minutes. Then he returned to Armbruster's fire. "Like I thought, sir." Then Armbruster grinned a little grimly. "But there's more. He thinks Fat Ass is fuckin' around with us, sir. Leavin' a trail here and there for us to find, then losin' us again. Chief thinks the bastards gonna run us around for a few more days—or until he gets tired of the game—and then wipe us out."

"There's a good chance he can do it, too. We're deep in his territory. We don't know a damn thing about these mountains, and they're like his backyard."

"What do you suggest, Lieutenant?" Cavannaugh asked blandly. He had no desire to give up now, but he wasn't about to go against his commanding officer either.

Armbruster thought that one over for a while. Then he smiled weakly. "I think we'll give Mister Fat Ass another day or two of his game—while we hunt out a suitable campsite. Then we stay put and let him come to us."

Cavannaugh nodded. "I think I like that idea, Lieutenant."

Armbruster found the spot he wanted the next afternoon—a small meadow surrounded by heavy stands of pines; a thin strip of a stream meandered across it;

mountains rising beyond the immediate trees that crept up a short slope.

"I'll use the tent this time, Sergeant," Armbruster said. "About there ought to do." He pointed to a sharp bend in the stream.

"Yessir." Cavannaugh detailed two men to raise Armbruster's tent; others to care for the animals, and the remainder to do whatever other work was needed in setting up the camp. Chief prowled around the fringes of the campsite, muttering.

With camp set up, the horses and pack mules hobbled and grazing, firewood stacked and fires burning, the men settled in to wait.

It wasn't long before the camp was found, but it wasn't Gordo Nalgas and his men who found it. The next afternoon, arrows started flying out of the pines.

Private Arthur Duncan fell over, three arrows in his back. Cavannaugh, who had been within a foot and a half of Duncan took one glance at Duncan and then bellowed, "Apaches!"

The men flattened on the ground, rifles ready. Trouble was, they couldn't see the Indians. At least not at first. Then they spotted three Apaches heading fast for the horses and mules.

Armbruster had dropped to the ground inside his tent and then slithered forward. He saw the Jicarillas speeding toward the animals. He jumped up and jerked out his pistol. "Skidmore, Kapp, follow me!" He raced toward the animals, hoping the two men would do as ordered.

Cavannaugh had gotten behind a log and was scanning the trees. He spotted Chief thirty yards over to the right, pointing. "Olson, Carlton, Williams, you follow me into the trees. Brown, Smith, lay down a coverin' fire."

"When?" Private Rob Smith asked.

"Now, goddammit!" As soon as the first shot came,

Cavannaugh was up and running toward the trees, zigging from side to side. He noticed that Chief had slipped into the cover of the trees. He hoped the Tiwa would be all right. None of the pueblo Indians that Cavannaugh knew of were fighters.

Cavannaugh felt an arrow tug at his shirt, and then another. He jerked out his two pistols—not exactly regulation, but he didn't much give a damn. He'd wear his one Colt Dragoon around the post, but out here, he wanted at least two of them.

An Apache screeched suddenly and jumped out from behind a tree at him with war club raised. Without even thinking, Cavannaugh dropped to the ground, wincing when a hipbone hit a rock. He rolled over onto his back and fired each pistol twice. The lead balls knocked the Indian back into the tree, and then he fell.

Cavannaugh leaped up and ran on. Gunfire popped from all around, but he could not worry about that now. He had to concentrate on flushing out the Jicarillas who were so well hidden in the trees. He blasted another Apache who seemingly popped out from nowhere. The Jicarilla had managed, though, to slice open Cavannaugh's left arm before the bullets put him down for good.

Cavannaugh heard horses, and then the gradual diminishing of gunfire. "Olson, report!" he roared.

"One Apache dead, Sergeant. I don't see no others." The voice sounded odd filtering through the trees.

"Carlton!"

"None dead here, Sergeant. But no livin' ones either, far's I can see."

"Williams! How about you?" He tensed when he got no response in a few seconds. "Williams! Report!"

"Dammit all to hell, Sergeant," Olson shouted. "Williams is dead."

"Shit," Cavannaugh snapped to himself. "Get him back into the camp and watch over him. Carlton, you help him."

More gunfire popped from over near the horses. Cavannaugh turned and ran, heading toward the herd. Suddenly he slammed into an Apache. He lost one of his pistols in the collision, and he just barely managed to get his head out of the way of the Indian's knife.

"Fuck with me, will you," Cavannaugh muttered. He tried bringing his other pistol up, but the Apache was kneeling on that arm. Worse, the warrior was raising the knife for another stab at him. He spit in the Indian's eye. It gave him an extra second or two to pound the warrior three times—twice on the side of the head and once in the ribs—with his free right fist.

The blow seemed to have no effect on the Apache. Figuring he was done for, Cavannaugh threw a desperate punch at the Jicarilla's throat. The Indian rocked backward a little, enough for the soldier to free his left arm. He got the arm up in time to block the Indian's next knife thrust. With his right, Cavannaugh smashed two more strong punches to the warrior's throat.

The Apache gurgled and tried another stab, but he had little strength left. Cavannaugh jerked his midsection upward, knocking the Indian off him. The Sergeant jumped up and then stomped a boot down on the warrior's throat, crushing it. Then he shot the Jicarilla in the face once. He retrieved his other pistol, spun and ran. Cavannaugh burst out of the trees, slightly above the herd. He stopped and grinned grimly.

Armbruster stood, looking as calm as he would in church of a Sunday, his pistol in hand and ready. In front of him knelt Privates Ike Skidmore and Arnie Kapp, also armed and waiting. Behind Armbruster were all the horses and mules. The animals were nervous, but Armbruster seemed to be paying them little heed.

Cavannaugh could see two dead Apaches near the herd. He also spotted two dead soldiers. "Damn," he muttered.

Armbruster had surprised himself with his instant call to action when the attack started. But he had no time to think about that or anything else but trying to save the animals, as well as the men guarding them. He was too late to save Frank Dudley, who was already dead. The other guard, Karl Schneider, was slipping through the horses, trying to drive them away from the side of the attack, and toward the trees.

Schneider was making progress, and seemed pretty well protected by animal flesh, but then an arrow suddenly appeared in the back of his neck. He fell and was trampled by the skittish animals.

"Dammit all!" Armbruster screamed, though it couldn't be heard over the sound of the stream, the animals and the gunfire. He skidded to a stop as he saw an Apache jump onto a horse's back. Armbruster threw his gun up and fired twice. The Jicarilla jerked and then fell. He, too, was stomped into the dirt by the nervous horses and mules.

Skidmore fired his rifle at one of the other two Jicarillas trying to get to the animal herd. He thought he hit the man but he wasn't sure. He tossed the rifle away and pulled his pistol.

Kapp, who had been pacing Skidmore, fired at the third Apache. He knew he hit the Indian, but he also knew the wound wasn't fatal. He also pitched his rifle aside and drew his revolver.

"Over here!" Armbruster screamed for the fourth time. Skidmore and Kapp finally heard it and looked toward Armbruster, who indicated that they should head toward him. They did.

"All right, men," Armbruster said calmly when the

two soldiers stopped. "Both of you kneel here. Skidmore, face west a little; Kapp, east."

"Where're you gonna be, Lieutenant?" Kapp asked nervously.

"Right here." He fired at the Apache that Skidmore had wounded.

Kapp fired at the same warrior at the same time. The Indian died, though neither Armbruster nor Kapp knew whose shot had been fatal.

"Keep your eyes peeled, men," Armbruster said. "I'm damn sure some of those bastards're still around."

Twice more, Armbruster or his two men fired at Apaches up in the trees, but none knew if they had hit anyone. Slowly the sound of gunfire from the whole area dwindled. Moments later Armbruster could hear Cavannaugh checking on the men. Soon after that, Armbruster looked up and saw Cavannaugh burst out of the trees up the slope in front of him and a little to the right.

Cavannaugh waved and was shocked when he saw Armbruster suddenly bring his pistol to bear on him. Before the sergeant could do anything, though, Armbruster fired. From just behind himself, Cavannaugh heard the distinctive splat of a lead ball hitting human flesh. A heartbeat later, a body crashed against his back, almost knocking him down. He watched as a dead Apache hit the ground and rolled a couple of times. The corpse came to a stop on its back, showing the bloody bullet hole just over the left eyebrow. "Jesus," he breathed. Then he headed down the slope.

Cavannaugh turned and headed to his left toward their camp. There he directed three-quarters of the men to fan out and search through the trees looking for wounded Apaches, and to see if another attack looked imminent. The rest he sent to help Skidmore and Kapp calm the animals. It wouldn't do to have stopped the Apaches from stealing the animals if they all ran away.

Then Cavannaugh walked slowly toward Armbruster, who was heading in his direction. Pain lanced into Cavannaugh's arm, annoying him. "I'm obliged, Lieutenant," he said as the two men stopped, facing each other, "for savin' my life." He smiled a little. "For a moment there, though, I thought you'd gone *loco*."

"It must've seemed that way. But there was nothing else I could do."

"Oh, I full well know that, sir. And I'm glad you did just what you did. I'll say one thing, though," he added with a mischievous grin. "I didn't know you could shoot that good."

"I didn't either, Sergeant," Armbruster said solemnly. "Let's go assess the damage," he added after noting the concern that had flickered ever so briefly on Cavannaugh's face.

⟞{ 19 }⟝

Privates Arthur Duncan, Cal Williams, Frank Dudley and Karl Schneider were dead. Sergeant Cavannaugh, and Privates Arnie Kapp and Rob Smith were wounded, Cavannaugh's being the worst. Chief showed up, unscathed, and Armbruster wondered if the Tiwa had fought anyone.

"Anyone here know how to patch up the wounded, Sergeant?" Armbruster asked.

"Skidmore's done it a few times, I think, sir."

Armbruster nodded. "Private Skidmore," he called.

The soldier looked up, eyes haunted. He and the other surviving soldiers had returned to report that they had seen no more Apaches anywhere. Then they brought the bodies of their companions back to the camp and lined them neatly up. The survivors were sitting nearby, at a fire, sipping coffee nervously. "Yessir?" he asked worriedly.

"I'll need you to doctor Sergeant Cavannaugh, Private Kapp and Private Smith."

"Yessir." Skidmore did not seem at all enthusiastic.

"Start with Sergeant Cavannaugh. He's the worst off of the lot."

"Yessir." Skidmore pushed himself up and went to the supplies for a medical kit.

"Privates Olson, Carlton and Brown, you're our burial party. Privates Smith and Kapp'll help as soon as they're patched up."

"You mean we're not gonna take 'em back to Fort Defiance for a proper buryin', Lieutenant?" Carlton asked.

"No, Private," Armbruster said flatly.

"But, sir, they deserve—"

"I know what they deserve, Private," Armbruster said more harshly than he had intended. "But we are two, three, maybe even four days' ride from the fort. In this heat, how long you think those bodies're going to last? What kind of send-off would that be for your friends?"

"I reckon not so good, Lieutenant," Carlton said. He was not happy about it, but what Armbruster had said made sense. "Sorry to have mentioned it, Lieutenant."

"There's nothing to be sorry for. You were looking out for your friends. Nothing wrong in that." He paused. "Rest a bit longer, though, while I find a proper spot for the burial." He turned and walked away.

Armbruster surprised himself a little as he went around the camp. He was calm and quite rational. He was sad that four of his men had been killed, but that was part of life, and he would worry about it later. Right now work had to be done.

He decided on a spot across the stream, on a grassy flat abutting a four-foot-high dirt bank. He walked back to the camp and told the men of the burial party of his decision.

Armbruster checked on Cavannaugh. Skidmore was almost finished sewing up the slash in Cavannaugh's arm. The sergeant was sweating, face tight against the pain. Skidmore had offered him some laudanum or whiskey to kill the pain, but Cavannaugh had refused.

Pain he could live with and still do his job. Drunk or unconscious, he would be of no use to himself or anyone else.

They spent two more days at that site, nervously keeping watch. Then they packed up and rode off, winding their way down out of the Chuska Mountains.

The day they left their camp—with its four fresh graves covered by mountain stones—they were attacked as they entered a narrow, steep-walled gulch.

Private Will Brown went down with two arrows and a rifle ball in his chest. He tumbled off his horse and lay on the ground.

Chief, who took an arrow in the shoulder moments after Brown was hit, flattened himself on his horse and slapped it, riding hell-bent down into the small canyon.

Armbruster shouted an order to follow Chief. There was nothing else they could do. They were exposed where they were, but if they could make it to the floor of the rocky canyon, they could find protection among the boulders and trees.

Surprisingly, they all made it. Hunkering down amid the rocks, Armbruster asked, "More Apaches, Sergeant?"

"Ain't sure, Lieutenant," Cavannaugh responded. "I suppose."

"No," Chief said from a few feet away. He had worked the arrow loose and pulled it out. He held it out toward the others. "Navajo."

Armbruster nodded. "Must be Fat Ass and his boys."

"You know, Lieutenant," Cavannaugh said sharply, "I'm gettin' damned sick and tired of being attacked by goddamn Indians."

"So am I, Sergeant." He paused. "Any suggestions on what to do?"

"Not really, sir. It might help if we could pop a few of 'em."

"Why's that, Sergeant?"

"From what I've heard, the Navajos are powerful afraid of the dead. Don't like to truck with 'em at all. I ain't sure it's true, sir, but I've seen some signs of it. Still, it doesn't seem to bother those bastards in the midst of war, so I don't know."

"Who's the best rifle shot here, Sergeant?" Armbruster asked.

"Private Olson."

"Chief, you think you could work your way up into those rocks," he asked as he pointed, "and flush out one of those Navajos? Just enough to give Private Olson a shot at him."

Chief nodded solemnly. Private Skidmore bandaged his arm some. Then the Tiwa slipped off.

Twelve tense minutes later, a Navajo appeared, jumping up from behind a rock. Olson, who had been waiting took only a second to aim and fire. Birds scattered, squawking, as the Navajo fell atop the boulder and lay still.

"Well," Armbruster said, "that might not turn those Navajos away, but it sure ought to give them something to think about."

Armbruster began to worry when Chief did not return for some time. "You think Chief's gotten himself killed, Sergeant?"

"Maybe, Lieutenant." Cavannaugh shrugged, continuing to keep watch over the boulder protecting him. "The one failin' he's got as a scout is that he's too peaceable."

An hour and a half later, Chief slipped into the haven again, stopping silently behind a boulder between Armbruster and Cavannaugh. "Navajo gone," he announced.

"All of 'em?" Cavannaugh asked. "You sure?"

"Yes, sure."

"How do you know that?" Armbruster asked.

A chilling, hard-lipped smile spread across the Tiwa's

face. He reached into a pouch hanging from his belt and withdrew something. Then he held it out.

Armbruster sat there a moment, wondering what this was all about. Then he noticed blood dripping from the handful of whatever it was Chief was holding. He edged closer. "Jesus H. Christ," he breathed as he spotted six bloody ears resting in Chief's palm.

"Well, I'll be damned," Cavannaugh added in the same whispery voice as he moved up, too. He looked at Armbruster. "You see that one with the long turquoise earring, Lieutenant?" When Armbruster nodded, Cavannaugh said, "That's Fat Ass's."

"You certain?"

"Sure am, sir."

"You were saying something about Chief being a peaceable fellow, Sergeant," Armbruster said dryly.

"I stand corrected, sir," Cavannaugh said without apology.

"All right, Sergeant," Armbruster said suddenly. "Get the men up and moving. For some reason I've got a hankering to get the hell out of the Chuska Mountains."

Cavannaugh nodded in full agreement.

Twenty minutes later they were maneuvering through the canyon. The only reason it took them that long was that Armbruster had the men round up all the stolen mules and horses. Then they headed for the far side, where they made the short, though difficult climb out of it.

Nightfall, however, still found them in the Chuskas, and they made an uneasy camp for the night. The men buried Private Brown there, making sure his grave was piled high with stones to keep the animals from digging the corpse up. They did not worry about the Navajos disturbing the grave. Even if what Cavannaugh had heard about the Navajos' fear of the dead was only half true, the Navajos wouldn't go digging up a grave.

Armbruster had them up and moving early the next morning, and they left before dawn. Around midmorning they finally hit the flats again, and Armbruster reveled, if only momentarily, as the grand, wide-open vista spread before him. They headed southeast, pushing hard, figuring to avoid Canyon de Chelly. Armbruster had considered heading back to the vast, beautiful canyon to find Anciano and kill the old man, but he decided there was little point to it.

Three days later, the battered, unhappy group rode into Fort Defiance, under the interested eyes of almost everyone who was there. As they rode toward the office, Armbruster said, "I'm planning to pull out again as soon as possible, Sergeant."

Cavannaugh glanced at him in surprise. Then he smiled. "Major Brooks might have something to say about that, sir."

"He can say all he wants about it," Armbruster said harshly. "I'm still riding out of here as soon as I can."

Cavannaugh stared at Armbruster for some moments, then nodded when he realized the officer was serious. "I'm with you, Lieutenant," he said quietly. "If you want me along."

"I wouldn't think of leaving without you, Sergeant."

"Thank you, sir."

"You want to stay overnight and leave in the morning, Sergeant?"

"I'm at your pleasure, sir. I get a quick change of clothes, round up some more men, draw rations and get a new horse and I'll be ready. An hour, maybe less."

"You don't want Doctor Fournier to look at your arm?"

"No, sir. He can't do no more for it than's been done. The stitches're holding, and the poultices've been keeping the wound from festerin'." He glanced askance at Armbruster. "What're you going to do if Major Brooks says you can't go, Lieutenant?" he asked.

Armbruster smiled grimly. "Change his mind. It might take a couple of days, but I'll cause enough trouble around here that he'll be asking me to leave the fort for a while."

"If he doesn't throw your ass into the guardhouse. sir."

"Oh, I'm not planning to break rules and regulations, Sergeant. Just be a regular pain in his ass. He'll get tired of it fast enough."

"You know something, Lieutenant," Cavannaugh said with a grin, "you're all right. For an officer, that is."

"Why, thank you, Sergeant," Armbruster said, laughing. "I don't know as if I've ever been complimented so highly."

They stopped in front of Brooks's office. "What do you want me to do, Lieutenant?" Cavannaugh asked.

"Have the men return the horses to the stable. Then dismiss them."

"And me?"

"Stay here, if you don't mind. I'm still hoping to convince the major to let me ride out again right away." Armbruster climbed down off his horse and stretched. His rear end was sore, and his back hurt, but he ignored them and headed into the office.

It took less than five minutes for Armbruster to make his report. Then he spent an uncomfortable half hour as Brooks ranted, raved and bellowed at him. Armbruster took it stoically, answering when he thought he had a chance to, keeping his face blank when necessary.

Finally, though, Brooks began winding down, as he had to. No one could continue such a tirade forever. He ended with, "Well, Lieutenant, what do you have to say for yourself?"

Armbruster shrugged. "Not much, sir. We killed a dozen Indians or so and recovered the horses and mules stolen from Sieneguilla de Maria."

"And lost half your goddamn command."

"Not to make light of the situation, sir," Armbruster said, "but those're the fortunes—or misfortunes—of war. We're out here to control the Navajos, and to a lesser degree the Apaches. That'll mean losses to our side, but we caused far more misery than we suffered."

Brooks glared at him for some minutes. Despite his tirade, Brooks's respect for Armbruster had risen more than a little. Few second lieutenants would stand up to that kind of berating and then answer so calmly—and rationally. What Armbruster had said was true; Brooks just hadn't expected to hear it from someone as young and inexperienced as Armbruster. "All right, Lieutenant," Brooks finally said. "Good work. Dismissed."

"I want to go out again, Major," Armbruster said.

Brooks's head snapped up and his eyes widened. Then he grinned. He would've done the same thing himself years ago. "I don't know if that's a good idea, Lieutenant."

"I do, sir."

Brooks nodded. "Rest up a week."

"No, sir. I plan to leave within the hour."

"I won't allow that," Brooks said harshly. A spirited officer was one thing, a disobedient one was another thing. "I might allow it in five days, say."

"Before dark, sir."

Brooks shook his head. Then he sighed. It would do him no good, he knew, to try to force Armbruster to stay the extra time. "First thing tomorrow, Lieutenant," Brooks said. "That's my final offer. You need at least some rest, and Sergeant Cavannaugh will, too. Take it or leave it."

"I accept, sir."

20

The first place Armbruster and his men went when they left the fort again was Sieneguilla de Maria, where they returned the small settlement's stolen horses and mules. That called for a fiesta, which the men enjoyed considerably.

Then for the rest of the summer, Lieutenant Edward Armbruster, top Sergeant Clancy Cavannaugh, and their varying squadron of men cut a wide swath through the land, from the Puerco River to the Lukachukai Mountains, from the fort west to the Hopi Buttes.

Shortly after Independence Day—one of the few times that summer that Armbruster was at Fort Defiance—Armbruster asked Brooks for permission to form his own squad of a dozen men, plus a sergeant and a corporal. After some thought, Brooks agreed, and for the rest of the summer the "Loco Squad," as the other men dubbed the fractious group, raised hell throughout the region.

The men of the Loco Squad took pride in that moniker, and soon sported variations of the standard uniform, sprouting colorful ascots and wide-brimmed hats with the left side of the brim pinned to the crown and complete with eagle feather. They wore black leather boots that came almost to the knee. Armbruster, Cavannaugh and Corporal Rick Bauer took to wearing fringed buckskin coats.

Each man carried a brace of .44-caliber Colt Army revolvers in flap holsters on his belt as well as a hard leather cartridge box on the belt. In saddle holsters they carried two more Army Colts, as well as a .54-caliber "Mississippi" percussion rifle. Each enlisted man also carried a substantial Bowie-type knife, while Armbruster and Cavannaugh carried short swords.

Without meaning to, the squad had become something of a guerrilla-style light cavalry force. The small group kept the hostile Indians—Navajo and Apache—on the run, until the region was calmer than it had been in years.

On their rare forays back to the fort for supplies and a day or two of rest, they were an arrogant bunch of men. And nearly every other man on the post—or any that considered himself a man—pleaded with Armbruster for acceptance into the elite fighting corps.

Many of the other officers, on the other hand, were rather displeased with the force, and even more so with Lieutenant Armbruster. Captain Gilmore was particularly incensed, seeing as how he was Armbruster's nominal commanding officer. These unhappy officers pestered Brooks incessantly in a bid to have the special force put out of business. Brooks, however, while not sure he liked the cocky attitude of Armbruster and his men, certainly could not argue with the group's success. Because of that, he warded off the pleadings of the other officers, though it grew wearisome.

As autumn approached, the unhappy officers began to cheer up. Surely, they figured, Brooks would disband the Loco Squad when all its men were confined to the post. They discussed the subject with some frequency, trying to convince themselves that it would come true.

Brooks even considered it. He did not want open warfare between his officers while they were all cooped up here for the winter, and so when Armbruster returned late in September for the winter, Brooks called him into the officer the next morning. "Sit," Brooks said. "I'd like this to be rather informal. A cigar?"

Curious, Armbruster nodded and took a cigar from the box Brooks held out. He lit it and leaned back in the chair.

"Perhaps you haven't noticed, Lieutenant," Brooks started, "but a good many of the officers here at Fort Defiance are . . . let's say unhappy . . . with your private little army."

"Perhaps, sir," Armbruster countered in a hard voice, "if they had the balls to go out and kick the shit out of some hostiles, they wouldn't be so unhappy."

"You've changed, Lieutenant," Brooks said. He knew now he should've seen it before, but he hadn't.

Armbruster didn't figure the statement required comment. It was obvious to anyone who looked at him these days. Armbruster had turned into a hard, experienced, well-blooded army officer. He was tough as a rifle barrel now. He was no longer the scrawny, gawky-looking young man—boy, still, really—he had been when he had arrived at Fort Defiance, was it only nine months ago. Armbruster didn't question it himself. He could not explain how he had, in one short summer, changed from a young man who had puked his guts out in his first battle into the hardened warrior he had become.

Brooks realized that Armbruster wasn't going to say anything, so he kept his own silence for some moments, wondering where he should take this. "I've got a problem here, Lieutenant," Brooks said quietly, staring at the tip of his smoldering cigar. "I can't have ninety-five percent of my officers irked because of one.

On the other hand, you and your men've certainly taught the hostiles some lessons."

Armbruster nodded. "I know you're in a difficult position, sir," he said apologetically. "But, begging your pardon, sir, that's your problem."

Brooks bit back the smile that threatened to spread across his face. "Yes, son, it is. I—"

"Look, sir, you have every right in the world to disband the unit. But to be blunt, I think you'd be a damn fool if you did it."

Brooks felt a flush of anger, then he nodded and smiled a little, his mind made up. "So do I, Lieutenant. I can't see messing around with something that's working."

"You're probably going to face a hard time with the others, sir."

Brooks nodded and tapped a shoulder. "That's why I have these oak leaves," he said. "Of course, it'd help me considerably if you and your men toned down your arrogance a tad."

"I'll order it, sir."

"Do so." He paused. "I'll give you and your men some leeway, Lieutenant. A considerable amount. But this is not your post, and I can only be taken so far."

"Understood, sir."

"Then there's just one other thing, Lieutenant," Brooks said with a faint smile. He rummaged in a desk drawer, drew something small out and pitched it to Armbruster. "Congratulations, *First* Lieutenant," Brooks said.

Armbruster looked down at the small cloth insignia with gold bars in the gold-ringed square, surprised. He had never expected to have been promoted so fast. He felt honored—and in some ways unworthy. "Thank you, sir," he said quietly. "I hope I can justify your faith in me."

"If I didn't think you could do that, Lieutenant, I

wouldn't have given you those." He paused. "Well, Lieutenant, I think we've about covered everything. Dismissed."

"Just one more thing, sir."

"Yes?" Brooks questioned, looking at Armbruster in surprise.

"Yessir. I'd be grateful if you were to allow the Loco Squad to escort the next courier heading to Albuquerque."

"What for?" Brooks asked, and then immediately felt like an idiot. "It's been a while since the men've been there, hasn't it?"

"Yessir. Not since spring for most of them."

Brooks nodded. "So be it. Are you going to lead them?"

"I had thought of it, sir," Armbruster said, his face pinking slightly. "It's been a while for me, too."

Brooks laughed. "Understood. The next express should be ready to leave in about four days, if everything stays on schedule." He paused. "Take a week. Two, if things're going well."

"Thank you, sir. For everything." Armbruster rose and saluted sharply, his cigar and his new insignia in his other hand. Then he left. He stopped outside and looked at the insignia, still not believing it. He felt like a boy as he walked—no, strutted; he and his men no longer walked—across the post toward the Company B barracks. A section of the barracks had been set aside for the Loco Squad, much to the chagrin of Captain Gilmore and Lieutenant Knudson.

The two officers were inspecting the Squad's men when Armbruster entered. The other men of Company B were standing around with amusement stamped on their faces. Sergeant Cavannaugh and Corporal Bauer were at attention, looking distinctly displeased.

Armbruster stopped for a minute to let his exploding temper fade to a simmer. Then he moved into the large room. "What the hell is going on here?" he roared.

Gilmore and Knudson turned, both looking smug. "These men are still part of Company B," Gilmore pronounced, "and I've found that many of them are out of uniform. So I'm inspecting them and their gear. I expect everything to be brought up to my standards posthaste."

"You don't get the hell away from my men, I'm going to kick your ass around the fort before I drop you in a latrine," Armbruster said tightly.

"You're through here, Armbruster!" Gilmore snapped, still smirking. "By the time I report the mess that this group of men is in, Major Brooks is going to cashier you right out of the service."

"Bullshit. I just left the major and he's agreed to leave the Loco Squad intact, as much as that might piss you off," Armbruster said with a sneer. "Captain."

"That's preposterous."

"It is, huh?" Armbruster pressed, walking up to stop right in front of Gilmore. "Then why'd he just give me these?" Armbruster held out his new first lieutenant's insignia.

Gilmore's eyes widened, and his mouth flapped a few times.

"Now, Captain," Armbruster said harshly, "are you going to get the hell out of here and leave my men alone, or shall you and I go on out back and settle the question once and for all?"

"Washington will hear about this," Gilmore puffed angrily.

"Before you go and do something that goddamn stupid, just stop and consider it for a bit, why don't you," Armbruster suggested. "Major Brooks gets wind of the fact that you went over his head—or even if you're just planning to—and you'll be busted down to buck goddamn private with authority over keeping the latrines clean.''

Gilmore shoved angrily past Armbruster. "Come, Lieutenant Knudson," he snapped.

Knudson avoided looking at Armbruster as he followed Gilmore outside. Armbruster turned and watched them go, then stood there surveying the rest of the barracks. "You boys find any more humor in this situation?" he asked. The men of Company B looked away, unwilling to answer.

When Armbruster turned back to his own men, they were grinning hugely to a man. "Jesus goddamn Christ, *First* Lieutenant," Cavannaugh said. He saluted. "Congratulations, sir."

Armbruster smiled, his anger dissipating considerably. "Thank you, Sergeant." He looked around at his men. "What I said to the captain was true. Major Brooks is keeping this unit together. It's going to be a long, boring winter sitting here, so I intend to make sure you men keep up your fitness and your morale. I also expect you to comport yourselves like the elite men you are. That understood?"

"Yessir!" the men answered in unison, proud of themselves—and of their leader.

"You men've earned some time off, too, so we will be escorting the next express courier to Albuquerque. We'll have two weeks there. We leave in four, maybe five days."

"I believe the men'll be ready, Lieutenant," Cavannaugh said, grinning.

"Just make sure they're not *too* ready, Sergeant. I'm not about to watch my back on the trip." He left as his men burst into laughter.

The Loco Squad made a hell of an impression on Albuquerque, too, and left behind several busted up fellow soldiers and Mexicans; more than two dozen brokenhearted strumpets; and a goodly portion of their summer's wages to pay for the damage to the saloons and brothels.

On the journey back, they were hit by an early fall storm—mostly chill rain and a biting wind—which was a harbinger of what was to come in the months ahead. A week back at the fort, and they got their first snowfall. Only two days later, amid more snowfall, Cruz Martinez and his daughter, Serafina, rode in. Armbruster, who heard about it from Cavannaugh, hurried outside his apartment and watched.

Martinez and Serafina stopped out front of Brooks's office. Serafina waited outside while her father went inside. Armbruster stepped into the light snow and headed swiftly toward Serafina.

The young woman was bundled up in a blanket coat, pulled high around her ears. It was warmer that way, but it also tended to shut her off from the men of the fort, few of whom she would trust.

"*Hola*, Señorita Serafina," Armbruster said quietly as he reached her horse.

Serafina's head popped out of the blanket and she looked around, nervously. Then she saw who had spoken and she smiled.

Armbruster thought the smile would melt all the snow in the area, it was so warm—and inviting. At least he hoped it was inviting. "I've been waiting for you to get back," he said, ignoring his recent trip to Albuquerque. He didn't think Serafina would be interested in that.

"It took us longer than usual," Serafina said. She held out her arms. "Help me down, Señor Teniente."

Armbruster did so with pleasure.

"There," Serafina said. "That's better." She looked up at Armbruster and her dark, soft eyes saddened. "But because it's so late in the year, Papa and I can't spend much time here. I will have little time with you."

"Then we must make the best of the time we have," Armbruster said reasonably.

"*Sí.*"

Martinez came out of the headquarters and saw Armbruster. He grinned, pleasured to see his friend. "Teniente," he said joyfully, as he came down the stairs, hand out. They shook. "It is good to see you here."

"I was just saying the same about Serafina—and you, of course."

Martinez looked skeptical, but he said only, "You have been making quite a name for yourself in these parts, Teniente. All the Navajos speak of the tall gringo soldier."

"Maybe it'll keep them from raiding some. If it does that, my job's been fulfilled."

"And that is needed." Martinez paused. "Would you like to have supper with us tonight, Teniente?" he asked.

"*Sí,*" Armbruster said enthusiastically.

"We'll see you then. Serafina, come."

⊰❨ 21 ❩⊱

For the first time in a couple of months, First Lieutenant Armbruster felt a little nervous. He didn't show it much as he trudged toward the small house set well behind the small stables behind officers' row. He paused for a moment and then knocked on the door.

Serafina opened it and smiled brightly at him. *"Hola, Teniente,"* she said. As always, her voice was husky and warm, its richness reaching deep into Armbruster's soul to stroke it into flame.

"Hola, Miss Serafina," Armbruster managed to squawk as he entered the room. He felt the same way he had early this summer—confused, unsure of himself, awkward of body and mind. Much of that he could ascribe to Serafina herself. Her dress was shoulderless, exposing a portion of dusky brown skin, and came only to midcalf, showing some of her shapely calf. She was barefoot, which surprised Armbruster a little. A necklace of hammered silver graced her slim, long neck. Her long black hair was tied in a long French braid that hung halfway down her back. With the hair pulled back, Armbruster could see the set of shiny silver earrings that matched her necklace.

"Ah, *Teniente,*" Cruz Martinez said with a smile. "Come in."

Only with extreme reluctance did Armbruster break his gaze away from Serafina and turn to greet her father. He shook Martinez's hand and then looked around. Armbruster had never been in the small house before, and he noted that there were three rooms. The one in which he was standing was the kitchen and dining area; the two toward the back were bedrooms. Armbruster knew that outside, attached to the back wall of the house was a storage room.

Armbruster was a little surprised to see the house so comfortable looking, since Martinez and Serafina had only arrived at the fort early that afternoon. He more than half suspected that she had worked as hard on preparing the house as she had in preparing herself. Of course, he also at least partly suspected that he might just want to think that she had gone through so much effort for him.

"Come, Teniente, sit," Martinez said, waving a hand toward the table. "Would you like a drink?"

Armbruster nodded. "That'd be nice. As would an answer, Mister Martinez . . ."

"But what is the question?"

"What's Teniente mean?"

Martinez laughed. "It is your rank—Lieutenant. Which I see has risen over the summer." He pointed to Armbruster's shoulders.

"Yessir."

Martinez poured them each a healthy portion of whiskey from a gray earthen jug into crockery glasses. He raised his glass. "*Salud*, Teniente!"

"*Salud*," Armbruster ventured, figuring he knew what that meant. "But, please, Mister Martinez, quit with the Teniente. Call me Ed."

"*Sí*. I will do this. And you must call me Cruz."

Armbruster raised his glass again. "To you, Cruz."

After they had drunk again, Martinez said, "You've changed much in this summer, Ten . . . Ed."

Armbruster nodded. "I suppose I have." He smiled crookedly. "Most folks here on the post think I'm nearly a completely different man than I was in April. But that's not so. Not really. Mostly what's changed is my attitude. Somewhere along the way this summer, I somehow managed to learn to be less afraid of things, and more aware of myself as a man, and as a soldier. Once my confidence increased, it began building on itself, I think, until I come across to others now as arrogant. I also seem to strike them as being bigger."

"You are bigger. Some."

"I suppose I've added a few pounds. Such a thing's to be expected for a man my age and with the work I do."

"And this new attitude and a few pounds have made you the scourge of the Navajo and Jicarilla?" Martinez asked with a grin.

Armbruster saw it as a serious question. "Mostly the attitude, I suppose. I just somehow, somewhere, decided that I was not going to be afraid of anyone." He stopped, face burning hotly as he realized Serafina was listening to every word he said as she worked around the kitchen.

Martinez nodded, still smiling. "That's half the battle of life. Trouble is, many's the *hombre* doesn't ever learn that."

"I must admit, it feels good at times to be so damned cocky."

"The way a man should be," Martinez agreed enthusiastically, and he took another drink. He set his glass down and then stared solemnly at Armbruster. "I understand that you want to visit my daughter," he said in questioning tones.

"Yessir," Armbruster said evenly, eyes locked on Martinez's. He was not about to back down now after talking about how arrogant he had become.

"We'll be here only a few days."

"You'll be back."

"I must tell you, Señor, that if you're planning to just use my Serafina and throw her away, I'll be 'plumb angered,' as some of you Americans might say it."

"Well, Mister Martinez," Armbruster said slowly, "I can't set here and tell you I'm going to marry Serafina one day. I hardly know her. What I do know is that I'm mighty attracted to her and. I like her more than a little. With time, that might grow into something substantial. Or maybe it won't. We can't know until we try."

Martinez nodded. "I'll allow it," he announced. "But listen to me, Teniente. If you hurt my Serafina, you'll pay for it."

"I'm not afraid of you, Mister Martinez," Armbruster said flatly.

"I know you're not. It's one of the reasons I like you. But I don't make idle threats, Señor. My daughter is more important to me than my own life."

Armbruster nodded. "You don't have to worry about me, Mister Martinez," he said evenly. "I'm not about to cause her any pain."

Martinez grinned again and raised his glass in one more salute. He refilled both their glasses and then put the jug away.

When he had resettled himself in his chair again, Armbruster asked, "How'd you come to meet your late wife, Cruz? If you don't mind my asking."

"I don't mind." Martinez said wistfully. He paused and took a small sip of whiskey. He made himself a corn-husk-wrapped *cigarillo* and lit it. "I've been a trader for many years, Ed. I started working with some men employed by a company at the time working out of Taos and Santa Fe—the Bent and Saint Vrain Company. Have you ever heard of it?"

Armbruster shook his head. "I've only been out here since I arrived at Fort Defiance."

"The Bents and Saint Vrains were good men." He shook his head sadly. "The oldest Bent, Charlie, was killed in the uprising in Taos back in 'forty-seven. The two youngest also died early. Bill Bent's still alive, the last I heard, living in Missouri. Ceran Saint Vrain's still living in Taos and Santa Fe."

Martinez paused a bit to collect his thoughts. "Despite an old man's ramblings, there is a point here somewhere." He smiled a little. "After five or six years of that, I could speak Navajo pretty well. Some other Indian languages, too, so I branched out on my own. A few years after that, I moved to Albuquerque to cut down on the time it took to get to the Diné villages. That's when I met Bonito Flor—Pretty Flower. Madre de Dios, but she was beautiful." His eyes were focused on the past now. "So beautiful."

"I know," Armbruster said quietly.

Martinez looked at Armbruster, a question in his eyes. "How could you know that?" he asked.

Armbruster merely nodded in Serafina's direction.

"Sí," Martinez said with a pleased smile. "I see you look at Serafina the same way I did at Bonito Flor. That's good."

"Many fathers wouldn't think so."

"True." He sighed out a stream of smoke. "We were married soon after and a year later, Serafina was born. We three traveled together much like Serafina and I do now—though there was no fort here then." He smiled, but it was tinged with sadness.

"What happened to Bonito Flor?" Armbruster asked. He could not help himself; he had to ask.

"I don't like to talk about it, Señor," Martinez said, voice full of pain.

Armbruster nodded. He still wanted to know, but he was not cruel enough a man to badger Martinez. "I'm sorry, Cruz," he said quietly.

The two men sat silently, Martinez full of remembrances. Armbruster was content to just watch Serafina at her work. She moved with the grace and smoothness of a cat. As she bent and moved and turned, her skirt flared out at times, exposing more of her calves, which Armbruster was surprised to see were, in addition to being well formed, quite muscular.

Then supper was ready. Serafina set out platters and bowls of various interesting-looking and aromatic foods. Armbruster's mouth watered as his salivary glands contemplated the feast sitting before them. He dug into the tamales, the corn and bean soup, corn tortillas wrapped around spicy meat and cheese, and several bean dishes.

Armbruster had always thought Bessie over at the officer's mess was the greatest of cooks, but he changed his mind now. He was willing to admit to himself, though, that his revised opinion might be colored just a bit by his feelings for Serafina.

After the meal, Martinez rolled himself another *cigarillo*, while Armbruster fired up his pipe. The two men smoked and sipped coffee while Serafina cleaned up, and then she, too, sat with some coffee.

Finally Martinez stood and stretched. He pulled out a pocket watch and looked at it a moment. "I'm going to go in my room and rest a little," he said. "Stay as long as you like, Ed."

Armbruster nodded, perplexed. On the one hand he was glad to have a little time alone—or mostly alone —with Serafina. On the other, Martinez was only a thin wall away. He and Serafina were alone, but they could do almost nothing.

"More coffee?" Serafina asked after her father had gone into his bedroom and closed the door behind him.

Armbruster nodded again, not trusting his voice again quite yet.

Serafina poured it and then sat at the edge of the

table at right angles to his chair. As his hands wrapped around the mug, Serafina tentatively touched them with a finger. "Do you mind?" she asked.

"Not at all," he said. The simple moving of her finger on his skin sent little bolts of excitement racing through him.

Soon his hands opened and captured the nearest one of Serafina's. He rested the back of her hand on his left palm and then he stroked her palm and fingers. Her hands were callused from hard work, and her nails were broken and cracked. It did not matter; to him they were the softest, finest hands he had ever touched.

After some time of that, he switched to her other hand, pleased at the look of pleasure on her face. Serafina's head was back a little, a small smile curled her full lower lip, and her eyes were closed.

Armbruster had to wonder about himself after a little. He had spent the past ten minutes softly stroking a woman's hands. The other men would laugh him out of the fort if they found out. He wasn't sure who would be worse—the men of his Loco Squad, or the men who hated and/or feared Armbruster's men. Then he decided he didn't care. The men would never find out about this, and he enjoyed it.

Finally, though, he stopped and leaned back. He noticed that his hands were shaking a bit as he reached for his pipe to refill and relight it.

"Is something wrong?" Serafina asked nervously. Her usually smooth face was creased with concern.

"No, no." Armbruster hesitated. "It's just that I can't go on touching you any longer. Not without . . ." He stopped, flustered.

"I understand," Serafina said, a touch of wistfulness in her voice. She had enjoyed the feel of his flesh on hers.

They sat for a little in silence. Then Serafina said quietly, "Papa doesn't talk often about Mama. He still misses her very much. That's why he didn't finish telling you about her.''

"Do you know what happened?"

Serafina nodded.

"Do you mind talking about it?"

"No. It was a long time ago, and I was young." Her tone belied her words at least a little bit. "Another reason why Papa doesn't talk about her death, is that he feels responsible."

Armbruster's eyes widened in surprise.

"We were crossing a wash over near Salahkai Mesa. Mama thought she had heard a storm earlier and warned Papa not to try crossing. But he said we'd be all right."

"You don't have to say any more, Serafina."

"I know. But . . . Now that I've started, I want to get it out." She sniffled a few times, but shed no tears. "Papa took me and some of the mules across. There was a little mud in the bottom, but no water. He went back across and got the rest of the mules. Mama was coming across at the end to make sure none of the mules got away. She was about halfway across when we heard a rumbling. Papa and Mama knew what it was, and Papa yelled at Mama to run."

Serafina stopped, dabbing at her eyes with the end of a sleeve. "The horses and mules heard it, too, and got skittish. Mama's horse reared and she fell off. Before she could get up and run, the water came. We never saw her again."

"Good Lord," Armbruster breathed. He didn't know what else to say.

Serafina smiled through her tears. "Well," she said, almost brightly, "I took your mind off of me, didn't I?"

"I guess you did." Armbruster rose and knocked the ashes from his pipe into the stove. He turned back. "Much as I hate to say it, Serafina, I think I'd better be going."

Serafina nodded. She came up to him and wrapped her slim arms around his middle. She looked up at him, mouth parted, waiting. She did not have long to wait before Armbruster's lips were on hers.

{22}

For the next week, Armbruster spent every evening at the temporary Martinez home. Soon after supper each night, Martinez would head for his bed, leaving Armbruster and Serafina to talk, something that for the first few days Armbruster found difficult to do being in such close proximity to Serafina.

After those days, though, he began to relax. He realized that Serafina cared for him as much as he did for her. And once he got over worrying about trying to do more than talk at these times, he settled down. There was, he knew, nothing they could really do but talk, no matter how much they might want to carry their relationship further.

The talks were rather enlightening for Armbruster, though, since he began learning some Spanish, and even tackled a little Navajo. He also learned a little about the Navajo people. The first thing—of many—that surprised Armbruster when he learned it was that Diné girls usually married shortly after reaching puberty.

"Why aren't you married then?" Armbruster asked with a knot in his stomach.

"Two reasons. For one, I'm half-Mexican. For the

other, Diné girls *usually* marry at that time; they don't *have* to."

"Haven't you found someone you wanted to marry?" Armbruster asked, worry still throbbing through him.

"Yes, I have," Serafina answered quietly, looking down. Then she raised her eyes to stare into his—a strange thing for a Navajo—male or female—to do. And she smiled softly, worried herself. "You."

Relief flooded over Armbruster, and he smiled hugely. "Thank God," he whispered. Then the worry returned. "You don't have a Mexican feller, do you?"

Serafina shook her head. "Do you feel the . . . same? About me, I mean?" Serafina asked tightly.

"Yes, I do," Armbruster said solemnly, but the truth of it was written on his joyous face and in his broad smile.

"And you have no wife or other woman back in the United States?" she asked, still worried.

"No, ma'am, I sure don't."

It was Serafina's turn to be relieved. She had not known how Armbruster would take her statement. She thought she knew what his reaction would be, but she knew she had to find out.

After some minutes of basking in the glow of their mutual feelings, Armbruster said, "Tell me more about the Navajo—Diné."

"What do you want to know?"

"I don't know," Armbruster said with a shrug. "Their beliefs, I guess. How they live."

"You've seen the way they live, at least to some extent. They mostly raise sheep. And horses, of course." She laughed a little. "You won't see most Diné walk more than a few feet if there's a horse to ride. They just plain don't like it. That seems odd to some folks, considering the Diné aren't plains Indians, like the Comanches. Most folks expect Comanches to be on horseback all the time. They don't think the same abut the Diné.''

"How many villages are there?" Armbruster asked.

"None," Serafina said, almost surprised. She stood to get them more coffee.

"But I've been in Diné villages," Armbruster protested.

Serafina poured coffee and then smiled at Armbruster. "They're not real villages. Members of a clan get together at times—for a healing ceremony, or for the annual sheep shearing. But they don't live in a village." She put the coffeepot back on the stove and sat. "Members of a family might build their hogans near each other for companionship or something. Especially a couple who've just married. They almost always live near the woman's mother, at least for a while. Those who marry are always of different clans, and they live with the mother's people." She grinned. "Women own the hogans and the sheep and much else."

Armbruster's eyes widened in surprise. "I thought all Indian women were little more than slaves," he said.

"Many white men think that. It might be true with some other tribes, but not with the Diné. Actually, Diné men treat their women fairly well—a lot better than white men treat their women, from what I've seen."

"Then why're you in love with me if white men're so evil?" he asked half-seriously.

"You're not like most white men," Serafina said simply. "That was clear right from the first. Well, maybe not from the first instant, but not long after." She smiled with a tinge of sadness. "Not too many white men'd come to the rescue of a half–Mexican-half–Diné woman like you did that time." She almost shuddered at the recollection of Private Fenton Heywood's bulk atop of her, and his persistent, groping hands.

Armbruster was almost embarrassed at the praise, and so he only shrugged.

"It meant a lot to me," Serafina said quietly.

Armbruster shrugged again. "I couldn't let any man do that to any woman—especially . . . especially one I . . . liked even then."

"Why?"

"Why what?"

"Why'd you like me even then?"

"I don't know," Armbruster said honestly. "I just did."

She smiled a little. "I remember you standing at the corner of officers' row watching Papa and me when we came into the fort back in the spring."

Armbruster nodded. "I'd never seen a woman like you before," he said. "One so beautiful, so . . . different. I know the former is one of the reasons I was attracted to you, but I think the latter was just as important. At least at the time."

"And now?" Serafina asked softly.

"Now," he said evenly, "I love you for being you." He couldn't believe he had actually come out and said that.

Tears welled up in Serafina's eyes, but her smile was as bright as the July sun. She rose, came around the table and sat on his lap. She wrapped her arms around his neck and rested her cheek against his chest near the shoulder and let her tears soak his shirt.

Armbruster let her stay that way a little while, then said softly, gruffly, "You better go back to your chair now."

"Why?" Serafina asked, jerking her head off his chest, worried.

"You stay where you are, and I won't be held responsible for what happens."

A mischievous smile spread slowly across Serafina's face. "I will," she offered.

"Uh-uh. I'm not about to have your father come out and kill me."

"Oh," Serafina said nervously looking around, "don't talk about death and dying!"

"Why?" he asked, surprised.

Serafina rose and went back to her chair. "The Diné fear death and anything that has to do with it. It's one of their greatest fears."

"Why? I mean nobody likes to think about death, especially that of someone they love, but still, we all have to deal with it."

"I don't think I can explain it all to someone who isn't a Diné," Serafina said sincerely. She paused to sip some coffee. She was plainly uncomfortable. But she finally went on. "The dead are dangerous. They can attract spirits—bad spirits—and witches and all kinds of evil." She shuddered.

"Don't say any more, Serafina," Armbruster said, taking her hands in his. "I didn't mean to cause you such anguish."

"It's all right," Serafina said, smiling bravely.

"Doesn't your religion deal with . . . them?"

"In some ways, I suppose. But the Diné religion—if you could even call it that—isn't like the Christian religion." She paused, gathering her thoughts. "The Diné believe in something they call *hozho*. It's the harmony of life. All things must be a certain way or *hozho* is disrupted. If that happens, one of the shamans must determine what is wrong, and then the proper sing must be held."

"Sing?"

"Yes. Our religious—or medicine—rituals, I guess you could call them. There are many, and most medicine men know only one or two, though a few know several. There's the Nightway and the Topway and the

Blessingway and many others. I don't think I could describe them to you, even if it were allowed."

Armbruster nodded. "I understand." He grinned. "I mean I understand that you can't talk about them. I haven't a clue as to what they're all about."

Despite having become more relaxed in just sitting and talking with Serafina because they could do nothing else, Armbruster found it a little more difficult each evening to leave Serafina. Each good-night kiss was longer and more intense than the one before, and Armbruster left each time a little more tense. Still, he was not about to stop seeing Serafina, nor was he about to forgo kissing her good night.

Another source of tension for Armbruster was the knowledge that Martinez would be leaving soon, and Serafina with him. In the week Armbruster had spent each evening at Martinez's, there had been two more days of snowfall, and temperatures were down considerably. If Martinez was to make it back to Albuquerque before full winter hit, he'd have to be leaving soon.

Armbruster's anxiety rose a little with each day, and finally it reached a peak. A week after Armbruster began going to the small house, Martinez finished his supper and then announced, "It's time Serafina and I were heading back to Albuquerque, Eduardo."

Armbruster nodded, unhappy. "When?"

"Day after tomorrow."

Armbruster nodded again, even more unhappy. He glanced at Serafina, who was cleaning up. She looked stricken.

Martinez rose and pushed his chair in. "And, since we'll be leaving soon, I'm going to check the mules," he announced. "And then I have some other things to do." He looked at his watch. "It's twenty minutes past five o'clock now. I'll be back by nine." He looked pointedly at Armbruster and then his daughter.

Serafina looked at her father, still shaken by his announcement about leaving, but then she recovered. She smiled as she went to kiss her father on the cheek. Then Martinez pulled on his coat and left. Serafina turned to look at Armbruster and she smiled warmly.

Armbruster was still rather taken aback by Martinez's earlier announcement, and his mind was struggling with Martinez's departure. "Did your father just do what I think—hope—he did?"

"What do you think he did?" Serafina asked mischievously.

"I think he just left us alone and bluntly told us he'd be gone for almost four hours."

"*Sí.* That's what he did."

Armbruster shook his head in wonder. "There's not any white man I know'd leave his unmarried daughter alone in a place—one with two bedrooms, no less—with a man who had a strong hankering for her."

"My papa isn't white," Serafina said. "Not in your world anyway."

"He approves of you and I being alone together?"

Serafina shrugged. "I don't know if he 'approves.' But he trusts you and he trusts me. But more important, my people—both my peoples—are much freer about these things than yours are. I could never understand how you keep your women all closed off from the world and the good things it has to offer."

"Like love?" Armbruster hinted, voice deep with a growing desire.

"Like love," Serafina agreed. She walked to him and sat on his lap.

Once again nervous, Armbruster lowered his head so he could kiss Serafina. She enthusiastically threw herself into the operation, and Armbruster's confidence began to return.

When they broke apart, Armbruster asked a little breathlessly, "I suppose you'd not object too strenuously if I was to suggest we go in one of the other rooms?"

"Now?" she responded in mock horror.

"Now," Armbruster growled, his voice thick.

"What do you think?" Serafina asked quietly, nipping him playfully on the nose.

Without a word, Armbruster surged to his feet, easily holding Serafina. He was a little surprised at how light she was. He turned and strode toward the bedrooms. He stopped. "Which one?" he asked.

Serafina removed one of her hands from around Armbruster's neck and pointed.

Armbruster moved into the small room and gently placed Serafina on the soft quilt over the tick mattress.

Serafina would not let go of his neck, though. Instead, she tugged, pulling him down on top of her. "That's better," she whispered.

Armbruster could only grunt an affirmative and he smothered her mouth with his.

Before long, they somehow managed to remove or loosen enough of their clothing to make their operation a success.

Lying back afterward, with Serafina lying on his front, Armbruster was almost stunned. He had had his share of women before, but never one who had left him the way he felt now—strong and drained at the same time. He felt more of a man than he ever had.

He stroked her hair a little, and she lifted her head. Resting her chin on the side of a small fist, she smiled at Armbruster. "I think we've got too many clothes on," Serafina said impishly.

"Oh, you do, do you?" Armbruster countered. He was beginning to relax, thanking whatever had brought Serafina Martinez into his life. "And just what do you propose to do about it?"

"Fix that problem." She swept off him until she was standing. Then she pulled off her dress—the only garment she was wearing. She smiled delightedly at seeing the look of desire in Armbruster's eyes.

"Your turn," Serafina said as she bent over to begin undoing the buttons of his shirt.

·❦{ 23 }❦·

"**Y**ou think your father'll leave us alone again tomorrow night?" Armbruster asked as he sat on a chair in the kitchen and pulled on his boots. With each article of clothing he had put back on, his sadness deepened at the thought that Serafina would be gone the day after tomorrow.

"There's a good chance of it," Serafina said. She, too, was fully dressed again. "Why?"

"Because it's the last time we'll see each other until spring."

"I have some thoughts on that, too," Serafina said firmly. "Now that I've got you," she added boldly, "I'm not about to let you go easily."

"What're you planning?" he asked, wondering.

"Don't worry about it. I'll talk with Papa tomorrow. You just keep smiling and show up here tomorrow evening like usual."

Armbruster was about to say something when Martinez walked in the door. Armbruster felt considerably guilty when he greeted Martinez. He knew Martinez had to know what he and Serafina had been up to, and it was hard for Armbruster to look Martinez in the face. But to look at Martinez, if he knew, he certainly didn't seem bothered.

"Well, good night," Armbruster said, and then he escaped into the cold, starry night. He had a considerable amount of trouble getting to sleep that night as thoughts of love consummated fought with thoughts of impending loss. He remained quite distracted the next day as he drilled his troops and went through his paperwork and the other mundane tasks involved in his job.

As he walked toward Martinez's small house, he had reached a point of hating himself for allowing the worry to overwhelm him. His anger, combined with the anxiety had him ready to explode.

Serafina opened the door before he had finished knocking, and he was shocked to see that she was beaming, bright and happy. His stomach soured even more. He could not believe that after last night she would be this joyful about leaving him for the winter.

Armbruster dully walked in and greeted Martinez. He sat and gulped down the entire crockery glass of whiskey Martinez had set before him. The move shocked all of them to some degree.

Still bubbly, Serafina served supper shortly afterward. Armbruster only picked at his food. Serafina noted it and felt a little hurt. "Don't you like your food?" she asked.

"Oh, it's not that," Armbruster said lamely. He knew she took pride in her cooking. "I'm just not hungry is all."

Serafina nodded, accepting it. She knew something was bothering Armbruster, and she was fairly certain she knew what, but there was nothing she could do about it now.

After finishing, Martinez pushed his plate away, leaned back and rolled and lit a *cigarillo*.

Great, Armbruster thought angrily, *he's not even going to leave Serafina and me alone tonight. Damn!*

"Are you done?" Serafina asked Armbruster. Her

enthusiasm was bubbling again, so she could not be too angry at Armbruster.

"Yes," Armbruster said in annoyance.

Within minutes, Serafina had cleared away the dishes and then sat back down. When she had, Martinez looked hard into Armbruster's eyes. "My Serafina tells me she wants to stay with you while I go back to Albuquerque," he said roughly. "Is that true, Señor?"

Armbruster was flabbergasted. His mouth flapped open as he stared at Martinez. Then he looked at Serafina, who nodded happily. "Yessir," he finally said, looking back to Martinez.

"*Bueno.*" Martinez didn't look any happier. "I want to know, Señor, if you'll take good care of my Serafina."

"Better than any other man except you, Cruz," Armbruster said honestly.

"Ah, *bueno.*" Martinez grinned. "I thought you would say that. And I believe you."

Armbruster nodded. Then he shook his head. "But I don't figure Major Brooks'll allow it, even if you would."

"I think he'll allow it, if you talk to him about it."

"You talked to him?" Armbruster guessed.

"A little. I have little power here, you understand. I'm but a poor trader—and a damned Mexican one at that—but I'm not without resources."

Serafina nodded her head. "Papa's the only one who'll bring supplies up here in the winter, if the fort runs low. And he's friends with Mister Webber, the sutler."

"What good's being the sutler's friend?"

"You and the other soldiers buy things at Mister Webber's?"

"All the time."

"Papa's the one who generally brings his supplies here, too." She almost giggled. "Papa and Mister Webber are partners in a place in Albuquerque, though almost no one knows that.''

''Poor trader, eh?'' Armbruster asked, squinting at Martinez. He was feeling considerably better, though he was still flummoxed by what he had heard this night.

''Sí,'' Martinez said with a laugh. He paused. ''Major Brooks knows Serafina staying here's liable to cause trouble, but he'll allow it grudgingly. You must ask him, though.''

''Why?'' Armbruster asked suspiciously.

''He wants to make sure you're behind the idea for one thing. For another, I think he wants to rant and rave at you for a while because of it. He can't do that with me. And I suspect he'll want to tell you that if there's trouble because of it, you'll pay for it.''

Armbruster nodded. It all was reasonable. ''Aren't you worried about trouble here, Cruz?''

Martinez shrugged. ''I always worry about trouble, Señor. But if I worried about it too much, I'd never be a trader.''

Armbruster nodded. ''You make any arrangements about all this?'' he asked.

Martinez shook his head. ''Other than she can stay here in this house.'' He stood. ''Well, I've got to go check on the mules again,'' he said. ''I have other chores, too.'' He grabbed his coat and left.

Armbruster sat looking at Serafina in wonder. His world had been turned topsy-turvy, and he was still a little awestruck. ''How'd you manage to talk Cruz into this?''

''I have my ways.'' Serafina grinned. She rose and came over to him. She took his hands and put them around her to rest on her buttocks. ''Now, let's worry about all these things later.''

He rose, leaving his hands on her buttocks. When he was standing, he kissed her.

* * *

The first thing the next morning, Armbruster dressed carefully in his uniform. He debated whether to wear his Loco Squad accouterments. Wearing them might inflame Brooks. On the other hand, those items gave him confidence. He also suspected that since his encounter with Brooks over keeping the Loco Squad together, Brooks also was a little in awe of the Squad's garments. He decided to wear them.

Then he marched over to Brooks's office. The major's face was cloudy with anger already. In some ways that helped Armbruster, who, once he saw it, stiffened his own resolve and defiance.

"I understand you have a rather unusual request, Lieutenant," Brooks said coldly.

"And I understand you have an answer already, Major."

"Don't smart-ass me, Lieutenant," Brooks snapped.

"Yessir." He paused. "I know, sir, that this is unusual, and I know it probably breaks a dozen army regulations. I—"

"Only a dozen?" Brooks asked sarcastically.

"Whatever, sir. I know this puts you in a tough position, but—"

"Goddammit, Lieutenant," Brooks snapped, "why don't you go find yourself a decent white girl and marry her. That'd solve all this."

"Because, sir," Armbruster said slowly, "I've found this girl. Would it help if I married her?"

"I don't think you could find anyone who'd perform the service."

"If I could?"

"I suppose that'd be marginally better," Brooks reluctantly acknowledged. "Still, where're you going to find one—besides in Albuquerque?"

Armbruster shrugged. "Looks like we're stuck, sir."

"Don't get cocky with me, damn you." Brooks

sighed, then almost grinned. "You're one of the biggest pains in the asses I've ever met, Lieutenant," he
said. "You remind me of me when I was your age." He
sighed again. "Look, this is bound to cause trouble, so
we need to minimize that as best we can."

"How, sir? I'm willing to do all I can."

"If you're willing to do that, you'll send the young
lady back to Albuquerque with her father."

"Correction, sir. I'm willing to do almost anything I
can to minimize the trouble."

"All right, here are the rules. She must stay in the
house as much as possible. She won't be allowed in any
of the other fort buildings, except one of the stables—
the one nearest the house—your quarters, if she is
brought in and out unobserved by others, the hospital
or the sutler's."

"That might be difficult, sir."

Brooks shrugged. "That's your concern, Lieutenant.
Not mine."

"Yessir. I can handle all the conditions except the
one abut her staying inside all the time. She's not a
prisoner, sir."

"Perhaps not. But I've become somewhat of a prisoner of your lust."

Armbruster felt as if he had been slapped. "There's
a lot more to my feelings about Serafina than lust,"
Armbruster snapped. "Sir."

"That doesn't change my mind or affect the rules
I've laid out, Lieutenant," Brooks said firmly. "I am
going well out of my way to accommodate your liaison
with this half-breed. Such things are immoral and
against God's nature. But because of reasons I can't
divulge, I am willing to bend over backward to make
these arrangements. There will be no negotiating on
these rules. You take them or leave them."

"I accept," Armbruster said, not very happy about it,

but far happier than he would've been had Serafina been forced to return to Albuquerque.

"I wasn't finished, Lieutenant," Brooks snapped.

Armbruster bit his lip, angry at himself—and at Brooks.

"The harshest rule in all this is that the first time there's trouble over this half-breed, she'll be shipped back to Albuquerque."

"That's not very . . . fair, sir," Armbruster said evenly. "There's many a man on this post that'll try to cause trouble with her just to get rid of her."

"That's your problem, Lieutenant. Any trouble at all, and she goes. You still accept?"

"Yessir." Armbruster felt boxed in. There was nothing he could do about the situation. If he wanted to spend the winter with Serafina, he would have to keep her locked up. If she objected to that, she would be gone from his life, at least for the winter.

"And, Lieutenant, I don't want you fighting over this woman. Someone gives her a hard time—or gives you a hard time about her—you swallow the insults and walk away."

"Yessir," Armbruster said dully.

Brooks almost gloated. He liked Armbruster and did see something of himself as a younger man in Armbruster. But he had a fort to run, and he could not do it easily with men like Armbruster bucking his rule. If only Serafina Martinez had been white, he figured, this problem would've never come up. That, he knew, was the crux of the matter—Serafina's nationality. Or, rather, nationalities. Perhaps if Serafina were half-white and half-Navajo, or even half-white and half-Mexican, there might be some civilization in her, and they could manage to turn her into a white woman. But she wasn't and there was no hoping that would change those things. "All right, Lieutenant, dismissed. Just heed my words."

"Yessir." Gloomy and irritated, Armbruster headed toward the house. Serafina was all smiles, but turned more solemn when she saw the look on Armbruster's face. "Mister Martinez," Armbruster said as he went in, almost ignoring Serafina.

"Things are all right?" Martinez asked, worried.

"I suppose." He quickly outlined the rules Brooks had given him. Finally he looked at Serafina. "If you can't abide by those rules, maybe you best go on back to Albuquerque with your father now."

"I can live with them," Serafina said firmly.

"Mister Martinez?"

"If she wants to live within the rules, I won't object." He paused. "More important is whether you can live within those rules."

"I'm not sure I can," Armbruster said honestly.

"Well, suppose you can't," Serafina interjected. "Then I have to go back to Albuquerque. I won't like it, but I'll go if forced. But," she added earnestly, "at least we'll have had a day or a week or maybe even a month together. That's something."

Armbruster nodded slowly. "Yes, Serafina. Yes, it is." He resolved silently to do as best he could in living within Brooks's rules. And if he had to break them at some point, he also vowed to make every moment with Serafina count as much as possible, in the case that she was forced to leave. He smiled at Serafina. "It'll be nice being with you all the time, Serafina. Even if that time is rather short."

"*Bueno!*" Serafina said, all smiles again.

"When're you leaving, Cruz?" Armbruster asked.

"Right now. I've just been waiting to see what you had to say about Brooks's offer. I didn't know what he was going to say to you, but I knew he was going to make this as tough on you as he could."

"He did."

"That's a fact." He shook Armbruster's hand.

"Good luck, Eduardo. And watch over my daughter for me."

"I will, Cruz," Armbruster said with a nod.

Martinez kissed his daughter, hugged her, and then walked out, leaving Armbruster and Serafina alone together.

It was a time unlike any Armbruster had ever experienced. It was not difficult for him to keep Serafina in the little house, since he was rather reluctant to leave it himself as long as she was there. He, of course, still had duties to perform, and was gone much of the day, but he got back to the house as much as possible.

The first signs of trouble sprang up quietly just short of a week later. Armbruster was heading toward the Company B barracks when he heard some noise—sounding like a fight—coming from behind the laundress quarters. He headed back there and found three men from the Loco Squad—Privates Tom Olson, Arnie Kapp and Klaus Nesselroad—having a rather spirited set-to with five other men from Company B while a dozen or so other men stood around watching, adding their quietly shouted support to their fellows.

Corporal Bauer was one of the bystanders. He spotted Armbruster and shouted, "Ten-hut!"

Those watching the fight snapped to attention immediately. It took those actively involved in the fracas a little longer, but soon they, too, were at attention.

"Would one of you boys like to tell me what this was all about?" Armbruster demanded.

"No, sir!" Bauer responded sharply.

"You men know there's not supposed to be any fighting." He almost smiled. "Unless there's good cause."

"There was good cause, sir," Bauer said. "Believe me, sir."

Armbruster nodded. "All right. You boys," he said, pointing to the men who had been fighting, "get yourselves cleaned up. Loco Squad, fall in over at the cliff in a quarter of an hour. We haven't wasted any powder in a while, and I expect it's time to do so. You men from Company B might want to find something to do, unless Major Brooks finds something for you to do." He turned and left, striding away, wondering what the fight was about. Then he put it from his mind, since he figured it didn't concern him anyway.

He went straight to where the cliff rose a hundred feet high on the east side of the fort. The cliff made a good backstop for practicing with either rifle or pistol.

Sergeant Cavannaugh was already there, with Privates Cecil Quinn and Don Vickers. They had a small cart piled with rifles, and boxes of paper cartridges. Soon after, the men of Loco Squad straggled up and formed something of a line, though all were slouched over.

Armbruster noticed that Bauer had gone straight over to Cavannaugh and talked to him for some minutes, face and hands animated. Cavannaugh nodded frequently, and cast surreptitious glances all around.

"All right, men," Armbruster said when all his troops were there, "have at it."

The soldiers walked up to the cart one by one, picked up a rifle and a handful of cartridges, and then formed a ragged line and began firing randomly. Armbruster didn't much care what they looked like, as long as their gunfire was accurate. He had no reason to want to see his men go into a fight with the Navajos or Apaches and try to form a battle line. That would be suicidal for a group such as his. He'd rather have them lined up where they felt most protected and firing at will, as long as they hit what they aimed at. And nine times out of ten, they did.

As Armbruster watched the men practicing their marksmanship, Cavannaugh moved up to stand alongside of him. Over the rattle of gunfire, the sergeant said, "I understand you found a few of them men fighting just a little while ago, sir?"

Armbruster nodded. "So?"

"I'd not be too hard on the men for it if I were you, sir," Cavannaugh said flatly.

"Why not?" Armbruster asked, looking at his top sergeant.

"I'd rather not say, sir." Seeing Armbruster's look of annoyance, he added, "Some of the men in B Company were makin' disparagin' remarks about someone, Lieutenant." He hesitated an instant. "Miss Serafina." He turned to face Armbruster.

Looking straight at Cavannaugh, Armbruster said, "You know there'll be hell to pay if Major Brooks hears about it."

"Yessir, I do know that. I also know that the men of Loco Squad ain't gonna say nothin' about it."

"You're probably right. But we can't say the same thing for most of the other men—those not in our little group."

Cavannaugh grinned tightly. "True, sir. But if one of 'em goes blabbin' to the major we'll lie through our teeth sayin' no such thing ever happened. And then later, we'll kick the shit out of whoever it was went and opened his mouth."

"That could cause even more trouble."

"We're used to trouble, Lieutenant," Cavannaugh said cockily.

"Listen, Sergeant," Armbruster said sternly, "there's no reason for you and the rest of the men to get run out of the army because of something like this. This is my problem to worry about."

"Yessir."

"Your sincerity is overwhelming, Sergeant," Armbruster said, fighting back a smile even though he was angry at the entire situation.

"Yessir."

"Besides, none of the men like Serafina anyway."

"Doesn't matter none to them, sir. She's your lady. You picked her. That's good enough for our men, sir. Their personal feelings don't matter much in this, Lieutenant. Our loyalty is to you."

"You, and all the rest of those damn fractious mongrels out there"—he pointed vaguely toward his troops —"are crazy."

Sergeant grinned. "That's why we're called the Loco Squad."

"You're also hopeless."

"We can but try, sir." Sergeant grew solemn. "A word of advice for you, Lieutenant?"

Armbruster nodded.

"Let us handle this, Lieutenant. You get involved and there'll be big trouble. A couple of the boys get caught fightin', we can explain it away. Hell, there's fights every day on this post and every other one I've ever set foot on. At most one of us boys might have to spend a couple days in the guardhouse. Most of us've done it anyway."

"As much as I hate to admit it, Sergeant, I think you're right." He sighed. "It's galling, though. But listen to my advice now, Sergeant," he added. "If the situation seems to be getting worse, you let me know. I can't have my men getting jailed or beat up—or both —to save the honor of my woman."

"Yessir."

* * *

His men and the others of B Company seemed to quiet down as winter covered the high country of Dinétah, at least as far as Armbruster was concerned. Armbruster wasn't sure if that was because the men saw little point in keeping up the simmering feud based on his living with Serafina. He hoped it was, though he suspected it was more because it was just too damned cold out most times to want to get into a fight outside, and they had no desire to wreck their living quarters.

The weather went a long way to keeping Serafina in her house—along with Armbruster as often as possible. Still, that was not nearly enough time for Armbruster, but he tried to remain reasonable about it. The worst times were when he had to take his troops into Bonito Canyon for firewood. The fort used a considerable amount of wood during the cold, dreary winter. It was an all-day job, which meant that Serafina would be all alone at the fort. He didn't like that at all. The job was also one that left him and all his men tired and sore. Serafina would treat him lovingly and kindly on those nights, but he felt himself weak.

The winter seemed to keep almost everyone else holed up inside as much as possible, and Armbruster found that a relief more often than not. It meant he had fewer jibes from fellow officers to take, fewer stares he had to ignore, fewer insults to take without reciprocating. In some ways, though, he didn't like being cut off from the others, since there were times when he missed male companionship. He had barely spoken to any of the other officers for almost a month.

Serafina's love and kindness kept him from being too lonely for friends most of the time. She was a fine companion in many ways. With her background, she had acquired skills and languages even most men did not. She was exotic, far more intelligent than most people would believe possible, and full of humor.

As the days and weeks passed, Armbruster even began to entertain notions that he would ask Serafina to marry him someday. He held back partly because of fear, but also because he was sure such a thing would not be well-received at the post. If Brooks denied him a chance to marry Serafina, Armbruster either would have to desert or he would most likely end up being shipped elsewhere, far away from Serafina.

He did hint at marriage a few times, basically feeling Serafina out to see how she would take to the idea, as well as the possibility of waiting three more years. His enlistment would be up then, and he could resign his commission. Then he would be free to marry her. She always indicated that she would wait, but Armbruster was still reluctant to take that final step and bring the subject into the open.

The only excitement at the fort was the occasional Navajo who wandered in looking to trade for some badly needed food. That and the regular—if that's what it could be called—express from Fort Marcy. On one of the latter, First Sergeant Carl Burghalter was along. He and Armbruster spent a couple of hours sharing a bottle of brandy and some talk. The sergeant had changed little, but he noted some of the changes in the lieutenant he had brought out here for the first time not much more than a year ago.

After each of these small incidences, though, the fort would fall back into its winter hibernation. It was then, with the winter strangling the land, that cabin fever began to build up. Fights became more common again, though Armbruster figured it had nothing to do with him directly, though he could never be sure.

At least that gave the men—and the officers—something to do. With each fight there followed at least one court-martial. If men from any Company but B were involved, Armbruster might sit as one of the hearing officers. He, however, was the defense for any member of the Loco Squad who was being court-martialed. In doing so, he compiled an enviable record—he won six of the first seven cases he had. That record of success, though, brought two challenges to fight from other officers, challenges which Armbruster gracefully turned down.

He almost issued one challenge himself, not to an officer, but to an enlisted man.

A Private Heinrich Gustav of E Company was awaiting his court-marital for fighting, and Armbruster overheard him say to a fellow private standing next to him, "If it vasn't for dot schtupid whore dot schtupid Lieutenant Armbruster's livink vit', ve—me und you—voulnd't even be here."

The other soldier was preoccupied and only nodded.

"Ach, I don't know vhat anyone vould see in such a bitch," the dull-witted Heinrich said.

Armbruster saw red and was about ready to take Heinrich outside and beat him to death when Corporal Bauer slipped into the breech between Armbruster and Heinrich. He never looked at Armbruster or said anything to his commander. He just leaned over Heinrich's shoulder and said quietly, "Another word like that out of your fat mouth, Mein Herr, and you'll be feedin' the fuckin' wolves before nightfall."

Heinrich turned his florid, fat face and saw Bauer's cold blue eyes staring at him, and he knew Bauer had spoken the truth. He nodded.

"Good," Bauer said. "When you get up there to tell your side of things, you say you and whoever you were fightin' were fightin' over a card game. Yah?"

"Yah," Heinrich said thickly. He entertained thoughts of killing Bauer, but then he realized it was not worth risking his life over.

Bauer turned, winked at Armbruster and moved away.

Despite his victories, Armbruster did not find the military trials very entertaining. They were usually dull and dry, the soldiers involved sheepish and as often as not hungover, the punishments severe. But there was no getting away from them, and they seemed to be held with ever more frequency. Occasionally, one would be called off for some reason or other, a time when Armbruster would rejoice and hurry out to be with Serafina unless other pressing duty called.

A little more than a month after Serafina's father had left the fort, one such case came up. The court-martial was delayed until one of the two combatants was released from Doctor Fournier's hospital.

With no other duty facing him, Armbruster began hurrying up toward the small house, thoughts of a naked Serafina rampaging in his mind. He was almost there when he heard Serafina scream. He ran, heading around the small stable at one end of the row of stables. Then he saw someone come flying out of the house, landing with a thud in the thin layer of snow.

"Hans!" Armbruster said, growing angry. He could not understand why Knudson would try to molest Serafina. It made no sense, considering how he felt about Serafina and her kind.

Private Fenton Heywood came swaggering out the door of the house. "I don't like bein' disturbed when I'm with a woman, boy," Heywood snarled. "Now I'm gonna fix your ass but good." He lurched off the porch and into the snow, heading for Knudson, seeming oblivious to the rest of the world.

Even from a distance Armbruster thought Heywood looked drunk. Armbruster skidded to a stop alongside Knudson. Heywood stopped, too, surprised.

Armbruster slowly peeled off his jacket.

╡ 25 ╞

Knudson scrambled for safety as Heywood charged like a wounded bear. Armbruster casually dropped his coat on the snow. At the last moment, he stepped a little to the side and swung, foot extended, as Heywood rumbled by. His foot caught Heywood on the rump and propelled him forward with a little more speed.

Heywood stumbled and fell facedown in the snow. He was enraged when he got up and turned to face Armbruster. Officers and enlisted men were racing in the direction of the house.

Knudson, Sergeant Cavannaugh and Private Cecil Quinn hauled out pistols. "Hold it, Heywood!" Cavannaugh snapped.

"Go ahead and shoot," Heywood said over his shoulder. "This little shit ball needs all the help you can give him."

"I'll shoot anyone who shoots him," Armbruster snapped. "Put those pieces away." His voice left no room for argument, even among the higher-ranking officers who had come along.

Even Brooks was there. "Holster your pistols, men," he ordered.

Cavannaugh, Knudson and Quinn slid their pistols away. Cavannaugh was nervous. He knew Armbruster had beaten Heywood once before, but Cavannaugh figured that was as much luck as anything. Cavannaugh also knew that Armbruster had grown in size, strength and experience in the past few months, but he was still not certain by any means that Armbruster could take the brutish, hulking Fenton Heywood.

Armbruster peeled off his gunbelt and dropped it alongside his coat. "Well, come on at me, you overgrown ox," he said with a sneer.

"Don't be in such a hurry to die, Lieutenant," Heywood growled. His eyes were wild, and he seemed half-crazed. He figured he had nothing more left to lose. If he was going to die by firing squad or hanging, he might as well take his time and kill Armbruster slowly.

"I'm in no hurry. I just don't want to freeze to death standing here waiting for you to decide what to do."

Heywood cracked his knuckles and then moved forward slowly. He was not about to be made a fool of again by charging and getting dumped on his snout. He closed in and suddenly swung a ham-sized fist at Armbruster's head.

The move took Armbruster a little by surprise. He darted his head to the side, but Heywood still managed to get a pretty good piece of him, knocking him down. As soon as Armbruster's back hit the snow he knew he was in real trouble. Footing was slick and getting up would be difficult, especially since Heywood was headed the few feet toward him, ready to stomp Armbruster into a pile of broken bones.

Armbruster rolled over and pushed up onto his hands and knees. But Heywood kicked him hard in the side, sending him rolling away. It hurt like hell, but Armbruster was grateful that it put him several feet away from the suddenly cocky Heywood. That allowed him a chance to get to his feet, even if he was a little unsteady.

Heywood was still pressing forward toward him, and

so Armbruster gave way a little, trying to give himself a few moments to recover. He knew he was going to have to be careful; there was no way he could stand toe-to-toe with Heywood and pound him into submission.

"Whatsa matter, Loo-tenant?" Heywood smirked. "Scared?"

Armbruster nodded. "I'm always scared when an ox tries to think." He stopped backing up and flicked a jab at Heywood's head. He didn't expect it to have much effect, if any, and it didn't. He tested the maneuver a few more times. Again it had little effect, other than to make Heywood smile a little. But it did keep Heywood's attention, which is what Armbruster wanted. Armbruster drove a hard right fist into Heywood's midsection.

The punch surprised Heywood with its suddenness and power. Heywood did not think Armbruster was that strong. He stood, somewhat stunned, for some seconds.

Armbruster took the opportunity to pound Heywood in the stomach, chest and face. All the while, he remembered what had happened to his hand the last time he had fought Heywood. But at this point he didn't much give a damn.

Heywood slipped on the slushy snow and fell on his rump. Armbruster darted in and tried to kick Heywood in the head. Heywood ducked and swept his legs in an arc low to the ground, knocking Armbruster's foot out from under him. As Armbruster fell, Heywood snarled, "It ain't gonna be that easy, you son of a bitch."

Armbruster managed to get up first, but he was limping a little, from where his hip had hit the earth. The pain in his face, leg and hip served to focus his mind, though, helping him forget the throng of men who had gathered. With his hate driving him, and the pain focusing him, he became more formidable.

As Heywood was rising, Armbruster stepped in and slammed a powerful punch into Heywood's face, smashing the private's nose flat and loosening several teeth. Heywood plopped back down on his rear, grunting. He spit out some blood and began pushing himself up again. Armbruster hammered him to the ground. The men went through the ritual twice more, both times with the same result. But by that time, Heywood was half-unconscious, and made no more move to get up.

Armbruster jumped on Heywood and grabbed Heywood's throat in his hands. Before anyone could really stop him, he had squeezed the life out of Heywood.

Then rough hands were pulling him from Heywood's bloated corpse, and Doctor Fournier was kneeling at Heywood's side. Fournier looked up at Brooks and shook his head.

"Fix Lieutenant Armbruster up, Doctor," Brooks said harshly. He looked at Armbruster. "I want you in my office in thirty minutes, Lieutenant." Then he spun and walked away.

"Inside, Lieutenant," Fournier said.

Armbruster picked up his coat and gunbelt and headed for the house. Cavannaugh and Corporal Bauer fell into step beside him.

"We'll have a couple of the boys watch over the house for a spell, Lieutenant," Cavannaugh said.

Armbruster nodded in appreciation.

Fournier ordered several men to remove Heywood's body, then followed Armbruster into the house. Ten minutes later he left, having found little to patch up on Armbruster.

Moments later, Serafina answered a knock on the door. Bauer stepped inside. "Lieutenant Knudson would like to speak with you, sir. You up to it?"

"Send him in, Corporal."

"You want I should stay in here, sir?" Bauer asked.

Armbruster smiled grimly and placed one of his pistols on the table near his right hand. "I don't think that'll be necessary, Corporal."

Bauer nodded, and a moment later Knudson tentatively entered. He let his eyes adjust to the dimness inside. Seeing Armbruster seated at the table, he pulled a chair up. "Mind?" he asked. When Armbruster shook his head, Knudson sat.

"You wanted to talk to me, Hans?" Armbruster asked levelly.

After pouring coffee for both men, Serafina came up behind Armbruster and stood there, her dark hands resting lightly, possessively on his shoulders.

Knudson nodded, though he said nothing. He fiddled with his coffee a little and finally said, "I don't know where to start, Ed. . . . May I still call you that?"

Armbruster nodded. "You can start by telling me what you know about this," he said harshly.

"Ed," Knudson said, staring at Armbruster, "I've been a goddamn fool. I guess I was more concerned about my goddamn career than about men who're supposed to be friends. Of course, none of that means anything right now. But I hope it will."

Armbruster nodded again, wondering what Knudson was driving at. But he would not press Knudson; he would allow his fellow lieutenant to proceed at his own pace.

"I noticed Heywood watching the house here every now and then," Knudson said flatly. "I should have said something to you, but . . ."

"That's over and done with, Hans. It can't be changed."

"Anyway, it seemed to me he was trying to find a pattern or something. Whatever he was trying to do, he decided that today was the day he was going to make his move against the half . . . Miss Martinez. I think he figured that you'd be tied up most of the day with court-martials, like we've all been so much lately. I saw him heading up here just after you went into the office. And I . . . I . . . followed him."

"Why?"

Knudson shrugged. "I'm not really certain. All I was sure of was that he was going to cause some deviltry. He knocked on the door, and when Miss Martinez answered, he shoved inside and kicked the door closed. I ran, and burst inside just as he was . . ." He looked embarrassed and stumbled to a halt.

"He was trying to rape me," Serafina said coolly. "I screamed. Then Lieutenant Knudson came in and pulled that animal off me."

"You did that?" Armbruster asked, surprised.

"Yes," Knudson said, smiling weakly. "I don't know who was more surprised, him or me. But he got up and knocked me clean through the door. That's when you came along. And a damn good thing, too."

"You did all that for a woman you hate?" Armbruster asked in surprise.

Knudson nodded and hung his head. Then he squared his shoulders and looked up again. "Like I said just a moment ago, Ed, I've been a damn fool. There's nothing wrong with Miss Martinez that I can see. I don't know how I could've held such hate in my heart for her simply because . . . because of her . . ." He clanked to a halt again. "Well, goddammit all, I just couldn't let that son of a bitch do what . . . what he was going to do to her."

Armbruster sat for a little, sipping his coffee and thinking. Then he looked up and over his shoulder. Serafina smiled at him and nodded. He patted one of her hands on his shoulder. "A man can always use friends, Hans. Especially a smart-ass first lieutenant who doesn't have many friends at Fort Defiance."

"As well as a dumb-ass first lieutenant who's turned his back on a friend for too long." He reached his hand tentatively across the table.

Armbruster smiled just a little, and even that hurt his face. But he shook hands with Knudson, who drained his coffee cup. Knudson looked relieved as he stood. "I guess I better get back to duty, whatever that's going to be today. Ed, Miss Martinez," he added, bobbing his head in their direction. Then he turned and headed for the door.

"Hans," Armbruster called. When Knudson stopped and looked back at him, Armbruster said, "Thanks." The word was simple, sincere.

Knudson nodded, smiled and headed out, feeling like a new man.

Armbruster entered Brooks's office and saluted.

Brooks returned it and then told him to sit. Brooks flipped Armbruster a cigar and lit one for himself. Once it was going, Brooks said, "You remember what I told you about what would happen if trouble arose over the woman, Lieutenant?"

"Yessir." Armbruster had dreaded coming here for this reason.

"The fights between your men and the others who were talking bad about your 'fair' lady, I could live with."

"You knew?" Armbruster asked, surprised.

Brooks nodded. "You're not the only one on the post who has people loyal to him, you know, Lieutenant."

"I suppose not," Armbruster said with a little regret in his voice.

"This, however, I cannot accept. Even if I agree with what you did to Heywood—and I do; as an aside, you won't be facing a court-martial over it—I can't let this go unpunished, as it were.''

"I don't figure there'll be any more trouble over this, Major," Armbruster said hopefully.

"That doesn't matter, Lieutenant. And you damn well know it." Brooks stared at the smoke curling from his cigar for some moments. "It reflects badly on me, and hurts my ability to command effectively."

Armbruster nodded. He hated this, but right now he could not argue it. For one thing, Brooks was right. For another, he was just too sore and tired. He and Serafina had talked about this possibility, since Armbruster had figured it likely, and, while both were reluctant to be parted, they knew better than to fight this particular battle.

"She'll be escorted off the post and back to Albuquerque. I think it best if she left first thing in the morning."

"Loco Squad and I will be her escort," Armbruster said flatly.

Brooks's hackles rose at the challenge, but then he calmed down. It was fitting that Armbruster be allowed to take Serafina back to her father in Albuquerque. He didn't like Armbruster having been so smug in saying he would do it, but no one else was around to hear it, and so it would do no harm.

"You'll be ready to leave in the morning, Lieutenant?" Brooks asked, pointing his cigar at Armbruster, indicating the bruises and such.

"I'd rather have a few days to recover, but . . . well, dammit, Major, to be frank, you've been a lot more understanding and have yielded to me a lot more than anyone would expect. I can't ask you to grant me more time to be with Serafina."

Brooks smiled. "I'll tell you what, though, Lieutenant, you and your men can have two weeks in Albuquerque when you get there. It's not much, maybe, but

it's about the best I can do under the circumstances."
He did not sound apologetic.

"That's more than fair, sir," Armbruster said. He
rose painfully and saluted.

{ 26 }

An irritated, rather heartbroken Lieutenant Armbruster rode back into Fort Defiance a little more than a month later. He and his men had taken their time in getting to Albuquerque, as Armbruster wanted to spend as much time as possible with Serafina. Then they had spent two weeks in Albuquerque, Armbruster quietly with Serafina and her father; his men raising hell in the *cantinas* and *casas de putas*. Then there was the relatively fast trip back, marred only by one storm that kept them holed up in a stand of junipers for most of a day.

Armbruster reported in to Brooks, which took less than two minutes, then rode to one of the stables behind officers' row. After leaving his horse with a soldier there, he stepped outside and stood for a little staring at the small house out back.

He wondered now if he had done the right thing down in Albuquerque when he had pledged his troth to Serafina Martinez. They would have to wait, he told her, until he could resign his commission—almost three years away. That had worried him most, since he wasn't sure Serafina would wait for him. She was young, beautiful, and moved through three different worlds, in two of which she was accepted.

"Of course I'll wait for you," Serafina said, surprised that he would even think otherwise. "Do you think me that kind of woman, to pledge myself to you and then go off with another man?"

"No," Armbruster said quietly. It was their last night together before Armbruster left to return to the fort, and they were naked, lying in Serafina's bed, holding each other close. Serafina's head rested on Armbruster's chest; he was stroking her hair. "It's just that I still can't believe that a woman who's got all your qualities would be in love with me."

"You have good qualities, too, my love." She smiled and ran a small hand across his chest under the blanket. "Besides, who can know the reasons of love? I love you, and that's all I need. You need not worry about me finding any other."

Armbruster had smiled then, as he smiled now in turning away from the house at the fort. He knew now that he had done right. He trudged through the chill, bright blue afternoon toward his quarters. His heart almost stopped when he heard something of a giggle when he entered the room. He scratched a match on the wall and lit the lantern on the wall just inside the door.

"Jesus goddamn . . . Get the hell out of here," he snapped angrily as he spotted a naked Alma Vickers in his bed.

The slovenly, fat laundress and wife of Private Don Vickers had the blanket pulled up to her chest in what she probably assumed was a demure manner. "But, Lieutenant," Alma said, her hoarse voice grating on Armbruster's ears, "don't you want me?"

Armbruster was revolted. "I'd rather copulate with my horse," he growled bluntly. "Now get the hell out of here."

"I could scream," Alma said with no pretense at coyness on her fleshy face.

Armbruster pulled out a pistol, cocked it and aimed it at the piggish woman. "Go ahead," he suggested. He frowned when he heard a snicker and a cut-off chuckle behind him. He turned and spotted Hans Knudson, who could no longer contain his laughter.

Knudson never really knew how close he came just then to being shot dead by Armbruster, who had to fight with all the willpower he could muster not to squeeze the trigger. "Got you again, goddammit," Knudson said, still laughing.

It took several moments—time in which Knudson began to doubt his sense in pulling this, or any other, prank—before Armbruster controlled himself enough to uncock his pistol and slide it back into the flap holster on his right hip.

"I'm sorry, Ed," Knudson said apologetically. "I thought that now that we were friends again, you wouldn't mind a little joke."

"It's not the joke, Hans; it's your timing that stinks." Armbruster turned. "I'll be back in five minutes, Mrs. Vickers. Be gone by then."

Knudson hesitated a moment, then followed Armbruster outside. "I really am sorry, Ed."

"I know." He stopped and looked at his friend. "When I was in Albuquerque, I asked Serafina to marry me," he said quietly. When Knudson had managed to control his surprise, Armbruster added simply, "It won't be for a few years yet. But I love her." He shrugged, indicating that there was nothing he could do about the situation. "I don't expect you or any of the others here to understand that. I'm not even sure I'd want your understanding. I know what everyone thinks of her. But I don't really give a damn."

"It's not that . . ."

Armbruster overrode Knudson. "She's been on my mind since I left her. Then I walk into my quarters and you have that pig waiting for me in there. Christ, Hans, how could you have put that thing in there?"

Knudson still thought it funny, but he was torn between the humor and his feelings of guilt. He had not meant to insult Armbruster, but that's the way it had turned out. "There's a few reasons I had her do it. For one, she was the only one I'd figured would go whole hog into it. For another, I figured you'd know as soon as you saw her that I had a hand in it. I hate to tell you this, but the other reason is that she's got a powerful hankering for you." He couldn't help himself, and he started chuckling again. "God help you," he added, breaking into laughter.

Armbruster wanted to strangle Knudson, but the humor of the situation finally got to him, and he laughed, too. "You're going to put me in my grave with these goddamn pranks, you foolish little bastard."

"Then I'd have to find another victim."

Winter took its own sweet time in leaving, and the longer it lasted, the more irritated Armbruster grew. He was tired of sitting around the fort, and looked forward to getting back to patrolling. He also wanted to see Serafina again. When he had left Albuquerque, they had arranged for her to be here for a week before leaving with her father to go trading. Armbruster had tried to talk Martinez into leaving her in Albuquerque instead of continuing to risk her life on trading expeditions, but neither Martinez nor Serafina herself would hear of such a thing.

The Martinezes arrived late in April, much to Armbruster's relief. Leaving Sergeant Cavannaugh and Corporal Bauer to run the Loco Squad for most of the time, Armbruster spent almost the entire week in the small house with Serafina. Their feelings for each other had not lessened over the lonely winter, something each had feared, but never expressed.

Armbruster got permission from Major Brooks to have the Loco Squad escort Martinez and Serafina to their first stop on their trading jaunt. In light of that, Martinez decided that he would stop first at Nazlini Creek, out beyond Rock Mesa. It was a fairly sizable journey, and would keep Armbruster with Serafina for close to another week.

Then the Loco Squad went off in its own direction. Bolder now, and knowing something of the Navajo language, Armbruster occasionally stopped in an encampment of Navajos, trying to build goodwill when he could. If not he wanted to instill in them fear of the *Escuadra de Diablo*—The Devil's Squad—as the men had learned at the village on Nazlini Creek that the Navajos had begun calling them.

It seemed to be working, too, they realized after two months, since they had far fewer skirmishes than they had the year before, at least with the Navajos. The Jicarilla Apaches, on the other hand, held no goodwill toward or fear of anyone, and they continued to raid in the area, oftentimes hitting Navajo sheep or horse herds.

Such raiding kept Armbruster and his men occupied enough, but they still made a foray back to the fort on occasion to lay in supplies and to see how things were going there. For the most part, the fort was calm. Only occasionally did a passing band of Navajos or Apaches raise a state of alarm. Until July.

Armbruster and his troop had pulled in and taken two days to rest. Armbruster was shaving, preparing to leave again the next day when he heard a commotion —a scream, several yells, and then some gunfire—out near the officers' mess.

Shirtless and with shaving soap all over his face, Armbruster grabbed a pistol and charged outside his quarters and around back. He saw several soldiers firing at a fleeing figure. There was nothing he could add to the disturbance, so he shoved his pistol into his waistband. He saw a boot lying on the ground around the corner of the officers' mess, and with sinking heart he walked slowly there.

He knelt, knowing before he did so that Jobo, Brooks's thirteen-year-old black houseboy, was dead. Though Jobo was but a slave, Brooks seemed to exhibit a certain fondness for the boy, enough so that there were rumors that he was actually the youth's father.

Armbruster rose and turned. Old Bessie, Jobo's grandmother, stood there in shock, mouth agape, hands clenched tightly on her thin breasts. "Get someone to come carry Jobo away, Bessie," Armbruster said quietly. "Now!" he snapped when she did not move right away.

Brooks trotted up, winded, and stopped. Rage coursed across his seamed face. "Lieutenant Armbruster, get a burial detail up," he commanded. "Volunteers only. We'll bury Jobo out behind the house back there." His voice was full of pain and anger.

"Yessir," Armbruster said, saluting. "You go on back to your office now, sir. I'll send someone for you when things're ready."

Brooks nodded and left. Armbruster looked at Bessie. "Do what I told you, Bessie," he said quietly. "Bring him into the kitchen for now, till our work's done. If he's got any decent clothes, maybe you and some of the others'll fix him up."

Bessie finally nodded and moved.

Armbruster turned. "You men get him?" he asked. When they all shook their heads, he asked, "You see who it was?"

"A Navajo they call Poquito," a man said. "He's around the fort a lot."

Armbruster nodded. "All right, all you folks get the hell away from here. There's nothing more for you to see here." He spotted Bauer. "Corporal, bring the Squad here, on the double."

Within moments Armbruster was standing alone. Then Bessie and two black men arrived, lifted Jobo's body and carried it off. Soon after, his men got there. "I need four men as a burial squad." He held up his hand as everyone began volunteering. "Before you speak up, I have to tell you that this is for Jobo."

"The major's black boy?" Private Ike Skidmore asked, disbelief that they would be asked to so such a thing in his voice.

Armbruster nodded. "I'm looking for volunteers. None of you want to do this, I'll understand. Then I'll go to the other men of B Company, or to the other companies. I'm not forcing anyone into this."

The men muttered amongst themselves for a while, before Private Klaus Nesselroad stepped forward. "What the hell, Lieutenant, if I can put up with this rabble," he said, indicating his fellow soldiers, "I don't see why I can't lay to rest one goddamn black skin."

Sergeant Cavannaugh and Corporal Bauer stepped forward.

"I'd rather have lesser ranking men than you two," Armbruster said, "but you're welcome to it, if we don't get any other volunteers."

"Hell, Lieutenant, I can throw in," Private Oliver Carlton said.

"Me, too," Private Claude Bates offered, stepping forward.

Armbruster nodded. "Looks like you're off the hook, Sergeant," Armbruster said. "Corporal Bauer, you're in charge of the detail. The major wants Jobo buried up behind the house. Find yourself a suitable spot for it and then get to digging. Old Bessie's preparing Jobo for his departure. When things're all prepared, one of you come get me, someone else get Major Brooks. Dismissed."

Armbruster went back to his quarters and finished shaving, having to resoap his face to do so. Then he dressed. Unable to just sit and do nothing, he headed toward the house. The men had taken off their shirts and were about halfway through with digging the grave. They were taking turns, two men digging for five minutes, two resting, and then switching off.

Armbruster paced while his men finished their work. It did not take long with four men working at it. As they were pulling on their shirts again, be said, "Private Bates, hurry to Major Brooks's and tell him we're ready here. Private Carlton, go tell Old Bessie we're set. *Pronto*. Then get your asses back here. There's more work to be done."

It wasn't much of a funeral ceremony. It was attended only by Brooks; Brooks's wife; Bessie and the five other slaves at the fort with their masters; Lieutenants Armbruster and Knudson, the latter who had come up quietly behind everyone; and the four grave diggers.

Jobo was laid in the grave, Brooks said a prayer and gave an abbreviated eulogy. Then one of the salves, Agamemnon, said some things in a language none of the whites understood. Finally Brooks nodded, and the four soldiers pitched dirt into the grave.

Brooks moved alongside Armbruster. "When this is finished, please report to me, Lieutenant."

"Yessir," Armbruster said, surprised.

As soon as the others left, the men removed their shirts once again and went to the burying with dispatch. Done with that, they piled some stones and wood on the grave.

When the soldiers were dressed, Armbruster looked around to make sure no one but Knudson was watching. He sidled over to Bauer and then reached into his uniform blouse. He extracted a small bottle of whiskey and handed it to Bauer. "For you and the others. Thanks for your help."

Bauer smiled a little, took the bottle and slid it away. "We'll enjoy it, sir." He turned and led his three companions toward the barracks.

Armbruster headed for Brooks's office. Knudson accompanied him as far as officers' row.

{27}

"I want the bastard who killed Jobo, Lieutenant," Brooks snarled.

"Yessir," Armbruster said, trying to make it sound noncommittal.

"Don't patronize me, Lieutenant," Brooks snapped. "I'm aware of the rumors about all this. I will say, though, that they are scurrilous enough that I won't dignify them with any response. It's enough to know that I'm enraged that someone would take some of my property."

"Yessir," Armbruster said flatly.

"Oh, hell, Lieutenant, loosen up. Have a seat."

Armbruster nodded and sat.

"Do you know who did it?" Brooks asked.

"One of the enlisted men said it was a Navajo named Poquito. He apparently comes around here a lot."

Brooks nodded. "I can't picture his face, but I know the name. From what I can remember, he's never caused any trouble before. I wonder what got into him."

Armbruster shrugged. "Could Jobo have caused some trouble with the Navajo, sir?"

He shook his head. "It's unlikely. Jobo was a quiet boy, and I've never known him to cause any trouble at all. It doesn't really matter, though. Jobo's dead, and Poquito must be made to pay for that."

"Yessir. But where do I come in?"

"I want you to go to Sarcillos Largos's camp. That's where Poquito is from. There or near about there. I want you to negotiate Poquito's surrender. Then bring him back here to be hanged good and proper."

"Why me?"

"Word of *el Escuadra de Diablo* is all over," Brooks said only a little sarcastically. "The fierceness of your troop is almost legendary already." There was more sarcasm in his voice this time.

"I'm overwhelmed, sir," Armbruster said in like tone.

Brooks nodded. "In all truth, Lieutenant, the Navajos know of your squad. It's one of the reasons things've been mostly quiet here, I figure. And so they probably will give you Poquito since they'd rather do that than fight you and your men. Or so I hope."

"What happens if they won't give him up?"

"Take him," Brooks said flatly.

Armbruster nodded. "How far do I go in negotiating the surrender with Sarcillos Largos?"

"Promise him anything you damn have to, Lieutenant. Once you get Poquito back here, I'll use my rank over you, as is my right, and do whatever I damn well want."

"I don't like it, sir," Armbruster said flatly. "That's going to make me look bad."

"I don't care."

"I do. My word's all I have sometimes."

"It won't be you going back on your word, Lieutenant. It'll be me overriding you."

"I'm not sure the Navajos'll get the distinction," Armbruster said, knowing he had no other choice.

"Then use your wit and your wiles, Lieutenant," Brooks snapped. "Just get the job done in any way you can. Obviously, I'd rather not start a full-fledged war. But this is one of those cases where I—we—cannot back down. Poquito isn't all that important himself. Neither is Jobo. But there's been talk out there of organized resistance."

"Organized?"

Brooks nodded. "The Navajos're clannish people, as you undoubtedly know. It's not unfeasible for them to join together to make war on us. Not that I think it's likely."

"But things've been plenty peaceful."

"It may be the calm before the storm, Lieutenant. I don't say it's so; only that it's possible. And I'm not about to back down on this and make it a reality if it is being considered."

"Yessir. When should I leave?"

"First thing in the morning." He had been tempted to send Armbruster and his troop out immediately, but that wouldn't accomplish much.

Armbruster entered Sarcillos Largos's hogan and sat across the fire from the Navajo. On his right was Sergeant Cavannaugh and on his left Private Rob Smith. The Tiwa, Chief, squatted just behind Armbruster. That would make it simple for him to lean over and translate into Armbruster's ear, if that became necessary. Corporal Bauer and the rest of the soldiers were in their own camp just outside the "village."

"Major Brooks, the soldier chief at the fort at Tséhootsooi—the Green Place Between the Rocks—is angry at the Diné. He is angry at one of the Diné in particular—Poquito."

"I know no one named that," Sarcillos Largos said evenly.

"I thought the Diné were honest people, ones who did not talk with the forked tongue like a snake," Armbruster said harshly. "Maybe I was wrong."

Sarcillos Largos would not look Armbruster in the eyes. Armbruster had thought that odd about Navajos at first. He thought it indicated a lack of respect. But Serafina had taught him it was the opposite. Navajos thought it an insult to look into another person's eyes.

Sarcillos Largos nodded. "The Diné are honest," he insisted.

"Honest men do not lie to one another," Armbruster pressed. "I know Poquito from his many visits to the fort. I know he lives here, or close to here. You can't lie and tell me you don't know of him."

Both men were speaking in Navajo, Spanish and some English, with Chief filling in the gaps when necessary.

"Ah, Poquito," Sarcillos Largos said with a nod. "Sí, I know him." He shrugged, face impassive. "The trouble when one man does not know another's language or way of speaking very well."

Armbruster grunted an acknowledgment. He knew Sarcillos Largos had understood him well enough; Armbruster could not mispronounce a name as easy as Poquito. Still, the Navajo had admitted—more or less —that he was wrong. Armbruster would let the matter drop.

"Why does the soldier chief want Poquito?"

"Poquito killed one of the people at the fort. A black-skinned boy who was important to the soldier chief."

"Poquito wouldn't do such a thing," Sarcillos Largos responded. "You know what his name means?"

"Something so small it's shy."

Sarcillos Largos dipped his head. "He was named that for a reason. And he would not kill someone. Not just outright like that. He must've had a reason."

Armbruster shrugged. "The reason doesn't matter. He killed an unarmed boy—only thirteen years old.

Now he must pay for it. Major Brooks will have it no other way."

"I can't give up one of my people to have him put in your jail."

"He's going to hang," Armbruster said flatly. "And if he comes willingly, he'll be the only one to die."

"You'll make war against the Diné over such a small reason?"

"Yes," Armbruster said harshly. "You know who I am, and you know about my men. We are devils, and we will sweep down on your people until this part of Dinétah is clean of Diné."

"There are many Diné, and only a few of *El Escuadra de Diablo.*"

"But a few of my devils are equal to many Diné," Armbruster said, every bit as arrogantly as Sarcillos Largos had spoken.

Cavannaugh and Private Smith shuffled uneasily. They could understand enough of what was being said to know of the boasts. While the Navajos did not live in villages really, there were several hogans gathered at this place, and more not far away down the small canyon. There were more than enough Navajo warriors in and around this hogan to take care of the three whites —and Chief—with little effort.

Sarcillos Largos did not look happy, but he knew the ferocity of this group of white men. He could kill the leader of those devils, and the others with him in the hogan, but that still left a dozen or so of the devils out in their own camp,. And with the death of their leader, they would be angry devils indeed. Still, it was not in his nature to give up one of his men to be hanged for killing an invader of Dinétah.

"How can I trust you? Or your soldier chief?" Sarcillos Largos suddenly asked. "I've never dealt with you before, and the soldier chief has lied to me."

"About what?"

"Earlier in the summer, soldiers killed some of Manuelito's cattle. The soldier chief said he would punish them, and make them pay restitution for the missing cattle. None has been punished. And none has made restitution."

Armbruster swore inwardly. He hated being put in a spot like this. He wished men were not so easily given to making promises they had no intention of keeping. He also disliked lying, but he was going to have to do so now. "The men were punished. I saw it with my own eyes," he said evenly, hoping that neither Cavannaugh nor Smith would give his lie away. "As for the restitution, I don't know. I'll ask the soldier chief when I get back."

Sarcillos Largos was still displeased, but it looked like he had little choice. What he needed was some time to think, to devise a plan. "I need time to discuss these things with my old men," he said.

Armbruster couldn't get back to the fort before dark, and he had planned to stay the night out here somewhere anyway. He didn't like camping so close to this many Navajos, but with his men alert, there should be no trouble. He nodded. "But let me warn you, Sarcillos Largos, that if you try to get Poquito out of here during the night, we'll hunt him down no matter how long it takes. And in the meantime, I'll take you back to Fort Defiance to pay for the death there."

Sarcillos Largos's face betrayed nothing of the anger that surged through him. He wanted to kill this white soldier, and then throw the body into a bottomless chasm where it would not attract witches and skinwalkers. He simply nodded. "Come back when the new day begins."

The men of the Devil's Squad had an uneasy night, though nothing untoward happened. Just after dawn,

Armbruster entered Sarcillos Largos's hogan again. "Well?" he demanded without preliminary.

Sarcillos Largos was amazed at how a white man could disrupt *hozho*—harmony—just by appearing. He decided that he would have to have a medicine man perform a sacred ceremony to restore his *hozho*, as soon as the white men were gotten rid of from here.

"We would like to deal with this situation," Sarcillos Largos said.

"How?"

"We will hang Poquito."

"You think I'll believe that?" Armbruster demanded. "You think I'm a fool?"

"No," Sarcillos Largos said hastily, trying to seem apologetic. "We will bring Poquito there—to the fort. We will hang him there in front of your soldier chief and all the others."

Armbruster thought that over for a few minutes. Based on what he knew about the Navajos, it seemed a highly unusual thing for them to propose. Maybe their fear of the dead was somehow lessened by performing the execution themselves, he thought. Perhaps there was some kind of religious rite they could do for him if they were present.

He decided it sounded like a good idea. His main problem now would be to convince Brooks of it. He nodded. "I'll take your words back to the soldier chief. It is for him to decide. I'll return tomorrow, in the afternoon, with my answer."

Brooks was not as difficult to convince as he had suspected it would be. "Look, Major," Armbruster said, "it'll save a heap of grief to do it this way."

"How's that?"

"We don't really want to go to war with the entire Navajo Nation over a slave boy, do we, Major?"

"Well, no, I suppose not."

"Well, that's just what's going to happen if we try to

take Poquito out of that village. You let them come here and hang Poquito for us and everybody'll be happy, more or less. You'll have your justice, and the Navajos won't be insulted."

"What happens if they've taken off? Or if they say they'll be here on such and such a day and then they take off?"

"Then I'll lead the Loco Squad personally and hunt them down. I also told Sarcillos Largos that if he spirited Poquito out of his camp when we left that I'd bring him in himself to hang for the crime."

Brooks almost grinned. "Well, that's something anyway. But they could've taken off as a unit."

"I suppose that's true, sir. But my men and I have something of a reputation now among the Navajos, and I think Sarcillos Largos believed me when I told him I'd find him—and Poquito—no matter where they ran. I think we're safe in this, sir."

"We better be." Brooks rubbed his weary face. He could not remember being this tired, and he had a fleeting thought of retiring soon and heading east to spend the rest of his days in a rocking chair on a wide porch. He pushed the thoughts away. "All right, Lieutenant," he said, "tell them I approve. But you better make sure they know I'll brook no horseshit with this. I want it done, and I want it done soon."

"Yessir."

Once more Armbruster and his men made the ride out to Sarcillos Largos's village, where Armbruster gave the Navajo Brooks's agreement—and warning. He ended with, "The hanging will be in three days. If you're not at the fort by then, we'll be coming for you straight off."

"I'll be there," Sarcillos Largos promised.

{ 28 }

The fort turned out en masse, lining up in a U around the east, west and south edges of the parade ground to watch the solemn procession of Navajos enter on horseback from the north. The Navajos—only about twenty of them—stopped at a simple gallows the soldiers had hastily made.

They made a great show of presenting a bound, gagged prisoner in a circle for all to see, though no one was too close. Sarcillos Largos had insisted that no one come too close; that it was bad enough they had to execute one of the Diné themselves, without having white men gawk too closely at the prisoner.

"The only other thing Sarcillos Largos asked, Major, is that we allow them time to leave the fort before we go pulling the body down."

"What in hell for?"

Armbruster shrugged. "Sarcillos Largos didn't say, but I assume it's because of the Navajos' fear of the dead."

"I suppose you're right." Brooks paused. "Well, I guess I can't quibble with that. What the hell, maybe leaving the body up there an hour or so might serve to keep other Navajos from causing trouble."

"It might."

So now the troops of Fort Defiance—the ones who were not out on patrol—were standing around watching as the Navajos made a little show of their kinsman.

The Navajos helped Poquito onto a small wagon, and two men got up there with him. One of the Navajos placed the noose from the gallows around Poquito's neck and made sure it was tight. Then he and his companion jumped off the wagon.

Moments later, Sarcillos Largos himself swatted the horse hitched to the wagon. The horse bolted, pulling the wagon out from under Poquito, where he jerked and twitched.

The horse got only a few yards before several Navajos caught it and stopped it. Then the Navajos were on their ponies and trotting away from the fort, leaving the wagon behind.

Brooks dismissed the men—except for Armbruster's troop, which was to stand guard, at a respectable though not too great distance, over Poquito's dangling corpse.

Just over an hour later, Armbruster had Privates Kapp and Bates bring the wagon up under the body. "All right, Private Krieger, you and Private Pettet climb on up there and cut the poor bastard down," Armbruster said. He remained beside the wagon to monitor the event.

"Goddamn!" Armbruster exploded as soon as Krieger and Pettet had the body laid out, faceup, on the wagon.

"What's wrong, sir?" Pettet asked, nervous.

"This isn't Poquito," Armbruster snapped.

"You sure, sir?" Krieger asked.

"Yes, dammit."

"I thought you didn't know Poquito, sir," Cavannaugh said. He had come running up at Armbruster's original bellow.

"I don't, but I know this isn't him." He pointed to the corpse.

"How do you know that?" Cavannaugh asked.

"Because this," he snarled, stabbing the body with a finger, "is a goddamn Mexican, not a goddamn Navajo. That's why I'm damn sure."

Cavannaugh looked at the body. "Damn, Lieutenant, you're right. That sure as hell don't look like any Navajo I ever saw."

"Besides, dammit, I saw this son of a bitch in Sarcillos Largos's village. He's one of that bastard's Mexican slaves."

"Jesus, Lieutenant, that Sarcillos Largos is some sneaky son of a bitch, ain't he?" Cavannaugh commented.

"Damn those bastards!" Armbruster snapped. He was enraged at being the butt of the Navajos' joke. "Sergeant," he added with angry urgency, "get the men saddled and ready. I want to pull out in an hour."

"I don't think that's wise, sir," Cavannaugh said cautiously.

"I don't give a good goddamn what you think, Sergeant," Armbruster snapped. "You just do what I tell you. If you don't, I'll promote someone else who will."

"Lieutenant," Cavannaugh said flatly, "I've been threatened by everything from a shave-tail son of a bitch like you was not so long ago to a full goddamn colonel. But I ain't about to take no orders from a man I respect but who's lost his reason for a few moments."

"So," Armbruster said angrily, "you think I've lost my reason, do you? Well, I have something to tell you, Sergeant."

"Let me finish, sir. After that, if you want to bust me back to private and promote Corporal Bauer in my place, then so be it."

Armbruster controlled his temper. "Speak your piece, Sergeant," he said tightly.

"Yessir. First, let me ask, what's the big deal with findin' out this ain't Poquito?"

"They played me for a fool, dammit."

"Beggin' your pardon, sir, but, so?"

"So, I've been made to look like an idiot. The Navajos know it, and they'll try it again. It makes me an easy mark for them."

"That might be, sir—once. They'll know soon enough you're on to 'em. But really, Lieutenant, do you want to start a war over hurt pride?"

"No," Armbruster grudgingly admitted. "But what about Major Brooks?"

"What about him, sir?"

"Once he finds out I've had the wool pulled over my eyes by those damn Navajos, he won't trust me anymore. And that, Sergeant, means we may well lose the Loco Squad."

"How's he going to find out, sir?"

"What's that, Sergeant?"

"How's he going to find out, sir?"

"Well, he'll . . ." Armbruster stopped, thinking. "He doesn't know what Poquito looks like, do you think, Sergeant?"

"Does it really matter, sir? We bury this body here and unless the major knows Poquito real well and Poquito shows his face here again, the major'll never know."

"And," Armbruster said, warming to the thoughts a little, "if Sarcillos Largos is as smart as I think he is, he'll have told Poquito to hightail for the far parts of Dinétah. I doubt we'll be seeing that young buck again."

"Right, sir." Cavannaugh paused. "One more thing, Lieutenant. I think that as soon as we head out on our next patrol, we ought to stop by Sarcillos Largos's village and let him know we're on to his trickery. At the same time, you can tell him that if he was stupid enough to allow Poquito to stay anywhere within a hundred miles of the fort, that he had better change his mind or we'll get him."

"Talk about a devious son of a bitch," Armbruster said with a grudging smile.

"It's a talent I have, sir."

Armbruster nodded. "All right, Sergeant, let's get this poor bastard buried."

There was no need to warn the rest of the Loco Squad to keep quiet about the deception, and Armbruster had little worry that anyone else at the fort would catch on. Most of the soldiers, even if they had met with Poquito close up, wouldn't know him anyway. They tended to not see people they felt were inferior, like Indians—or Mexicans.

They buried the Mexican off the fort property in a grave they covered with rocks. Not only did Armbruster want to discourage animals from disinterring the corpse, he also wanted to make sure no person dug it up.

Two hours later, Armbruster strode into Brooks's office. He was nervous, but thought he was hiding it well. "All done, sir," he said evenly. "Poquito's buried and I have some men from B Company taking down the gallows." He hoped he didn't stumble over Poquito's name when he said it.

"That was some spectacle, wasn't it, Lieutenant?" Brooks said.

"Yessir," Armbruster said noncommittally.

"No hitches in anything?"

"No, sir."

"Good, good."

"Would you object if me and the Loco Squad were to pull out again tomorrow, sir?"

"Eager to be on the prowl again, eh, Lieutenant?" Brooks asked. He seemed in great humor.

"Yessir."

"Well, then, go to it, Lieutenant. And go safely."

"Thank you, sir."

Though Armbruster relaxed considerably after leaving Brooks's office, he still was a little tense until after he had been gone from the fort for two days. By then he figured that if Brooks found out about the deception, he would not be able to send anyone out for him. And by the time he got back to the fort, it should have blown over.

The troop pulled into Sarcillos Largos's small community not long after the Navajos had. Sarcillos Largos was surprised to see them, but covered it well as he asked, "What do you want here now, Lieutenant?"

"That was some trick you pulled on us, Sarcillos Largos," Armbruster said flatly. "No wonder you wanted to do it yourself, and didn't want anyone getting too close. But you've been found out."

"I don't know what you're talking about, Lieutenant."

"Horseshit. We talked about truth and honesty before, Sarcillos Largos." He smiled. "I was angry when I learned I had been deceived. But on the ride out here, I've come to appreciate the macabre humor of what happened."

Sarcillos Largos ventured a smile. "I thought it would be humorous," he said quietly.

"It was. But a warning," Armbruster said. "Don't try such a thing again. At least not with me. And one other thing: If Poquito's still around here, tell him to move far away."

Sarcillos Largos smiled again. "He's been gone since the last time you were here."

The troop was kept busy—chasing, but doing little fighting. There were always reports of trouble somewhere else. Armbruster liked to think the trouble was always elsewhere because of the reputation his men had among the Navajos.

As they had the year before, they showed up at the fort again every once in a while, and once they rode down to Albuquerque for a spree of debauchery.

Their arrival at the fort in mid-June brought their biggest surprise, though. As they were trotting across the parade ground, they suddenly spotted creatures unlike anything they had ever seen before. And if they were surprised, their horses went crazy.

"Jesus, Lieutenant!" Cavannaugh shouted. "What the hell're they?" He was fighting his horse, as were all the other men of the troop.

"Don't know," Armbruster squawked as he tried to get control of his animal.

The men finally got to the stables, and turned their horses over to the soldiers on duty there. To a man they headed for the parade ground, eager to find out what the large, ugly creatures were, but yet a little frightened of the strange beasts.

Armbruster spotted Knudson and he gravitated toward him. They greeted each other, as Armbruster's men grouped up behind the two officers, wanting to be sure they heard everything.

"All right, Hans," Armbruster asked as soon as he and Armbruster had said hello, "just what the hell are those ungainly monstrosities?" He pointed to the beasts.

"They're camels," Knudson said with authority.

"Is this another one of your stupid pranks?" Armbruster asked skeptically.

"Oh, come on, Ed," Knudson said with a laugh. "How would I be able to set something like this up?"

"I'll be damned if I know, but I suspect you're right this time. What're they doing here?"

"A guy named Ed Beale came with them. They're desert animals. From what Beale says, they can go for days and days without water. And they can subsist on what scrubby brush is out here, even greasewood."

"That'd come in handy," Armbruster said thoughtfully. "Horses and mules suffer something awful out here from the lack of water and decent forage."

"That was the army's thinking. Beale says they started this experiment down in Texas a year or so ago. Beale's here to plot a road from the fort here all the way to California, using the camels. Beale calls it the Camel Road."

"He use those . . . camels, did you call them? . . . for packing? It sure doesn't look like anybody can ride them."

"Beale rides them. He's got a couple of real foreigners—fellows from Turkey land or Persia or something—who ride them with ease."

"You ain't gonna get me on one of those goddamn things," Private Arnie Kapp muttered, drawing forth a laugh from his companions.

"When's he leaving?" Armbruster asked.

"Day after tomorrow."

Armbruster laughed a little. "If they didn't spook my horse, I might like riding along for a while. Those goddamn things're bound to scare the living shit out of the Navajos."

{ 29 }

Fall began to edge into Dinétah, and Armbruster turned his men for the fort, for what should be the last time from a patrol that year. He was planning on one more trip—down to Albuquerque, with Serafina and Martinez. That was the major reason he was eager to get back now: Serafina should be arriving soon, too. It was already early September, and winter would not be long in coming.

He also rode to the fort with a little trepidation. Knudson would be expecting him, and more than likely would have thought up some annoying prank. Still, the anticipation of spending a little time with Serafina overrode his expectation of one of Knudson's pranks.

He entered his quarters warily, expecting . . . he didn't know what. Knudson had been at it again, he found out when he lit the lantern. He grinned a little when he saw the pile of bones neatly arranged in his bed, capped with a horse's skull on his thin pillow.

"Gee, Ed," Knudson said, poking his head in the door, "you sure you want to take up with a sack of bones like that?"

"One of these days I'm going to get you back for all these pranks, Hans," Armbruster said with a laugh.

Knudson helped him clean up the mess, and the next day Armbruster fell back into the dull routine of the fort. He noticed that more Navajos were coming and going these days, and that the men still out on patrol were reporting more raiding than ever before by the Navajos.

Five days after he got back to the fort, Serafina and Martinez arrived. Armbruster was antsy the rest of the day, waiting for the Martinezes to get settled in. He worried that the long summer had changed Serafina's mind about him. He was one happy man when he learned that such a fear was unfounded.

Serafina was overjoyed when Armbruster came to the house that afternoon, and she practically bubbled as she prepared supper. She found it hard not to just drag Armbruster into her back bedroom the first minute she saw him. She, too, had been afraid on the journey to Fort Defiance that Armbruster might have decided that he did not want her any longer. But she could see at first glance that he still loved her.

They spent a week together, reveling in each other's company, even if it all was behind the closed doors of the small house. They ventured out only rarely, not wanting to cause any more trouble at the fort, and when they did go out, it was generally at night, trying to catch a cool breeze tinged with the soon-to-arrive autumn.

Armbruster once again got Brooks's permission to escort Martinez and his daughter to Albuquerque, where the men of the Loco Squad had themselves a ten-day spree.

When Armbruster and his men arrived back at the fort, it was into October. The air was frosty at night and in the mornings, though the days were still warm enough as often as not.

Before Armbruster could even go to his quarters to

freshen up, a B Company private came to tell him that Major Brooks wanted to see him immediately.

"Shit," Armbruster muttered. He slapped some dust off his hat, blue wool pants and fringed buckskin coat as he hurried toward Brooks's office. Captains Ambrose Gilmore and Josiah Goodwin were there, as were Lieutenants Knudson, Frank Saxbury and Andy Emerson.

There was also an officer Armbruster had never seen before. When he saw the officer's rank of lieutenant colonel, he was a little worried, thinking that perhaps Brooks was being replaced. Brooks might not have been the best commanding officer a man could ask for, but he had been more than fair with Armbruster, who appreciated that.

"Sit, Lieutenant," Brooks said without preliminary. When Armbruster did, Brooks pointed to the officer Armbruster did not know and said in a neutral voice, "Lieutenant, this is Lieutenant Colonel Dixon Stansbury Miles of the Third Infantry. He is here to conduct a fall campaign against the Navajos. Colonel, Lieutenant Edward Armbruster."

Armbruster stood and saluted, surprising Miles a little. The colonel returned it and Armbruster sat again.

"You're the one in charge of the bunch called the Loco Squad, are you not, Lieutenant?" Miles asked noncommittally.

"Yessir," Armbruster said proudly.

"You and your men have some reputation. We've heard of you at Fort Marcy and even farther east."

"Yessir." Armbruster didn't know what else to say.

"Some of the other officers here," Miles said with a vague wave of the hand to encompass Armbruster's fellow officers, "think that this Loco Squad is overrated and causes more trouble than it solves."

Armbruster hesitated only a moment, just long enough to decide to throw caution to the wind. He figured he had little to lose. If Miles liked his feistiness, the Loco Squad would go on. If Miles thought him a troublemaker, the worst he could do would be to run him out of the army. At the moment, Armbruster didn't think that was such a bad idea, since it would allow him to marry Serafina all that much sooner.

"That's because some of my fellow officers are chickenshits, Colonel."

Knudson stifled a chuckle, as Miles's eyes raised. Then the colonel smiled a little. "So, Lieutenant, you think your men make an effective fighting force?"

"Yessir. The best you'll find in Dinétah."

"Dinny-what?"

"Dinétah. The land of the Navajos. The Navajos call themselves Diné. It means The People. Dinétah is the land of The People."

"Hmmm," Miles said. "Yes, now I recall—you're affiliated with the Navajos, aren't you?"

"No, sir," Armbruster said flatly.

"But Captain Gilmore said—"

"Captain Gilmore doesn't know his ass from his hat," Armbruster said evenly, looking steadily at Gilmore. "Sir." He turned to look at Miles. "I have a . . . shall I say a friendship . . . with a woman who's half-Navajo. She has taught me a little—very little, actually—about their ways. She has also taught me a small amount of the Diné tongue, something that's come in handy a time or two. Sir." The last word was tacked on, almost as an afterthought.

"I see," Miles said in a musing tone. He paused, then, "So, Lieutenant, do you think you and your men are objective enough as a unit to do battle with the Navajos? Some here think it'd be better to break up your little group and absorb you and your men back into the lines of B Company."

"Sir, I said much the same to Major Brooks some time ago as I'm about to say to you. As commander of the Third Infantry, you have the right and power to disband the Loco Squad. But, as I said to Major Brooks, you'd be a damn fool if you did it.''

Miles let loose a loud, hoarse laugh. "The major told me you'd say something like that," he said, when the laughs had dwindled. "Well, Lieutenant, from what Major Brooks told me, from the reputation your men have, and from seeing what pusillanimous creatures some of your fellow officers are, I tend to agree with you. In fact, Lieutenant, you and the Loco Squad will lead the charge when we make our assault on the first Navajo stronghold we find."

"Which will be?" Armbruster asked warily.

"I hear a fellow named Manuelito has a village some thirty miles from here. Is that right?"

"That's where he and some of his clan winter, yessir. It's southwest of here, at a place called Kinlichíi. It means 'Red Pueblo.' It's along Pueblo Colorado Wash."

"They live in pueblos?" Miles asked, surprised.

"No, sir. But there's pueblos all over Dinétah. Damn near every one of them is abandoned. They seem to have been there forever. The Navajos say they are the former homes of a people the Navajos call the Ancient Ones, a people who vanished many, many years ago." Armbruster shrugged. "At least that's the best I can understand it."

"Interesting," Miles said.

Armbruster was not sure if the colonel was serious or not, so he said nothing.

"When can you be ready to ride, Lieutenant?" Miles asked.

"Morning, if necessary, sir. The day after'd be preferable, though. My men can use a little rest."

"Understandable, Lieutenant. But you seem reluctant."

"I am, sir, a little. Making war on women and children doesn't set with me very well."

Miles cast an angry glance at Gilmore, who had snickered at Armbruster's statement. Then Miles looked back at Armbruster. "To tell you the truth, Lieutenant, I'm not very fond of attacking a village where there's women and children about, but we have no choice. We've had reports of Manuelito raiding frequently and in many spots." He almost grinned. "Seems he keeps away from wherever you are at any given time, Lieutenant." He sighed. "We've also had word that he and a Navajo chieftain named Huero are planning a lot more deviltry for the spring."

"Yessir." Armbruster still didn't like it, but he knew it was necessary. "My men and I'll be ready."

Miles nodded. "So it shall be, gentlemen," he added. "Now, where can a thirsty man find a drink around here?"

"You don't have to go far, sir," Brooks said as he pulled a bottle of Scotch whiskey out of his desk and set it on top.

Companies B, C, E and G, plus the Loco Squad made camp less than two miles from where Manuelito's village was. It was late in the afternoon, and darkness was less than an hour off. Lieutenant Colonel Miles wanted plenty of daylight in his attack on Manuelito's village, so he had called a halt for the day.

The men were up, had eaten and were saddling their horses by the time dawn broke. Then they pulled out, riding slowly, making an effort to keep the noise down. Less than half an hour later, they pulled up beneath a barren, rocky ridge.

Armbruster dismounted. With hand signals, he motioned for Private Ike Skidmore and Frank Pettet to head up the ridge and check out the camp. The two men slung their rifles across their backs and cautiously moved up the ridge.

"Think they'll ever make it to the top, Lieutenant?" Gilmore asked *sotto voce*, from just behind Armbruster.

Without looking at the captain, Armbruster said over his shoulder, "Use your goddamn head for something other than a place to keep your hat for once, Captain. My boys go running up there, they'd knock all kinds of rocks and shit loose. Those, in turn, would tumble down the ridge, kicking up more rocks as well as dust. By the time all that garbage hit the flat down here, the horses'd be spooked. Between the noise they'd make and the dust rising, the Navajos'd know we were here."

"I thought you liked to fight Indians," Gilmore said tightly.

"I don't know where you got that cockamamie notion," Armbruster responded, still not looking at Gilmore.

"And you have the gall to say the rest of us're too scared to fight Indians?" Gilmore said, face livid.

"Big difference between being afraid to fight Indians and not liking fighting Indians. I'm not afraid of fighting them anywhere, anytime. I don't have to get any pleasure out of it, though."

"So if you're not afraid of fighting them, why're you so worried about them finding out we're here?" Gilmore asked smugly.

Armbruster finally turned to look at Gilmore, stabbing him with a baleful glare. "Good Christ," Armbruster said in surprise, "you are a dumb bastard, aren't you?" He shook his head, wondering how Gilmore could have ever been promoted to captain. "If we lose the element of surprise, we'll lose more men. That what you want?"

"Well, no, but—"

"Shut your trap, Captain," Armbruster said harshly, turning away from him again.

"I'll do no such—"

"Shut your trap, Captain," Miles said flatly. "Lieutenant Armbruster's right."

Minutes later, Skidmore scrambled down the ridge as carefully as he had climbed it. Pettet stayed on the ridge, keeping watch.

"It don't look like the place's full, Lieutenant," Skidmore said. "A few hogans're empty, and there's not as many sheep and horses as there ought to be."

"Manuelito there?" Armbruster asked.

"His hogan looks occupied, sir."

Armbruster nodded and turned. "Your call, Colonel. We can go get them now," he said sourly. "Or we can wait till there's more of them."

"Might as well do it, Lieutenant. It's what we came here for. How shall we do it?"

"Where're the horses, Private?" Armbruster asked Skidmore.

"West side of the village, sir. In a makeshift corral. The sheep're a little farther west, with two boys watchin' over them."

Armbruster nodded. "All right, Colonel," he said, "have a few men creep around the camp there and get into position over by the sheep herd. When everythin's set, have them start shooting sheep."

"Shooting sheep?" Miles said, amused.

"There's two things that really matter to the Navajo, sir: sheep and horses. Somebody starts shooting their sheep, the Navajos're going to come running out of their hogans, leaving them open for attack."

"Makes sense," Miles acknowledged. "Anything else?"

"Send another small detachment toward the horses. As soon as the first bunch starts firing, have the second group stampede the horses."

"Then what?"

"Then me and my boys head over the ridge and do what needs doing, sir. Keep the rest of the men here, or nearby, just in case."

Miles nodded.

"Just one more thing, sir. I'd warn the men shooting at the sheep to watch where they're firing. We don't really need to go killing children."

Miles nodded again. He turned and began issuing orders to Gilmore and Goodwin.

❧❴ 30 ❵❧

"**I**'d like to go with Lieutenant Armbruster's men, Colonel, if I may," Knudson said, surprising just about everyone who heard.

"That suit you, Lieutenant?" Miles asked, turning to Armbruster.

"Could be sticky, sir. I'm used to commanding my own force."

"I'll have no problem following your orders, Ed," Knudson said.

"All right, Hans," Armbruster said with a small smile. "Best make sure your hat's on tight, though."

Knudson nodded. He shoved past an angry Captain Gilmore to get his horse.

Men were moving, two small detachments heading south to get around the ridge and then cross a small open space before moving along another ridge that would give them an open field of fire at the horses and sheep. One detachment was to move a little farther northwest along the second ridge to get near its end. That way they could move swiftly around it toward the horse corral.

All the rest of the men, except for Armbruster's troop, began moving horses and gear out of the way, checking rifles and preparing to wait, something they were all too familiar with. Skidmore went back up the ridge to tell Pettet the plan. The two would stay where they were to relay orders via mirrors or hand signals, and also to keep an eye on the overall battle, ready to throw more men at the Navajos, if needed.

Armbruster and his men moved north to come around the tapered end of the ridge. They would sweep around that edge, on the flat and straight into the camp.

Finally all was ready and everyone in position. Armbruster signaled to Lieutenant Colonel Miles that he and his men were ready. Miles nodded to Captain Goodwin, who signaled Skidmore on the ridge. Skidmore, in turn, tapped Pettet on the shoulder. Pettet caught the sun in his small hand mirror, flashing a signal across to the other ridge.

Moments later, gunfire broke out as soldiers began firing at sheep. Then the entire region erupted.

Armbruster led the charge toward the camp, spurring his horse hard, reins in his left hand, pistol in his right. His men were right behind him, spreading out some as they sped toward the village.

Across the village, Armbruster could see half a dozen soldiers riding hard from the other ridge toward the horses. Then the horses were loose and fleeing in all directions.

Navajos were streaming from their hogans, the men armed and shouting, the women herding children and old people in whichever direction they thought they might find safety.

Dust swirled around the village within moments, making it hard to see. Noise added to the wildness of the situation.

Armbruster and the Loco Squad were used to fighting in such conditions. Each man had enough sense not to fire indiscriminately, lest he kill one of his comrades. They were calm enough, too, in the heat of battle to not just fire at anything they saw moving. Whether the men agreed with it or not, Armbruster had a standing policy that women and children were to never be killed if it could be avoided at any cost other than the soldier's own death or that of a comrade.

"Halt!" Armbruster bellowed, trying to be heard over the cacophony. "Dismount!"

The dust was beginning to settle, making it easier to see. The Navajo horses were racing off in all directions, and the village seemed empty, except for three Navajo bodies—all males—lying around.

Armbruster tossed his reins to Private Claude Bates and he ran, bent over, into Manuelito's hogan. He found no one and he stepped back outside. All the gunfire had stopped. The men who had raided the horses stood around looking uncertain as to what to do next.

Armbruster was about to give some orders when the rattle of gunfire erupted again. One of the soldiers at the corral fell off his horse. Private Oliver Carlton, one of Armbruster's men, crumpled to the ground, the front of his uniform bright with new blood.

Armbruster did not have to give orders then. The men scrambled for the protection of the nearest hogan's log and dirt walls. "Anybody see where that firing's coming from?" Armbruster asked.

"The way Ollie went down, sir," Sergeant Cavannaugh called, "it's got to be comin' from the northwest. One of those two hogans yonder."

Armbruster edged around Manuelito's hogan as a few more shots rang out. The horse raiders were racing for the ridge, but another was shot before they made it. "Right you are, Sergeant," he said. "All right, Corporal Bauer, you and Arneson, Quinn and Nesselroad lay down a covering fire. Hans, you go with Sergeant Cavannaugh, and take Smith and Krieger with you. Head for that hogan toward the ridge there. And listen to Cavannaugh. I'll take Olson and Vickers with me and go for the hogan just to the north. Bates, you and Kapp move as many of the horses inside the hogan here as you can. Keep the other ones behind the walls. Everyone got it? Good. Now!''

As three men fired steadily and smoothly, the rest made their moves. Sweating and puffing, Armbruster pulled up behind another hogan, with Vickers and Olson half a step behind. Armbruster looked and saw that Knudson and his group had made it. The ones who had been shooting were hastily reloading.

Armbruster edged around the hogan toward the north. "Private Olson!" he shouted. "There's two Navajos in the doorway of a hogan to the west. You see them?"

Olson crept around the southern end of the hogan and stopped. "Yessir."

"You take the one to the south. I'll get the other."

"Yessir. Give me the word."

"On the count of three. One . . . two . . ."

Behind the hogan near the ridge, Knudson was peering around one of the shelter's roughly octagonal edges, trying to spot any Navajos still out there shooting at the soldiers. He saw Armbruster doing the same in the hogan almost directly west of him. Private Tom Olson was around the other side of Armbruster's hogan.

Knudson saw Private Don Vickers moving up slowly behind Armbruster, but he thought little of it—until he saw Vickers raise his pistol and aim it at the back of Armbruster's head.

Knudson's mouth went dry and his palms grew sweaty. He could not believe what he thought he was seeing, but if he was seeing it, he was the only one who could help Armbruster. He tried to yell, but that didn't work well. Warily he raised his cocked pistol and braced his arm on the hogan. Saying a quick, silent prayer, he squeezed off a shot.

The cloud of powder smoke obscured his vision for a moment, but when it cleared he saw Vickers on the ground and Armbruster turning toward Vickers in surprise.

". . . Three." Armbruster fired, but at the moment he did so, something, or someone fell into him, knocking his aim off. He got a fleeting glance of the man at the south side of the hogan's door go down. The other one slipped outside and ran hell-bent around the hogan.

"Shit," Armbruster muttered. Then he turned and saw what had hit him—Private Don Vickers. "What the hell?" he said aloud.

Vickers was still alive, but didn't appear to have much of a chance of surviving. Armbruster grabbed his shirt and hauled him around and into the hogan and dropped him. Back outside, things seemed quiet. "You see any more of them boys in the hogans, Sergeant?" he yelled.

"No, sir. I ain't sure, but I think they all skedaddled."

"Well, I'm not of a mood to sit here all day and wait to find out. Bates, Kapp, start bringing those horses to us."

When each man had his own horse and had his pistols reloaded, Armbruster said, "Mount up, men." Then they were trotting west—the only direction the fleeing Navajos could have gone—leaving a dying Vickers behind in the hogan.

They rode down on three Navajo warriors who had stopped behind a cracked pile of boulders and were firing arrows. Armbruster was winged in the left side by one; Bauer took one in the arm; and Private Emil Krieger was knocked off his horse by another.

Then Armbruster and his men were swarming around the Navajos' small haven, and before long the Navajos were dead to a man.

"We ride some more, Lieutenant?" Cavannaugh asked.

Armbruster shook his head. "No, Sergeant. I suppose whatever Navajos we could catch up to now would be women and children. We've got wounded to look after." The more Armbruster thought about the idea of this raid, the less he liked it. It was one thing to strike at a war party, a group of warriors anticipating battle and so wary. But to attack them when they were in their homes seemed wrong somehow to Armbruster. Especially when noncombatants could all too easily get caught in the crossfire. He turned his horse back toward the village.

Krieger was dead. The arrow had gone through a lung and he had choked to death in his own blood. Private Quinn broke off the arrow shaft, and then he and Private Nesselroad put his body across his horse. They and the rest of Armbruster's men gathered at Manuelito's hogan.

Within minutes, a jubilant Colonel Miles rode in with the rest of the soldiers. "Well done, men!" he crowed. "Well done!" Then he saw the blood on Armbruster's left side, along the middle ribs. "You're wounded, Lieutenant," he said. "Doctor! Surgeon. Quickly."

"It's nothing, sir," Armbruster said, managing to keep his composure. He repeated the statement when Captain Fournier, the post surgeon, hastened up.

Fournier took a quick look and pronounced Armbruster's diagnosis basically accurate. Then he asked, "Have you other wounded?"

"Yessir. It's too late for Private Krieger," he said, pointing to the body still lying across the horse. "Corporal Bauer's wounded, as is Private Vickers. He's by far the worst off. He's inside the hogan here."

Fournier nodded and headed for the hogan. Miles was occupied with talking to other men, and Armbruster used the opportunity to get away from the colonel. He checked each of his men, making sure they were all right. He ended with Knudson. "You have any troubles, Hans?" he asked.

"Not me, no."

Armbruster looked at him, a little surprised. "That supposed to mean something, Hans?"

Knudson jerked his head. "Let's get away from these people, Ed." When a puzzled Armbruster had followed Knudson a little away from the others, Knudson stopped and said, "I hate to say this, Ed, but I saw Vickers about ready to blow your brains out."

"That's ridiculous," Armbruster said.

"Is it?"

Armbruster wondered. Vickers had seemed a little sullen of late. But not enough to kill him, or so Armbruster had thought. Every man got a case of the sulks once in a while; it didn't usually lead them to kill people. Still, Armbruster had to wonder what Vickers had been doing close enough to him that when he got shot he fell into him. That made no sense either. And, who had shot Vickers? Armbruster looked sharply at Knudson. "You shot him, didn't you?" he asked with certainty though not with any accusatory tone.

Knudson nodded. He still looked a little shaken.

"I guess I ought to be thankful," Armbruster said. Then he shrugged. "Well, by Christ, I am," he said. "For you to have hit Vickers with a pistol at thirty yards like that is a goddamn miracle."

"You son of a bitch . . ." Knudson started. He stopped when Armbruster began to laugh.

"Got you, didn't I, dammit," Armbruster crowed. He was still angry down deep—angry at Vickers. Knudson had to be right; there was no other explanation. Now he wanted Vickers to live—just long enough to find out why he wanted to do it, and then to kill him.

Fournier found Armbruster and said, "There's not much I can do for him, Lieutenant. I'd say he doesn't have more than an hour at most."

"Thank you, Doctor," Armbruster said. "I'll go talk to him in a moment." When Fournier had left, Armbruster said, "Come on, Hans, let's go see what Vickers has to say for himself."

Armbruster and Knudson knelt on each side of Vickers. "Lieutenant Knudson says you were about ready to put a bullet in my brain just before you were shot, Vickers. That true?"

"Yeah," Vickers croaked, anger in his voice despite the pain.

"Why?" Armbruster asked, surprised.

"You were fuckin' 'round wit' my wife, damn you."

"I was what?" Armbruster asked. He did not think he would have been able to be more surprised, but he was.

"It was all over the post, dammit," Vickers growled, "how my Alma was awaitin' for you naked in your bed when you come back from one of our patrols, you connivin' son of a bitch."

"That was a practical joke, Private," Knudson said. "I paid Alma two dollars to wait in Lieutenant Armbruster's bed then. She was clothed." He didn't mind the lie, since it had been her idea to shuck her clothes. "As soon as Lieutenant Armbruster saw her in his quarters, he told her to leave, while I stood back and laughed at his surprise."

"Horseshit."

"It's true, Private. Lieutenant Armbruster didn't get any closer to her than his doorway."

"Horse—" Vickers coughed and choked. When he stopped that, his breathing was labored and rough.

"Horseshit," he managed to wheeze. A moment later he was dead.

Armbruster and Knudson rose. "I think we can keep all this quiet, Hans, don't you?"

Knudson nodded. He felt terrible that one of his pranks had been so misunderstood and had led to this man's death.

"We'll write it up that he was killed by a Navajo," Armbruster continued. "Hell, maybe he even saved someone's life in the doing."

"Don't get too carried away with this, Ed," Knudson said with a weak smile.

"I won't."

-❧{ 31 }❧-

Armbruster sent the bodies of Privates Vickers, Carlton and Krieger to the fort for burial. Armbruster also offered Bauer a chance to go back with the B Company detachment. The corporal refused.

"If you ain't going back, Lieutenant," Bauer said firmly, "neither am I. My wound ain't no worse than yours, sir."

"You die trying to be a goddamn hero, Corporal, and I'll have your nut sack for a tobacco pouch."

"Yessir," Bauer said with a grin.

"Go see Doctor Fournier and get patched up." When Bauer had left, Armbruster turned to Cavannaugh. "Sergeant, set our camp over there," he said, pointing to a clear spot near the foot of the ridge on the east side of Manuelito's village. Armbruster winced as pain bit into his side. It wasn't all that bad a wound, and he tended to forget about it—until he turned a certain way, when it would give him an unwelcome reminder of its presence. As his men began making their camp, Armbruster walked to Miles's tent. Miles had called a staff meeting to consider their next moves.

"Ah, Lieutenant," Miles said jovially when Armbruster entered.

"Colonel." Armbruster gingerly took a seat. He was

aware of the other officers' eyes on him, but he ignored them. Or at least tried to.

"Well, Lieutenant, what do you think we should do next?"

"Depends on what your goals are, sir."

"To teach the Navajos a lesson, boy. What other goal would we have?"

Armbruster ignored the temptation to tell him what he thought about the army's goal here. "I think you should send out a few patrols and see what they rustle up. Send the rest of the men back to the fort."

"Why?"

"For one thing, sir, this many men on patrol will be hard to feed and supply. We'd also make a hell of a lot of racket, which can either leave us vulnerable to ambush, or would drive the Navajos out of their homes until we passed by. I also think the fort's open to attack."

"You think that's likely, Lieutenant?" Miles asked, somewhat intrigued by the possibility.

"No, sir. But with the fort's layout and that damn cliff overhanging almost the whole eastern side of it, if the Navajos ever take it into their minds to attack, the fort's real vulnerable."

Miles thought that over, then nodded. "I suppose you want your men to be among those on the move?" he asked with a hoarse laugh.

"Yessir," Armbruster said, not seeing any humor in it.

"But your ranks are decimated, Lieutenant."

"Not quite, Colonel. We lost three men, that's all. The only wounded are Corporal Bauer and myself, neither seriously."

"Still, Lieutenant, the loss of a fourth of your men is considerable."

"Several men from B Company have expressed an

interest in my squad, sir. I'd rather have them get some training first, but they can learn by doing.''

Miles nodded. "So be it, then. How long will you be gone?''

Armbruster shrugged. "Hard to say, sir. But I suppose we should be back at Fort Defiance by Christmas, certainly by the new year.''

"Provisions?''

Armbruster pondered that. "Since we've brought little in the way of provisions with us, we'll arrange to meet a detachment bringing supplies from the fort. We'll make do until then.''

Armbruster and his enlarged but battered squad rode into Fort Defiance two days before Christmas. Miles had made sure that the men who had been killed at Kinlichíi were replaced, and several weeks later, at a rendezvous for provisions, he had insisted that Armbruster take most of B Company with him—with Armbruster in command.

Captain Gilmore had been most displeased with that, and Miles had finally told him to go back to the fort. Miles had briefly considered making Armbruster a brevet captain, or even a brevet major, but when Gilmore agreed to go back to Fort Defiance, Miles had stopped pondering that.

Of the forty-two men who had served under Armbruster's command in the two-and-a-half-month campaign after Kinlichíi, nine did not make it back.

"And how many hostile Navajos did you remove, Lieutenant?'' Miles asked when Armbruster had reported to him.

"Fifty, maybe sixty, Colonel.''

"Then your losses were insignificant in comparison, Lieutenant. You gave those hostiles something to think about over the winter.''

Armbruster nodded. "Still, sir," he said, weary, "I don't know as if it'll do any good."

"Why?"

Armbruster shrugged. "I'm not sure, sir. It just seems that they're different. Like they're planning something. Or maybe like they're just tired of all the trouble and aren't going to back down anymore."

"That sounds ominous, Lieutenant. Are you afraid of that?"

"Not so much afraid as . . . hell, I don't know. I guess it's just that if the Navajos decide to go to war, there's going to be a lot of people die—on both sides. It's not something I'd like to see." He shrugged and grinned sadly. "Maybe I'm just gloomy, sir. It seems like I've been out there fighting Navajos for years."

"I understand, Lieutenant," Miles said genially. "But you'll feel different come spring. You'd better anyway."

"Why's that, sir?"

"I'll be heading back to Fort Marcy soon. Just after the new year arrives, I expect. And you, my boy," Miles said, standing and putting a strong hand on Armbruster's shoulder, "will be taking the lead in fighting the hostiles."

"But what about . . . ?"

"Don't you worry about Captain Gilmore, or even Major Brooks. I've seen how you command men in the field. Gilmore's a deskbound fool. Brooks, I believe, has enough sense to let you go your own way to a great extent. I'll warn Gilmore and anyone else who might want to be a pain in the ass about this."

"Yessir." Armbruster didn't know what else to say.

"You see many men of B Company who might make real Indian fighters, Lieutenant?" Miles suddenly asked.

"Some. Why?"

"I'd like you to take the rest of the winter to train at

least twice as many men as you've had in the Loco Squad. Think that's possible, Lieutenant?"

"Possible to train them, sir? Or possible to even find ones worth training?"

"Either. Or both."

"If I can find men who've got it in them like the men of my small group, I can train them. Whether I can find another dozen or more of them, sir, I don't know."

"How many do you think you can find?"

Armbruster thought about that a little. "There's been eight, maybe nine who've shown in the past couple months that they've got some sand in them. I think they'll probably take to the training. Of the others, though, I don't think there's much . . . quality . . . to be found there."

Miles paced, thinking, then nodded. "All right, Lieutenant, you take those eight men and meld them into Loco Squad. Train their asses hard over the winter. Come spring, I want you and your men running roughshod over the Navajos."

"No, sir," Armbruster said flatly.

"What's that, Lieutenant?" Miles asked, shocked.

"I said, 'No, sir.' " Armbruster paused. "I'm not going to train men to run roughshod over the Navajos or any other Indians."

"Hell, son, you know I don't mean indiscriminate killing of Indians. Just hostiles. I want you and your men to run the hostiles to ground. Break them if necessary, bring them in as prisoners if you can."

"I suppose I can do that, sir," Armbruster said, smiling weakly. He was unsure about all this. Miles was setting him above many of the other officers at the fort, men of higher rank, longer time of service, or both. That was not going to sit well with some of them, and when Miles was gone, Armbruster knew he would be on his own. He did not look forward to it.

"Good. Good," Miles said jovially. He took a close look at Armbruster. "Something bothering you, Lieutenant?" he asked. "Any other man'd be happy as a clam with your assignment."

Before Armbruster could respond, Major Brooks entered the room. "Ah, Major," Miles said with a laugh. "Just the man I want to see."

Brooks was getting just a tad weary of Miles, but he kept that to himself. "What for, Colonel?" he asked politely.

"I'm putting Lieutenant Armbruster in complete charge of the Loco Squad, with orders to expand and to train the new men over the winter. And in the spring, he and his band of men will lead the fight against the hostile Navajos."

Brooks was not surprised. Nor was he unpleased with the thought. He was, however, less than happy at just being summarily ordered to accept it. "A good choice, sir," Brooks said evenly.

"Yes, so I thought, too." Miles yawned. "Well, gentlemen, it's about time this old soldier was abed. So, if you'll excuse me."

Brooks and Armbruster saluted and left. As soon as they were outside the door, Armbruster said, "This wasn't my idea, Major."

Brooks glared at Armbruster for a moment, trying to find the truth. He thought he did. He nodded. "I'm sure it wasn't."

Armbruster stopped. He waited a moment for Brooks, who had kept walking. When the major stopped and turned to face him, Armbruster said, "If you'd prefer, sir, as soon as Colonel Miles leaves the post, you can relieve me of the duties he's saddled me with here."

"Is that what you want, Lieutenant?" Brooks asked after a moment's thought.

"No, sir. I think the idea's good, and I think I'm the

right man for the job. On the other hand, I can understand if you and the other officers . . . well, you know, sir."

"Yes, Lieutenant, I do know." He looked up at the dying day, then back to Armbruster. "Trouble is, I also think it's a good idea." He sighed tiredly. "No, Lieutenant, I think I'll let you go on and do what the colonel suggested. I don't look forward to having to explain the facts of life to the other officers, but that's neither anything new, nor any of your concern. All I ask is that you do the job as best you can. That way none of us'll look too damned foolish."

"Yessir," Armbruster said, relieved.

"Just one more thing, Lieutenant." Brooks paused. "Do you think all this is overdoing it?"

"No, sir. As I told Colonel Miles a few minutes ago, I think the Navajos're getting antsy,"

"So you think they'll cause trouble."

"I'm afraid so, sir."

"Afraid so, Lieutenant?" Brooks asked, eyebrows cocked in question. "You're not going soft on me, are you, Armbruster?"

"No, sir," Armbruster said solemnly. "But we've lost a number of good men already. The Navajos go on the warpath, especially in large numbers, and more of us'll get killed. And more Navajos. It's all such a damn foolish thing. But it's coming."

"You sound as if you don't like war," Brooks said in accusatory tones.

"I don't," Armbruster said flatly. He didn't much care what others thought of his ideas, but he really didn't like being challenged about it.

"Good," Brooks said. "I don't much like officers who enjoy war as an end to itself. It's a necessary thing more often than not, but that doesn't mean reasonable men have to enjoy it." He smiled a little.

"I agree, sir." He paused. "A question, though.

Since I'm supposed to be the high muckety-muck of this new Indian fighting army, I'd like to have the freedom to make promotions.''

Brooks cocked an eyebrow at him.

"I don't plan to make too many changes that way, sir, but I feel that with a larger group to deal with I'll need a second sergeant. I have a corporal I'd like to promote, which means I'd have to promote somebody to replace him. I also think I'll need another corporal, which means one more promotion."

"Is that all, Lieutenant?" Brooks asked with another small smile.

"Yes, sir, I think that ought to do."

Brooks nodded. "You make your choices and bring them to me. I'll make them official."

"Thank you, sir." Armbruster wandered toward his quarters almost dazed at the way the evening had gone. It was so odd, he thought. The more he considered leaving the army and trying to make a life with Serafina Martinez, the better he seemed to do in the service of his country. And with that came added responsibilities. He was not sure he liked that, but he seemed to deal with it in an easy, natural way.

He sat at his desk and thought for a little while. It did not take long, since he had thought all this out before. Quickly he wrote down his suggestions for the promotions, and then he headed to bed. Still, with all that had gone on that evening, he had a considerable amount of trouble getting to sleep.

❧ 32 ❧

Armbruster got the men of Loco Squad together in the barracks. He made sure that everyone else from B Company—including Captain Gilmore and Lieutenant Hans Knudson—also was there.

"Men," Armbruster said, "there's going to be some changes to Loco Squad. The unit is being expanded, and so some of you men in B Company'll be joining my crew. If you've got a problem with coming along, you let me know straight off. I don't want any chickenshits in my outfit." He paused, looking along the ranks of men.

"Most of you who fought with us during the fall campaign against the Navajos know what kind of man I am now, and what kind of commander I am. You don't think you fit in, don't try."

Armbruster paused again, waiting to see if anyone had anything to say. No one did. "The first order of business—the men being asked to join Loco Squad. As I call your name, step over to the unit's side of the barracks. Sergeant."

Sergeant Cavannaugh nodded, stepped forward and took the paper from Armbruster. He turned to face the men. "Johnson, Sandberg, Latham, Sundstrom, Womack, Gehringer, Sullivan, Dunn, Tuttle, MacDonald, O'Leary, Kazmierczak, Scoggins." He stopped and looked at all the men whose names he had just called. "Any of you want to opt out?" Cavannaugh asked.

When no one responded, Cavannaugh nodded, handed the paper back to Armbruster and then retook his place off to the side a little.

"There's one more transfer," Armbruster said. "Corporal Goettle, if you'd like to join us, we'd be happy to have you."

"Yessir!" Goettle said enthusiastically. He moved to the Loco Squad's side of the room.

"I have a few more changes to announce," Armbruster said. "But first I'd like to make something clear, just in case it's not. Sergeant Cavannaugh is my right-hand man. He has been and will continue to be, Loco Squad's top sergeant. There is—and will be—no one in Loco Squad I trust more that Sergeant Cavannaugh. Fuck with him, and you fuck with me." Armbruster glared from face to face, making sure they understood his sincerity.

Satisfied, he went on. "And to reinforce his importance to me and to this unit, you men will now report to Sergeant Major Clancy Cavannaugh. Sergeant, come and take your new insignia."

Cavannaugh stood in stunned silence, chewing on his mustache, not knowing whether he should laugh, cry or jump for joy. Finally he walked to Armbruster and woodenly took his new stripes. "By Christ, I don't believe it," he whispered as he walked back to his position.

"Now," Armbruster said, "I haven't discussed this with the next person I'm about to mention, either, though I have talked it over with Major Brooks. He is in full agreement. As is Colonel Miles." He made a quarter turn. "Lieutenant Knudson, I extend an offer for you to be second in command of Loco Squad, if you're willing."

Knudson's eyes lit up. He snapped off a salute. "I sure as all hell would be, Lieutenant." He strutted over to the others of Loco Squad.

Armbruster nodded and smiled. "There's more, men, but not much. And it's all good news. I think." He smiled again. "Loco Squad will be broken into two units of ten privates each. The seven members remaining from the original Squad, plus Womack, Tuttle and O'Leary will form First Unit. The rest of the privates will form Second Unit."

He paused. "Corporal Bauer," Armbruster said, "step forward." When Bauer had done so, a little nervously, Armbruster grinned. "You'll run the first unit. Congratulations, *Sergeant* Bauer."

He handed a set of stripes to Bauer, who took them, a little dazed. Bauer remembered to salute and then lurched back to the ranks, staring at the three stripes that would replace the two he wore as corporal.

"Corporal Goettle. Front and center." When a dazed Goettle moved up, Armbruster said, "You'll run Second Unit—as a sergeant, of course. Both you and Sergeant Bauer will report to Sergeant Major Cavannaugh." He handed Goettle his new stripes.

Shaking his head in wonder, Goettle took them, saluted, and walked back to the line of men.

"And, finally," Armbruster said, "since we have no more corporals, we'll need one for each unit. Private Skidmore, you're now Corporal Skidmore, and with the First Unit. Private Olson, you have the honor of working with Sergeant Goettle and the Second Unit as a corporal."

Armbruster dismissed the men, then. He knew they would have much to talk about, and he wanted them to get used to all the changes. Cavannaugh would know what to do with them once the talk dwindled—and once the new sergeant major recovered his own equilibrium. Besides, they wouldn't be doing all that much before the new year turned. That would be in only a few days. Until then, the men could slough off a little, and then celebrate. After that, training would begin.

"Ed! Ed!" Knudson called, hurrying to catch up to Armbruster. "Buy you a cup of coffee over at the officers' mess, Ed?" Knudson asked.

"Sure."

They walked silently toward the mess, making haste to get in out of the cold. When they were seated and sipping some coffee, Knudson said, "I don't know how to express my thanks to you, Ed. I—"

"No thanks're necessary."

"Yes, they are. After all the pranks I've pulled on you and—"

"And what?"

"I'm afraid I haven't thought very highly of your choice of woman all this time."

"I know that," Armbruster said flatly. "And I don't expect this to change your mind. Remember, all I've done for you with this move is to make you subordinate to a man with less time in service."

Knudson laughed, somewhat uneasily. "I never looked at it that way." He thought about it, and decided he could live with it. He told Armbruster so, then added, "You sure took me by surprise, though."

Armbruster nodded. "I figure I did. But I wanted to get everything done before someone changed his mind. I'll tell you, though, I didn't make any of those changes this morning without discussing them with Major Brooks . . . and Sergeant Cavannaugh." He hesitated only a second. "Even your move," he added bluntly.

Knudson wasn't sure he liked the idea of a sergeant having a hand in deciding his fate, but then he realized that Cavannaugh had been in the army far longer and had seen far more action that Knudson had. He nodded. "Think I'll fit in?" he asked, worried.

"If I didn't, you wouldn't be a member of Loco Squad."

Knudson nodded again. "I'm not sure," he said slowly, carefully, "that I can change my opinion of some of your personal choices." He was still worried, but he felt some relief that it was out in the open.

Armbruster thought they had gotten beyond Knudson's problem with Armbruster's relationship with Serafina. Especially after Knudson had stopped Heywood from assaulting Serafina. Still, Knudson had to live with his conscience, just as Armbruster had to live with his. "Just do your job is all I ask, Hans. You don't agree with what I do in my personal life, we don't have to socialize. I'm not trying to break you to my mold."

Knudson felt better. "A man can't ask no more than that, Ed."

Over the winter, the new men in Loco Squad took to their training pretty well. Knudson also showed himself to be an alert and effective officer, especially in administrative duties, something Armbruster hated. With Knudson doing much of the paperwork and other administrative folderol, Armbruster could spend time training his men.

The winter also gave Armbruster time to worry. As the weeks progressed toward spring, he felt more and more strongly that there would be big trouble with the Navajos once the weather broke. Though it was only a hunch, he pushed his men, wanting them to be tough and resolute when—or if—the war with the Navajos came.

Spring seemed to get an early start that year, and he looked forward to seeing Serafina again. When she arrived, though, he began to feel like a fool with all his worries about war with the Navajos. He had expressed those concerns to Serafina almost immediately—well, after they had coupled twice.

"I think you're worrying unnecessarily," Serafina

had said. "I have heard from the Diné that they are planning a *Natch'it* up at—"

"A what?" Armbruster knew some Navajo, but this was a new word to him.

"A *Natch'it*. It's a sort of political-religious gathering. Big medicine among the Diné. It lasts nine days."

"Not a war council?"

"No. It's not really a peace council either, but with that much time spent in ceremonies, maybe *hozho* will return to the Diné."

"That'd be nice—if it came true." Armbruster sighed, both in contentment at being with Serafina, and with a lingering worry. "Where's this going to take place?"

"Tsin Sikaad."

"Tree Setting Up?" Armbruster asked, trying to work out the words themselves as well as inflection.

"Very good," Serafina said with a small laugh.

"Where is it?"

"Near Tsaile Lake and Tsegi."

"When?"

Serafina shrugged. "I'm not sure. A couple more weeks. Maybe a month. Why?" she asked, suddenly worried. "You're not planning to go up there and stick your nose in where it doesn't belong, are you?"

"I might just mosey on up there and keep an eye on things. I promise I won't interfere, unless it looks as if they're going to make a heap of mischief."

"I don't like it, Eduardo."

"Me either. But it has to be done."

"But, I—"

"Hush," Armbruster said. Then he covered her mouth with his.

The day after Serafina pulled out with her father, Armbruster went to Major Brooks. He had been glad to see Brooks keep his word about Loco Squad, even though

Lieutenant Colonel Miles had left four days into the new year. Now Armbruster wanted to test Brooks's resolve just a little more.

Armbruster explained about the meeting the Navajos were planning. "I'd like to take my men up there and see what's happening." Before Brooks could say anything, he added, "And, no, we're not going to cause trouble, sir. Just observe."

Brooks thought about it a little while, then nodded. "I see no harm in that, Lieutenant," he finally allowed. "But there's one condition."

Armbruster felt his stomach twist a little.

Brooks grinned. "Take me with you. I am so goddamn sick and tired of being cooped up in this goddamn office that I could just spit. I need to get away from here for a little. Feel a saddle instead of a chair under my ass."

Armbruster was considerably relieved. "You sure that's safe, Major?" he asked.

"Are you saying that I'm too soft, Lieutenant?" Brooks asked.

"No, sir," Armbruster responded hastily. "I meant are you sure it's safe for the fort. And for your family here."

"My family is used to army life, Lieutenant. You should know that. And if all the Navajos in the world are at this big ceremony, we don't have to worry about the fort."

"Now, sir, I never said all the Navajos in the world were going to be there. I understand that many of them will."

"You're splitting hairs, Lieutenant. Now, are you going to take me along?" He grinned impishly. "Or are we all going to stay here at the fort for a while?"

"When can you be ready to leave, sir?" Armbruster countered with a chuckle.

"Whenever you want, Lieutenant." He paused.

"And rest assured, Lieutenant, I do not intend to usurp command of the Loco Squad on this venture. Especially if fighting should break out."

"Thank you, sir."

⊰❴ 33 ❵⊱

The Loco Squad's view of the *Natch'it* from across Tsaile Lake several hundred yards away was not very good, but Armbruster did not want to bring the troops any closer. That might precipitate a fight. Still, through telescopes it didn't seem that much was going on in the sprawling camp of temporary shelters. Nothing ominous, at least.

The ceremony was under way when Armbruster and his men arrived, so they set up camp and began observing the Navajos. Twice in the six days of the ceremony that the army was there, Navajo leaders rode to their camp to chat with the soldiers.

"They certainly seem friendly enough, Lieutenant," Brooks said after the first visit by Navajos.

"Yes, sir, they do," Armbruster said flatly. "But I'd bet every cent I have that they're coming over here to size us up."

On the third time, Manuelito was among the visitors. Armbruster was certain now that the Navajos were trying to figure out just how vulnerable the army was out here. Brooks also was convinced of it.

Armbruster decided to test his theory. "What do you want here, Manuelito?" he asked harshly as the three

Navajos and three officers—Armbruster, Brooks and Knudson—sat for a council.

Manuelito showed no surprise. He simply shrugged and said, "We want to see that the soldier chief is comfortable."

"Your lies're as transparent as your foolishness," Armbruster responded flatly.

"These are not good words you say to me," Manuelito countered somewhat heatedly.

"Nonetheless, they're true." Armbruster paused. "How many men you have over at your *Natch'it?* Two hundred? Three?"

Manuelito shrugged. "You can come and count them, if you want," he challenged.

"That's not necessary." He paused, allowing Manuelito to gloat a few moments. "Now, let's stop the nonsense, Manuelito. I know you're here to find out what kind of resistance we can put up. And I'll tell you exactly what you face here. We have twenty-eight men, each armed with two sidearms, a bowie knife, two saddle pistols and a Mississippi percussion rifle. We are *El Escuadra de Diablo,* and we will kick the shit out of however many hundred warriors you have in that camp."

He let Manuelito think about that for a few seconds, ignoring Brooks's quick sucking in of breath at Armbruster's manner and tone. Then Armbruster added, "Now, we aren't here to cause trouble. We're just here to watch your celebrations. But if you want trouble, you'll get a lot more than you planned on."

"The soldier chief does not send *El Escuadra de Diablo* out to just sit and watch the Diné," Manuelito countered, angry that his purpose had been found out.

"*El Escuadra de Diablo* is sent out to do whatever is necessary. If that includes battle, we're prepared. Like that time last summer at your camp down on the Kinlichíi. If you and your people don't want war, then all

El Escuadra de Diablo will do is visit and patrol and see that things remain peaceful.''

Manuelito grew more and more angry, though he never actually acknowledged the truth of anything Armbruster said. But when he finally left, though, he had decided that there would be no attack on the whites. Manuelito was absolutely sure his people would crush the soldiers, but he was equally certain that the cost would not be worth it. Not here, not now. There would be other times.

''You certainly have a way with words, Lieutenant,'' Brooks said as he and Armbruster watched Manuelito and his two friends walk away. While much of the talk had been in Navajo or Spanish, Brooks had gotten enough of it to know at least some of what Armbruster had said. His tone and demeanor made even the words he did not understand quite intelligible.

''One thing I've found about the Navajos, sir, is that they believe in the harmony of their world. They call it *hozho,* and it's hard as hell for a white man to understand really. I don't understand it very much at all, though I think I have the basic idea of it. What I did with Manuelito today was to let him know in no uncertain terms that if he started a fracas, then his *hozho*—and that of all his people over there—was going to get trampled into the dust. There aren't enough medicine men to perform the ceremonies needed to restore their *hozho* after that.''

''I suppose that makes some sense, Lieutenant,'' Brooks admitted, though it was as clear as river mud.

''The only one it really has to make sense to, sir, is Manuelito. It's unimportant that you or I have no real concept of what it is. I know just enough of it that I can speak to him in a way that *he* will understand it.''

''So, you don't think they'll attack, Lieutenant?''

''No, sir, I don't.''

"You'll have men, though, standing guard through the night?"

"And day, sir," Armbruster said flatly. "I'm not a fool, Major."

Brooks smiled a little. "No, Lieutenant, you certainly are not."

They left a day before the ceremony was to end anyway. There was nothing more to see, and neither Brooks nor Armbruster could see any reason for staying there.

The column took its sweet time heading back toward the fort. Brooks was in no hurry, enjoying his time out here. So they took a rather circuitous route. Less than a day's ride from Fort Defiance, they found a small Navajo village. The Indians invited them to stay for a dance that night. Armbruster agreed without asking Brooks, and explained it to the major later. Brooks thought the idea splendid. Since the soldiers had shot five deer that day, Armbruster donated them to the Navajo band for the dance.

The soldiers set up a camp a few hundred yards from the outermost hogans. Sergeant Cavannaugh had the unpleasant duty of assigning men to guard the horses and the camp during the festivities.

As darkness began to fall, the soldiers who were not on duty headed for the Navajo camp. They sat on finely woven blankets, made by the women of the village of wool taken from their own sheep and then dyed. They ate dishes of deer meat and mutton.

Armbruster sat, interested in everything that went on. For a while his eyes were drawn to a beautiful young woman who was dancing with a happy abandon. He shook his head in annoyance after a while, thinking himself somehow unfaithful to Serafina.

His attention was drawn to the young woman again a little bit later when an angry shouting overrode even the music. Armbruster looked and saw an old man berating the woman. "What's going on, Rojo Piedra?" he asked the camp headman who was sitting next to him.

Rojo Piedra scowled. "Old Piño Grande doesn't think his woman there is acting quite as wifely as he thinks she should."

"I haven't had a good look at him, but from what little I've seen, isn't he a mite old to be married to a girl so young?" Armbruster asked.

"*Sí.* Her name is Vientito."

"A most inappropriate name," Armbruster commented, watching the tableau playing out.

Suddenly Piño Grande angrily stripped Vientito bare right in front of everyone.

The action seemed to have little effect on Vientito, who went right back to her dancing.

Others, however, were not quite so nonplused. Armbruster, for one, could feel his palms suddenly dampen at the sight of the woman's flesh flickering in the firelight. She had a sheen of sweat that glistened, and dancing shadows heightened the erotic effect. Armbruster knew most of the other men must be feeling like he was. He finally tore his eyes away, and saw Piño Grande slinking away into the darkness. He still had not gotten a good look at the old man, not that it mattered.

"What's going to happen now?" Armbruster asked, pointing to Piño Grande's retreating figure.

"That depends. If she reforms to his liking, it'll all be forgotten soon," Rojo Piedra said.

"You don't sound like you think it'll happen."

Rojo Piedra shrugged. "I don't. And so I fear for some unfortunate's life."

"How's that?"

"Diné custom won't allow him to kill her, so he'll have to find an 'outsider' to kill to release his pent-up anger," Rojo Piedra commented.

"That doesn't bode well for my men," Armbruster said flatly.

"I doubt Piño Grade will bother your men. He's an old man and will look for someone who perhaps can't fight back too well."

"Then you don't think I should pull my men out of here?" Armbruster asked. He certainly didn't want to precipitate a war by tempting one half-crazed old warrior too much.

"No. Not if your men are alert."

Armbruster nodded. He turned to Cavannaugh, who sat on his other side. "Spread the word, Sergeant," he said quietly. "The first man tries something with that naked young lady will become a gelding."

Cavannaugh cast a surprised glance at the lieutenant.

"The old man who stripped her is her husband. Apparently she's not acting wifely enough for him, so he figured he'd shame her into changing her ways. It ended up with him being more shamed than her. And there's no goddamn reason I can think of to increase that shame."

"Yessir."

Armbruster was rather relieved when, a few minutes later, a young Navajo man took Vientito into the darkness beyond the firelight. Soon after, Armbruster ordered his men back to their own camp. The men who had to stand guard were even angrier than they had been, once the tale of Piño Grande and Vientito was related. But they were used to such disappointments. They caused little trouble, though one almost started a fight with a friend who took some convincing to stop taunting the unfortunate soldier. It finally took Lieutenant Knudson telling both men that they would face the lash—and be drummed out of the Loco Squad—if they didn't start to behave.

They rode into the fort about midafternoon the next

day. Despite his desire to get out of the fort, Brooks looked rather relieved to be back—and out of the saddle. He had gotten out of that habit, and now was suffering for it.

Two days later, Armbruster and his men were preparing to leave when the bugles and drums rang out. The Loco Squad raced toward the parade grounds, pistols out. They saw other men headed toward the large stable on the post's southwest end, and they joined in the rush.

"What is it?" Armbruster demanded, shoving through a circle of enlisted men. He came upon the body of "Little Joe," the post's handyman. Little Joe was a quiet, unassuming man of uncertain lineage. He was, almost everyone believed, at least half-Indian, though he might have Mexican mixed in there, too. He was a harmless fellow, who had never caused anyone any trouble. He was . . . helpless, Armbruster finally realized. A chill ran up his spine.

Brooks came up moments later, puffing though he had had but a short distance to come. He realized he wasn't getting any younger. He stopped and looked down at the body. "Anybody know what happened here?" he demanded, certain he would not get an answer. He didn't.

Armbruster knelt next to the body and carefully looked it over.

"When I find which one of you bastards killed old Little Joe here, he'll hang," Brooks said. "I promise that." He had no special feeling for the handyman; he just hated having such things happen at his post.

"I don't think anyone here's responsible, sir," Armbruster said as he rose.

"What do you mean?" Brooks demanded.

"I'll tell you later, sir. Let's get Little Joe taken care of and the men back to their duties."

Brooks nodded, issued a few orders and then stalked away, Armbruster in his wake.

"Now, Lieutenant," Brooks said when he and Armbruster were in Brooks's office, "would you mind telling me what this is all about." It wasn't a question.

"I'm not sure, sir, but I think Little Joe was killed by a Navajo."

"What makes you think that?"

"For one thing, it doesn't look like a white man's job of killing, sir. I can't explain why exactly, but it doesn't."

"That's not much to go on, Lieutenant."

"No, sir." He paused and then plunged ahead, telling the story of Piño Grande and Vientito. "Rojo Piedra said that it was against Navajo custom for the old man to kill her so that he'd have to find someone outside the tribe."

"But why Little Joe? And why here at the fort?"

"I'm just supposing, sir, but I think because Piño Grande was so old, he needed someone who couldn't fight back much. Someone who was pretty helpless, someone—"

"Someone like Little Joe," Brooks finished.

"Yessir. As for the fort, the only thing I can think of is that he knew he could find someone helpless here. Maybe he knew about Little Joe, maybe not. But he had to know there were women around here."

"Damn."

"I also think he did it here so he could look like a bigger man when he gets back to his people. He can say he snuck into the fort, and killed someone right under the noses of the soldier chief and all us Something-Sticking-Out-From-the-Foreheads."

Brooks looked at Armbruster, puzzlement on his face.

"It's what the Navajos call the soldiers. From the visor on the enlisted men's caps."

Brooks nodded. After some thought, he said, "I want you to ride out to Rojo Piedra's and bring that old bastard back here so we can stretch his neck. He might think he's something special, but all he is to me is another goddamn murdering savage."

"Yessir."

❧⁑ 34 ⁑❧

Armbruster and his men rode boldly into Rojo Piedra's small village and stopped in a semicircle around the headman's hogan. Rojo Piedra came out, mystified and worried. It was unlike Armbruster to not dismount and pass some pleasantries before getting down to business.

"I want Piño Grande," Armbruster said harshly.

"But why?" Rojo Piedra asked, still baffled.

Armbruster dismounted and tossed his reins to Corporal Skidmore. "Let's talk inside," he said to the Navajo leader. He had decided in an instant that Rojo Piedra really was baffled, and so deserved some explanation.

Once he and Rojo Piedra were inside and sitting, Armbruster said, "I believe Piño Grande killed a man at the fort."

"No!" Rojo Piedra appeared to be truly surprised.

"Yes," Armbruster answered. "I think he killed the handyman there because he could not by custom—as you told me—kill Vientito. Her scandalous behavior drove him to it, I suppose, but that doesn't mean he should get away with it."

Rojo Piedra sat in thought. He was certain that Armbruster was right, but he could not just give Piño

Grande up to the army. Even if he could find him right now. That was one reason he believed Armbruster—Piño Grande had been gone for a few days, and had not returned. If Piño Grande had killed someone at the fort, there was a good chance he might not be back in the camp yet, if he took a circuitous route.

"That's hard to believe," Rojo Piedra offered, not knowing what else to say but knowing he had to say something.

Armbruster shrugged. "I can't prove it. At least not right now. But I'd wager a year's pay that he's the one who did it."

Rojo Piedra sighed. Piño Grande had once been a great chief, and had the respect of all the Diné. But time had treated Piño Grande harshly. When his old wife of many years died, he had brought Vientito into his hogan. But his age and his deteriorating physical condition would not allow him to meet the young woman's needs. Now it had come down to this.

"He's not here," Rojo Piedra said quietly.

"Where is he?" Armbruster asked, voice growing harsh again. He had the feeling that the Navajos were hemming and hawing.

"I don't know," Rojo Piedra said honestly. He hesitated. "But even if he did this thing, why should we give him to you?" he argued.

"He must be punished," Armbruster said flatly. "He just can't go around killing people—especially people who never did anything wrong."

Rojo Piedra nodded. "That's true," he said solemnly. "But why is it only true for the Diné?"

"What does that mean?" It was Armbruster's turn to be puzzled.

"A few weeks ago, the soldier chief at Fort Defiance ordered Venado Negro whipped for—"

"Major Brooks ordered a Diné whipped?" Armbruster interjected incredulously.

"No," Rojo Piedra said. "The other soldier chief."

Armbruster thought for a moment. "Gilmore? Captain Gilmore did that?" His incredulity rose.

"Sí. He is the one."

Armbruster found it hard to swallow, but the more he thought about it the more he believed it possible. It would've been while Brooks was on patrol with Loco Squad. Gilmore, who had been angry for much of the past couple of years, probably saw his temporary command as a chance to show how tough he could be. This could be trouble.

"You know why?" Armbruster asked.

"A misunderstanding. Venado Negro traded some furs and corn for flour and coffee at Webber's. Then he stayed around to look at some other things. When he walked out, the soldier chief, who had just come in, thought he was stealing the flour and coffee. The soldier chief got some men and arrested Venado Negro. Though Webber tried to explain that it was a misunderstanding, the soldier chief had Venado Negro whipped." Rojo Piedra's voice had become bitter.

"Dammit," Armbruster muttered. "I'll take it up with Major Brooks when I get back. I don't know that there's much he can—will—do," he added bluntly. "Either way, it doesn't mean you can just sit here and not give us Piño Grande."

Rojo Piedra's face was hard. "That soldier chief also told the Something-Sticking-Out-From-the-Foreheads to shoot at Amarillo Luna."

"Why?"

Rojo Piedra shrugged. "All he wanted to do was talk to the agent. He heard the soldier chief shout something, and then the Something-Sticking-Out-From-the-Foreheads shot at him. He ran."

"Was he hurt?"

"No."

"That's something anyway," Armbruster said lamely. He considered his options. There were several, nearly all almost guaranteed to precipitate a battle, if not a war. "I'll tell Major Brooks of these things," he finally said. "Maybe he can do something." Armbruster went outside and mounted his horse.

"We're going back without the Navajo?" Knudson asked, trying not to sound peevish. He had been hoping for some action, even if it was just dragging some decrepit old chief back to the fort to be hanged.

Armbruster nodded. "For now. Let's ride."

At Fort Defiance, Armbruster reported on what Rojo Piedra had told him. It did not impress Major Brooks.

"You should have come back with the old reprobate," Brooks insisted. He was not quite angry, but he wasn't happy either.

"He wasn't there," Armbruster said flatly.

"You know that for sure? Or are you just relying on the headman's word."

"The latter, but I'm still sure of it."

"Why?"

Armbruster shrugged. "If old Piño Grande's guilty, as we figure, I doubt he'd have gone running back to the village. I suspect he'd want to see what was going to happen here. He probably followed us—at a safe distance, of course. When we left the village, he probably hid. He might be back, or he might be waiting a few days to see if things quiet down."

"Then go out there in a few days."

"Yessir."

"Look, Lieutenant," Brooks said wearily, "I've got superiors, too. And they're breathing down my neck. Apparently you aren't the only one who thinks things might explode out here."

"I understand, sir," Armbruster said honestly.

"Good. You go back out there in three days, and you

give the Indians an ultimatum—they hand over the murderer or they face the consequences."

"At the risk of war, sir?" Armbruster asked flatly.

"Damn, you're annoying today, Lieutenant," Brooks said. "No, not war. If it looks like big trouble'll start, come on back. But if that happens, I'll send out damn near the fort's entire compliment."

"Yessir."

Three days later, Armbruster led his men back to Rojo Piedra's village. Rojo Piedra once again refused to surrender the old chief, saying that Piño Grande still had not returned.

"Let's search every damn hogan," Knudson said.

Armbruster looked around. There were a heap more warriors than there had been the other day, even though most of them were inside the hogans, staring out curiously. "No."

"Dammit, Ed, are you turning chicken?" Knudson asked angrily.

Armbruster took a few moments to bring his rage down to a controllable level. "Lieutenant, you should open your eyes more often and your mouth less often," he said harshly.

Knudson looked as if he had been slapped. He started to jerk his horse's head around, but Armbruster stopped him.

"Take a look around, Hans," Armbruster said quietly. "A good look."

Knudson did. Despite his anger, he began to see the partially hidden warriors. "Kind of outnumbered, aren't we?" he asked, ashamed.

"Maybe not outnumbered," Armbruster responded, "but there's enough of them here that we'd lose too many men even if we won. I'm not about to risk most of my men to show these Indians how tough I am." He grinned savagely. "But I'll remember this."

They rode out. An hour's ride away, Armbruster called a halt at Bear Springs and ordered camp to be made.

"You have something in mind, Ed?" Knudson asked, curious.

"No real plan. I just thought we might set here a day or two. Most of the warriors in Rojo Piedra's village aren't from there. I expect they'll want to get back to their own hogans soon."

"Makes sense. So we sit it out a couple days and then go back in there and get this Piño Grande fellow?"

"If things work out, yes." Armbruster smiled wanly. "Of course, where such things are considered, they don't very often work out as planned."

The Navajos attacked just after dawn two days later, making a fast horseback raid into the soldiers' camp, and then back out again, dashing behind the boulders strewn across the flats not far from the spring.

"Second Unit, the horses!" Sergeant Major Cavannaugh roared. "First Unit! Form two skirmish lines diagonal from the spring narrowing outward. Keep low."

Within moments the horse herd in the little stand of small junipers was surrounded by ten soldiers led by Sergeant Goettle and Corporal Olson. About the same time, two lines were formed in a V shape, with the opening toward the spring. Instead of kneeling, the men were lying on their stomachs. Some were fortunate enough to have logs or rocks in front of them, offering some protection. Sergeant Bauer and Corporal Skidmore were among the men.

Armbruster squatted behind a stunted tree at the edge of the spring. Several feet to his right, Cavannaugh was hunkered down behind some brush. To Armbruster's left, Knudson tried to find protection in some reeds.

Suddenly arrows began flying out from the rocks.

The soldiers waited it out, each man hoping he would not be hit, since there were no real targets to shoot at.

Time dragged, and the heat rose. The men in the open sweltered as the sun beat down on their backs. An hour or so before noon, Armbruster had had enough. "Sergeant Goettle," he called, "have six of your men ease up to where they can see the rocks where those Navajos're hiding. At my command, lay down a covering fire."

"Yessir!"

"Sergeant Bauer, lead your men in a dash for the rocks when Second Unit begins firing."

"Yessir!" He seemed even more enthusiastic than Goettle had.

"Hans," Armbruster said, "you're in command here. Pay attention to what Sergeant Cavannaugh says."

"Where're you going?" Knudson asked.

"With First Unit."

"That's stupid, Ed. I mean, Jesus—"

"Now, Second Unit!" Armbruster roared, cutting Knudson off. Then he was up and, with pistols in hand, running flat out for the boulders across the dusty, barren flats.

Private Klaus Nesselroad tumbled to the ground. Armbruster noticed an arrow sticking out of Nesselroad, but he could not see where in the man's body it was.

An arrow struck Armbruster and he sucked in his breath in shock. Still running, he glanced down to see the arrow sticking out of his wide leather belt. The very tip of the arrowhead was poking through, scraping his belly flesh a little. Without slackening his speed, he jerked the arrow out and threw it aside. Then he was among the rocks.

A Navajo, bow drawn, suddenly loomed up in front of him. "Shit," he muttered. He fired twice without aiming. Both balls hit the Navajo, but Armbruster was not sure how seriously hurt the Navajo was. The Indian fell, the arrow from his bow twanging off to the side somewhere.

Armbruster thought to stop and check the Navajo, finishing off the job, if needed, but another warrior crashed into him from the side. He went down, mostly on one side, with the Navajo atop him. Armbruster never really knew how the Navajo's war club missed his head. It was sufficient for him to know that it did.

Armbruster managed to cock his right arm up toward the Indian a little. He fired. The ball barely grazed the Navajo's left cheekbone, but he jumped up with a start. Armbruster rolled over onto his back and kicked the Indian in the groin.

The Navajo hissed and started to wilt. Armbruster brought up the pistol in his left hand and fired twice, hitting the Navajo in the stomach with both bullets.

Armbruster rose unsteadily and walked to the first Navajo he had shot. The warrior was still alive. He had a compound fracture of the left leg and was trying to crawl to safety. Steeling himself, Armbruster walked up behind the Indian and shot him in the back of the head.

When Armbruster looked around again, he could see Navajos riding hard away from the spot. Some of the men were still firing at the fleeing Navajos, but Armbruster shouted for them to stop. They were doing nothing more than wasting ammunition.

"All right, men," he finally shouted. "Let's get back over to camp and take stock."

Nesselroad was not seriously hurt. The arrow he had taken had barely pierced the skin of his hip. Two other men had minor gunshot wounds. They tallied six Navajos slain in the engagement.

"I'm not sure if those damn Navajos'll be back," Armbruster said. "But we'd better get back to the fort.

Nesselroad, Bates and Womack need their wounds treated, and we need to reprovision.''

"For a longer campaign, sir?'' Cavannaugh asked.

"Yes, Sergeant. The Navajos have been pushing, and now we're going to push back. Hard.''

{ 35 }

An emissary of Rojo Piedra arrived at Fort Defiance the next afternoon and asked to meet with Major Brooks. The commanding officer agreed, but made sure Armbruster was in the room at the time. Privates Pettet and Gehringer also were there, acting as guards, in case the emissary—Hablador—tried something.

"All right, Hablador, what've you got to say?" Brooks asked curtly.

"We have caught Piño Grande—the man you seek."

"Then why isn't he here?" Brooks asked harshly. He was angry and frustrated, and in no mood for games.

"He was wounded in the fight with *El Escuadra de Diablo*. Very badly wounded."

"Then Lieutenant Armbruster will come and get him, if he's unable to travel."

"No," Hablador said hastily. "We will bring him here. Rojo Piedra had me come here to ask that you not send El Diablo"—he pointed at Armbruster— "and his men to return to the village to get Piño Grande."

"Why not?" Brooks demanded.

"The Diné are afraid," Hablador said flatly. *"El Escuadra de Diablo* has caused much blood to be shed among my people."

"If Rojo Piedra had done as we requested at the beginning, no blood would've been shed," Brooks retorted.

"It's too late to change that now."

"Indeed. When will you bring the murderous old bastard in?"

"In three days. He should be well enough to travel by then."

"If he's not here by dusk Thursday—three days away —El Diablo and his men will ride to Rojo Piedra's village at dawn the following morning," Brooks warned. "Is that clear?"

Hablador nodded. Minutes later he was on his horse and trotting out of the fort.

"What do you think, Lieutenant?" Brooks asked.

"I really don't know, sir. It could be true. We killed six Navajos the other day, but we might've wounded a hundred. Or none."

"Well, dammit it all." Brooks suddenly grinned just a little. "I suppose waiting a few more days won't hurt anything."

"Probably not, though it could give Rojo Piedra time to move his people."

"We'd find them. Or, more realistically, you'd find them. It might take a little while, but I have no doubt that you'd do it. I think Rojo Piedra will think the same. He seems to be an intelligent man—for an Indian—and I suspect he'll know that if he runs that we're going to be in the worst of humors when we track him and his band down."

"I suppose you're right, sir." Armbruster stood. "We'll know for sure in three days." He paused. "One other thing troubles me about all this, sir," he finally added.

"What's that, Lieutenant?"

"Well, you told Hablador that he and Rojo Piedra were responsible for the bloodshed the other day. And that's true. But I think there's more blame to go around.''

"What's that mean, Lieutenant?'' Brooks asked grumpily.

"Captain Gilmore. If he hadn't acted like such an asshole with those two Navajos while you were on patrol with us, Major, then Rojo Piedra might not've been so reluctant to turn Piño Grande over to us.''

"Lieutenant,'' Brooks said sternly, "you've been at this post several years now. You and Captain Gilmore have never gotten along, and I can understand that. I don't expect all my officers to be bosom friends with each other. But even you can see how worthless court-martialing Ambrose Gilmore would be.''

"Why would it be useless, sir?'' Armbruster asked. "It'd show the Navajos that we are men to be trusted. That, I think, will keep down the amount of blood spilled in the future.''

"A telling point, Lieutenant. But answer this first: Do you think you could get a conviction against Gilmore? Especially considering that the court-martial would be held here?''

"I suppose not,'' Armbruster admitted reluctantly.

"You're damned right, not.''

"So you're not going to do anything about Gilmore having brought us to the brink of a full-fledged war with the Navajos?''

"Not to save your wounded pride or your wounded sense of justice, Lieutenant,'' Brooks snapped. He did not like having his decisions questioned. Still, he liked Armbruster a lot, and did not want to be too harsh with the junior officer. "Look, Lieutenant—Ed—that's all water under the bridge now. Things've gone too far to turn back. It's unfortunate, but looking at it realistically, this time war with the Navajos probably was inevitable. Rojo Piedra's thrown down the gauntlet. And no matter what the reason, whether it was Captain Gilmore, or the hard edge on Loco Squad, the gauntlet has been thrown and it won't be picked up again.''

Armbruster knew Brooks was right, but he didn't have to like it. He reluctantly admitted to himself that it was at least partially his dislike for Gilmore that pushed him to question his commanding officer the way he had. "I suppose you're right, sir,'' he allowed. "I can't help but wish it could've been otherwise, though.''

"So do I, Lieutenant. So do I.''

Dark was less than half an hour away when the Navajos arrived. The main body of Indians stopped at the edge of the fort, while three men came forward, towing a horse which dragged a litter behind it.

Armbruster, Knudson and Cavannaugh—joined by Major Brooks—waited at the post's flagpole. The three men stopped, and Armbruster glared. They were not Navajos, but captured Mexicans who were slaves in Navajo camps.

"Piño Grande died on the way to the fort,'' one of the men said. He, like his two companions, looked scared to death.

Armbruster nodded. It would make sense for the Navajos to stay away if the old chief really had died. Still he could feel anger rising in his chest at the remembrance of the last time he had thought that. He walked forward a little, stopped next to the horse-drawn litter and looked down. He did not even need to pull away the blanket.

"Something wrong, Lieutenant?'' Brooks asked, moving up to Armbruster.

"This isn't a goddamn chief. Hell, it's not even a Navajo,'' Armbruster snapped.

The four white men looked up, and noticed that the Navajos were gone. "Shit,'' Armbruster snarled.

"I'll get the men, sir," Cavannaugh said. "We'll be on their asses before they can get to Bear Spring."

"No," Armbruster snapped. "I'm not risking the men out there at night, Sergeant. Besides, they'll probably be expecting that. Maybe we can confuse them a little if we wait a while." He paused, thinking.

"Yessir," Cavannaugh said, sounding a little disappointed. Then he looked at the body. "Damn, Lieutenant, ain't he that damn Mexican who's been loiterin' around the fort here the past couple weeks?"

"I think you might be right, Sergeant," Armbruster said absentmindedly. "Not that it matters any."

Doctor Fournier, the post surgeon, came up. "Want me to take this thing off your hands, Major?" he asked.

"May I, sir?" Armbruster asked, looking at Brooks. When Brooks nodded, wondering, Armbruster said, "Doctor, I want you to examine the body."

"What for?" Fournier asked, surprised.

"See what you can tell me about the wounds."

Fournier shrugged. "Sure, Lieutenant." He called several men over and directed them to cart the body to the hospital.

Armbruster looked at the three Mexicans who had brought the body in. "You boys want to go back to the Navajos?" he asked in Spanish.

All three shook their heads vigorously.

Armbruster nodded and then pointed. "Take your horses over there to the stable and care for them. You can keep them—as long as you ride them out of here soon. You can stay in the stable overnight. I'll have someone bring you some food."

"*Gracias,* Señor Teniente," one said.

"*De nada.* You're to be off the post by an hour after daybreak. *Comprender?*"

"*Sí.*"

"All right, get going." Armbruster turned to Cavannaugh. "Sergeant, have one of the men rustle up B

Company's cook and have him get some food to those Mexicans. Nothing elaborate. Beans and bacon or something. And coffee. Also make sure they've got a little salted beef, salt pork or jerky for their journey.''

"Yessir." Cavannaugh walked off.

Brooks, Armbruster and Knudson walked to Brooks's office and sat. Brooks broke out a bottle and filled three glasses.

"You come up with a plan yet, Lieutenant Armbruster?" Brooks asked after a few minutes to reflect over the whiskey.

"Not much of one, sir. We'll be going after those bastards, certainly. I thought maybe we'd leave an hour or so before dawn. Loco Squad should be able to pull out fairly quietly. If the Navajos are waiting for us out there somewhere, we might be able to get past them without them knowing it. If they have men watching for us to follow them, it might really befuddle them when no one leaves tomorrow after dawn. After that, we play it by ear."

"I'm afraid your concerns are coming true, Lieutenant."

Armbruster nodded. He had no reason to be smug about it.

"Make sure you take sufficient ammunition, Ed," Brooks said quietly. "And take a couple extra men from B Company as couriers."

Minutes later, Doctor Fournier joined the group. He pulled up a chair, grabbed the shot of whiskey Brooks had poured for him and bolted the drink down. He refilled his glass and set it on the desk.

"Well?" Armbruster asked.

"The unfortunate soul was killed less than half an hour before he was brought into the fort, as best as I can tell. Perhaps it was a little longer than that, but he certainly was not hurt several days ago as the Navajos had said."

"Well, that at least confirms it," Armbruster said. He finished the whiskey in his glass, and then stood. "Well, sir," he said to Brooks, "I have work to do, so if you don't mind."

"Of course, Lieutenant," Brooks said. "If I don't see you again before you leave, good luck, and God go with you."

"Thank you, sir. I'm afraid we'll need all of His help we can get." He left, with Knudson on his heels. At the barracks, Armbruster outlined his plan—such as it was—for all the men. It did not take long. "So you boys better get yourselves some rest. You'll be up early."

Armbruster left, and with Knudson and Cavannaugh went to the quartermaster's to make arrangements for the next morning. It was almost midnight by the time Armbruster got to bed, and it took a while to get to sleep, since he was rather wound up.

It seemed like he had hardly gotten to sleep when Bauer woke him. "Thanks, Sergeant," Armbruster grumbled as he swung his legs out of bed. He rubbed his face, thinking he might not ever be able to shed the tiredness. He forced himself to get up and pour some water in the basin. After splashing water on his face and then shaving, he felt a little better.

Armbruster took time getting dressed. For some reason he began to feel this was a special occasion, though he didn't know why. Still, he dressed with care. Then he headed to the officers' mess. Old Bessie was there and had breakfast—and more importantly, coffee—ready.

Knudson entered minutes later and sat at Armbruster's table. He, too, looked tired and grouchy, but he perked up after a few healthy swallows of coffee and eggs. Neither man saw any reason to talk.

Still silent, they went outside. It was a warm but pleasant morning. They headed to the large stable, where Cavannaugh had assembled the men of Loco

Squad, plus two volunteers from B Company. The latter would act as couriers between the column and the fort, if necessary.

The mules were loaded and most of the horses saddled already when Armbruster and Knudson walked up. "Good work, Sergeant," Armbruster said with an approving nod.

Armbruster was surprised to see the Tiwa scout, Chief, squatting silently with his back against the stable wall. Armbruster walked to him and squatted in front of him. "Haven't seen you in a long time, Chief," he said quietly.

"I went away," the Tiwa said.

Armbruster accepted that. "Glad to have you back," he said with a nod before rejoining Knudson.

Minutes later they were riding out of the fort, heading west for the mouth of Bonito Canyon. The men had tied down all their loose equipment and made little noise as they worked into the canyon. There were some sounds that could not be masked—the creak of leather, the occasional clunk of a pack hitting a cliff wall, the horses' slow hoofbeats, a sudden, involuntary sneeze by a man—but they couldn't be helped.

Just before dawn, Armbruster called a halt. The men moved into a copse of trees along Bonito Creek. They did not unpack the mules, nor unsaddle the horses. They did loosen the saddles to give the horses some breathing room. But Armbruster did not plan to be here long. He just wanted to wait until full daylight, and then see what Navajos—if any—were around.

Armbruster sent Chief to scout the area. The Tiwa left his horse and moved out on foot. Half an hour later, he came trotting back.

Watching him coming, Cavannaugh said, "He looks about done in, Lieutenant."

"He sure as hell does, Sergeant," Armbruster answered. "Privates Quinn and MacDonald, hurry out there and help Chief."

The two soldiers trotted out. Before they got to Chief, though, the Indian fell facedown in the dirt. Everyone in the army camp could see the arrows sticking out of Chief's back.

"Shit," Armbruster snapped.

When Quinn and MacDonald dragged Chief into the copse, Armbruster and Knudson knelt next to him. The others gathered around. Chief raised his head weakly. "Many Navajos," he gasped.

"How many? And where are they?" Armbruster asked urgently.

"Maybe three hundred. All in rocks. On cliffs. All over." He tried to say something else, but died before the words could form.

"Shit," Armbruster snapped again.

⟨ 36 ⟩

Armbruster was about to begin issuing orders when fifty or so Navajos suddenly rushed the soldiers' position. The men did not need the bugler to let them know what to do—they just went into a defensive posture, pouring a deadly fire into the ranks of Navajos.

The Navajos lost at least a dozen men in that first assault before they retreated back to the safety of the rocks. But Armbruster had lost Privates Scoggins and Latham. There was not much could be done about that now. He nodded, mind made up.

"Lieutenant Knudson," he said urgently but calmly, "you and Corporal Olson take four men from Second Unit and hold down the left flank. Sergeant Bauer, you and four others from First Unit, plus Corporal Skidmore, take the right flank. Sergeant Goettle, take the other four men in Second Unit and guard the horses. Sergeant Cavannaugh, you and I and the rest of the men will stand fast in the center."

The noncoms and Knudson swiftly picked their men and moved into position. When they had done so, Armbruster called Private Garrett, one of the B Company soldiers acting as couriers. "Private," Armbruster said, "I want you to haul ass back to Fort Defiance. Tell Major Brooks we're pinned down by perhaps three hundred Navajos and that I request reinforcements posthaste."

"Yessir." Garrett did not look at all happy about his duty.

"Now, Private!" Armbruster said a little harshly when Garrett did not move immediately. That got the courier moving.

The Navajos tried another frontal assault, but they lost several more men. That kept them behind the rocks; Armbruster's men were just too good marksmen to risk losing any more warriors.

The day dragged on, with the heat rising steadily and cruelly. The men in their wool or buckskin clothing sweltered, not finding much solace even in the shade of the trees or cliffs. The only saving grace about their position was that they had the creek at their back. They would not suffer from thirst.

As the hours passed, Armbruster began to wonder what had happened to Private Garrett. Near noon, he decided that either Garrett had not made it or that Major Brooks was not planning to send reinforcements. That didn't make sense to Armbruster, except possibly if the fort itself was under attack. Even then, though, Brooks would've certainly sent word back that such was the case. He had hesitated all morning to send Private Pomeroy, the other courier, but by noon he felt it was necessary. While the Navajos had not tried another frontal assault, they had periodically poured rifle and arrow fire down on the soldiers. Two men had been wounded.

Finally he could wait no longer. He called Pomeroy and gave him the same orders as he had Garrett and sent the private on his way. Then he settled back to wait some more.

Two hours later, Armbruster summoned Knudson, Cavannaugh, Bauer and Goettle and held a council of war. He opened it by saying that he figured both Garrett and Pomeroy were dead and that he thought they should make a run for it.

"I don't cotton to runnin', sir," Cavannaugh said without apology.

"Neither do I, Sergeant," Armbruster said with a weak grin. "But the mark of a smart man—one who survives—is knowing when to fight and when to run off with his tail between his legs. Considering that we're outnumbered maybe twelve to one, I think this is such a time."

"I expect you're right," Cavannaugh admitted. He thought for a minute, then said, "If I may, sir?"

"Dammit, Clancy," Armbruster said, "you know you can speak your mind to me any goddamn time. Even if I don't want to hear it."

"Yessir. The more I think about it, the more I think you're right that we should cut and run. But doin' so all at once'd be plenty foolish."

"So what do you propose, Sergeant?"

"Leave me and a handful of the boys to protect the rear. We'll hold 'em off as long as we can, then chase after you."

Armbruster shook his head. "Too dangerous. Damn near suicidal."

"Yeah, it could be that, all right," Cavannaugh agreed. "But better to sacrifice a few men than endanger the entire outfit, sir." He paused. "But it doesn't have to be. Me and the boys're pretty good fighters, sir. We might not be so bad off as you think."

"Another possibility, Ed," Knudson said, "is using a small detachment, like Sergeant Cavannaugh mentioned, but as a decoy, rather than as a rear guard."

"Beggin' your pardon, sir," Cavannaugh said, "but that's an even dumber idea than mine."

Knudson's anger flared. "And just why is that, Sergeant?" he demanded.

Armbruster listened with interest, wanting to hear Cavannaugh's reasoning.

"With your way, Lieutenant," Cavannaugh said evenly, "the detachment'd be out in the open more likely than not. We'd—they'd—be ridin' hard probably, which meant they'd not be able to raise much of a defense. Hell, sir, shootin' from the back of a horse don't do a hell of a lot for accuracy. But fightin' a rear guard action, we'd be able to set up a defensive position. With the right spot, we might be able to hold those bastards off for quite a spell. Maybe even long enough that we could use darkness to get out of here ourselves."

"He's got you there, Hans," Armbruster said. "Not that I like either idea very much." He paced a little, mulling it over. "The one thing that really puts me off about the idea," he finally said, "is that if Privates Garrett and Pomeroy didn't make it, there must be Navajos toward the canyon mouth."

"There probably are, sir," Cavannaugh said. "But if so, there's more than likely not more'n a couple of 'em. You should be able to take care of 'em."

Armbruster paced some more. Then he stopped and shook his head. "No, I'm not going to sacrifice any men. Not as long as there's a chance of getting us all out."

"But, sir . . ."

"No buts, Sergeant." Armbruster sighed, trying to settle his decision in his mind. He almost smiled. "But you'll have a chance for some heroics, Sergeant, I'd wager." Suddenly he was all business again. His decision was made and he was comfortable with it. "Hans, you and Corporal Olson start having a few of the men walking the horses toward the canyon mouth a couple at a time. Send four men with the first batch, and have two stay there to guard the horses as they arrive. The other two can do the ferrying. Oh, and leave the mules be. I want this done as swiftly as possible, but with a minimum of fuss. I don't know how well this's going to work even if everything goes right. There's no reason to make it known that we're up to something.''

Knudson nodded. ''Then what?''

''We'll worry about that when the time comes.'' When Knudson had left, Armbruster said, ''Clancy, pick two men—good ones . . .''

''They're all good ones, sir,'' Cavannaugh said quietly but with considerable pride.

Armbruster smiled and nodded. ''Yes, they are, Sergeant. Pick two of them and send them out prowling near the canyon mouth, let them see how many Navajos are out that way. Tell them to be cautious, though. I don't want to lose them. If there're only one or two there and they can dispatch the hostiles without endangering themselves, tell them to do so. If not, or if there're too many, have them report back here as soon as possible.''

''Yessir.''

It was almost an hour before everything was ready. All the horses were set. Privates Pettet and Kazmierczak had returned to report that they had spotted only two Navajo warriors and had dispatched them.

Armbruster nodded. ''All right, I want all the men—except those with you, Sergeant,'' he said with a nod toward Cavannaugh, ''to move quickly and quietly to the horses and wait there, prepared to fight and mount up. Hans, you're in charge there, at least until I get there.'' He paused. ''And make sure the bodies of Private Scoggins and Chief are tied down well on their horses.''

Knudson nodded, face tight.

Within minutes, Armbruster, Cavannaugh, Bauer, Skidmore and four privates were the only ones left in the camp. He explained his plan, such as it was, and soon they had gathered up the mules, which were still packed except for ammunition, powder and ball. Armbruster took one last look around, then nodded.

The enlisted men suddenly shouted, swatted mule rumps with their hats and fired a few shots at the ground. The braying mules bolted, racing away, packs flapping. The men spun and ran the other way, heading for the horses.

As Armbruster neared the waiting men from his unit, he roared, "Mount up, men! And ride!"

The men acted swiftly and certainly. There was no panic, just the knowledge that they needed to move. The horses broke into gallops, the men riding in ranks of two. Knudson led the way, with Sergeant Goettle and Corporal Olson right behind him. Armbruster and Cavannaugh brought up the rear.

Through the cloud of dust, Armbruster suddenly noted that Knudson had disappeared. He knew that Knudson had gone down when he saw the enlisted men separating to go around something on the ground. Over the pounding of hooves, Armbruster heard a rifle shot, and then another. He looked up, eyes frantically searching the canyon walls for the source of the gunfire. He saw a Navajo and he jerked with all his strength on the reins. The horse nearly tumbled over backward in trying to stop, but Armbruster was paying the animal no mind. He had slid off the-horse, rifle in hand, while the animal was still squatting on its haunches.

Armbruster dropped down to one knee and brought the rifle up. He ignored the sweat rolling down his face as he aimed, waiting for the Navajo to show himself again. When the warrior did, ready to shoot at the soldiers once more, Armbruster fired. He had a tense moment before the warrior fell, bouncing down the rock-studded slope of the canyon wall.

Armbruster swung about, dropping his rifle and

reaching for a pistol at the sound of someone approaching. He relaxed minutely when he saw that it was Cavannaugh.

"Time to go, sir," the sergeant said tightly. "The men're waiting."

Armbruster nodded. "Lieutenant Knudson?"

"Dead, sir," Cavannaugh responded flatly. "Shot through clean. The men have him on his horse."

Armbruster nodded again. He and Cavannaugh jumped into their saddles, and within moments, the whole column was racing off again. Armbruster looked behind several times, expecting pursuit, but none was in the offing.

"Sendin' the mules out there must've worked, Lieutenant," Cavannaugh shouted as they rode. "Them Navajos're probably still going through the packs."

They finally slowed some, keeping their pace to a good trot, and less than an hour after leaving their camp in Bonito Canyon, the troops rode back into Fort Defiance.

Armbruster walked right into Brooks's office, without knocking, and sat. Brooks looked annoyed, but said calmly, "You're back rather sooner than I expected, Lieutenant. Trouble?"

"Privates Scoggins, Garrett and Pomeroy are dead," Armbruster said. "As is Lieutenant Knudson."

Brooks's eyebrows raised.

"Chief's dead, too. Before he died, he told us we were facing maybe three hundred Navajos. They had us pinned down since first thing this morning. Private Scoggins was killed early in the fighting. I sent Private Garrett here with a request for reinforcements."

"He never arrived."

Armbruster nodded and took the glass of whiskey Brooks had handed him. "We found his body on the way back. Pomeroy's, too. I sent him back here several hours after Garrett."

"So, what's our next . . ." Brooks started. He stopped when Captain Gilmore entered the office.

"Well, Lieutenant," Gilmore said smugly, "I see you and your crack outfit out there could've used some help from us regular soldiers in B Company." He didn't quite sneer, but it was close.

Armbruster carefully placed his glass on Brooks's desk. Then he stood, turned and punched Gilmore in the face as hard as he could.

Gilmore staggered out through the office door, across the narrow width of the hallway, and out through the front door of the building. He stumbled on the steps and fell to the dirt. By the time he landed, Armbruster was on him again.

Armbruster grabbed a handful of Gilmore's shirt and half hauled him up, then pounded the captain's face steadily. Until Sergeants Cavannaugh and Bauer pulled him away from their fellow officer.

Armbruster almost regained most of his senses. He stood there, chest heaving, and glaring at Gilmore. "You ever say anything that fucking stupid to me again, Gilmore, and I'll pound you to death."

Gilmore mumbled something that was unintelligible. He was clinging to consciousness only by a thread.

"Sergeant," Brooks snapped, "get Captain Fournier over here to take care of Captain Gilmore. On the double."

"Yessir." Bauer spun and spouted orders.

"Come on, Ed," Brooks said, tugging on Armbruster. When they were back in the office, Brooks pushed Armbruster into a chair and then handed him the glass of whiskey. "Drink," he ordered. When Armbruster did, Brooks sat and said, "Dammit, I wish you hadn't done that."

Armbruster shrugged, unconcerned.

"He's going to push for your court-martial as soon as

he can, you know," Brooks said. He was annoyed but not too worried.

"If you had let me finish the job, we wouldn't have to think about that," Armbruster said flatly.

"Indeed." Brooks paused. "As I was starting to ask before Gilmore imposed on our hospitality, what's your next move?"

"Only thing I can think of to do, Major, is to send out the men in force. It's imperative we kick the shit out of the Navajos a few times. We don't and we'll never be shed of the problem. But if they can put together three hundred warriors to throw against us whenever they want, our patrols're going to have to be a lot bigger."

"And a lot more aware of what's going on around them," Brooks added. "I can't believe Chief missed that many warriors."

"Me, too, but I think it was mostly that we never expected the Navajos to do such a thing. We—I—won't be taken by surprise again."

"When do you want to start?"

"Morning." He paused. "Lieutenant Knudson needs to be avenged, and the sooner the better."

⌁{ 37 }⌁

Armbruster and the Loco Squad—augmented by two dozen men from B and E Companies—went on a rampage for the rest of the summer. They were merciless in the pursuit of hostile Navajos, raiding villages, camps, strongholds, wherever they could find the enemy. It wasn't so much that Armbruster was devoted to Knudson; it was only that despite their differences, Hans Knudson had been the closest thing to a friend Armbruster had had out here. Indeed, Knudson had been nearabout the only friend Armbruster had had in years.

But even Armbruster's anger had limits. By late August, the men were beginning to wear down from the constant riding and fighting. Armbruster also felt the stress of a too-long campaign. He also wanted to be there when Serafina arrived at the fort, so in early September, he finally turned his men toward the fort.

Armbruster felt a little regret at having dumped the problem of Captain Gilmore's desire to court-martial him on Major Brooks, but that was the post commander's job, Armbruster figured. Still, it was the one reason he was reluctant to return to Fort Defiance. He and his men had, of course, gone back to the fort several times during the summer to reprovision, but they had not stayed long, and Brooks had always kept Gilmore and Armbruster apart on those occasions. But now that winter was on its way, Armbruster would be confined, more or less, to the fort, and there would be no avoiding Gilmore. Armbruster did not fear a court-martial, but he would hate to go through one. For one thing, it would mean he had lost to Gilmore, no matter the actual outcome of the court-martial. And, since there was little doubt that he had hit Gilmore, he most likely would be found guilty. With luck, he would only be cashiered. That would not bother him, but if he were sentenced to prison, he would not be able to be with Serafina, and that would certainly displease him.

Armbruster made sure his men were taken care of before he reported to Brooks. The major had a cigar and a glass of whiskey waiting on the desk for him. Armbruster gratefully gulped down the liquor and then lit the cigar. Brooks shoved the bottle toward him, and Armbruster poured himself another brimming glassful.

"Well, Lieutenant?" Brooks asked after a bit.

"I'm not certain, sir, but I'd estimate we killed forty hostiles. We lost another ten men total since the fight in Bonito Canyon."

"A reasonable ratio."

"No, sir, it's not," Armbruster said flatly. "If we killed a hundred hostiles for each man lost it wouldn't be a decent ratio."

Brooks nodded. "Still, men die in war, and when we can keep our own losses low, so much the better." He rubbed a hand across his face, looking every bit of his fifty-six years. "As much as you might want to admit it, Lieutenant, you've done well."

Armbruster nodded as he sipped his whiskey.

"Anything else to report?"

"Not really, sir," Armbruster said wearily. "Everyone performed well, especially Sergeant Major Cavannaugh and Sergeant Bauer. It wasn't for them, we'd of really been up shit creek more than once.''

"You should put them up for citations, Lieutenant.''

"I will, sir. As soon as I catch up on my sleep.''

"Well, then, how about some good news?''

"That would be a relief, sir," Armbruster said, meaning it.

"Captain Gilmore has been reassigned to a post back in the States. Missouri, I believe.''

"That is good news, Major," Armbruster said honestly. "But can't he still cause me grief from out there?''

"I don't think that's likely. His records contain several notations about his being unable to get along with fellow officers, as well as notations about ineffectualness and subordination.''

"That should make a difference," Armbruster agreed, considerably relieved.

"I thought you'd see it that way," Brooks said dryly.

"In all seriousness, sir, I do appreciate what you've done. Not only with this but with all the other times. I know damn well I've been a burden on you. I don't really mean to be, but . . .'' Armbruster shrugged.

"I could've done with a little less of the trouble you've caused," Brooks said with a chuckle. "But it could've been a lot worse, too.''

It was early October before Serafina and Martinez returned to the fort. Armbruster joined them at the house for supper that night. While they were eating, Martinez said, "The Navajos aren't happy, Eduardo.''

"That's news?" Armbruster responded sarcastically.

Martinez nodded. "There's much talk among the Navajos of the *loco teniente* and his army. You have caused considerable anger in the Navajo people—''

"That doesn't bother me.''

". . . and much fear.''

"That's good."

"You may be right about that, Eduardo. The Navajos who're talking peace seemed to be gaining the upper hand as we headed back here."

"Peace'd be nice, I suppose," Armbruster said quietly. "But I don't expect to see it any time soon." He went back to eating, thoughts awhirl. He was not sure he was done killing Navajos yet, and that bothered him. But neither was he certain that he wanted to kill any more. He had little heart for it; was tired of it; and didn't want to see more of his men slain.

Later—after Martinez had gone out ostensibly to check the mules; and as he and Serafina were lying together in bed relaxing—Armbruster said, "I'm afraid there'll be more blood spilled before the war with the Diné is over."

"I know," Serafina said sadly. She didn't want any more of her mother's people killed, but she found she could not be too worried about that. It seemed sometimes as if she were losing touch with the Diné, and she wasn't sure how she felt about that. There were times when she thought it was a good thing. While she was treated well by the Diné, she had never been completely accepted by them, even when her mother was alive. She also knew that soon she would have to break away from the Diné completely. Armbruster wouldn't be welcome in many hogans, even if he was a trader with her father instead of a soldier.

Though she did not want any more Diné killed, if at all possible, she was in some ways glad that her man was the one leading the war against the Navajo. She knew that Armbruster would try to ensure that no women or children were killed. He would make every effort to attack only war camps or wandering war bands instead of villages whenever possible. It was odd, she knew, perhaps even ghoulish, that she was almost thankful for the man fighting her people. However, she figured that was far better than the alternative.

"It'll be over in a year or so, though," Armbruster said quietly, hopefully.

"Oh?" Serafina responded, heart pounding in scared anticipation.

"I've decided that just after next summer I'll resign my commission. Then I'll marry you." He paused a heartbeat. "If you want."

"Of course I do," Serafina said, happiness pouring through her body. She reached out to touch his face, and then gently kiss his lips. "But do we have to wait until the end of summer?"

"You'll be with your father trading with the Diné until then. I can't just sit around here with nothing to do while I wait for you."

"I suppose I can last that long," Serafina said somewhat sadly.

"You better," Armbruster growled.

"I could say the same for you, Eduardo. You're in a far more dangerous position than I am."

"I'll be all right. With winter coming on, the Navajos'll quiet down."

"They didn't last winter."

"True. But my men and I didn't kick the snot out of them the summer before like we did this year," Armbruster said a little sourly.

"That might make them more angry."

"Your father seems to think otherwise." Armbruster sighed, partly in annoyance, partly in contentment. "There's nothing I can do about it anyway," he said. "If they cause trouble, I'll be duty-bound to go after them."

"I know," Serafina said simply. "That's why I worry for you."

Armbruster pulled her close. "Well, quit worrying. We've got better things to do."

* * *

Armbruster decided that his men needed one last fling in Albuquerque before winter set in. They had fought hard, well and long over the summer, and had managed only one trip to the city's pleasure palaces. Major Brooks, reassured by Martinez's talk of peace forces becoming stronger among the Navajos, allowed the men several weeks.

The trip was relatively fast, though the men certainly made their mark on Albuquerque again. It was only the fact that they were well-armed that kept the constabulary away from them.

While in Albuquerque, though, Armbruster officially asked Martinez for Serafina's hand in marriage. Martinez was not surprised, but he paused before answering, not wanting to appear too eager—or too pleased.

Serafina sat nearby, outwardly calm, but her insides were dancing in worry.

"I think I will allow this," Martinez said with dignity. "If my daughter wishes it." He looked toward Serafina.

The young woman was about to burst from excitement, but she kept her demeanor serene. "I think I would like that, Papa," she said, voice quivering with joy.

"Then I give my consent, Señor Teniente," Martinez said.

Armbruster grinned. He had not wanted to admit it, but he had been nervous. That was foolish, he knew, but he could not help himself. Now he was relieved. "I won't be a *teniente* by then, Señor Martinez."

"This will make you sad?"

Armbruster nodded. "Some. I trained for a long time to become an officer, and I've become a damn good one. But in many ways I won't miss it much. There's too much killing and bloodshed for any reasonable man."

"A strange thing coming from a man like you." Martinez's smile was a little off-center. "You who have become something of a *demonio* to the Diné."

"I don't kill Navajos, or anyone else," Armbruster said carefully, "because I'm a demon. I'm not even bloodthirsty. I do it because it needs doing. And because by doing it I can keep my men—and hopefully some innocents—from getting killed." He knew that was an inadequate explanation, but he did not think he could do any better.

Martinez didn't know how to respond to that, so instead he asked, "When will the wedding take place?"

"First I have to ask if you're still planning to take Serafina trading with you next summer?"

"*Sí.*" Martinez smiled a little. "It will be the last time she and I go together, yes?"

"Yes." Armbruster thought a moment. "Well, I don't know if this'll give us enough time," he said, "but how about the autumnal solstice?"

"A fine day, Eduardo," Martinez said happily. "*Sí,* a fine day. I will make sure we're back by then."

Armbruster nodded.

Suddenly Martinez appeared crestfallen. "You're not Catholic, Eduardo?" He made it sound like an accusation.

"No," Armbruster said flatly. "Is that going to be a problem?"

"No!"

Armbruster and Martinez turned to look at Serafina in surprise.

"No, Papa," she added firmly. "I'm going to be Eduardo's wife. The padre will marry us, or we will go someplace where we can find someone who will."

"You are certain of this, *mi hija*—my daughter?" Martinez asked sternly.

"*Sí,* Papa," Serafina answered. There was no doubt in her voice or demeanor.

Martinez threw up his hands. "What is a man to

do?" he asked somewhat plaintively. He looked at Armbruster and winked. He was not such an upstanding member of San Felipe de Neri Church or any other church, for that matter. He would be able to persuade one of the padres to perform the ceremony, though not for nothing. "It'll cost you a little, though, Eduardo," he said. "The padre, he'll want a little something to look the other way."

Armbruster nodded. "You set it up and let me know," he said seriously. "But you tell that padre that if he tries to steal from me, he'll regret it," Armbruster added in warning.

"There will be no trouble," Martinez assured him.

As winter approached, Armbruster was glad to see that the Navajos apparently were keeping to themselves. And right around the advent of official winter, two Navajos arrived at Fort Defiance and asked to speak to the soldier chief.

Brooks called Armbruster, Captain Josiah Goodwin and Lieutenants Frank Saxbury and Andy Emerson to the small council room in the commander's building, then ordered the two Navajos to be brought in.

"We want peace," Rojo Piedra said. "We're done fighting the soldiers."

"How can I be sure of this?" Brooks asked harshly.

"The Diné will come when the grass greens and sign peace papers with the blue coats."

"If there's any trouble before then, Rojo Piedra, I'll let El Diablo"—he pointed to Armbruster—"and his men loose on you."

Rojo Piedra nodded. He was nervous, since he was far from convincing all the Diné to seek peace with the white men. Still, he hoped to do so by the spring solstice. Unhappily, he and Hablador—who had done much of the translating in the short meeting—left the fort, heading back to their people.

⟨ 38 ⟩

The peace—if that's what it could be called—lasted less than a month. Then several hundred warriors, led by Huero, attacked the soldiers guarding the fort's beef herd just outside the fort.

The drums rolled and the bugles blared, and men tumbled out of their barracks. Seeing that he was the only officer around, Armbruster sent the men of Loco Squad out on their own, led by Sergeant Major Cavannaugh. Then Armbruster took command of B, C, E and G Companies, at least until the other officers came along.

By the time Saxbury and Emerson arrived at the battlefield, such as it was, Armbruster and the men under his command had driven the Indians off. Two of the men guarding the cattle were dead, as were one man each from G and E Companies. The soldiers had killed four Navajos that they were sure of.

"What do you think of this, Ed?" Brooks asked when it was over and the officers were seated in Brooks's office.

"I think that the Navajos have decided they don't want peace," Armbruster said dryly. "Sir."

"Don't be a smart ass with me, Lieutenant," Brooks snapped. "Just answer my question."

"I did, sir. If what you're really asking is where I think this'll lead, or what I think we should do about it, then ask that, sir."

"Shit," Brooks said testily. He settled himself and then asked, "All right, Lieutenant, where do you think this'll lead?"

Armbruster thought about it a few minutes, ignoring the signs of impatience on Emerson, Saxbury and Goodwin. This was the first chance he had really had to ponder it. "I think it means trouble, sir," he finally said. Then he held up a hand to stop any retort from Brooks or the others. "It seems to indicate the Navajos're losing their fear of the fort. It could mean they're testing us to see the chances of overrunning us."

Everyone else remained silent. Then Armbruster added, "Of course, sir, I could be full of shit, and it could be an isolated incident."

"But you don't really think that, do you?"

"No, sir. I figure that if they could bring together two, three hundred warriors in the middle of winter, that they've got more on their minds than grabbing a few cattle or killing a few soldiers."

"I think you're right, Lieutenant," Brooks said without hesitation. "But what do you suggest we do about it?"

"Increase the number of men guarding the cattle considerably, sir. Keep the number high until we're sure what all this is leading to. And keep the herd as close to the fort as reasonably possible."

"Agreed. Now, when are you and the men of Loco Squad leaving to run down these hostiles?"

Armbruster hesitated. "I don't think that'd be wise, sir."

Saxbury snickered, but a cold look from Brooks stopped him.

"Your reasoning, Ed?" Brooks asked.

"If they're testing the fort's defenses, our leaving would weaken the fort too much, sir. I think what we should do is to send out small patrols, but only far enough to spot another war party of Navajos, if one comes, and spread a warning."

"I think it'd be better to cut them off before they come against the fort, wouldn't you?"

"Maybe, sir. But remember what happened last summer in Canyon Bonito. They may just be sitting out there waiting for us again."

"A good point. Still . . ."

"Sir, let's just sit it out a while. A couple of weeks, maybe a month. If there're no more attacks on the fort, I'll ride out and kick some ass wherever I find it."

"What about Rojo Piedra?" Brooks asked. "You told him in no uncertain terms that you would hunt him down at the first sign of the promised peace not holding."

"I did," Armbruster agreed. "And I will. But now's not the time. It's another reason they might've attacked the fort. That wily son of a bitch knows I'm a man who keeps his word. He might be counting on that."

"A trap," Brooks said.

"Yessir. But I'll be damned if I'll take the bait—if that's what it is. If it's not," Armbruster added with a shrug, "we'll probably never be sure. But I'll still get Rojo Piedra, though in my own damn good time."

"All right," Brooks said after a few moments' thought, "we'll do it that way. I want you and your men to take the first few patrols, though. Go as far as you think is necessary." He half-smiled. "But I think you should avoid Canyon Bonito."

"I'll do that, sir."

Within half an hour, Armbruster and his men were riding out. They spent the rest of the day patrolling the area, but saw no sign of the Navajos still being in the area. Just before dawn they returned to the fort. First thing the next morning, they were on horses and riding again. Armbruster decided to ride a little farther afield.

They surprised a band of three dozen Navajo warriors at Bacon Springs. But the Indians had a pretty good defensive position, and held the soldiers at bay. For four days the two sides sniped at each other, neither causing the other much damage.

An hour after the skirmish started, Armbruster sent Private Rob Smith back to the fort to report. He grew more and more annoyed as that first day drew to a close, and he vowed to himself as he went to sleep that he would end it first thing the next day.

But the Navajos were far more entrenched and tenacious than Armbruster had counted on, and all his vowing and fuming were for naught. That afternoon he sent Private Nick Arneson back to the fort to report and to see if the fort was in any danger.

The fort wasn't, but Brooks was afraid such a danger could pop up at any time, so he was reluctant to send reinforcements. That didn't bother Armbruster. In fact, he thought it best. He figured that's all he needed was somebody else coming to his rescue again. But Armbruster kept open the line of communication with the fort, in case the Navajos he was facing got reinforcements, or in case the fort was attacked.

Armbruster waited it out throughout the third day, but on the fourth he angrily ordered a full-scale assault on the Navajo position. It worked, and his men pushed the Navajos out. The soldiers killed two Navajos and drove the rest off without their supplies and some of their horses. Armbruster was relieved to find that only two of his men had been wounded, neither critically.

Armbruster turned his men back to the fort, where they rested up for several days. Other patrols were sent out, but each stayed within a quarter mile of the fort's "boundaries." Then Armbruster and his men were back out again, taking the major role in the patrols, as they had for the past several years.

After a week of no trouble, everyone at the fort began to relax a little, and the patrols once more spread out a little farther, and nine days later Armbruster's troops found another band of Navajos creeping up on the fort. They easily routed the fifteen Indians without the loss of a life on either side.

Despite the tranquillity that spread over this part of Dinétah, Armbruster began to dread the coming of spring. If the Navajos had been this fractious during the winter, once warmer weather came there was a good possibility of them going on a rampage.

His feeling was only reinforced when he and his men, accompanied by a dozen men each from B and G Companies, had another skirmish with Navajos two miles from the fort.

Tensions were still running very high at the fort as the end of April approached, when Martinez and Serafina arrived, and Armbruster was testy about it all. "You're late, Cruz," he said to Martinez in an accusatory tone. "What kept you?"

"You know how bad the mud gets out here sometimes," Martinez answered calmly. "It was worse than usual and slowed us down."

Armbruster nodded, accepting it. He knew it to be true, but he still didn't like it. He explained what had gone on over the winter and the early spring.

Martinez nodded, but would not change his plans any in light of the new information.

Armbruster was unhappy—or as unhappy as he could be around Serafina—when Martinez and Serafina prepared to pull out a few days later. He was mighty reluctant to let Serafina leave. "It's a damn fool idea, Cruz," Armbruster said to Martinez.

"We'll be safe. Serafina's one of the Diné."

"Not enough of one when they're on the prowl like they've been."

"We'll be all right," Martinez insisted.

Armbruster glared at the small, tough Mexican trader. "All I can say to you then, Cruz, is that if the Diné do anything to Serafina, you better hope the bastards kill you at the same time, because if they don't, I swear to Christ I will."

"You worry too much, Eduardo."

"Maybe I do, but I've got good reason to." He looked at Serafina and smiled a little. She returned it.

The next morning she was gone, riding out on her chestnut mare as she always did, holding the ropes to most of the mules carrying the trading goods. Both Martinez and Serafina seemed unconcerned.

Armbruster turned after he could no longer see them, and went to the barracks. "Sergeant Cavannaugh," he said roughly, "I'll be in my quarters the rest of the day. I don't want to be disturbed by anyone."

"Anyone, sir?"

"Anyone."

Cavannaugh looked at Armbruster oddly for some time, then nodded. "Yessir." He suspected what the problem was, but he also figured that Armbruster's reasons were none of his business.

"Thank you, Sergeant," Armbruster said stiffly. He left, went to his quarters and proceeded to drink himself into a stupor. He felt like hell the next morning, and it took him most of the day to recover from his hangover. Once he did, he sought out Cavannaugh again. "I'm grateful for your keeping folks away from me," he said quietly.

"No trouble, sir." He cocked an eyebrow at his commander. "You feelin' all right now, though?"

"Yes, Sergeant. It was just something I felt compelled to do. No matter how stupid it seems in retrospect."

He sighed. "But I think it's about time we got back on patrol. We'll leave the day after tomorrow. You can spend tomorrow having the men prepare and draw supplies."

"Yessir."

The long, persistent rumble of the drums calling the Long Roll woke Armbruster from a deep sleep the next morning. By the time his socks hit the floor, he was already reaching for his pants. He had just gotten them pulled on and was sitting pulling on his boots when Sergeant Major Clancy Cavannaugh burst into his quarters.

"It's the goddamn Navajos again, isn't it?" Armbruster asked, looking up while jerking on one boot.

"Yessir," Cavannaugh said. "And I reckon we're in for one hell of a mornin'."

Soon after, Armbruster and some of his men were in the sutler's store, watching the attack from the safety of the building's thick adobe walls. But Armbruster was antsy. There was no action here, and he and his men were too used to action. He could not see himself sitting here all day waiting for someone to attack the sutler's place.

Despite the fact that it was still rather dark, he caught a glimpse of some Navajos easing up on Brooks's house. "Shit," he muttered. He gulped down the entire mug of coffee Mrs. Webber had handed him less than five minutes ago. He set the cup down and spun, mind made up. "Sergeant, let's move. The major's quarters. *Pronto.*"

"Yessir."

"John," Armbruster said hastily to Webber, "will you be all right here by yourself?"

"Goddamn right," Webber growled. "You go on and do what you need to. I'll watch over my family."

"Get the door for us, John," Armbruster said firmly.

Then, "Let's go, men." With pistols in hand, he led the way out, dashing across what suddenly seemed to be miles of emptiness toward the rear of officers' row. His men, silent, well-armed and deadly, were a step behind him.

Armbruster and his six men blasted their way into the middle of nearly a dozen Navajos trying to get into Brooks's quarters. Then they were fighting hand to hand, knives clacking, men grunting in the semilight beginning to creep over the camp.

Within minutes the surviving Navajos were fleeing, those unhurt helping the wounded. Five warriors lay where they had fallen.

Armbruster pounded on the door with the hilt of his sword. "Major!" he roared. "Major, you all right in there?"

"Get the hell away from my door," Brooks's voice boomed from inside, "or I'll shoot you dead right where you are!"

"Major! It's Lieutenant Armbruster."

"Well, why the hell didn't you say so," Brooks snarled as he jerked the door open.

"Everyone all right in there, sir?" Armbruster asked.

"Yes, son. How's the battle going?"

"Not sure, sir. If you want to check for yourself, I'll leave some of my men here to watch over your family."

Brooks hesitated only a moment, then nodded.

"Corporal Skidmore, you and Privates Sullivan, Mac-Donald, Smith and Bates are to watch over Major Brooks's family. The rest of you come with me. Let's go, Major."

Armbruster, Brooks and Armbruster's three remaining men—including Sergeant Bauer—ran along the side of the house and then out onto the parade ground, where they stopped. Swiftly Armbruster and Brooks surveyed the battlefield. Many soldiers were still running around seemingly confused. Little leadership seemed evident. Arrows and lead balls rained down on the parade ground from the cliffs. *Come on, Sergeant,* Armbruster thought, *get up there and start taking those bastards out.*

"Privates Pettet and Tuttle," Armbruster snapped, "go get me the buglers and the drummers from each company."

"All of them, sir?" Tuttle asked.

"As many as you can find in three goddamn minutes. Drag them back here if need be. And check with Sergeant Goettle to see how things're going. Skirt the buildings going and coming."

As the two men raced off, Brooks, Armbruster and Bauer edged backward until they were just about touching the wall of Brooks's house, figuring to keep in the shadows as much as possible while they waited.

"Didn't I order you to guard the east side of the fort, Lieutenant?" Brooks asked.

"Yessir. Sergeant Goettle's at the base of the cliff with some of the men. Sergeant Cavannaugh's headed up to the top of the cliff to bring the fight to the Navajos up there."

"Why aren't you with them?"

"I thought I could be of more help elsewhere," Armbruster said flatly. "Sir." He turned a steady, hard gaze onto Brooks. "If you think it'd help, though, I'll be glad to take my men and go over there."

Brooks grinned tightly. "That won't be necessary."

Tuttle and Pettet returned with three buglers and one drummer. All were puffing from their run. Armbruster took them around to the back of officers' row. "Summon your companies, boys," Armbruster ordered the musicians.

The buglers and drummer looked at Brooks. "You heard him, men," Brooks snapped. "Do it."

As they began using their instruments to call their companies into formation, Pettet said, "Sergeant Goettle's just fine, sir, though he's more than a mite put out that he ain't seeing any action."

"He'll see some before the day's through, Private. Thank you."

Within minutes most of the soldiers of the post were in formation in front of Brooks's quarters. Goodwin saluted Brooks and asked, "What's this all about, Major?"

"It's time we defended this fort properly, Captain," Brooks snapped. "Lieutenant Armbruster will direct that defense."

"A lieutenant?" Goodwin protested.

"For this battle, Brevet Major Armbruster," Brooks responded coldly. "Dismissed."

Goodwin didn't like it, but he knew that if he uttered another word of protest Brooks would see that he was court-martialed—if he were lucky. Silently he went back to his men and waited.

"B and G Companies," Armbruster roared, "get as many wagons as you can round up and put them between all the buildings to help cut off the chance of Navajos overrunning us. Captain Goodwin, take E Company and take positions near the commander's officer and storerooms. You'll stand in defense of the southern perimeter of the fort. C Company, spread out along the east and west sides of the fort. Your ranks'll be filled out when B Company finishes with the wagons."

When the soldiers had hastened off to their duties, Armbruster said, "Private Pettet, go bring Sergeant Goettle and his men here. I want them to watch the north perimeter here. I—"

Armbruster stopped when a new outbreak of rapid gunfire caught his attention. He looked up, suddenly worried, then smiled grimly as he saw in the burgeoning dawn several Navajos plunge off the hundred-foot cliff. "Sergeant Cavannaugh and his men," he said quietly. He looked at Pettet and nodded. "A change of orders, Private. Go tell Sergeant Goettle to send half his men here. He's to join Sergeant Cavannaugh up on the cliff with the rest of his men—and you, if that's where you want to be."

"Yessir!" Pettet said before charging off, dodging arrows and bullets with something that approached magic.

The Navajos tried to overrun the fort at three of the four sides—skipping only the eastern edge, considering its proximity to the cliff—starting with the north. Armbruster and his men drove them back that time, causing heavy losses to the Indians in the process. The Navajos then proceeded to try the west and then south.

They managed to break through into the fort at the latter. A few warriors even managed to gain safety in a few of the fort buildings, but the majority were caught in a deadly crossfire between Armbruster's men on the north and Goodwin's E Company on the south. Those who weren't killed or wounded swiftly deserted the field of battle, racing off toward the west. A few soldiers died when Navajos caught them from behind as they guarded the perimeter. But most of the Indians were interested only in getting away from this frightful spot.

It was almost full daylight now, and against the glare of the rising sun, Armbruster could still see Navajos occasionally falling off the cliff after having been shot. Then Sergeant Cavannaugh was standing at the edge of the cliff. He cupped his hands around his mouth and shouted, "They're gone, Lieutenant!"

Armbruster nodded, mostly for his own benefit, since Cavannaugh would not be able to see it. "Track them to make sure they're really gone," he bellowed. A moment later Cavannaugh disappeared.

Armbruster sent men out to each of the three other perimeters to check on their welfare. Armbruster's men also carried orders to have those other commanders send out small patrols to see if the Navajos truly had fled from all sides. The rest of the men were to remain at their positions until given word that they could stand down.

Then Armbruster took what men of his were left at the fort—except for the contingent still watching over Brooks's family—and they began going from building to building, searching for Navajos. They killed two who ambushed them and chose to continue the fight, and captured fifteen others who surrendered peaceably.

Once that nerve-racking task was completed, Armbruster allowed Doctor Fournier to go about tending to the wounded soldiers. After putting their prisoners in the guardhouse, Armbruster and his men went after the other prisoners—those Navajos who had been wounded and either wanted to surrender or could not get away.

It was a time-consuming job, and before it was com-

pleted, the patrols had returned. Each reported that
the Navajos had indeed left the area. With that, Armbruster enlisted almost all the other men in moving
wounded Indians, guarding captives, removing dead
Navajos and then burying them in a mass grave, and
cleaning up after the battle.

Shortly before noon, they were done, and the fort
was back to normal, except for the one hundred twelve
prisoners chained up in several of the small stables at
the north end of the fort.

As he was checking the men guarding those prisoners, Armbruster glanced up at the small house not far
away. He stopped, staring. Then he turned and ran
toward Brooks's quarters, calling to his men as he did.
Armbruster stopped and settled himself a moment before knocking on Brooks's door.

Brooks answered and indicated that Armbruster
should enter.

"I'd rather you stepped outside, sir," Armbruster
said quietly.

Brooks's eyebrows raised, but he came out and shut
the door softly behind him. "What it is, Lieutenant?"

"I'm going out after Serafina and her father," Armbruster said harshly. "Sir."

"You think she's in danger?"

"It's a possibility."

"But she is a Navajo. At least partly."

"She's that, sir. But after the whipping we just gave
the Navajos, they're going to be some goddamn angry
Indians out there. They just might take that anger out
on anyone they come across."

Brooks did not hesitate. "Go, Lieutenant. Take what
men you need. Oh, and Lieutenant," he added as
Armbruster started to leave, "I want you to come see
me as soon as you get back."

"Yessir." Armbruster turned and saw Cavannaugh
trotting up with Armbruster's horse in tow, a dozen

men from Loco Squad following. Armbruster flung
himself into the saddle and then he and his men gal-
loped out of the fort.

It took them three days to find the trader and his
daughter, but they finally came across them in Nazlini
Canyon. The two were alone but alive. Martinez was
surprised to see Armbruster. He was even more surprised when Armbruster told Martinez that he was taking him and Serafina back to the fort.

"But why?" Martinez asked, angry.

"A thousand Diné—maybe more—attacked the fort
a couple days ago. We kicked hell out of them and sent
them packing, but I don't know as if they're going to
be favorably disposed toward outsiders—even one like
Serafina."

"I told you before, Eduardo, we'll be all right."

"Cruz, I don't want to say this, let alone do it, but
you and Serafina are going back to the fort with me.
You can sell your goods to John or sell them at his
place yourself. But you're going back to the fort."

Martinez, who could be as tough as anyone when the
need arose, glared at Armbruster, his dark eyes blazing
hotly.

"Eduardo is right, Papa," Serafina said. She was no
more scared than she ever was, but with her father
growing a little older, and her own marriage impending, she was becoming more cautious.

Finally Martinez nodded slowly. "I'm getting too old
to tempt the fates any longer," he admitted. "We'll
leave in the morning."

"I wish you'd reconsider, Ed," Brooks said.

"I know you do, sir. But my mind's made up." As
soon as returning to the fort with Martinez and Serafina, Armbruster had gone to see Brooks. Without preliminary, he told Brooks that he was resigning his
commission immediately and would be leaving the fort

with Martinez and Serafina as soon as he thought traveling would be safe.

Brooks rapped his fingertips on the desk in angry annoyance. Lieutenant Edward Armbruster was perhaps the best fighting officer Brooks had ever seen. "We're still short a captain, from when Captain Gilmore was reassigned," Brooks said quietly. "The rank is yours for the asking."

Armbruster was a little taken aback, and for a moment he actually considered it. Then he shook his head. "No, sir. Not unless people change their attitude."

"Miss Martinez?"

Armbruster nodded. "Our wedding day is set, sir. I love her and she reciprocates the feeling. Our differences don't matter to us, but because they seem to be so important to others, I have no other choice."

"Think of what you're throwing away, Lieutenant," Brooks insisted.

"I have, Major. And, while there're some good things I'll miss, there's also a plentiful of things I won't —all the bloodshed and death, spending frigid winter nights out on the trail, poor food, the weight of so many regulations . . ."

"But I can really use your help here, Lieutenant," Brooks said.

"I suppose you can. But you'll find someone else to take my place."

"I doubt that," Brooks said with a small smile.

"I'm flattered you think that, Major. I really am. But look at it realistically. How much longer are you going to be stationed here? And what're the chances of my next commanding officer being as lenient in allowing me a free hand with my men and how we go about our business?"

"Not very good," Brooks grudgingly admitted. He sighed wearily, then stood and reached across the desk.

As he shook Armbruster's hand, Brooks said, "I'm sure going to miss you, Lieutenant."

"And I you, sir."

Three days later, Armbruster, Martinez and Serafina left Fort Defiance. They were escorted by every member of the Loco Squad. Armbruster felt a little odd in the civilian clothes given to him by John Webber. He still wore his calf-high boots, the buckskin jacket and the jaunty hat from his Loco Squad service. But now he wore a simple calico shirt and a pair of stiff new Levi-Strauss pants. He stopped just outside the fort's borderless confines and looked back.

Serafina stopped next to him. "Will you miss this place, Eduardo?" she asked.

He smiled at her. "Perhaps a little. I served with good men here." He saddened momentarily at the remembrance of Lieutenant Hans Knudson. Then his smile returned and widened. "And I met and courted you here." The two turned and rode slowly off, side by side.

AUTHOR'S NOTE

Fort Defiance was established at Canyon Bonito in 1851. The army officially recognizes the date as September 15, 1851. At the time, this was part of New Mexico Territory. Today, the town of Fort Defiance lies in Arizona, only a few miles from the New Mexico border, on the giant Navajo Reservation.

Though the army had chosen the fort site well—as far as wood, water and grazing were concerned—the soldiers called it Hell's Gate or Hell's Hollow. The Navajos—who called themselves the Diné—called the spot Tséhootsooi, which means the Green Place Between the Rocks.

The fort site is bounded on the west by a draw through which the Bonito River flows. On the east side is a steep, rocky cliff about a hundred feet high. To the north, the land rises gradually to the Chuska Mountains. And on the south is rolling land dotted with massive rock formations.

Real people are scattered throughout the novel, most prominently Major Thomas Brooks. I have, however, taken considerable liberties with him as a character.

Other real people include the Navajos Sarcillos

Largos and Manuelito, as well as the fort sutler, John Webber.

A peace meeting was held in 1855 at Leguna Negra, but starting in 1858 or so, a number of small incidents began occurring between the Navajos and the soldiers. Each pushed the fragile peace a little closer to an end. One such event was the slaying by a Navajo of Brooks's slave boy. When Brooks demanded of Sarcillos Largos that the killer be turned over, the Navajo complained that the soldiers who had killed some of Sarcillos Largos's cattle some weeks earlier had not been punished.

In October of 1858, Colonel Dixon Stansbury Miles led the Third Infantry on a raid in which Manuelito's camp was burned. Afterward, Miles continued the campaign, in which seven or eight soldiers and an estimated fifty Navajos were killed.

In spring 1859, the Navajos held a *Natch'it*—a sort of political-religious gathering. At the *Natch'it*, Manuelito tried to push his tribesmen into warring on the whites, but Sarcillos Largos argued against it. Things settled down until January 1860.

By this time, Brooks was no longer commander at Fort Defiance, but I have left him in that position for the purpose of this novel. Beginning in January 1860, the Navajos began pressing the soldiers some. On January 17, the Navajos skirmished with soldiers who were guarding beef cattle. Another skirmish erupted at Bacon Springs with an estimated three hundred Navajos. This lasted from January 18 to 22. Other fights took place on February 8 and April 5.

All this warfare culminated in the big fight for the fort on April 30, 1860. The real fight was not as dramatic as the one depicted in this novel, but it was a tension filled time for the soldiers involved.

About half an hour before daybreak, a thousand warriors under Manuelito attacked from the steep cliff on the east side of the fort. A number of them quickly got control of the fort gardens, and there they found cover behind fences and wood piles. Within minutes, all one hundred thirty-eight men stationed at Fort Defiance at the time were engaged in the battle.

Once daylight had come, the soldiers managed to drive off the Navajos, losing surprisingly few men in the process. The Navajos had never really gained control of much of the fort, having gotten in charge of a few buildings before being driven out.

The fight for the fort did point out Fort Defiance's vulnerability. Captain (Brevet Major) Oliver Lathrop Shepherd, who was in command of the fort at the time of the attack suggested that the fort be abandoned because it was located with a ravine on one side and a cliff on the other.

The fort was not abandoned for another year, and when it was, on April 25, 1861, it was the Civil War that brought the abandonment. The fort was temporarily used by Kit Carson's troops in 1863. They called it Fort Canby. Some years later, Fort Defiance became the first agency on the Navajo Reservation, and today some of the buildings that had been reconstructed over the years are used for the Bureau of Indian Affairs and Navajo Nation offices.

Today, Fort Defiance is a sleepy speck of a town about two miles from Window Rock, the Navajo Nation capital. It is only a few miles from the New Mexico state line. The Navajo Reservation is the largest and most populous in the United States. It is situated mostly in northeastern Arizona, though it runs into New Mexico on the east and Utah to the north.

TERRY C. JOHNSTON
THE PLAINSMEN

THE BOLD WESTERN SERIES FROM
ST. MARTIN'S PAPERBACKS

COLLECT THE ENTIRE SERIES!

SIOUX DAWN (Book 1)
92732-0 _____ $4.99 U.S. _____ $5.99 CAN.

RED CLOUD'S REVENGE (Book 2)
92733-9 _____ $4.99 U.S. _____ $5.99 CAN.

THE STALKERS (Book 3)
92963-3 _____ $4.99 U.S. _____ $5.99 CAN.

BLACK SUN (Book 4)
92465-8 _____ $4.99 U.S. _____ $5.99 CAN.

DEVIL'S BACKBONE (Book 5)
92574-3 _____ $4.99 U.S. _____ $5.99 CAN.

SHADOW RIDERS (Book 6)
92597-2 _____ $5.99 U.S. _____ $6.99 CAN.

DYING THUNDER (Book 7)
92834-3 _____ $4.99 U.S. _____ $5.99 CAN.

BLOOD SONG (Book 8)
92921-8 _____ $4.99 U.S. _____ $5.99 CAN.

THE FIRST FRONTIER SERIES
by Mike Roarke

At the dawn of the 18th century, while the French and English are locked in a battle for the northeast territory, the ancient Indian tribes begin a savage brother-against-brother conflict—forced to take sides in the white man's war—pushed into an era of great heroism and greater loss. In the tradition of *The Last of the Mohicans*, *The First Frontier Series* is a stunningly realistic adventure saga set on America's earliest battleground. Follow Sam Watley and his son Thad in their struggle to survive in a bold new land.

THUNDER IN THE EAST (Book #1)
_____ 95192-2 $4.50 U.S./$5.50 Can.

SILENT DRUMS (Book #2)
_____ 95224-4 $4.99 U.S./$5.99 Can.

SHADOWS ON THE LONGHOUSE (Book #3)
_____ 95322-4 $4.99 U.S./$5.99 Can.

Coming Soon:
BLOOD RIVER
(Book #4)